The Landmark Library
No. 15

THE OPPIDAN

The Landmark Library

THE OPPIDAN

Shane Leslie

Obruerint citius scelerata oblivia solem
Quam tuus ex nostro corde recedat honos
CLAUDIAN

CHATTO & WINDUS

LONDON

Published by
Chatto & Windus Ltd.
London

*

Clarke, Irwin & Co. Ltd.
Toronto

First published 1922
This edition first published 1969

© Shane Leslie 1922

SBN 7011 1557 2

Printed in Great Britain
by William Lewis (Printers) Limited
Cardiff

TO
E. S. P. HAYNES
AN OPPIDAN TO A
COLLEGER

PREFACE TO NEW EDITION

Fifty years ago I made a humble effort to write an Eton novel based on memories of boys and masters at the turn of the century. Many went back into rather dim times. In those days old masters survived till they reached the oldest ages possible. Many of these were alive when I became an Etonian in Queen Victoria's reign. It was often possible to see the old Queen driving in her carriage through Eton School and turning away to the Playing Fields and disappearing towards Slough. All boys then wore top-hats to Class and Chapel, and naturally saluted their ancient Sovereign.

Only Etonians, I fear, will know what *Oppidan* means: that is — an Etonian who is not a gowned scholar but one of the big majority of the School's population.

Time has passed and only a handful of boys and certainly no masters now survive. It may be curious and amusing to give the real names of some of those who figured in my novel. Here they are:

The Vice-Provost was Mr Warre-Cornish.

The School Clerk was Mr Gaffney.

'Mr Morley' was Mr Allcock, so called after his Dame.

'Mr Lamb' was Mr Ramsay (afterwards Master of Magdalene College, Cambridge).

Dr Lloyd was School Organist.

'Mr Winterstown' was Mr Somerville (afterwards an M.P. for Windsor).

'The Flea' was Mr Austen Leigh (Lower Master).

'Jenkinson' or 'Muggins' was Mr Macnaghten.

'Mr Maxses' was Mr Maximilian Dyer.

'Mr Christopher' was Mr Arthur Benson (afterwards Master of Magdalene, Cambridge).

'Mr Pecker' was Mr Peake Rouse.

'Mike' was Mr R.A.H. Mitchel.

'Mr Munford' was Mr Walter Durnford.

'Mr Redley' was Mr Radcliffe.

'Dr Borcher' was Doctor Porter (Science Master).

'Mr Gill' was Mr Hill (Zoologist).

'Mr Bunny' was Mr Hare.

'Mr Daughan' was Mr Vaughan.

'Herr Blitz' was Mr Ploetz.

'Mr Clinton' was Mr Brinton.

'Mr Broadpen' was Mr Broadbent.

'Mr Robertson' was Mr Robeson.

'Billy Johnson' was Mr Cory.

'Stiggins' was Mr James.

'Sammy Evans' and 'Sidney Evans' were part of Miss Evans' family.

The Miss Gullivers and Miss Evans were the last of the original Eton Dames.

'Arthur Jack' was another Mr James.

'Friar Tuck' was Mr Tuck.

'Hoppy Daman' was Mr Daman.

'Stephen' was J.K. Stephen.

'Quills' was Mr C.M. Wells (who coached the cricket XI).

'Ullathorne', a contemporary Etonian with me, was Ronald Knox.

'Lord Charleston', another contemporary, was Lord Ribblesdale's son.

PREFACE TO FIRST EDITION

THIS novel dealing with the Eton of twenty years ago carries no claim for greater accuracy than is found in a work of Sir Walter Scott. Historical names and characters may be retained in what is fiction, while the use of pseudonyms elsewhere does not mean that historical truth is wholly disguised. Real and false names may be mingled, a period telescoped, and even anachronisms strewn among the pages within the scope of one novel. For the novel should be the means of preserving much that cannot be conveyed in strictly historical works.

In modern time all specialised spheres of life become subject to the novelist, though his name be Bungle and his hall-mark Botch. Within the cosmos are a thousand worlds. Within the little world of England there are worlds within worlds, minute in time, unique in space. But to those who inhabit them they are the world, and to those who pass from them they remain sacred. The Eton world is such. Where life becomes stereotyped or traditional, the material of a novel may be found. The more restricted, the more difficult and interesting a novel should become. There is no English novel so technically correct as Zola's *Débâcle*, and no British sport has inspired the accuracy with which Ibanez describes Spanish bull-fighting. In the absence of the great Cricketing Novel, which has never been written, the National Institution called the Public School has been treated some forty times, not as a whole, but by subdivision into the species

—Harrow, Rugby, Winchester, Shrewsbury, etc. The
field is still open to the Eton novel. Disraeli's account
in *Coningsby* hardly conveyed more than a veneer of
local colour gathered during a stay with an Eton Tutor.
A novel called *The Etonian* might with the necessary
changes in vocabulary have just as well been called the
'Harrovian.' *A Day of my Life at Eton* is the genuine
thing, but no novel. Its humour was successfully intended, but perhaps not its underlying satire. *About Some
Fellows* is as dull as most sequels. It was, and is, Eton's
misfortune to miss description from a great literary artist.
The father of Thackeray and the son of Dickens were
Etonians, but their great relatives immortalised other and
lesser Schools.

The Public School canvas is certainly limited. There
could be nothing duller than a school novel true to life.
Conversation is as restricted among boys as among clerks,
and by reason of school slang rather less intelligible.
Against the general background the precocious boy
seems more brilliant than he is and less popular than
he deserves. School life can be totally monotonous and
the train of events devoid of plot. Breakage of rules
affords perpetual incident and expulsion the occasional
tragedy. The only conversation of literary interest is
either priggish or Rabelaisian.

Character again is more discernible among masters than
boys. The boy is moulded to convention and lives in
mild terror of being thought quaint, talented, or pious.
The school novelist finds it necessary to caricature the
worthy masters and to exaggerate the unworthy boys.
Incidents which could only occur at intervals have to be
brought together in quick succession on the chance of
improvising a plot. Instead of boring the reader with the

record of twenty excellent Houses at Eton, the failings attributable to at least three failures have been piled to illustrate the agony of one. The House described in this novel is the like of none yet known on field or flood. Disorder, however, is the more attractive theme both to the novelist and the physician. Disorder in corners implies the general health, and health (the sane mind in the sound body) was the ideal of the Eton of Edmond Warre, which moulded thousands of Etonians living and dead. It was an athletic and, according to its code, an honourable tradition, but it levelled more than it elevated. As long as the world seemed laid specially for the British Empire, and the Empire to be constructed like a shell round the Eton kernel, Eton was successful and unchallenged. The Eton which bred Viceroys and Rulers could only be compared to the Academy of Noble Ecclesiastics in Rome, which affords the Church a nursery of Cardinals and Nuncios and is based rather on a combination of breeding and tradition than on a superiority in brain or morality over less gilded institutions.

It seems impossible that Eton can hold again the prestige of power she held under Hornby and Warre, who themselves have become legendary. To have been at Eton at the turn of the century was to drop into the mould which their rather narrow genius imposed on the School. Theirs was an Eton differing as profoundly from the Eton of Keate and Hawtrey as from the Eton of the future. Following the feeble interregnum of Balston and Goodford, the School fell into the hands of two successive rulers, whose rule was that of the Philistine and the Philathlete, but who nevertheless made modern Eton great. It is not for the novelist to decry the past or prophesy the future. Eton is subject to evolution, and even her slang has changed as much as her institutions. Not architecturally only has Eton been much replaced during the past fifty years. The change in the boys' language is mysterious and symbolic. No modern Etonian would dream, for instance, of calling money *pec*, or a lie a *bung*, or a tip a *pouch*, but no glossarian can date or explain their obsolescence. Printed boat-lists, however, establish the change from Steerer to Cox in the year 1854. Eton is always evolving. Eton began in the fifteenth century as a Charity School under Papal benediction, and her Founder was a late mediaeval saint. When in addition to his Scholars the Oppidans or 'townboys' flocked to share his teaching, Eton became the training-ground of the Squirearchy and the nurturess of Church and State, who repaid their nurture in honours and prestige. The nineteenth century found Eton as rough as a workhouse school, in College at least, but as intellectual as the Athenaeum. Those heroic days were marked by the reign of Keate.

With the nineteenth century new movements, religious, athletic, and aesthetic, arose at the Universities, and a Public School like Eton, which was also part of the national tradition, might have become the stamping-ground of the prophet or the prize of the pioneer. Eton might have become the second home of the Oxford Movement and given new life to the Church to which she gave Pusey. As it was, her Bishops passed into Melanesia. She might have made a political reality of the 'Young England' movement to which she contributed the brilliant George Smythe. But Etonians held the two Houses of Parliament for their class and not for the people. Eton compromised in every direction save athletics. Her religion became neither High nor Low, but remained a splendid possibility. As the Classics slowly fell from their high estate, the literary promise of earlier days in the century was stifled. Etonians like Fielding, Shelley, Hallam, Milman, Kinglake, Leslie Stephen, and Swinburne had no successors. Hornby did not aim at fine *littérateurs*, and Warre was ashamed of Swinburne as an Eton product. The School touched his ambition of the thousand mark under his successful reign, but no literary giants were bred. Arthur Benson and Bridges' poetry, Rosebery and Curzon's speeches, the novels of Julian Sturgis and Hugh Benson, the plays of Robert Vansittart and Maurice Baring, and the satires of Gilbert Frankau fill a lonely front rank. But on the other hand, the great prizes of the State fell steadily to Eton. Etonians seemed to inherit the Empire their forefathers had made. Etonians were paramount in diplomacy, statecraft, and consulship. They were commanders of the Army until the Boer War, which was the climax of Warre's Eton. Never had Eton borne so great and gory a mantle. With the reign of the Seventh Edward military and political power began to be more equably divided with other Schools. The solid Eton phalanx which was returned to the Commons in 1900 was considerably dispersed in the Radical sweep of 1906. After Roberts came no Eton Marshal in the field, and Balfour sounded the knell of the long-held Eton Premiership. The national Church had already ceased to appeal to Etonians, whether it was that she seemed to pay less in one or other of the worlds. Muscular Christianity had scarcened Etonian clergymen, but the Eton clientele had been changing with the century. The fine old yeoman and county family names outdating the Peerage grew scarcer in the School Lists, while, unfortunately, financial finesse and Semitic snobbery have too often filled their place. It was perhaps inevitable that millionaires and magnates of industry, the social adventurers, Orientals, and Continentals, should wish their offspring to share the enviable prestige built up by landed and leisured gentry during three centuries of Eton history. A comparison of the modern School Lists with Austen Leigh's *Register* during the last half of the eighteenth century or Stapylton's nineteenth-century *Lists* affords a curious contrast in names. It is for a novelist to describe and not discuss, but the pious hope may be permitted that Eton will one day prefer the children of poor tradesmen and old-fashioned squires as of yore to Jews, who are ashamed of their race, or Catholics, who are ashamed of their own Schools. Perhaps Eton is in transition. Certainly the contrast between mediaeval and modern Eton could not be greater, if Eton were to pass wholly under secular influences, with her Head Master appointed by each incoming Government, with H. G. Wells as Chairman of her Governing Body, and the Chapel in which candles were once burned to the Blessed Virgin given over to the clouds of chemical work and the blouse of the workshop ousting the gown of King Henry's Collegers. Whatever betide her, *esto perpetua* !

It only remains to say that, in dealing with a past period now historical, the names of such as Warre, Hornby, and Miss Evans have proved too great to pseudonise. The pseudonyms cover only types and figures, shadows reconstructed from the past. The cricket matches described against Winchester and Harrow are fact, but the races are fiction. The finale of a fire was a necessity to any novel of a time, for even a world in flames has not burnt the recollection of the fire of 1903 out of Eton memory ; but the site, time, occasion, and victims have been so altered that no personal identification remains with the real tragedy. In many ways faulty and distorted, this book has been written remembering that Eton is beyond laudation or dispraise. And in any case it reflects an Eton which has passed away.

CONTENTS

CHAPTER I

ARRIVAL

PADDINGTON STATION resembled an iron-wrought hive, with its glass comb turned uppermost, as Peter Darley jumped out of a hansom on his initial trip to Eton in January of 1899. Like giant bees the industrious engines buzzed in and out, glittering in the winter sunshine, while an army of tiny drones rushed about the hive in aimless confusion. Peter had dropped his old nurse in Praed Street to avoid any appearance of disgraceful company. He was unsuccessful in his attempt to take a ticket to Eton. There was no such station, and he was given the choice of Slough or Windsor.

He had thought that only the Queen took tickets to Windsor. Slough he only vaguely associated with *Pilgrim's Progress*, and the word connoted sudden despond to his mind. 'Well, Slough then,' he told the booking-clerk. 'First-class, sir?' Peter turned, and, sighting three or four boys in a similar plight, plumped for first-class. It might be the right thing to do. Officers were bound to travel first. Perhaps Etonians ought as well. As he dragged his bag and rug along the platform, he saw the other boys ensconced in a third-class carriage, and became confused with shame at his own snobbery. Thank God, he had avoided a farewell scene with his nurse.

Alone at last, he pulled some notes out of his pocket which he had been learning all day. The excitement of becoming an Etonian at express speed was paid for by the menace of the Entrance Examination, in which he stood shortly to disgrace or honour his name, his guardians, the gamekeeper at home, his parents in heaven, and his nurse sobbing in Praed Street. These were grave thoughts, and between the glimpses of Wormwood Scrubbs and other glories of suburban scenery connected with God-forsaken places like Acton and Ealing Broadway he tried to con some tags of Latin verse. He had been well prepared during the holidays. The good old mediaeval art of cheville still flourished among crammers, and Peter had been provided with a number of poetical phrases warranted to wind up a Latin hexameter, or set the backbone of a pentameter, it being well known that a copy of good Latin verses at Eton covered a multitude of scientific or grammatical deficiencies. Eton was not a Grammar School. Peter's wandering Muse had just fitted together a line which ended—

' dicuntur et Acton *et* Ealing'

when Slough was called by the porters, and he ceased the feverish game of trying to make advertisements and place-names scan according to the rules of prosody. As he prepared to rush for a cab, his ticket was violently taken, he was informed he was all right for Windsor, the door was slammed, and the train was off. His eyes fell to the left, whence a gigantic dream city, like a picture he had seen of St. Michael's Mount, swam into his gaze. Towers and pinnacles, battlements and roofs cut the horizon as though suspended in the sky, for a light mist obscured all touch with earth. Like a beetling battle-ship concentrated under a gigantic turret, from which a short mast thrust a languid flag into the air, Windsor Castle burst upon Peter with all the strength of anchored magnificence revealing itself to travelling youth. Not imagining this was not his destination, Peter tried to decipher the Head Master's lodging somewhere in all that portentous array of stone. Engulfed by the vision, he never noticed the series of low-built houses set behind a storm-gapped row of giant elm-trees. Not until the train had swung over a ridiculous sequence of bricked arches, not until the scream of an iron bridge, laid like a crushed toast-rack over a silver streak of river, had rattled in his brain, did it dawn upon him that he beheld the Royal Residence of England, and that Eton must be the cluster of buildings round the graceful Chapel, which rose like a shapely, mastless trireme above the billowing trees farther down the River.

Between the College and the moving train his eye was caught for a moment by a circular clump of enormous elms close to the waterside. Farther back stretched the unending vista of hideous brick arches, presumably lifting the railway above the possibility of floods from the River. Tradition laid the arches to a masterful Provost, who furiously forbade the direct approach. And the curve represented the railway striving to obey the royal beckoning from Windsor in spite of the Eton potentate. Others said that they were erected by the Provost and Fellows of Eton on the model of a Roman aqueduct as a visible encouragement to Classical studies.

The train stopped. Peter hopped out and handed his bag to two porters, who, assisted by a third, found his luggage and summoned a fly driven by the most villain-ous-looking flyman Peter had ever seen outside a Cruik-shank etching. ' Drive to Morley's House,' he called out, proudly conscious that he was an Etonian crossing the Eton frontier. Annoyingly the flyman took not the slightest notice, save for a leer, and sat signalling like a bus conductor for other fares. His gesticulations brought three others into his net. Three times a year he reaped an easy and honest harvest by charging double fares to parties of four boys. New boys were obvious game, though an older bird would often throw him his legal fare with an oath that no flyman could equal. Piled with boxes and boys they ambled forth. Peter found himself driving up against the Castle walls, but a sharp turn to the left sent them down the hill of cobbles and round the mountainous base of the Curfew Tower. The flyman's eyes were fortunately set at the convenient angle necessary to see round corners while approaching them.

' 'Anging and tortures in that there winder,' and the flyman pointed out with his whip in the direction which Peter had located from the train as possibly the Head Master's suite. Another turn to the left. 'This is Damnation Corner, gents, owing to the trains lost by gents paying at the toll gate.' As they passed a gloomy Georgian house planted behind railings up to the street, the flyman motioned horribly: ' 'Aunted 'Ouse there. Sign up To Let.' Almost immediately they were on Windsor Bridge, and the flyman was showing them the octagon stone kiosk where, till recently, a gatesman had laid terrible toll on Eton pockets and tempers. ' At last a gent, knowing the law, broke the curse and drove a 'igh-stepping 'orse slap through and there ain't no toll since.' The vision of some very perfect Etonian flashed on Peter's mind, driving full tilt with a light blue ribbon on his whip before a cheering school. As a matter of fact, it was a legal-minded shopkeeper, a Protestant born out of due time, who had challenged the toll and freed the bridge. Let his name be blessed of all who have passed the bridge in the many years since !

Over Windsor Bridge they lumbered down a street, which seemed to thrive on the luxuries as well as the necessities of school life. There was a fishing shop, a naturalist's, a gunshop, an antiquary, tobacco stores, and approaching the College that solemn roll well known to Old Etonians—Ingalton Drake the publisher ; Denman and Goddard, tailors ; Devereux the hatseller ; Paine the bootseller ; W. V. Brown, and New and Lingwood, fancy haberdashers and purveyors of those coloured caps by which the status of an Etonian is irrevocably fixed in this world and in the life to come. Who but a choir-boy in Bedlam would want to exchange a School-colour for a halo anyhow ? At the end, on the right, was the lodging of Tom Brown, a tailor, whose schooldays remained unending and lucrative. Passing over a Bridge and

Pool, piously named after Barnes, a deceased confectioner, they drove into Eton proper. On the left were a succession of little foodshops and a jeweller. There was the shop of Rowland devoted to the fleshpots, and Meyrick, seller of those *pots* which only flesh contending against appetite could win in field or flood.

From Barnes Pool Bridge Peter obtained his first view of Eton. The road broadened into a triangle out of the stone-coped railing and branched to right and left of an island of low white-washed houses which looked neatly cut out of pasteboard. Gables broke the red roofing, and odd groups of brick chimneys seemed to have been added to give them an appearance of height. To the left the street ran between buildings strung together at no particular time, and with certainly no consistent plan. Only their chimneys combined in a feeble rivalry of the Chapel pinnacles, whose serried order against the skyline outdistanced the lime-trees stretching across the School Entrance. The last shop before the boundary stone, embossed with the College arms, was Clark's, the deadly rival of Rowland. The strange variety of Eton Houses followed. With wondering eyes the new boys, packed into the fly, drank in the scene. They had learnt something of each other's destinations. A well-built, dogged-faced fellow, Socston, was to accompany Peter to Morley's. The third announced himself as Lord Charleston of Miss Evans's House, and a perplexed curiosity came to Peter, who had hitherto believed that Lords were all grown up. The fourth confessed with much shame that he was not an Oppidan, hardly a real Etonian, only a Colleger, and was not going to any House. His name was Ullathorne, and he had taken a scholarship the previous year. Though he was excused the Entrance Examination, and passed direct into Fifth Form, all three felt that he was an object of intense pity.

' Morley's ! ' shouted the flyman as he stopped in front of a tall sham-stucco building that neither resembled a private house nor a public institute, but was known as the

' gin-palace.' While Socston scrambled out, Peter's eye fell on the old Churchyard opposite. Dishevelled yews and iron rods concealed forgotten graves. It was comforting to have that to fall back on in case of failure in examinations. Rallying himself by hasty reflexion drawn from the tombs, he prepared to enter the silent house of his Eton life. It was labelled with the antique legend, ' ERECTED 1844,' displayed as an escutcheon in commemoration of the seventh year of the Victorian era, but for no other reason particularly, unless to mark the building of the front of the house, for behind the pretentious exterior lay vastly inferior specimens of the builder's art. The strips of Italian plaster concealed a mean rearwork held up by sloping brick buttresses, that rare accompaniment of late carpenter's Gothic. But no doubt the date inspired parents with a sense of modernness and even novelty, which had not worn off, though several letters were damaged and presented a constant inspiration to catapults over the way. There was a dignified front door, but the boys used a back door or tunnel to the right that a self-respecting tradesman might have declined to enter. As the fly drove on amid promises to meet again, Peter and Socston groped their way into an atmosphere compounded of darkness and smell, out of which suddenly shot a gnome-like creature with a geranium-red face and ears like ship's ventilators, obsessed with a furious desire to snatch up their luggage in its paws and, pending Mr. Morley's arrival, to offer an effusive welcome, as well as a good deal of information useful to young gentlemen coming to Eton at such an unexpected time of the year as the end of the holidays. Important was the fact he promptly confided that old hands tipped him at the beginning rather than at the end of the half. ' I bet they wait till the term is over,' ventured Peter. With a purple convulsion the odd creature replied, ' We call it the 'alf at Eton, gentlemen, always 'alf.' And for this precious information each parted with half a crown. The Eton year is divided into three halves, for the same scholastic reason, perhaps, that the Charterhouse year is composed of three quarters.

Willum was one of Mr. Morley's domestic agents, and he proceeded to convey their luggage into an inner darkness illuminated only by his sanguine features. He was polite and fantastical, combining most of the motions appropriate to apoplexy and idiocy. Nothing fitted in his mortal compost, as he swayed, slipped, or sidled in front of the new boys in the excitement of bringing them face to face with Mr. Morley. 'New gentlemen, sir!' he panted as though he had picked them up at the station like a hotel-tout and expected remuneration per head. A squat, square figure with bristly moustache and spectacles appeared in the doorway and said decisively, 'Now one of you is Darley and one is Socston. Tell me immediately which is which.' As both bewildered boys replied simultaneously, 'Please sir, me,' Mr. Morley was not enlightened. 'I expect you are Socston,' he said, making a right guess, 'as I hear you were the best footballer at your private school—Willum, you may tell the Dame,' he added with as much show of inspiration as was perhaps possible for him. Willum stood beaming and rubicund. 'Yes, Willum?' he mentioned impatiently, and Willum rushed away, leaving a trio of whom the shyest was Mr. Morley. His interior discomfort took the form of drying up any exterior sources of conversation on the spot. He looked like one of those accurate but crusty clerks, whose extremest philanthropy might take the form of telling urchins the time of day, as he stood fumbling his watch with a hand on Socston's shoulders. 'I hope you will both take high,' was his inconsiderate reminder of the next day's horrors, 'the last lot took Third and Lower Fourth, very low, low—low—low,' and he repeated each word with a twitch of Peter's ears at which Peter started, not recognising the humour, which was unsignalled on Mr. Morley's face, and was stricken so dumb that Mr. Morley immediately referred to a visit which the Dame was expecting from them and for which they were already late, late, very late, and for which lateness he would certainly be blamed. Two years later Peter would have hailed the underlying facetiousness, but his present instinct was to prevent Mr. Morley's collision with the Dame at all cost. Mr. Morley never became more serious than in the delivery of pleasantry, but fortunately Willum reappeared and the new boys were drawn in his jubilant wake toward the Dame.

Mr. Morley sat back making mental notes of his two young friends. They might be athletic. He no longer hoped for scholars. He was only anxious that new boys should not be scamps, for his present set tended that way. He sat back ruminating. Not an Etonian himself, he had qualified for his Eton mastership by a wonderful piece of bowling against the Australians at Cambridge which had won the endorsement of a Lyttelton ten years before. Being a Mathematical master, he could never be a real Eton Tutor. He was allowed a House and the privilege of boarding boys, provided they were tutored by younger Classical masters. Eton phraseology accounted him a ' Dame ' for that reason, a kind of mule-tutor, which rankled albeit peacefully in his mind. Mr. Morley, being unmarried, was compelled to hire the services of an imposing housekeeper, charitably called Dame, to whose mysterious authority and possibly ungiven summonses he was accustomed to refer boys under any given difficulty or stroke of shyness. Parents were liable to be surprised, on remonstrating against the mediaeval ventilation or traditional food prevalent under his rather expensive auspices, to be hurried off excitedly to the Dame as a final and perfect court of appeal. Mr. Morley's voice used to become very shrill at such suggestions, and he used to cackle like a hen as he invoked his partner, who was found to weigh fifteen stone and to resemble a duchess dressed as a governess. But parents found that there was no appeal from her. All questions of health and nourishment were settled by her with a dignified surprise that anybody could mistrust the solidarity of the Eton tradition.

The Dame received the new boys with consoling exuberance and simulated Scotticisms. ' Puir laddies, puir laddies, ye 'll find Eton a hard place till ye gae into Fifth Form, but ye 'll be excused fagging for a fortnight. Come to yer auld Dame when ye 're sick,' and her voice rose, 'but na shamming, na Friday fevers cured by a Saturday half-holiday,' and she laughed, as though to imply medical second-sight in the detection of the least fraud. On a table near by were placed the few necessary bottles to cure all the ailments of boyhood, while Biblical Dictionaries tucked into every corner gave visitors to understand that the spirit as well as the body was among the Dame's absorbing cares. It would not be befitting here to mention the many good works which were directed from that room, for the same brain directed the food supply of the house, chose and inspired its staff, dictated to the cringing tradesmen, upheld Mr. Morley's feeble authority, received the foolish parents, and invented the official excuses which had to be furnished whenever healthy boys desired to stay out of school. And her script was more powerful with the Head than Mr. Morley's word. While she was Dame none ventured to complain, or to criticise Mr. Morley's House.

Inspection proving satisfactory, the Dame announced, ' Mrs. Sowerby will show you your rooms,' and she added, with alarming seriousness, ' obey the Master and respect the Holy Ghost.' Overwhelmed by these directions, Peter and Socston were retiring, when a strange little figure appeared in the doorway, looking like a resuscitated mummy of Queen Anne turned by secular drippings into candle wax. ' Mrs. Sowerby,' the Dame sighed, ' Mrs. Sowerby, unpack for these puir laddies, and show them the ways of the House, and remember, laddies, to put on a clean collar every day, and never to call Mrs. Sowerby the Hag, or I 'll speak to the Captain.'

Mrs. Sowerby, whom Peter had as much intention of addressing in terms of revilement as of endearment, led the way through a green baize door into inner darkness.

The exchange of lead for carpet betokened they were in
the boys' quarters. The impression of smell was intensi-
fied. In the gloom of each chilly landing invisible
females, whom the boys associated with a penitential
home in Windsor, one of the Dame's good works, were
expiating their past, if past they had, not with offerings
of spikenard, but with fiercely redolent soaps. A steady
scrub and steam and splutter ascended from each landing,
and from stairs, worn by generations of boys and sustained by crossbars of iron. On the third floor Mrs.
Sowerby, whose bunch of keys and uniform made her look
like a wardress going her rounds, switched at a tangent
into a long crooked passage, whose walls leaned heavily
to one side. On the other, however, they were pierced
with windows affording a sudden vista of the Castle,
shot with the red glare of sunset. Another twist, and
Peter found himself crouching in a low room, whose
ceiling must have suffered in the same geological cata-
strophe as the outside passage. The room was no doubt
commodious, when not entirely occupied with a table,
a bureau, a Windsor chair, a can, a footbath, and a curious
cupboard which opened in order to vomit a bed. A thick
smoke was the only indication that a fire had been previously lit. Mrs. Sowerby opened the window, and Peter
looked round at his furniture. The bureau was the most
curious. It was a carpenter's chimaera of threefold
construction. Its head was a book-case, its belly was a
writing-desk, and its tail was a chest of drawers. Under
the table was an awkward box upholstered in drab purple,
which Mrs. Sowerby addressed as an ottoman. It proved
to be the local hybrid between a sofa and a packing-case,
rather neatly combining the deficiencies of both. Mrs.
Sowerby began pitching out his clothes and books at
lightning speed, looking closely all the while, as she said,
for contraband. ' Any cigarettes or catapults ? ' she
asked, with a ferrety gleam in her wax face. Peter
immediately asked leave to retain a model engine which
required methylated spirits. ' The boys won't leave that

long,' she grinned, ' or that either,' as she pulled out the blue-and-white striped cap of his private school. ' You must ask the Dame for an order to buy a *scug*-cap.' She then indicated that tea was procurable from a hanging hutch on the wall, which she called a *sock* cupboard. Such stores as he had brought were bundled into its cavity. Socston joined him, and they both sat down in the spirit of silent grandeur befitting Etonians at tea. ' We must remember to call it *sock*,' remarked Peter, ' only private schools call it grub.' ' I hear they half kill you if you use the wrong words here,' remarked Socston, who was a cheerful pessimist, that is, by expecting the worst he could always accept any situation short of such. Peter was one who rather enjoyed his griefs, and could sup on sorrow, however high his expectations had been.

At this moment a wild shout rang down the passage, followed by the thud of boots or bags striking hostile substances and the full cry of a pack of boys. ' Dear me, the other boys must have come back,' said Peter, ' at least the Lower Boys. Fifth Form don't come till to-morrow.' ' They must have caught a new boy,' reflected Socston. ' Hadn't we better give ourselves up and be tossed in blankets, which is what they do, my father told me ? ' Peter opened the door, and they were relieved to find that Willum was the victim of this horse-play. Whether he had dared to suggest tipping while there was wherewith to tip or not, he was being driven along the landing with blows and fearful suggestions as to his paternity. ' I never knew Eton boys were allowed to swear,' observed Peter, who had once overheard a drunken woman address a policeman. Socston grinned and shrugged his shoulders. ' My *Pater* told me I would hear harder swearing at Eton than all the rest of my life. His advice to me was, never mind what they say or what you say. Take care what they do and what you do.' Peter was an orphan, his father having died while exploring in Egypt, and he began to long for an interview with Mr. Socston, senior, to reveal the ropes and pitfalls of the Eton arena. His nurse had given him a leather-bound Bible, his guardian a sovereign, and an aunt had begged him to send word whenever he was in need of a plumcake, and, above all, not to spend too much time rowing in the Eton Eight.

But beyond bursting into their rooms the old boys offered the new no annoyance. Having hurled downstairs the unhappy Willum, apparently about to belch purple and threatening to tell the Dame, whom they knew he was far too awed to approach, they inquired the names of those who had added themselves to their number with an appearance of lifelong curiosity, and spoke menacingly of the Fifth Form heroes, who were expected the following night. ' Wait till your fortnight is up. You 'll probably be tanned straight off.' ' What do you get tanned for ? ' asked Peter a little bravely. ' For doing lessons badly, or offending Mr. Morley ? ' A howl of laughter followed. ' You get tanned for shirking *footer*, or spoiling toast, or ragging the Hag. Wait till they get back. Come on, let 's go and drop bags on Willum when he rings the supper bell.' And they slouched on like the great men they temporarily were.

In the Eton pool every fish sports and swims in awe of another minutely bigger or socially distinct. Remove scorns the Fourth. Fifth Form disdain and ignore both. Upper Fifth condescend to *fag* and belabour Lower Boys. Upper Fifth look up to the House Captains, and they in turn admire a deity known as the President of *Pop*. The Houses are divided into Houses with the right to House-colours or not. The wearers of House-colours rank above Lower Boats, and a little below Upper Boats. All yield to the wearers of School-colours. The hierarchy of games and colours awarded for games finds climax in the Captain of the Boats, who alone has a colour, a peculiar cap and coat, of his own. With the Captain of the Eleven and the Captain of the Oppidans he composes a Trinity that no young scoffer has dared to deride, no sceptic has rashly questioned, and no heretic, save at dire cost, has ever withstood. All these important truths Peter quickly picked up in his first hours at Eton, and hung round greedy for more. He learnt the important differences which his neighbours distinguished between *swipes* and *swiping*, between *whiffs* and *stinks*, before he was finally sent to bed by Mrs. Sowerby, deputising for the Dame, and officially visited by Mr. Morley, whom he learnt from Mrs. Sowerby to call 'the Master,' and from the boys to call 'the Man.' Reflecting on this puzzle, whereby the same individual could be Master and Man, he fell asleep, only to dream uneasily that Willum and the leering flyman had proved to be his examiners in the Entrance Examination, and that he had been placed in the School in exact accordance with his pecuniary offerings to each.

CHAPTER II

PETER was awakened the next morning by the scratching
of a match as Mrs. Sowerby lit his candle and cried the
hour with the unruffled dignity of the extinct Charley.
' Quarter to seven and a fine morning ! ' Mrs. Sowerby
cherished a complete indifference to heaviness of swearing
and sleeping. Shrill of voice and tidy as a corpse, she
went her remorseless way, awakening reluctant youth to
Early School. Of ant-like proportions and disposition,
she had passed her life in the vain endeavour to choke
the sloth of young gilded grasshoppers, to say nothing of
some developing night-hawks. Once only during the
Victorian era had she overslept herself, and she had been
consistently chaffed ever since the Dame had spent a
famous morning writing reams in her illegible handwriting for the line of Praepostors who arrived demanding
excuses for every member of Morley's House. With his
heart fluttering like a moth round the solitary candle
which she left burning on his table Peter dressed and,
balancing a sheeny top-hat on his head for the first time
in his life, stumbled down the dark passage to a corner
of the landing where he found Mrs. Sowerby under a gas-
jet regaling Socston with a bun and coffee, about equally
warm. After swallowing this slight fortification both
boys were consigned to the gloating care of Willum, who
looked none the worse for his ragging. His rubicund
features were still bursting with self-importance and local
information. He knew well that this was the last time
he could address his charges without being hung over a
gas-bracket or crushed behind a door. ' Cheer up, sir,'

14

he remarked, 'Mr. Morley's ain't very successful. They almost all take low.'

They crossed the street in the dark and came under the shadow of colossal buildings, which shot far above a line of lime-trees. A flicker of subdued gaslight revealed the upper story of long, casemented windows set with diamond glazing, under which they plunged through a huge gateway of scarred monoliths. Peter was reminded of the scene in passing Traitor's Gate in an Ainsworth novel. From every direction of the Eton compass groups of thoughtful new boys were being conducted by motley butlers and valets, the Sancho Panzas of the House masters and the silent rivals of the real College servants, who took over their charges at the School Gate. These very important individuals prepared the Bills of Absence, checked the work of the Praepostors, presided over the School Pound, where Epics could be obtained for a few pence and the veritable *Gradus* or steps to Parnassus for a shilling, and moreover were mysteriously acquainted with the modes and means of corporal discipline. Younger masters as well as boys relied on them for direction. College servants also ministered to the invisible services of the Head, the Provost, and other incumbents of the great red battlemented towers which Peter could discern across the School Yard. They included the snow-haired College Butler, who carried on a curiously twofold existence. On the one hand he presided over the mortal dietary of the Collegers, which would class him among superior majordomos, but at the sound of the Chapel bell he flung down trencher and carving-knife and, assuming the robe of a sublimated verger, seized the heavy silver wand called the 'Holy Poker,' descendant of that with which Mercury directed the immortal gods, and conducted the Provost and Vice-Provost to devotions. An old soldier called 'the Fusee' stood in the offing as the new boys came in, and glanced at Willum with such portentous superiority that Willum and his fraternity were content to deliver one glare before retreating. More important still was the

c

School Clerk, a grizzle-bearded and ubiquitous factor, who under less useful circumstances might have been a mathematical genius. Mr. Gaffney was *de facto* Head Master of Eton. All Praepostor books came under his red and blue pencils. All exeats and excuses passed through his hands. Given times and names, he could calculate the whereabouts of any single boy. He could detect an inaccuracy in a Praepostor or a faulty alibi with ghastly prescience. Through his delicate touch passed the birches of the exact Eton calibre and gracefulness. With scrupulous care he wove four birches to the hour. But the grave cast which long associations with punishment had given to his dignified features was tempered by the benevolence accruing from the conduct of a little home for lost and battered books. Seeming to offer an official welcome, he motioned Peter to the right, and Peter slightly bowed. He was throbbing like a minnow drawn for the first time into mid-stream. The other boys swept him round a corner and up three short flights of heavy oaken stairs. He clutched an iron ramp which stuck out of the mouldering stonework. At the top was a pointed Gothic door leading into the Antechapel, but the tide of boys thrust him into a prodigious chamber opposite. Like the School Yard below it seemed enormous, and the fifty new boys were swallowed in its centre. As they entered, the School Clock boomed through the mists and various Assistant masters, looking youthfully severe, bobbed out of huge wooden witness boxes. Heavy red curtains stretched on rods and divided the room, while long chandeliers hung from the spider-ridden ceiling. The masters wore black funereal gowns, which had the same effect on Peter as the dress of undertakers or executioners. Every boy found his name at a desk with paper, ink, and a packet of those beautiful quills with which Etonians have written Latin verse since the middle ages. A white printed questionnaire faced each whiter face. Peter had no time to look up at the forbidding busts of the mighty dead, poised above the dark panelling. He had never heard of Pearson or Hammond. He could not have recognised Camden, the Eton Lord Chancellor. Neither Porson nor Gray inspired him from their blank plaster eye-sockets, nor could Wellington nor Canning awe him. He could not have quoted :—

> 'Here where young Hammond learnt to pray
> Chatham and Fox were wont to stray.'

An hour later he showed up his first paper with many misgivings, and had time to notice that like the desks every inch of the panelling was carved and surcharged with the names of boys. Here were names bright in the roll of fame, if he could have deciphered them. Here were graven Shelley and Gladstone. Here were the two Walpoles. Here was scratched Pitt. Here were cut on a desk the first recorded Eton Eight of 1820. Here were hundreds of carven autographs, many of whom were well known in their day, and many hundreds more whose names had not become better known since the day when their owners chiselled them in the wood of Upper School, which was all the world had to remember them by a hundred or fifty years later.

There was an adjournment for breakfast, and the sight which met Peter was calculated to appal him. To right and left gigantic buildings rose in the misty light. Under Upper School stretched enormous cloisters of cyclopean masonry, carved and cut by generations of boys, though presumably designed in their defiance. Every boy for centuries must have picked out a crumb as he passed, some flicking with a penknife, others hacking with a hatchet to judge by the holes and slashes gaping in the blackened stone. The colonnade was not unlike the *vomitoria* of the Roman Coliseum. Peter looked out into a huge quadrangle, in the centre of which a railed statue of the blessed Henry the Sixth, girded with Sword and Garter, was barely visible, while the grey river mists still shrouded the double clock tower and the soaring pinnacles of the Chapel, out of whose side a flight of stone stairs descended to the cobbles. The new boys returned to their papers in a bright winter sunlight to find a crowd of curious Lower Boys, who received them with good-natured derision. One careless or uninstructed youth gave his name as Charley, and after every paper there were cries of ' Where 's Charley ? ' The Christian name is not used at Eton except under romantic or very exalted conditions. A real sensation was provided by an unlucky boy in a bowler hat, whose Dame, however, mercifully bought him a top-hat later in the day. The next day brought Greek Translation, drawing audible accents from some of the victims. Peter glanced at the two pieces of prose and verse, and suddenly his heart began to beat. It was a paper that had been set before, and he remembered he had done it very carefully with his crammer. With trembling fingers he rushed a version out of memory. In half an hour he had scored a bull's-eye, and had time to turn his translation of Greek verse into English rhymes. Then he sat deliciously still, and a confidence came to him, which never left him again in his school examinations. He had acquired a morale in face of examiners. He was only disturbed from his brown reverie by a resonant voice from the nearest witness box, ' Darley, if you have finished all you can do, you are allowed to show it up.' He rose and showed up his papers as in a dream dreamed years before. He felt a curious subjective paralysis of the mind, as though another than his real self was handing up the papers. ' Come here a moment,' continued the voice, and Darley watched himself obey. He was standing under a young Assistant master, who said he hoped he had not been puzzled by the Greek, as he was his Classical Tutor. He asked him to write his name in full in one of those books which all young masters keep in hopeful enthusiasm of generally disappointing pupils.

Mr. Lamb was an agreeable contrast to Peter's House Tutor. He was a gentleman of literary taste and high Classical attainments. He had been educated on the Eton Foundation and tasted King Henry's bread both at Eton and at King's College, Cambridge, which for centuries had been the nursery of Eton masters of the good old Classical brand. Eton was his religion, which in view of the conflicting theologies of the day was sufficing. Vulgarity and fanaticism he disapproved, as he disapproved Science or Mathematics, for the good reason that they were all too certain, too cocksure. But when Eton was in question he would confess to a little suppressed adoration. Under his clear eye and cheery manner he had minimised emotion. When he was puzzled or amused, he twisted a silky moustache. On the last day of the Examination, Peter and Socston were invited to his rooms, which were pleasantly situated in Weston's Yard behind an old brick wall engaged in the task of propping a leaning acacia. Under a solitary chestnut-tree a back door led out of the Yard to three pupil-rooms arranged kennelwise, whither Peter was invited to submit any brilliant little pieces of Latin or Greek composition he might happen to improvise during the next few years of his life. Mr. Lamb was full of encouragement. Their places in the School would not appear till next day. Mr. Lamb's pupils generally did remarkably well, they were informed, and they were not likely to prove exceptions. Their looks belied all prophecy on their behalf. Meantime, Mr. Lamb was anxious to try their knowledge of Greek Testament. Socston was immediately and hopelessly stuck in the passage at which Mr. Lamb opened in the blue-coloured volume which has made the Evangelists disliked by Fourth Form boys. Higher up in the School boys felt avenged on learning what inferior Greek the Gospellers wrote compared to Xenophon or Thucydides. Peter, however, had been fortified by his crammer against the exigencies of Eton theology, and had learnt the English text by heart, with a long list of Greek tags, on striking one of which he promptly began to recite from memory. Mr. Lamb became wreathed in smiles, and congratulated him on his knowledge of Greek. Eton struck Peter as bewilderingly lucky.

Mr. Lamb was left with a pleasant impression of his new pupils. He liked the immediate gratitude and filial obedience of new boys, the quick and innocent response which all boys in their first year make to a master's kindness or interest. For that reason he preferred teaching in the Fourth Form to dealing with the shell-backed Fifth, who disdained to be interested, and sometimes failed to appreciate a master's humour in class. He loved the soft clay of boyhood, fresh from the mysterious and unaccountable Potter, who planted the seed of such different flowers in such same-sized pots. Mr. Lamb was refined but academic, generous but a little sanguine, conventional to Eton standards and as artistic as he dared. His aesthetic side found harmless vent in the most exquisite of handwritings and in a facility for Latin verse which Cardinal Bembo might have envied. His only hobby was a blue Persian cat named after the Founder, and a grey parrot with a vermilion tail, which one generation of boys had taught to call 'Lamb!' and another to say 'Damn!' There was a tradition that he had entertained a desire to enter Parliament, but had been so shocked by overhearing a false quantity dropped in the House that he abandoned the idea and became, what Nature and Grace had intended, an Eton master. His Classical training, his amused courtesy with boys, his delicate perceptions of their etiquette, his subdued contempt for impossible parents, and his loyal satisfaction in the Eton tradition made him a finished specimen. The Greek proverb said of any one who disappeared, that he had died or become a schoolmaster. Mr. Lamb had contentedly died to all outside the world of Eton.

He was at the first and joyous stage in the Eton master's career, which was bound to lead to the solid success in the second, and if all developed according to the laws of Eton evolution, he would perhaps, thirty years after, make one more addition to that celebrated gallery of live curiosities and dead geniuses who live embalmed in the humorous section of Eton memory. For generations there had accumulated an Eton Zoo, many of whom had been quaintly drawn by ' Spy ' in *Vanity Fair*, but some of the most quaint and precious had gone uncharted to their graves. There were ' Hares ' and ' Badgers,' ' Woolly Dogs,' and ' Fleas,' and ' Bulls,' and ' Piggies,' according as boys discerned a likeness between masters' names or features and the animal kingdom. In the days of Dickens the School had been enriched by a ' Turvey-drop ' and a ' Stiggins.' Others had received the compliment of an adjective, such as ' Oily Ben ' or ' Mad Moses.' There were others indeed who were outside even the reach of schoolboy metaphor, and resembled nothing except caricatures of themselves.

The old Classical men presented a curious instance of academic inbreeding. Their predecessors had resented the election of every Head Master as a reformer, and lived to regret him as a Conservative. They had resented the break in the tradition when Hornby, who had been an Oppidan and not a Colleger, nay, even an Oxonian instead of a pure-bred Cantab, had been raised to the Head Mastership. To their mind the general demoralisation of the century had permitted astonishing intrusions. French masters had been clothed in gowns, and Mathematical masters, even of non-Etonian origin, had been allowed to keep boarding-houses. Modern languages had been steadily introduced at the expense of the old Classics, as though it were not the privilege of foreign diplomatists to learn English. Advanced Mathematics were taught, as though the land were not encumbered with the produce of sound commercial education. What could it profit to triumph in that world which figureth and giveth in figures ? Times had changed, and the Classical course, with its ironclad grammar, immense saying lessons, and ponderous sweep through the old literature, had been undermined, but not replaced. Boys acquired a smattering of several subjects and an ignorant dislike of others. Teachers of the ungentlemanly sciences had been introduced. A generation back the old guard had pardoned

Austen Leigh and Dupuis, the first masters to appear in
flannels and play cricket with the boys, but it was a bitter
wash to their eyes to see a Science master pedalling a
bicycle with his sacred gown flying in the air. To this
old Collegiate world it was a profanation, like umpiring
in a surplice. A Science master was not far removed
from a conjurer, who might be very amusingly and properly introduced to the boys about Christmas time.
Rumours brought word that the present Science master
took photographs like a bagman at the Windsor Fair.
He would want to take pupils next. To these cloistered
souls Latin and Greek had been the Alpha and Omega,
the golden sun and the silver moon of education. Gloomily
they watched the slow changes made in deference to Progress, or to its curious educational synonym, the require-
ments of the Universities. On a day marked Ichabod
in the Eton Calendar Huxley was placed on the Governing Body. The old men remembered when boys were
proud to spout Homer or Horace. Now they were grubbing at fragments of German and French, since the Prince
Consort had set prizes for his horrible language. In the
old days boys asked nothing better than to be ' sent up
for good ' with a copy of Latin verses, written as an
Anglican gentleman should be able to write them. Now
boys were sent up for correct conic sections. One had
actually been sent up for chemically analysing a sixpence !
Why not teach him to forge the coin outright ? A
Science master had wished to send a boy up for dissecting
a frog. There was no end to the beastliness which the
Governing Body had allowed to creep under the curriculum since they had superseded the Eton Fellows as
guardians of the shrine. Eton was now threatened with
the terrible possibility that these Mathematical masters,
not content with being allowed to take boarders, would
one day want to turn them into pupils, miscorrect their
Latin verses, and even prepare them for Confirmation.
Good heavens ! Was it not known that half of those who
mastered the binomial theorem immediately abandoned

all belief in the Deity ? This desire for equality with
the Classical masters was the thin end of the wedge of
a whole modern side. After all, were there not women
who desired equal rights with men ? It was true that they
could only be very immoral women. Nevertheless, some
people thought atheists immoral, and it was well known
that mathematicians who persevered to the awful con-
clusions of their science frequently became atheists. It
was well to realise that Mr. Lamb was no fogey. He
respected the old men, whose mantle and whose faith
would soon fall to him and the younger Classical masters.
Reforms he saw were coming inevitably, but he took his
own line. It was bound to be a time of transition. The
final struggle he expected would come in his day between
the Classical Tutors and the Mathematical Dames, between the Greeks and the Trojans. He specialised in
pupils from the Houses of the latter, and made rather a
point of keeping on terms of careful politeness with them.
If he could not respect a ' Dame,' he avoided a clash by
avoiding his pupils. He prepared his soul for strife, if it
should ever come, by voting regularly for Greek at Cambridge, and editing a perfect edition of Catullus. It was
a refined edition of a refined poet, and a labour of love
can cover many dislikes. In pupil-room Mr. Lamb's
whole soul was faithfully given to inspiring the uninspired
and getting indifferent boys out of the clutches of the
Furylike superannuation, which dogged them from Block
to Block through the School, as their years waxed and
their knowledge not at all. Mr. Lamb did not believe his
duty to his neighbour was complete unless he left an
abiding love of Catullus with each pupil. Mr. Lamb had
no enemy among masters, and deserved none among boys.
At present most of his pupils were Lower Boys chewing
inky and undigested husks of Ovid and Xenophon, but
he was looking forward to the day when he would read
Pindar and Catullus with advanced Fifth Formers and
a well-beaten pad should establish itself between his
pupil-room and the Chambers of the Head, the track of

boys 'sent up for good.' Hitherto his experiences had
chiefly been of tearing verses and ripping up proses for
their ghastly mistakes. Almost every pupil raised and
defeated the same hopes. Would he one day write a
good set of Latin verses ? Would he ever win Distinction
in Trials ? Would he one day be 'sent up for good ' ?
Would the School List one day teem with entries such
as :—

	House Tutor.	*Classical Tutor.*
Bumpkins minor (3) † 4	Mr. Morley.	Mr. Lamb.
Chumlinson (5)	Mr. Winterstown.	Mr. Lamb.

Such hieroglyphics indicated that a mythical Bumpkins
minor had been 'sent up for good ' three times, and an
unborn Chumlinson no less than five times, also that
Bumpkins had four times attained Distinction in Trials.
Such was the tenour of Mr. Lamb's meditation, when a
piece of paper was handed to him by the ruddy-haired
member of the College Office. It was written with purple
copying ink in the well-known and beautifully quilled
characters of the Head. It was a list of the new boys
and their places in the School. He hurriedly glanced for
the names of his new pupils. His eye caught Socston in
Middle Fourth. He glanced uneasily to Lower Fourth and
Third Form. No Darley ! Then he began reading from
the beginning. Good heavens ! he had taken Remove !
His surprise and pleasure roused his parrot's mirth. ' Ha !
ha ! ha ! poor old Lamb ! ' ' Say, good boy, Polly, very
good boy,' for Mr. Lamb felt as pleased as Punch.

That night Darley slept in agony, knowing that the
dreaded result must appear on the morrow. He had
remembered a false quantity in a dream and wept. Again
and again that day he had tried to cheer himself with
vain thoughts. Twice he had written without finishing
tear-blotted sheets home to his guardian and his nurse,
assuring all who loved him and stood to incur social
honour or disgrace by the results of the Examination that
all was well. Tea had left a lump in his gizzard, and he

had been unable to eat a morsel for supper. Another lump had grown in his throat, and he had gone to bed curled up into many yet more miserable lumps, wondering whether suicide was preferable to shame. But at any moment his hot pillow could have been transformed to paradisal down under his aching head and his cell of pain to the antechamber of bliss, could he only have known where his name stood in the purple-writ scroll signed by Edmond Warre. In default of one whisper of inside knowledge he was destined to pass the most miserable instead of the happiest night of his. Sleep abandoned him and he began to recall his past. Left an orphan by his father's early death in the East, he had been brought up without brothers or sisters by an old nurse under the supervision of his uncle as guardian and the more human agency of a gamekeeper. If he failed in the Examination, it was, he felt perhaps, almost as well that both his parents were dead. He wished he could remember his father enough to imagine the sort of advice he would give him now. Against his assumed inclinations he would really have loved to have seen his nurse again. She knew all about his father, though she would never speak about him except in a mysterious way. Once she let slip that Peter had a sister, born while his father was exploring. His mother had died at her birth. That was all he was allowed to know. She had become a dream sister.

Again and again he rose and peered out of the window until the moist dawn rose out of the riverine meadows. He could see the slowly appearing battlements and stone cross of Lower Chapel pitched between two pinnacles. To the left and right rose the shapeless silhouettes of other Houses. He wondered if any shared his misery. The immediate prospect was a stable yard belonging to the old Christopher Inn, that desirable property, which with its timbered galleries, twisted stairways, and tap-room had been utilised in a brilliant fit of economy in order to house and teach boys. The famous hostelry itself with its signboard had been

sent down town, and though the smell of beer was no
more, the concomitant fragrance of horse-flesh remained.
Peter's eye was amused for a moment watching two
gigantic rats feeding on the top of the stable under his
window. In the yard itself a herald of the Eton dawn
was whistling that music which is so attractive to horses'
ears. Peter recognised the leering flyman, and the events
of the last few days flashed upon him just as a lifetime of
events reels through a drowning man's mind. The
journey, the arrival, his companions, the Examination,
every question, his answers, Mr. Morley, Mr. Lamb,
Mr. Lamb's parrot, Willum, and the Dame danced wildly
through his mind and left him hanging over the abyss of
dread that concealed the impending result of examination.
In agony of soul he lifted the window-sash and prayed
with a mixture of boyish faith and of a cynic's gamble,
until the mists melted away and the stone symbol of a
God's pain stood clearly cut in the crisp light. Simply
and reverently he tried to bargain with God for a good
place at Eton. His nightshirt was wet with the drops
which the mist had left in the air, and a shock of surprise
crossed Mrs. Sowerby's face when she found the unusual
sight of a boy kneeling out of bed before he was called.

There was no Early School on Saturday, and Peter
crept down to breakfast amid the extravagantly con-
descending and contemptuous looks of boys who had
been in his position a few months previously. He took
his seat at the bottom of the long table where the Lower
Boys sat with their backs to a narrow imprisoned alley
called the Dame's garden, into which the only approach
of light was tempered by a twelve-foot wall. Some dead
flowers in their blackened and cat-trodden bed seemed
to have expired in the effort to rival the ivy shoots which
crept up the wall, to meet equal disappointment, for they
also were dying at the top. Four large panes on the level
of the wall let a dim light into the dining-room, which
needed, without obtaining, artificial light most of the year.
Peter's neighbours kindly gave him an interesting outline

of the normal week. 'There's a half *hol.* on Tuesday, Thursday, and Saturday. And there's a whole *hol.* every Red Saint's day. There's only Matthias this half and St. David's Day. When a whole *hol.* hits a Saturday or a Monday, then is the best week-end for Long Leave. You can go for Short Leave any half *hol.* or whole *hol.*'

'I didn't know you had so many holidays,' murmured Peter. 'Not nearly enough by a damnside,' replied his informant. 'I suppose we have to work a good deal in our rooms if we are not in class?' Peter asked. 'Depends if you are up to a slack *beak* or not. There's not much work done in this House after tea,' was the cheery reply. 'When do you think is the best time for work?' asked Peter. 'Oh! after lights, or, if you're rushed, before the Hag comes round to call you!'

Peter returned to his breakfast and began to digest some important knowledge. Mr. Morley avoided the boys' breakfast, but the Dame poured out endless cups of hot coffee which belied the adjective and the name. At the main table sat the Fifth Form, for Mr. Morley's House was not represented in the Sixth. There was a fine crop of Lower Fifth, somewhat pruned by judicious expulsions and a little retarded from rising to the Upper Fifth and fagging rights by the distractions of sport. Boys left the room when they liked and Peter stole out to scout for the Examination list. He made up his mind to peruse it in lonely terror and then to bury common grief with Socston in the foodshop at Barnes Pool, where strong fruit-ade could be bought for a penny. In spite of his Greek translation he felt uneasier and uneasier. Immediately outside his House was Ingalton Drake's bookshop. There were several notices in the window which drew the eye of every boy every time he passed. He entered to inquire.

Within the shop a surging mob of boys were scrambling for books and paper, which were being distributed somewhat as oranges are scrambled in the last moments of a school treat. Boys were loudly demanding pens and ink or forms of paper such as *Deriwag* or *Sunday Q. Bumf* or

Broad Rule, a beautiful double sheet with a *Floreat Etona*
watermark. They made no payment but addressed a
partly invisible clerk by thrusting orders from their
Tutors under his frenzied eyes. 'Now then, hurry up,
little man!' 'My turn next, where the devil is that
bumf?' At these cries there shot from under the desk
the Little Man, so called, though zoologically it would
have been more correct to call him a large insect. He
snatched up two fresh orders, simultaneously depositing
two sets of supplies on the desk and, before he could be
detained under a top-hat or flattened out by a larger sized
dictionary, he had ducked, hopped, and disappeared into
a further room, where an old gentleman could be seen,
half after half, sitting at accounts. His beard had gone
grey in the process and he clove to his chair never looking
up once as the little man aforesaid danced, twirled, and
twittered to the right and then to the left of him, balancing
Lexicons and Grammars, juggling bottles of ink, secreting
boxes of nibs in his sleeves, and dashing pyramids of paper
within an inch of the old man's nose. Rumour held that
this was a Mathematical master sacked for speculation on
the Stock Exchange who had been condemned to tot
school accounts for the rest of his natural life. Certainly
he represented the passive side of the shop, while the Little
Man, as far as a physique adapted from the stronger lepi-
doptera would permit, displayed the activity of the firm.
Peter came to the conclusion that if bookworms hatched
into any sort of wingless thing, this was as likely to be
the produce as anything. A few minutes later the Little
Man made another reappearance, again snatched orders
from many hands, and amid a cloud of chaff and chivying
returned to drop himself and a pile of stationery on the
counter, whence with another hop and a glide he proceeded
to repeat the movement.

At his fourth appearance Peter hazarded the inquiry,
'When will the list be up? I mean where will the new
boys be up?' 'Up to anything!' flashed the insect, and
was gone chuckling. On his next return he twittered

between the crash of books, ' Try the School Office or Head's Chambers.' ' Where ? ' pleaded Peter. ' Ask the Head ! Ask the Head ! ' and his voice grew fainter in the recesses saying over and over again, ' Ask the Head !' until it died down into a cheep. Following the clue Peter set out for the School Yard across the street, which from a deserted route had in two days become the busy focus of Eton life, Eton energy, Eton slouching, Eton fashion and gossip. Boys were meeting each other after the holidays with a mixture of added swagger and reserved delight. Lower Boys were scuttling down town on errands from invisible fag masters. Gaily garnished members of the Eton Society called *Pop* were coming out of the Christopher Yard like newly hatched dragon-flies. Fifth Formers were loftily discussing prospects of sports, beagles, fives, and running. Everybody was wildly interested in everybody and everything except in one subject, which remained a matter of total and crushing indifference in the School, the new boys. They could be recognised by their slow, peering motions as they stood about uneasily watching their fellows and ludicrously grateful to any one who treated them as a little better than malodorous lepers. Until they were placed in the School they were without destiny or destination and merely drifted on the mighty current of Eton. Like straws on an eddy they floated around before they were absorbed into the tone and atmosphere and slowly but indelibly stamped with the outward gloss and inward attitude which mark all Etonians and can be acquired by experience only or, in the case of some old Etonian families, by an hereditary instinct. They soon learned that if they showed the least sign of being unconventional in dress or taste, they were pecked by the others and worried as birds worry another wearing a ribbon attached by some human owner. Persistence in oddity or pride in originality was liable to the severe penalties that the birds of the day-time administer to an owl, unfortunate or foolish enough to show itself matutinal.

Peter soon realised that he was surrounded by many pit-falls of taboo, by unwritten laws, which had to be sought or guessed, by customs, which were stronger than the Ten Commandments but, unfortunately for new boys, not recited on Sundays. First Peter had to learn how to cap or salute a master, by touching the brim of his hat. The old salute had been to remove the hat to a Classical but only to touch the brim to a Mathematical master. Only when speaking to a master was the whole hat removed. The Head and the Provost continued to receive the full salute. The Head never saluted within his realm. When Goodford was raised from Head to Provost, the promotion was made known to the boys by his answering salute as he came from election.

Eton jackets of course may never be alluded to as ' Etons,' which is the term used by the outer world. Clothes are important at Eton. They have been built up by tradition. The side-pocket came in with pegtops, the top-hat with the House of Hanover, overcoats with the severe winter of 1865. Sweaters were once the privilege of *Pop* and the *Victory* boat. They were allowed to the common herd after a boy nearly died of a chill. The *Victory* sweater survived with its blue border on the person of the ninth man in the *Monarch*, Ninth of the Ten as he was entitled. In two days Peter had learnt a good deal though not nearly all. He had not set foot one yard down town before he realised that boys only walked on one side of the street, and that to walk on the left side to Windsor was as odd an action as standing on one's head. Mimetically he had begun rolling up his trousers and un-buttoning the last button of his waistcoat. He observed that umbrellas must remain unrolled except in very exalted hands. The first time he turned into New and Lingwood's to have his hat *lushed* by old Solomon, he learnt that his narrow silk band must instantly be re-placed by a thick band of mourning for his late Majesty King George the Third, and antiquaries would have told him that the black tail-coat worn at Eton only came into vogue when the boys had their blue swallowtails dyed for the same reason. The black band for King George is as rigorously worn by Eton boys as the mourning for Nelson which is still carried by the British sailor. Taboo, which is the pith of etiquette and the nurse of superstition, is as strong at Eton as in the most remote African clan. An Etonian would rather say his prayers backward than appear with a coloured tie in School. Solomon with his white cap and flat-irons was as well known as the Head. He and his father had *lushed* hats at Eton since the beaver. Without Solomon half the hats of Eton would have collapsed before their time. Peter thanked him for his advice, and feeling his way cautiously through the visible and invisible regulations of Eton life, and trying to look as much alike to everybody else as possible, he made for the School Yard, when he was suddenly run down by a figure darting out of the entrance. It was Socston gasping, ' Darley, you have taken Remove ! Mr. Lamb has sent for us both. I 've only taken Middle Fourth ! '

They both turned to the left and joined the crowd of new boys intently scanning the entrance list. Stunned with sudden bliss, Peter allowed himself to be led off to his Tutor. The School Yard burst into radiant beauty before his eyes. What had seemed a gloomy fortalice became filled with golden light. The statue of the Founder seemed to beckon with benevolence instead of threatening with the iron rod which he held in suspended jurisdiction over the heads of generations. The great turrets of Lupton's Tower shot up like an arch of triumph. A downward rush of pigeons from the Chapel ledges filled the air with gaiety and speed. Youth flowered in his heart. He felt that already success feathered his cap.

Socston did not seem a bit disappointed, taking cheer from failure, as he remarked he had expected to take lower still. As they crossed the cobbles and slipped through Fourth Form passage, a narrow panelled run between the two Yards, friendship sprang up between them. They had suffered together from anxiety and hope,

D

anxiety's timid sister. Now they were temporarily free from the bondage of scare. One form of examination at least could never hurt them again. They felt as light and alert as the pigeons wheeling in the air. They promised each other always to *mess* together and stick by each other. The first keen joy of Eton life lifted the path under them, and they trod the very ether. They were Etonians at last. Into Weston's Yard they tripped, where the old chestnut met them like an old friend. Through the door they went into m' Tutor's garden and, climbing upstairs, were met by Mr. Lamb with a cheery laugh, 'Good boys, you have both taken higher than I expected. Your Tutor likes good boys, and good boys like your Tutor.' At which the parrot broke into ironical laughter punctuated by 'Lamb, Lamb!' Mr. Lamb was in good humour and apologised, 'You mustn't listen to what he says. He is a very bad parrot and ought to be complained of to the Head Master. Eh, Polly?' The parrot was only more amused at the idea than ever. 'By the way, I had a look at your paper, Darley. Your Latin verses were very fair, but your Tutor's boys are expected to do wonderful verses. There are two points of honour among my pupils. They do wonderful Latin verses and they never use Dr. Smith's abominable English-Latin Dictionary. Your Greek translation was by far your best paper, remarkably good indeed!'

Peter flushed to the roots of his hair with a conscientious scruple that, as he had seen the translation paper before, he was hardly entitled to praise, and, unwilling to commence his Eton career with deception, he blurted out, 'Sir, I saw the paper before at my crammer's. Perhaps I ought to tell the examiners.' Mr. Lamb was a little taken aback by this unexpected candour. 'No, no! I do not think you need mention it. Still, you did right to tell me. My pupils tell me everything.' This was not wholly exact, and Mr. Lamb, no less conscientious himself, added, 'at least I like to think they do.'

Peter discovered later that it was not Etonian to make

confessions to one's Tutor even of one's own failings, lest one might be one day tempted to cross the deadly line and touch on the sins of others. Eton form demanded perfect but reticent politeness to the tutorial race. Lower Boys were liable to be over-intimate and to pour forth their infant griefs, but the Fifth Former treated his House master as something between a hotel manager and a domestic chaplain, while Classical Tutors were expected to perform the functions of consul and coach, of a protector and a corrector at the same time. Of course there were always men of the necessary character, tolerance, and wisdom to make a success of their Houses, but there were some who were regarded by boys as escaped lunatics temporarily endowed with magisterial powers which could be always slighted. Though not yet in charge of a House, Mr. Lamb possessed all the imponderable elements of success with boys.

There were so many matters that a sacred law forbade being mentioned to a master that Mr. Lamb thought it was not well to encourage any further confidences for the time, and passing over Peter's little lapse proceeded to congratulate him on the Examination. It was a very satisfactory beginning and would reduce his fagging days to the minimum of a year. Mr. Lamb beamed over the Classical prospect, and then inquired his tastes in English literature. Peter racked his brain for the stiffest books he knew. 'Please, sir, I have read Shakespeare and Ruskin.' He happened to have read extracts in a reader. 'No Scott?' inquired his Tutor kindly. 'Oh yes, on Sundays.' Mr. Lamb thought Scott was nice and Stevenson nicer but Milton was nicest. He had been reading Milton with his pupils. All his pupils loved Milton, though they could never write quite such good Latin verses as Milton. This half he was going to read Stevenson's 'Bottle Imp' at Sunday *Private*, whatever that form of entertainment might be.

Peter felt the strangest half-pity, half-amusement stirring under his heart for this simple, smiling personage, whom he had expected to be so formidable and who showed pleasure in authors whom Peter connected with the nursery. He guessed Mr. Lamb must have been fond of *Robinson Crusoe* once, which would account for the parrot. ' And by the way,' he went on, ' there is to be a practice in Lower Chapel this evening, which you boys must attend. You must find the position of your seats and try to please Dr. Lloyd by good singing. Here are orders for all the books you will each need this half. Have them stamped with your names in gold letters at Ingalton Drake's. And you will notice that your Tutor writes a beautiful hand.' Peter glanced at the exquisite lettering signed with a long-tailed cipher. ' All my pupils learn to write beautiful hands. You may go. . . . Sandy! Sandy! down, you wicked dog,' and King Henry the Sixth barely escaped the rush of an Irish terrier by leaping on to Mr. Lamb's shoulders. As the boys descended the old-fashioned stairs they could hear the derision of the parrot, ' Pretty Poll! Damn! Ha! Ha! ' For alas, the wicked bird feared neither man nor the Head, and blasphemed accordingly.

As Peter passed back through the School Yard, he noticed an elderly mariner accompanied by a barrow and two leaping collie dogs making violent signals to him. The ancient's cap bore the legend ' College Porter,' and Peter felt anxious to employ him by writing an order on the slate which was thrust into his hand, when he realised that it was to poetry not porterage that his attention was being called. The slate was devoted to strange drawings of masters and to some very flattering verses comparing the writer to a Busy Bee. This was Porter Blake, the deaf Eton poet. Peter read the lines, shouted his satisfaction as politely as shouting can be shouted, and hurried on. He looked back and saw the Porter pointing out his latest effusion to the School Clerk, who to his honest rage scribbled ' Rubbish ' across the slate.

Blake was a privileged character and allowed to occupy the entrance into School Yard, over which he kept very careful watch lest any parcels were smuggled out of College without due use of his barrow. On one occasion there was a terrible scene at the gates. Some unkind Collegers had not only written a bitter parody of Blake's ode to himself on the slate, but the barrow had been hidden in the Playing Fields, whence it was brought back by an anxious search party. Blake's great aversion was cruelty to animals, and if he kept one eye on parcels, the other was kept on passing carters. At all hours he would run out to stop overloaded horses and order their drivers to the ground, happily regardless of their oaths, for his hearing had been totally destroyed by gunfire in the brave days of old.

CHAPTER III

CHAPEL INTERLUDE

PETER and Socston went their way, renewing defensive alliance and eternal friendship in view of the possibilities of the Morleyites. They found Willum swinging the dinner bell in the echoing passage with ponderous contortions passing through his febrile body. His face was swollen purple and threatening to discharge torrents of impure blood. He used the bell both as a summons to food and as a weapon of defence to drown the insults and oaths which were thrown at him by the descending boys. The more unconsecrated their language, the more vigorously he swung the bell over his head, until a final crescendo of peals heralded Mr. Morley, who clucked a short Grace and the meal began. The new boys took their new places, Socston half-way up the Lower Boy table but Peter shyly at its head. A buzz of comment followed— then stony silence.

'Good God!' muttered a Fifth Former languidly consenting to examine the new boys, 'one of them has taken Remove.' There was a burst of amusement, and conversation turned to more serious topics. Peter quickly realised how thoroughly unpopular his achievement was. While Socston had already been accepted into comradeship by his neighbours, Peter found himself ignored by the boys at the top of the table, who were two years senior and by their dress and manner made him feel a hopeless and uncouth subaltern. Their hair was pommaded, their collars were immaculate, and their black sailor ties were of knitted silk not of plain cloth. Their jackets were tailor-pressed and their trousers elegantly striped.

Their boots, as he noticed afterwards, were carefully buttoned, for a profound philosopher once observed that Etonians were divided into those who wore buttoned boots and those who did not. In a School, where dress was dictated with the precision of military regulations, there was scant choice left to the individual taste, with the result that between the buttoned and unbuttoned of foot lay the slight gulf that separates the smart set in all societies. In her visit to Eton Mary Wollstonecraft found ' nothing but dress and ridicule going forward,' while De Quincey chiefly noticed ' a premature knowledge of the world.' These certainly were the sum of Peter's first impressions, and as Lower Boys were divided as keenly among themselves as Uppers Peter was destined to remain in paralysing silence at meals during the rest of the half.

The afternoon Peter spent with Socston furnishing his room. They bought themselves candles and candle-sticks, for the lighting at Morley's was still mediaeval. They purchased heavy match-boxes with the Eton arms in heraldic colours, the most beautiful and symbolic of coats of arms—three lilies on *sable* and in chief a fleur-de-lys on *azure* with a lion *or* upon *gules*. They also chose some Thorborn prints of game-birds, and in a burst of originality a picture by Lady Butler of a cavalry officer charging to the cry of ' *Floreat Etona!* ' while a sudden loyalty to the School prompted Socston to buy, at an extravagant price, a framed cartoon from *Vanity Fair* of the Head Master reading ' Absence ' at the foot of the College steps. It was Edmond Warre to the life, the soundest, thickest-skulled, and noblest of Olympians, with his back as straight as a long life devoted to rowing could make it, facing the respectful School with innocuous defiance.

On their return, Socston introduced Peter to a number of Fourth Form friends, acquired during lunch—Philips, Ormton, and Camdown minor, a hulking fellow wearing the ' charity ' tails sometimes permitted to bulk without brain. They agreed they would all go together to choir practice that evening, Philips hinting that there might be a sport taking the mysterious form of ' rotting the Flea.' This puzzled Peter, until Philips, who was a humorist, explained that the ' Flea,' or Austen Leigh, was the Lower Master, and so called because his success at *swishing* Lower Boys seldom failed to draw blood. Apparently he was a very formidable person, and had also the requisite authority or musical gifts to preside at a practice in Lower Chapel, though whether he wielded birch rod or baton Peter was left to imagine.

Tea was a noisy hour at Mr. Morley's. From their large rooms overlooking the street, the Churchyard, and Upper Chapel, the fag masters bellowed in a lordly fashion, and fags began to run up and down the obscure boy-runs at the back of the house. The custom was that every fag had to be called by name, but the Captains indulged in calling ' Boy,' at which every fag within hearing was expected to make a rush and the task was, by a refinement of policy, allotted to the slowest. Tea required much expenditure of labour, with results which one French waiter could have probably obtained in half the time. Lower Boys bolted up and down the stairs, waving tea-pots and all but impaling each other on toasting-forks. Toasting-forks were conveniently used to chastise male-factors of burnt toast, and, as the round end of their handles, when properly applied, left a bright-red bruise of similar shape, the punishment was known as the giving or receiving of a *cherry-bum*. In consequence the standard of toast was high. Peter watched the scene with nervous edification. He only hoped he would prove as agile and satisfactory one day when his turn came. After tea, the Dame distributed tickets for the boys allowed to attend Chapel after *lock-up*. Peter came in for a good deal of stifling congratulation, followed by an exposition of the perfect Lower Boy's duty to his God, as well as his duty to his Dame. The latter included a clean collar every day and saluting his Dame in the street. She was very in-

sistent on this point, for at heart she had a secret griev-
ance. As there was caste between boys, between *saps*
and *bloods*, and between Classical and Mathematical
masters, so there was unrevealed and undreamed feeling
amongst Dames. Since the old Dame who kept the
boarding-house had become extinct, with one exception,
a new race of Dames had sprung up. These were worthy
matrons, retired gentlewomen or masters' wives. Sad to
say, among themselves they were divided into ladies and
those who were not thought to be quite ladies. Wherein
the difference lay, the gross eyes of the male, master or boy,
were happily not called to judge, but Mr. Morley's Dame
was classed with the latter, and neither Mr. Morley nor the
Head could prevail on other Dames to return her call.
So she had fallen back on good works, and Mr. Morley's
wardrobe, and the spiritual care of domestics and other
ecclesiastical by-pursuits. Willum incidentally had been
triumphantly confirmed, though a waif of Wesleyanism,
and Mrs. Sowerby had been admitted to the Clewer branch
of the English Church Union.

Upon each boy she adjured reverence and hearty
singing, but only Peter and Socston could have said
Amen. Meantime, Willum had unloosed the weighty
chains and bolts, which always made the open window
a preferable means of egress at night, and immediately
took refuge behind the door itself, which had fortunately
been manufactured to withstand puerile assaults from
within or without. As it was, twenty Lower Boys
instantly compressed themselves through, and Willum
behind, the self-same door at a rush. In a second they
shot down the tunnel, and were whooping through the
street. They wheeled to the left, down Keate's Lane,
past Houses which were also discharging musical aspirants
into the night. Peter was swept along between Socston
and Philips, innocently trying to remember the names of
the musical notes he had learnt as a child. He felt he
could join very tolerably in singing in a familiar hymn.
How he hoped they would have one of his favourites, and

then he could show them his voice. Other boys seemed
equally interested and keen to be in time for practice, for
they were scurrying as hard as they could. 'That's Miss
Evans's!' shouted Philips, as they passed a low, old-
fashioned building, with a bow window from which a
mellow ray shot into the street. 'And that's Ainger's
at the corner, and over the road is the dead dog lab.'
Some Evansites ran out into the crowd, and accidentally
one was tripped up by the passing Morleyites, whereat
much amusement to the latter and some unhappy references to the place of Mr. Morley's in the football ties from
the former, also to Mr. Morley's probable place in the next
world. Both estimates seemed to Peter undesirably
low, and for the first time his face flushed with indignation
and loyalty to House and House master. They were
now outside the shadowy exterior of Lower Chapel.
Slender buttresses, with Gothic battlements, rose in the
night. Lights were beginning to illuminate seas of
coloured glass. The Antechapel was crowded with boys
studying their places on a printed chart. Peter found
himself placed under the organ. Philips and Socston
were in the next section. Peter's pleasure became
complete on finding a Psalter, a copy of Church Services,
and a Hymnal with tunes, such as he had always longed
to possess, waiting in his place, stamped with his name in
gilt characters. Socston was already making signals to
him, and, friendship struggling against reverence, Peter
permitted himself to wave back his hand. A steady buzz
of conversation filled the Chapel, while Dr. Lloyd, the
eager organist, trotted up and down the aisle, trying to
engage the whole congregation in amicable conversation,
and at the same time discover if any new boy could sing.
Having failed genially in both quests, he retired to the
organ-loft, and drowned the buzzing tongues with a rush
of sound which broke through the building like the
breakers of the returning tide. Then he ran down from
the loft to renew his queries. 'New boys who can sing,
stand up!' he cried, and clapped his hands. Instantly

all Remove stood up and waved eagerly. ' New boys only, I said.' Everybody sat down except Peter, who was pulled down by his neighbours. ' Oh dear, oh dear, aren't the holidays over ? ' and he tripped back to the organ. The buzz broke out again, to be quelled by a greater power than Lloyd and Orpheus together. A dead hush marked the entry of the Lower Master from the vestry at the east end. Stalwart and plump, he looked like a rubicund old-fashioned hunting squire, who early in life had found the happy proportion between hard riding and good claret. He wore a surplice and spats. He had a round skull covered with short grey hair, a cricketer's keen eyes, a strongly-fashioned jaw, a certain stoop, and a curious swaying gait which in connection with his glowing face and the contrast of his plum-coloured features against the light-cherry and lily-white complexions of boyhood gave an unmerited impression of mild drinking. The religious silence was broken by the sound of his breath, which he exhaled as a strong swimmer breathes in the water. When he lifted his voice and spoke with a rich nasal twang which would have qualified him for American citizenship within sound of Sandy Hook, the effect was decidedly comic, and had been so in the opinion of several generations of boys. ' The Flea ! The Flea ! ' whispered the old boys to the new. Like a muttered toast the word passed down the line—' The Flea ! '

' We will now practise the Psalm for to-morrow's divine service,' he twanged with a nod to Lloyd and took his place in the carved desk under the organ. Lloyd began fluttering like a hen over her nest. ' The twenty-second morning, boys ! ' he piped in a voice which sounded in amusing contrast to the Flea's sonorous croak. After some further fidgeting in the organ-loft the noble psalmody rang out. Lloyd was no duffer with the keys, and he gripped the boys' voices into unison. The tune was a mixture of Gregorian and ale-chorus, and the boys lifted a merry noise skyward :—

' O give thanks unto the Lord, for he is gracious and his mercy endureth for ever ! '

They sang the verses of the Psalm antiphonally from one side to the other, and the movement caught Peter to ecstasy. The organ notes seemed to pick up the boys' voices and hurl them heavenward. The Psalm rolled on:—

' Let them give thanks, whom the Lord hath redeemed and delivered from the hand of the enemy !

' And gathered them out of the lands from the east and from the west, from the north and from the south ! '

The monosyllables beat time, and Peter thought he had never heard anything so delightful. The organ stopped and Lloyd rushed down with some instruction. In an anti-musical philathletic school he was always anxious to impress the new boys. The boys, with whom he was a favourite, listened to what he had to say and were resuming song, when the Lower Master, remembering that a Music master is a little lower than a French master in the Eton Hierarchy, must needs add a note not of music but of authority. The cackle of the Flea impressing the boys with the duty of pronouncing their words distinctly produced a general titter. The Flea's cheeks visibly swelled and after a heavy puff collapsed, while his little eyes stared at the boys as though he was ready to be provoked to anger and chastisement. The boys glared back. The challenge was taken up, and from that moment any real practice was out of the question, though they sang the next verse good humouredly, ' They went astray in the wilderness out of the way and found no city to dwell in ! '

But the organ notes for the following verse rang against empty air, for the bigger boys in Remove had struck, and the voices of the rest died down. Lloyd came to an abrupt finish, all his flourishes yielding to flurry. ' Sing better, boys, sing louder,' he entreated from above, striking a roll of music loudly in the palm of his hands. ' Yes, boys,' intoned the Flea, ' sing that louder.' Once more the organ pealed, but a handful of boys instead of uttering the winged words whistled the tune shrilly in the silence. The Flea turned an autumnal purple and left his desk. It was a false move, for he no longer commanded both sides of the Chapel. As he peered furiously down one side, the opposite side took up the whistling without a quiver or a twist to their lips. The excellent Lloyd drove versicle after versicle out of the organ, but he could reap no more harmony from the boys, charm he never so wisely. The Chapel had become an arena between the infuriated Flea and the calm cunning of the boys, who sat grinning in their tiers like the spectators of a baited bull. Once or twice the Flea made a rush and tried to pick out an obvious culprit, but as the culprit invariably was laughing, he could prove he could not have been whistling. The Flea had had long enough dealings with boys to know when he was beaten, and calling off Lloyd's music, he gave orders to the boys to return to their Houses, after which he stalked down the centre in passive indignation, his breathless sides causing him to pant and snort more than ever to the renewed merriment of the boys. Thus was the Flea memorably incited, baited, ragged, and rotted, and what could he do except to remember to *swish* harder during the coming months ?

Besides, Lloyd good naturedly begged the Flea not to requite the evening's proceedings on the boys. As a matter of fact, Lloyd had greater difficulties in Upper Chapel, where not only the bigger boys scorned to sing but one of the masters could not be persuaded not to. In vain Lloyd arranged choir practice to coincide with his pupil-room hours. He invariably joined the procession on Sundays and sang steadily a form of note Lloyd used to call ' Eton flat.' Only occasionally and with a pained delicacy Lloyd ventured to point out a slight harmonic inaccuracy in the choir singing. The culprit held his own, and being a senior Classical master was inexpugnable.

Though the irreverence of the scene had tingled at the bottom of his conscience, Peter had enjoyed himself enormously. This was the wonderful Public School life he had heard of! What next? he wondered. He felt that a pillow-fight would prove the perfect end of the best day of his life. Meantime the week's construes had been posted on every landing, and with a throbbing heart he flung himself into the work of preparation. A few heads looked in, and on hearing that he was doing Remove construes expressed amused satisfaction. One added the mysterious threat, ' Darley, you damn well look out every word in the Dictionary. We don't want you to *spout crib* words.' Peter promised readily and was left alone for the rest of the night. But how he wished he had a father or a mother to write home the story of his Eton day. Other fellows had parents and sisters. As he lay back in bed he yearned for the sister whom his nurse had told him he would one day find. In this wide but amusing and lonely world he felt conscious of some sweet kindred spirit with whom he could share all the pleasures and worries of the amazing life around him. But oh, the loneliness of his soul in the Eton crowd!

CHAPTER IV

SUNDAY QUESTIONS

PETER found himself placed for School and Chapel in Division XXV., at the bottom of Remove, up to Mr. Jenkinson, one of a far-famed Eton family, all of whom were known immemorially as ' Juggins.' First contact had produced Sunday Questions, which Peter had taken away to answer on the beautiful double sheets in time for Early School on Monday. His first Eton Sunday was an industrious one. Disdaining the long lie in bed, which almost made Sabbatarians of Etonians, so deeply was it prized, Peter rose and spent an hour before breakfast hunting for answers to mysterious queries out of the First Book of Samuel. One question left him at a loss. He was expected to quote from Byron's *Hebrew Melodies,* which was one of Mr. Jenkinson's ways of slipping a little English literature into the Sunday curriculum like a sandwich between the dry study of the two Testaments.

There was enough light to work by, but the low-lying mist still considerably obscured the breakfast meal. After breakfast the boom of the Chapel bell began to galvanise the world of Eton into preparation to meet its God or at least His deputies. There was a general movement towards the two scenes of divine worship. The Lower Boys sped down Keate's Lane, while the Fifth Form stalked in their glossy tails to locate their names on the new chart in Upper Chapel. Only the greatest swells loitered by the wall, reserving the right to enter at the last moment before the Sixth Form. The mists wound away skyward leaving the Chapel clear like a great grey galleon, which had for three centuries ridden the fog and cloud, wind and storm of Eton without turning the shadow of a point out of her steadfast course. Anchored, she still rode in the Sunday peace beside the great breakwater formed of Upper School, while Lupton's Tower rose above her like a double lighthouse, save that the great central eye signalled time and not place, urged hurry not caution. The long pinnacled outline of the Chapel lay above the irregular roofs and trees of Eton, and the vanes tipping the eastern turrets were lit like golden arrows pointing Etonians to the roads of future fame. The bell tolled for ten minutes, so that Peter had time to glance at the venerable weather-worn Chapel, which stood like some spireless and unfinished torso of a Cathedral, before he ran off to Lower Chapel. Nine mighty buttresses of lime and ragstone held up the eight gaudy windows of Upper Chapel with three-tiered props on each side. The east window hung like a glass tapestry between the two end-buttresses, which were crowned with neat wooden belfries. From the midst protruded Lupton's Chapel which, with the side entrance and steps descending into the yard, filled three of the interstices between the buttresses. Along the whole precipitous height the pinnacles rose like flowerless stalks. The stone fabric was much spotted and patched where it had been renewed or where wind and rain had soaked and crumbled its surface. The outer garment of stone seemed to Peter like a symbol of the whole School. The separate stones, some old, some new, some large, some tiny, were like the boys, not one of whom would be missed if removed, for another would immediately be found to take his place. The eighteen great buttresses, each divided as it were into three tiers representing Upper and Lower Fifth Formers pressing down upon the Lower Boys at the foot, corresponded to the different Houses. The battlements might be compared to the First Hundred and the pinnacles to Sixth Form and the School Captains in their soaring glory and uncommanded eminence. Yet they all combined to make one ever-changing, ever-renewable whole, at the same

time hoary with years, grey and beautiful in Time's lichen-
coloured livery. As the clouds moved overhead and the
bell vibrated life through the solid stone, the Chapel
seemed to swing from her earth-planted moorings and to
move slowly but surely upon her holy way.

Peter looked round. Collegers were pouring out of
their New Buildings like Levites in the surplices which
they alone of the boys wore on Eton Sundays. Masters
in immaculate white ties and flowing silk gowns were proceeding to 'Desks' or observation points in the Chapels,
where they sat like academical warders over the dear boys
and received the Praepostors' books. At the close of
service they gave minute signals to the different Blocks
of boys to take regulated flight like mobs of starlings. It
was a grief to Peter that he was not allowed to attend the
more glorious of the two Chapels, but that remained a
privilege worth working for. Since the School had swelled
to the thousand mark under the rule of Warre, it had
become necessary to cloister the Lower Boys like two
hundred sparrows in a stone cage of late Victorian Gothic.
For a time Lower Boys had attended the Mortuary
Chapel in the new Cemetery without any noticeable effects
on their spirits, which were still effervescing as Peter
deposited his top-hat amid hundreds of hats and sat
watching the Praepostors standing in groups to mark the
names. The Lower Master with a clergyman-attendant
entered the seats of the mighty under the organ. The
Flea read the Lessons to a dreamy or respectful congregation. There was no sermon, and the lads scattered to their
Houses before twelve to elucidate the puzzles and riddles
of Sunday Questions or to plot fresh juvenile mischief.
Peter began to prepare the Greek Testament for Early
School on Monday with a zest which was cooled by the
entry of Philips and Frencher, who removed his Lexicon
and gave reasons : 'You can do your Greek Test. after
lights. Nobody touches the muck during the day.'
'Don't mind him,' laughed Philips, ' come out with us.'
'All right,' said Peter, very anxious to please, putting aside

E

his Testament until the hour of surreptitious candle-light. 'Apologise first for your disgusting conduct,' stated Frencher, who had just crawled into Fifth. Peter apologised, and then inquired what for. ' For taking Remove. You must be an awful *sap*. Why don't you go and live in *Tuggery* ? ' And this was a question Peter was often to ask himself during his Eton career.

At this moment another young Fifth Former, whose name, Mouler, was on the next door, leaned in for a look at his new neighbour and condescended to join the converse of his inferiors. From him Peter learnt that the *Tugs* or Scholars were separated from Oppidans by the same gulf that lay between Professionals and Gentlemen in the world of sport. Peter remembered nervously that he had arrived with one of these pariahs and even promised amity. A *Tug* was something between a *scug* and a hireling chorister, he gathered. He was actually paid for being a *sap*. That, Mouler explained, was why *sapping* was unnecessary, so unpleasant even, on the part of a member of Mr. Morley's House, and why he must confiscate Peter's Lexicon as a warning. Peter tried to snatch it back, and Mouler, unable to bear the least rebuke from a new boy, smacked his face and damned his eyes. ' New boys have got to be civil,' explained Philips kindly, and grabbed back his Lexicon for him. Mouler having laid the basis of future relations moved off for a walk with a friend, who summoned him at this moment. Peter turned gratefully to Philips and asked when was he expected to do his work. ' Oh, any time except after twelve, in *sock*-shops or after Prayers or on your way to School.' Peter sat back in despair, as he thought of the unknown Jenkinson and the expectant Lamb. ' You see,' said Philips, ' the fellows don't like it. Nobody *saps* here except Tudor, and even he uses *cribs*, for I 'm his fag and know where he hides them,' explained Philips, who, being a parson's son and in most matters virtuous, was tolerant of all lack of virtue in others. ' Is there nothing worse than being a *sap* ? ' asked Peter. ' Yes, you might be a *Tug* altogether and have to wear a *beak*'s gown round your neck.' ' But what is worse still ? ' asked Peter, desirous to probe the depths of infamy. ' Well, you might be a cad and have to go to Harrow.' Peter remembered with a shiver that his grandfather had been at Harrow.

In order to discourage any tendency to *sap* Philips suggested they should go and loaf round the Castle. Peter accepted, only too glad to be seen in company with an older boy down town. Across the Bridge they aimed at the rat-hole which runs into the Castle at the top of the Hundred Steps, with a view to visiting the Curfew Tower, with its solitary gun commanding the Bridge and the cumbrous clockwork which rings the nightly curfew, when they ran into half a dozen boys from Morley's, who announced they were on their way to a hotel between Castle and Bridge. ' It's out of bounds,' whispered Philips, ' but as long as nobody sees us going in it does not matter.' One of the new party slipped back to watch the Bridge, while another sauntered towards Damnation Corner. The rest took the corner towards Romney Island, and disappeared into a private door. Peter found himself pushed in by Philips. They passed into a private house, which reeked of beer and resounded to the cheery click of billiard balls. In a rancid inner room Frencher and Camdown major were playing. Camdown minor and Mouler were acting as markers. Camdown major was of that numerous clan at Eton, tall and good-looking, who accomplish little good and not much harm, unless possibly to themselves. His mouth was like a girl's, though nothing very feminine proceeded from it. The light hair over his quick features was pasted with ' bear's grease,' and he moved like a lithe cat round the table, missing every stroke. When he cannoned he observed, ' Priceless ! ' or ' That was a crisp one ! ' Frencher played no better, and only ' hashed a number of sitters.' It was obvious they played not for love of the game, but for hate of the rule forbidding them to play at all. Frencher's amusement was too perpetual even to find its source in

Camdown's play. He was the esteemed practical joker at Morley's, and being accustomed to cause mirth, giggled himself at everything he did. His imitation of the Man having a fit round a corner had more than once deceived and drawn the Dame. Mouler was less harmless than Frencher. He had a number of points in common with a ferret and a Chinaman. He looked so sharp and so innocent. He had the thickest caked tongue in the School. As Peter and Philips entered, he curled his lips with disgust. ' Who brought the kids ? ' he asked, and the game languished. Frencher, as a matter of fact, was giggling over practising his next practical joke. ' Who will roll a billiard ball across the table at Prayers to-night ? ' he asked. There was general approval of the scheme, though to carry it out many were willing and no one anxious to be chosen. ' Do it yourself ! ' shouted Mouler. ' I will, by Gad ! ' said Frencher, but he was the only one not to join in the laugh which followed. As it was approaching two, they began sneaking home up the High Street. Peter felt sick with anxiety to reach the First Book of Samuel and be in time to learn his Greek chapter of St. Mark. Frencher was also a little anxious, for a borrowed billiard ball lay a little heavy in his pocket.

That afternoon, while the whole House paired for a walk, Peter sat down and strenuously finished his first Sunday Q.'s in copperplate. A single blot was removed at the edge of an eraser. Before the bell began ringing for Evening Chapel he was well into St. Mark. In Chapel he felt relieved again, and listened to the Flea reading, without caring whether his voice was among voices what the banjo is unto lute, shawm, and such like. He made mental resolves to avoid all forbidden things in future. He decided that he disliked nothing at Eton except Mouler. Tea followed Chapel. In peace he sat down to tea, and listened to the fag masters shouting like angry elephants, ' Bo-o-hoy-hoy-hoy ! '

After tea he finished his Greek, and was able to offer a helping hand to Philips in his Q.'s. It was a mistake, for rumour spread that the new boy would volunteer a *spout*, and a number of gentlemen in Remove arrived with their Classical books, and put Peter through the construes he had so laboriously prepared on Saturday evening. Towards supper-time there was a more general scramble to write out Sunday Q.'s. At nine Willum performed his bell feat to announce food and, half an hour later, Prayers. The *bloods* sat lazily in the Library, watching the other Fifth Formers assemble, while the herd of Lower Boys shot down the lead-carpeted stairs. Their speech was languid, and after the manner of *bloods* somewhat bloodiwise. They were discussing the character of boys in the next House a little libellously. The last of their inferiors were crushing into the dining-room. Peter was among them, and found himself jostling Mouler in the doorway. Willum, hating Mouler, pressed the door inward, and in a second both boys were engaging like terriers. Peter felt two punches before he struck back. Strange to say, encouragement was shouted to the fighters, both from within and without. A ring was being formed, when Peter, lifting his hand to his nose, found it crimson. There was nothing to be done but to retreat to his room and a basin of water. The next day Willum congratulated him on the science he had put into his solitary hit on Mouler, but he realised that, on the whole, it was not wise for a new boy to win a fight. Running upstairs, he spent a wretched ten minutes bleeding into cold water, and wondering whether the Captain or Mr. Morley would send for him first. He had not heard the amused cheer from the Library as he fled in shame. All he remembered was that at a private school fighting was a high crime and a misdemeanour.

Suddenly Socston strode into his room, against the rule, to tell him he had missed one of the most amusing scenes in the history of the House. ' It 's all right, Darley, you are quite forgotten. There 's a fine row on. They ragged the Man, as they call Mr. Morley. He had got half-way through Prayers, when Frencher rolled a billiard ball across the table to Camdown major, who opened his hands like a pocket. He tried to push it back with his finger, but it miscued and went down the table. The Man pretended not to see, but it crept slowly down the table like a white mouse, till it touched Tudor's hands. He was praying hard, and it gave him an awful start. Tudor put it in his pocket, and after Prayers the Man asked who put the fives ball on the table, and Frencher said, " Please, sir, I did not put the fives ball on the table," and the Man said he never said he did, and the House roared like mad. I tell you you missed an evening's sport.' Peter gasped, but he decided he had already enjoyed his share of Sunday sport in the afternoon. His head still swam with the blow he had received. He was as amazed as Socston that a master could be treated and flouted so, and said, ' I suppose he will tell the Doctor to-morrow.' ' Oh, call him the Head, not the Doctor,' entreated Socston, ' and masters are *beaks*.'

No sooner had Socston finished his tale than the rustle of bombazine was heard in the passage and the Dame, duly informed by Mrs. Sowerby, who heard it from Willum, appeared in person with restoratives. ' Puir laddie, did they pull a laddie's nose ? I hope they did nothing wrongful in the sight of the Lord.' She caught sight of Socston hiding under the table. ' Ah, the bad laddie, if the Master knew you were in another laddie's room after Prayers, I do not know what he would do.' Nor ever did Socston, for a minute after the Dame's departure Mr. Morley arrived and expressed himself equally puzzled to know what the Dame would do, could she see Socston at that hour in Peter's room. And in quest apparently of that information he passed on his way. ' I wonder if the Man is as big a fool as the boys think,' said Socston as he returned to his room. ' Good night ! '

The Man having completed his nocturnal round and lights being extinguished, the passages became singularly thronged with life. Lordly *bloods* discussed the athletic prospects of the half. Friends visited friends. Uppers

came out to borrow books out of which to finish belated
Sunday Q.'s. Lower Boys turned over to sleep, and a
little before midnight Tudor, putting away his *crib* to
Aristophanes, called down the passage for silence and the
last murmur died away.

The Eton world slept, and a soft moon flooded the little
hamlet, silvering the bare branches of the secular elms,
illumining the empty little thoroughfares, and bathing the
sheer steep of the Chapel in lambent argent, which gave
the stone a crystalline look against the darkness of the
windows. The stone might be glass, the glass black
marble. Not a stick stirred, not a cobble rang in the still-
ness. Peace and Beauty had here made their dwelling
place. The great buttresses, caught in the freezing en-
chantment of the moon, seemed to pour like icy waterfalls
from the Chapel roof, thickening in their fall, until they
touched the white lunar lake which filled the School Yard.
The weather-green statue of the Founder threw a sharp
shadow, as with raised wand he gazed watchfully toward
his beloved Collegers in Long Chamber, whom he still
fostered financially upon earth and with a Saint's powerful
prayers in Heaven. Like upright icicles the pinnacles of
the Chapel pierced the night air. There was no sign of
life. Nothing moved save the heavy, regular breathing of
the School Clock. In summer-time and winter-time, in
seed-time as in harvest, during the three halves of the
School year, Lent, Easter, and Michaelmas, during holiday
and in the night-time, when there was none to hear him,
the old Clock kept vigil. Boom ! Boom ! Boom ! Boom !
he struck the four quarters, and then one by one the
measured resonancy of midnight.

In the dreams of Old Etonians all over the world, some
lying in the houses of state, some in the pioneer's fevered
hut, in the beds of the wealthy, in the camp, or in the
cloister, the booming of the old Clock echoed, and for unconscious moments in their sleep the years were rolled
back.

CHAPTER V

SURROUNDINGS

PETER arrived ten minutes before the hour for Early School on Monday. Jenkinson's Division was placed in the low, white-plastered room known as the Black Hole, to the left of the entrance of School Yard. The grime of the eighteenth century added to its charm as well as to its opacity. In spite of the picturesque old-fashioned wooden tiers rising almost to the roof, and the heavy diamond-paned casements looking on the Long Walk, it would have been condemned by the London School Board at sight. Nevertheless, Peter soon realised that Jenkinson teaching in a coal-hole was better than the cream of State pedagogy filtered through a scientifically lighted class-room.

While the Clock boomed the hour, Jenkinson turned the corner collecting his division from the colonnade in the sweep of his gown. Thrusting a key as big as St. Peter's into the rusty lock, he preceded them into the mildewed atmosphere of the holidays, which even the incandescent gas could not expel. Mr. Jenkinson was a tall invalid. The effect of his height was lost in his scholar's stoop, but the wide brow bespoke the winning of the Newcastle Scholarship and a Trinity Fellowship. For some years he had taken Sixth Form as the Head's understudy, very much to the Head's reputation as a scholar. He was now condemned to drive second-rate writers like Xenophon and St. Mark into third-rate learners at the bottom of Remove. The drift and dregs between Fifth and Fourth Form together with the new boys in Remove were closeted under his guidance. Cheerily and wearily he faced the struggle of the half. The handsomeness of his youth was

still visible in his face, the scholar's pallor was under-
written by enthusiasm, and under the grey curls his eyes
flashed keenness and rectitude, honour and sympathy.
In his manner he was another such as Socrates, ascetical
and careless of bodily hardship and at the same time deeply
intellectual. Just and scrupulous, he spared himself least
and rather optimistically expected boys not to spare themselves either. But in this he was mistaken, and probably
preferred to be mistaken than to realise the slackness,
cribbing, and general avoidance of work which character-
ised Lower Remove. Perhaps he was too busy to be disappointed, for by his untiring and sleepless industry in
class and out he carried his whole division of blockheads
a little farther on the despised road of learning.

Jenkinson had the faculty of throwing himself into
whatever he did, and, what was rarer, into whatever others
did. He was ready to enjoy everybody's success and
always mildly depreciated his own. Masters showing
originality roused his keen admiration. It pleased him
no less in a boy, though he knew that officially he was
intended to modify or suppress originalities. He could
throw himself with an infectious zest into any Classical
characters drifting by on the weary wash of daily work.
A Roman Emperor like Caligula, a Latin poet like Catullus, or the memory of the first Marathon runner carrying
word of victory lived again on his lips. Even at the dreary
performance known as Classical French, when Classical
masters were brought to bear on a language they neither
knew nor liked, Jenkinson could throw accent to the wind
and leap into the spirit of Alphonse Daudet. He was
rumoured to have driven round Paris in a cab in search
of local colour to transmit to his division. And the whole
map of Greece flowered at his touch. Little as he knew
it, his influence was beginning to move in the School.
Masters, as well as boys, were affected by that white
selflessness. A master took more trouble with corrections
that were to pass under his eye, and a boy often thought
it worth while to please ' Juggins ' with his Latin verses,

for he was showing them up to the truest poet at Eton. Jenkinson stood for the spirit, and his influence unseen was stronger in the School than even the visible power of Dr. Warre. Jenkinson's House was in its athletic infancy, but he followed its first and feeble efforts with the loving heart of a fanatic. He was always ready to cheer his Lower Boys through the muddy process of the Lower Boy Football Cup, or to stick to a race on the River like a martyr. Entrants for the lower forms of aquatics, who might have entered for a joke, or out of curiosity, were stimulated into seriousness by the anxious appearance of Jenkinson on the River bank, hobbling along and administering steady applause during the race and sterling consolation at the end. His football playing consisted of lone and forlorn charges up the field. He played solely for his side. He was a splendid optimist, and except for *cribs*, lumbago, and snobbish parents, the universe to him was very jolly indeed.

Peter's first week was one of solid industry. He spent every available minute preparing the tasks of Remove, construing them to Mr. Lamb in Mr. Lamb's *puppy-hole*, and finally waiting for his turn in School. He had read his first lines in the two greatest world poems. With much dictionary grubbing he had deciphered the first twenty lines of the *Æneid* of Virgil, as well as a chunk of Homer's *Odyssey*. Only the pencilled, thumb-printed page testified the struggle he had made, while older hands had arrived at much more correct versions with the silent aid of Messrs. Kelly and Giles's *Keys to the Classics*. A year passed before Peter glanced at one of these well-established preventives of brain fag. In his endeavours to be punctual he pasted a printed time-table into the lining of his top-hat, and wasted cumulative hours by rushing to School ten minutes too soon. He accepted the guise of nonentity. He wore the dull garb and cap of the boy in the street. He rightly felt that etiquette required him to look undistinguished. His vanity was not offended by the *woolly-bear* or hideous great-coat, which was imposed on all new boys until the Eton Society, who rule fashion as well as games, announced by an act of sartorial clemency that all boys were permitted to wear their town overcoats. Within a fortnight Peter's blue and black *scug*-cap had been soiled to look like the property of an older boy, and he himself had been admitted to the menial offices of Tudor's fag. His duties did not consist of more than the emptying of cold, soapy baths, and the lighting of not much warmer fires with damp fire-lighters. Few incidents occur to a Lower Boy who follows in the obscure groove of industry. Unless he remains long enough in the School to hatch into Sixth Form glories, his career through Lower School is that of the much-squashed caterpillar, and through Fifth Form of the self-contained chrysalis. Peter felt about as distant from Sixth as from *Pop*, the Eton Society, who alone constituted *bloods* of the blood. Mr. Morley's swells were swollen only in Morleyite eyes, but *Pops* were the athletic oligarchy who ruled the School under the symbol of their knotted canes, tied with light blue ribbon into the form of *fasces*. They alone enjoyed the privilege of wearing coloured waistcoats and flowers in their coats. But in their lowly name they bore the mark of a lost intellectual origin when they met over a *Popina* or cook-shop for intellectual discussion and debate. The Captain of the School himself, a Colleger and a super-*sap*, had almost become a survival from a less athletic age, but he was, in deference to Dr. Warre, admitted in an honorary capacity into *Pop*. Dr. Warre had recently hinted that the early intellectual aims of the Society were not fulfilled by preferring athletes low down in the School to the leading scholars. Warre brought this Nemesis upon himself, for the whole athletic system had sprung up since his coming to Eton. If the Captain of the School was colourless, it was sometimes arranged for him to wear the blue and white cap of the *Monarch*, a clumsy ten-oar survival in the boating world, in order to prevent the sad sight of a *Pop* wearing a *scug*-cap. The lowliest colour may no more be assumed by the unathletic than a military decoration by a civilian.

Peter's first mistake had been to attend an Evening School, when cap is worn instead of top-hat, wearing the cap of his private school, which unfortunately happened to have the same stripes as the *Monarch*. As a result he was mobbed, as jackdaws mob one of their number ill-advised enough to carry a peacock's feather in his tail.

On Mondays only there was a survival of Evening School, an hour of mathematics after *lock-up*, dating from the days when maths. were an extra, to be learnt with fencing or Italian in odd hours and corners from odder assistants. In this case the assistant was particularly odd, a reverend Mr. Jones, whom the boys called ' Jumps ' J, because he neither walked nor crawled. He looked like Socrates. Eccentric in gait, features, and speech, he seemed the last person capable of instilling formulae into boys possessed of any sense of the ludicrous. The most famous jest ever played on Mr. Jones had been a solemn letter written to the *Field* over his honoured name, describing the havoc he had seen wrought by cows munching young partridges. On Sundays he squeaked the Epistle in wondrous contrast to the sonorous gospelling of the Head. Peter came to the conclusion that his voice was a mimetic result of perpetually scraping the blackboard. ' Infant, infant,' was his address to all sizes of boys. The hour up, the boys clustered round for their tickets to be initialled, for every Eton master adopts a cipher, more or less difficult to forge. As they passed out, one youth caught sight of Peter's coloured cap. ' Holy Jack the Ripper,' he exploded. ' Does he think he is coxing the *Monarch* ? '

Peter slipped on his cap and escaped in the night with the whole class in quick pursuit. He heard cries—' Off with it ! ' ' Rub it in the mud ! ' ' Throw it on the Burning Bush ! ' This last strange suggestion was favourably received, and before he had crossed out of New Schools he was tripped, and his cap carried away in triumph to a curious excrescence of ironmongery supporting a lighted lamp in the middle of the street. Biblical experts had long agreed that it was a fair replica of the Burning Bush after which it was named. One boy climbed upon the shoulders of another, and the erroneous headgear was placed where it could not trouble its owner or his critics again.

Otherwise incidents were few in Peter's closely regulated existence. The mighty traditional and almost mechanical world of Eton gathered him into her system, gave him her commandments, set him little tasks, plied his minute ambitions, permitted little liberties, traced each hour, and fulfilled his day. Boys are kept busy between Division masters and fag masters, but they know that as they progress up the School tasks will lessen and liberties grow. Peter found himself following his nose by certain paths daily, to School, to the School Yard, to Chapel, to the *sock*-shop, and on half-holidays he went down to the naturalist's shop at the Bridge, where he deposited seventeen and sixpence for a course of extra studies in bird-stuffing. Houses not in the athletic forefront were inclined to go to the dogs, or rather to the guinea-pigs. When Uppers took to pipes, Lower Boys took to pets. Morley's House was too insignificant to rouse any of the splendid rivalry that was provoked by a House like Miss Evans's. The only rival to Morley's was Maxse's, the little run-down house of red bricks, which the School knew generally as 'the Synagogue,' owing to the number of scriptural names and important city connections which it housed. It was said that some boys wandering into the House by mistake overheard the House Debating Society speaking in a tongue which they mistook for a class in German. Peter was glad to think there was another House which as a Morleyite he could still disdain.

Bad blood spurted between the two Houses, Morley's and Maxse's, whenever they crossed each other's trails. When they met in shops there were scuffles, and when there was snow they waylaid each other at the entrances of their dens. In the opinion of the School both had been voted vile and low, and once an Eton House has been given a bad name, only an infusion of Olympic victors and Newcastle Scholars enables it to lift its head again. Jenkinson's House was waiting, equally small and insignificant, at the bottom of the ladder, but it was not shunned as Maxse's was. It had yet to make its character.

Part of Peter's immediate education lay in becoming familiar with the different *beaks*, learning the House-colours associated with some, and the legends of Lower Boy fiction pertaining to others. Every morning between schools the didactic body hurried into the Head's low, ill-lighted Chambers at the corner of the School Yard and discussed with lightning rapidity the behaviour and penal possibilities of numberless boys. Division masters complained of boys, and their Tutors tried to defend them. Bargains as between gentlemen were made, masters letting down each other's pupils unless the offences were too appalling for excuse and the Tutor was unable to avoid counter-signing the complaint to the supreme authority, entailing the time-honoured penalty, which is chiefly honoured in the breach.

Philips took Peter to stand under the colonnade of Upper School, and named the individuals in that extra-ordinary academic rout. Some masters came striding, some slouching, some strutting, some strolling on their way to give account of their stewardship to the Head. Little by little Peter picked up their characteristics. There was old Ainger at the head of the list, a gaunt, sweet-smiling Ovidian, compiler of the Eton *Gradus*, and an Eton patriot. He had written the *Carmen Etonense*, which Etonians remembered when they forgot Horace. Ainger was the poet among Etonians, as his colleague Christopher was the Etonian among poets. They were supposed to be equally rivals for the Head Mastership and the national position of Laureate. There was Mr. James, the well-loved 'Arthur Jack,' a tall white-moustached leader of boys who remained his pupils to the end of their lives. He was the Eton artist, and had illustrated the scenes of the Eton floods with irresistible caricature. Often an exercise shown up to him was returned marked with a humorous or sarcastic sketch. In more serious moments he compiled the Grosvenor Guide to Latin Prose.

There was ' the Pecker,' whose House had gone down like a pirate's ship. There had been days when Pecker-ites poached Ditton Park at night for game, and when a black flag was hoisted each time a boy was expelled. His talents were now occupied as Senior Mathematical master with preparing Chapel Lists, and his House in Common Lane was occupied by the famous Mitchell. Old ' Mike ' had coached the Eleven from his youth unto old age, and resembled a bent piece of cricket willow. *Vanity Fair* had made his caricature a national posses-sion. He cherished a lifelong grudge against Harrow, since as a boy he had twice suffered an innings defeat at Lord's, and he still crawled round thinking of Harrow wickets with their bails off. But it was now six years since Harrow had been defeated, and during a quarter of a century Eton had only won four times. ' Mike's ' hair consequently had turned white, and there were murmurs that he was too old, not so much for teaching as for the responsible task of coaching the Eton Eleven. His soul stood for one supreme end. ' Of one thing,' wrote the celebrated author of *Eton Cricket*, ' I am certain. We all have one object in view, the improvement of cricket at Eton.' ' Mike ' regretted that Eton liberty would not allow cricket-fagging to improve the fielding. Win-chester fielding had been built up like the pyramids by hours of serf-labour. Harrow slipped coaching into the middle of the day, whereas nets at Eton were in the even-ing. That possibly was the worst of having a *wet-bob* Head. ' Mike's ' ambition had been to introduce a School Office for games with a permanent clerk, until somebody suggested a Boating Bursar ! As it was, he dominated Eton cricket with his theory of forward play and style, until, recalling the military defeats following Lord Peterborough's use of the best text-books, the Eton Eleven found themselves irreproachable except for the annual draw or defeat at the hands of Harrow. 'Mike' was waiting for a victory such as that of 1869, which closed an era of disappointments, and inspired old Provost Goodford to dance in front of the Pavilion at Lord's like David before the Ark.

There was Mr. Munfort, a spruce and popular old gentleman with an eagle eye and the genial features of Punch, in which he bore a curious resemblance to Keate, greatest of Eton Heads. With some assistance from the House of Lords, whose first-borns crowded to his House, he had won the Football Cup and could assume some of the respect and popularity which pertains to the owner of a Grand National winner. By his stride into Chambers it might be guessed that the Cup was on his dining-table. There was Mr. Redley, a Mathematical master with nicknames drawn both from the vegetable and animal kingdoms, for Peter was given to understand that he could allude to him either as 'Spadger' or 'Radish.' Mr. Redley was rumoured to have the mysterious power of seeing what was happening behind his back through the reflectors of his glasses against the blackboard. Science was represented by Dr. Borcher and Mr. Gill, from both of whom Peter came to learn avidly in time. Mr. Gill occupied the Museum as a Darwinian outpost and supplied the most exhilarating information about extinct animals and prehistoric men. His lectures were as good as a Jules Verne novel. Peter had had no idea what steps Eton had made to keep up with modern science, and in his excitement at the exhibition of a neolithic skull dredged from the Thames in school he mistook and noted it as that of a drowned College waterman. Dr. Borcher, who was in charge of the Laboratory, was an even more romantic character. He taught chemistry with a little sleight of hand and a considerable fund of humour. He was fond of pointing with a rubicund smile to bottles whose contents had only to meet for the neighbouring College to disappear in space. He was believed to have preached once, but not a second time, in Chapel, on the probable gases let loose at the Creation.

As the masters poured out again from the presence of the Head, Philips pointed out the gentle Mr. Hare, surnamed 'Bunny,' who had taken Third Form for twenty years. Having developed a vocation to suffer fools gladly, he had remained without ascending the scale, devoted to his life's work of saving the future pillars of the Empire from superannuation. He had never bullied or browbeaten a boy. He had never been known to raise his voice. Beside him walked Mr. Daughan who, coming to Eton without the athletic prowess necessary to awe the normal boy, had set out to win a reputation as the most daring rider of his day. Indeed it was rumoured among his pupils that he had been offered several mounts in the Grand National. As it was, he was content to win the respect of the sons of the horse-riding class. Close on their heels followed two Frenchmen, one distressed and gesticulating, the other bearded and cracking jokes. With grim dignity Herr Rudolph Blitz paced behind them. French and German were here at least united in their defensive tactics against the Eton boy. The Eton masters were always a strangely assorted regiment. Out of their number had sprung Colonial Bishops, melancholic Deans, Jesuits, Balkan adventurers, humanitarians, poets. Among them they offered an excellent though generally rejected course of learning. The system to which they were tied fortunately left the discipline of the School in the firmer and more consistent hands of *Pop*. The athletic boy who ruled the School was not subject to the eccentricities of genius. Hard players did not keep gentle hearts to those who were subject to them.

Boys and games were not the only subjects of masters' discussion. A great turning of the way was visible on the horizon. Masters, whether they swallowed or rejected the

F

present system, were already wondering who would be the next Head Master. It was obvious that the keystone of their arch must be replaced within a few years. As Rome canvasses the *Papabili* when the Pope grows old, so all Eton wonders and wishes and watches when the eye of the Head grows dim and his tread becomes slow. As the new century approached, the little world of Eton buzzed within its tiny bounds, and the old century, whose second Head was Keate, drew near to its close under the renowned Dr. Warre. Already four successors were in the field! Boys and masters found a mystical interpretation in the hymn lines :—

> ' When comes the promised time, O Lord,
> When *war* shall be no more !'

Dr. Warre had reached the last stage of his Eton career. Like Newborough, the Eton Head Master who trained Walpole, he could have written for his epitaph, ' Master of Eton, which he made greatest in the world.' An Oxford oarsman and Fellow of All Souls, he had reigned for fifteen undisputed, almost uncriticised, years, since he assumed office in 1884 and received a blue-ribboned birch from the Captain of the School. As the crosier thrust into the hand of a consecrated Bishop, as a sceptre given to a King, so is the rod to the Head Master of Eton, and of those three symbols democratic days have only spared the authority connected with the Eton Birch. Within his sphere a Gladstone or Plantagenet could not soar higher. His wisdom was that in an era of reform he had not been obstinate. He had even introduced reform before it could assail or overwhelm him. And his reforms had been transmuted into custom, while he himself had become part of the tradition. Modern Eton was the mirror of his career. He had rowed, and Eton had become the greatest rowing school in the world. He had encouraged athletics, and masters had abandoned a furtive existence out of school in gowns for flannels and joined the boys at their games. Ushers became coaches. The gentle herd of exquisite scholars was reinforced by 'Varsity oarsmen and first-class cricketers. On great occasions the Head would appear on the River wearing his dark Blue and rowed by his stalwart sons. The oar had become part of the Eton tradition, and the mind of the Head dwelt constantly on the modelling of rowing boats. A wondering staff had beheld his famous reconstruction of the Greek trireme, and his pupils were in the habit of puzzling University examiners by drawing accurate designs of the raft of Odysseus as re-rigged in the Homeric imagination of Dr. Warre. He wrote a noble handwriting, and masters, who loved the tradition, cultivated beautiful hands. The Head had been a rifleman, and the School became semi-militarised. According as Dr. Warre had set the mark, Etonians practised with oar and rifle and pen, heedless of the machine-gun and the typewriter, which would shortly make two of them obsolete. The Eton Volunteers were his handiwork, and he viewed them as proudly as Frederick the Great his gawky grenadiers. It was a long day since a common brake could contain the Eton Volunteers and their Colonel, or since the famous day when beer had been ordered for a Field day on the Warrean theory that two quarts made a pint, with the result that a bayonet was passed through the big drum. Chaff and criticism had rained on Warre from the older school, but with time he had prevailed. The School Volunteers had risen to three or four hundred strong and the Drill Hall had been added to the Eton monuments. Field days and Camps entered into the life of the School, but whereas athletics were compulsory, military knowledge was voluntary. As an encouragement to attend the Parades in summer-time the Volunteers were even excused a Monday Chapel. As the School had not yet taken military training seriously, it would not have been wise to have docked the time from the cricket pitch or the River. The risk that the God of Eton was a jealous God had to be taken.

With the achievement of all his ambitions the Head was inclined to live apart from boys and masters, remote and unseeing. He sat at the heart of the School, but he was the last to know if a limb was unsound. Innumerable complaints and cases were brought to him in Chambers, but they were all the traditional peccadilloes, which he could prune with his birch. It was rare that a serious case came to his ears. Very rarely would he inflict the dread punishment of expulsion on a boy, or remove a master for incompetency. To discontinue one of the Houses seemed to him as serious as plucking a stone out of the walls of Chapel. So he stood within his sacred ground and prayed for the peace of Jerusalem. To him Eton was a chosen little flock to be sublimely led in the direction of their destinies by himself and the Provost, who had been no less providentially chosen than Moses and Aaron.

Peter soon discovered that a Lower Boy had as much commerce or converse with the Head as with the Man in the Moon. He was very solemnly expecting to be sent for and congratulated on the place he had taken. He had even meditated his demeanour of mingled piety and loyalty as he felt a strong arm laid on his shoulder and a voice bade him continue as he had begun. However, a notice was received that the Head would address all new boys one morning in Upper School. With his new suit and his conscience both in spick-and-span condition, Peter attended the levee of boys, already far changed from the timorous and nervous candidates for the Entrance two weeks previously, while for twenty minutes the Head uttered a melodious booming sound. The construction of his oratory was awkward, however sonorous the note, and few sentences reached his deeply attentive audience. Half-frightened and half-amused, they heard him out, but what he said, beyond that it was a *pi-jaw*, remained a mystery. Nevertheless it was not without a certain mesmeric effect. That mighty mumbling figure in cassock and gown clearly symbolised law and even dimly portended punishment.

Thenceforward the Head disappeared for Peter into

Olympian backgrounds. If he saw him occasionally in the distance, it was only to remove his hat as to the Sovereign. But the Head was rigid in the etiquette never to return a boy's salute. It was necessary to the Eton system for the boys to feel, as a Head Master once explained to his King, that there could be nobody greater than himself.

CHAPTER VI

THE LENT HALF

THE new boys began dabbling in the amusements of the Lent Half. Beagling was beyond their pace, and rather the privilege of Fifth Formers who enjoyed wearing smart beagling *bags*. Besides, as fags they had to wait at the afternoon Absence, and take their masters' hats and overcoats home. Attending Eton Absence, like asking a question in the House of Commons, entails wearing one's hat, and the beaglers were allowed to appear with their hunting kit concealed with overcoats, while they momentarily brandished silk top-hats to their name.

Peter and Socston found they had a choice between playing fives or going for runs across country. Eton fives originated at Eton, being based on the game played for centuries at an irregular point between two of the Chapel buttresses. Every detail, including the jutting end of the inside balustrade leading down the Chapel steps, was reproduced religiously in every Eton fives court. This was indeed the stone, rejected by the builders from the sacred building, which had become the famous Pepperbox and cornerstone of Eton fives. Its vital consequence was that it broke the monotony of hitting a ball against plain walls. Imagine the variety of strokes which a cut-off corner would add to a billiard table ! It was this discovery which burst on some mediaeval Eton boy, with results as long-lived as those which followed the movement of Newton's apple.

Peter spent his afternoons watching the hundreds of players in the double row of courts playing four to a game, with the same Pepperbox performing the function of an inscrutable fifth player, throwing off balls with mathematical precision from his edge or consigning them to Dead Man's Hole at his base. There was something hypnotising in the constant click of hundreds of balls. The scene could only be compared to a large Benedictine monastery, where scores of priests with their acolytes perform Mass in each of a long row of tiny chapels without paying heed to each other, and the spectator only knows that in every alcove of the walls the same rite, the same sounds, the same service is proceeding.

One afternoon the two friends were perambulating the old fives courts on the Eton Wick road, when they perceived Mr. Jenkinson playing for dear life with a nervous Lower Boy for partner, against two very bored-looking grandees dressed like harlequins. 'Juggins' waved a ragged fives glove towards Peter. ' You *scug*, why aren't you playing ? ' 'Too many construes to prepare,' said Peter truly, but Jenkinson looked a trifle pained. He tried to make *saps* into athletes as often as athletes into *saps*. A few days later he induced Peter to enter, with a little practice, for a competition known as Jenkinson's Division Fives. Peter had the misfortune to draw the best player in Remove, who could often get balls up after Peter had missed. Peter hid behind the Pepperbox, and left every stroke to his partner. Occasionally the ball came for him like a bullet, and he had to strike or duck. He generally ducked. In this way they reached the antefinal, and the active partner, having some hopes of a little silver cup, and none of Peter's improvement, asked a few friends to attend to Darley by word of mouth during the game. As a result, Peter realised a terrier's experiences in a tennis court, for every time the ball approached him, he was assailed with threats before and after he missed it. The oaths which followed each miss seemed to dovetail into the oaths minatory of the next. His brilliant partner had no breath to waste in exclamations, but between games he kicked Peter as hard as his toe could move india-rubber through the air. They lost, and Peter came home feeling like a burst fives ball, which in Eton parlance is called a *blackguard*. Peter felt so *blackguardly* that he decided to take to running in future.

After this Socston and Peter began to take runs across country towards the Shooting Butts. The landscape was sometimes dotted with Morleyites, armed with pipes and catapults, and kindred souls from other Houses, of whom the more industrious dug up the old bullets in the Butts to melt down into ammunition. But Socston began to develop running power, and decided to train for the Junior Steeplechase, while Peter paced him as well as he could. The even flow of the Lent Half was only broken by the Athletic Sports and occasional Lectures in the evening. Like all new boys, Peter applied eagerly for lecture tickets. They could be desperately dull, but they gave a chance for those who wished to be out after *lock-up*. Peter attended a lecture on Damascus, innocently expecting some tips for Sunday Q.'s. The clerical lecturer began enumerating the products named after Damascus, such as Damsons, Damascene blades, Damasks, Damsels. At the first syllable of each word he was cut short by a hearty cheer, and ended his list of Dams— in a roar of applause seldom conceded to the cloth.

A lecture from the Bishop of London on Russia drew a large audience, including Peter, who learnt that Russia was a country perfectly different from any other, that the Bishop had been struck by the immense size of the country, that the peasants' houses were made of wood and heated by stoves, that the peasants had a great veneration for their Emperor, and were very melancholy. In conclusion, as he well might, the Bishop urged his hearers to find out more about Russia. As Peter came out of the Drill Hall, he met a number of Morleyites, whom he had missed during the lecture. ' Hullo, Darley, we 've been out all the time. Did the Bishop give you a *pi-jaw* ? ' ' No, but there were not many adventures,' said Peter. ' If you want adventures,' threw in Frencher, ' you may come with us. We are going back by Slads, and round past the Cemetery.' And they all slipped past the House which was Donaldson's.

The moment they were in open country, the company drew pipes and resumed various stages of smoking. They took a wide detour and returned by a long palisaded passage with Donaldson's garden on their left and the Eton Cemetery on their right, that forlorn acre, which is as crowded as Chambers with Eton masters treasuring up complaints against the Last Day. Unfortunately, some live masters lived in the locality, and were returning from the Bishop's lecture from another direction. The parties collided in Judy's Passage, an artery dedicated to a deceased Lower Master.

' *Cave! cave!* ' Peter shrieked with piteous apprehension. Frencher and Camdown cleared the fence. Mouler awkwardly slipped, and fell swearing to the ground. Philips bolted, and was held in stronger arms than his. Peter and Socston, not feeling particularly guilty, gave themselves up. The young masters seemed more amused than angry. ' Now, you young fools, what are your names ? ' The four fools gave them, except that Mouler gave Frencher's instead of his own. ' Where do you board ? ' ' Mr. Morley's, sir.' This really amused the masters, who looked at their tickets and sent them home. They made no inquiry as to the others who had escaped, being content like sportsmen with two brace out of the covey.

' Just what we were talking of,' said Mr. Robertson, a recent recruit from the 'Varsity boat. ' Morley's as usual,' said the other, a young Classic. ' The whole crew smoking. Ought we to tell Morley or the Head ? ' Robertson had recently put down an attempt to rag his first school by distributing Georgics as mildly as buns at a school treat. He was inclined to be severe. ' Wouldn't Morley resent our going over his authority to the Head ? ' asked the other. ' He hasn't any, I believe.' ' That's true. Mathematical masters don't seem to be able to keep better order in their Houses than, than—' 'Than a French master!' Mr. Robertson finished his sentence, with a laugh. 'No, no, old fellow,' said Classics, 'you are a Briton, and one of us. I mean our French colleagues. They could never keep discipline since Crecy.'

At the same time they were not sure what to do. Morley's was going down the hill, and they did not like stabbing him in the back. Sooner or later he would glide to the bottom. But if they did not speak to the Head, it might leak out through the boys themselves. They decided to consult Mr. Munfort, whose House was at the end of the passage. Feeling almost as sheepish as the boys they had caught, they rang up Eton Tradition in the person of Munfort. They were ushered into a snug study crammed with bachelor comfort, in the midst of which a spruce little man was writing to one of the Victorian Premiers on the general state of his hopeful, who, he was glad to report, showed some promise of getting into the Eleven if he stayed another half.

'Come in! Delighted to see you if I may finish this letter of some importance.' Robertson tried to keep his eye off the addressed envelope, and seeing the name turned red with apology. 'Oh, it's only a small matter, sir: we caught a lot of Morley's boys smoking red-handed round the corner. Do you think we should report them to the Head or to Mr. Morley?' 'I shouldn't worry the Head awhile,' said Eton Tradition kindly. 'Or Morley perhaps?' They were so anxious to learn. Eton Tradition spun round in his chair. 'Has Morley asked for their names?' 'No, sir.' 'Then let them go to blazes!' 'But if he asks for their names?' 'Send him to blazes!' And he spun back into his original position. He was the most popular master at Eton.

'Have a little claret?' and he had rung the bell before they could refuse. Then he began. There were some masters who were not Etonians. Eton could be trusted to lick an odd boy into shape, but an odd master was beyond her. Morley's boys were what they were because Morley was what he was. The same boys would turn out well in a good House. A bad House master never had a good House or a bad House a good House master. It was simple.

Eton turned out boys good and bad. The good were very good, and the bad were mighty bad. That was the tradition. It was the business of the Head to pick good House masters and turn the incompetent clean out. Would they regard this as confidential? Good night. And two young masters went to bed wiser than they had risen.

Meantime Peter returned feeling sick at heart. That deadly feeling assailed him of a row impending. His companions took it lightly enough, but he had visions of his Tutor being informed, and of a memento being made in his book. Besides, smoking was a *swishing* matter and would bring him to the Block. It was true he had not smoked, but he had been present at smoking, and it would never do for him to exculpate himself while leaving the others in the lurch. He was in for it, and he crawled miserably to his room. With a choking throat he turned over his Xenophon. Mouler and Philips had rejoined those who had escaped and were rushing round the House boasting of their dare-devilry. As they were bound to be *swished*, they might as well reap some credit for it. What with the retelling of their different stories, the Lower Boys were whispering at Prayer-time about a free fight in the Cemetery, and of a couple of masters left for dead among the tombs.

But the days passed, and no dread summons came from the ominous Praepostor. Masters, knowing that Morley's was going downhill, had got into the habit of not pressing charges against Morleyites. When a House at Eton starts foundering, nothing can stop it. Masters refrain from holing a sinking ship, not knowing what kind of a ship they may yet have to steer themselves. But hints reached Morley, and from time to time his quick ear, trained to overhear boys, overheard colleagues whose conversation died down in his presence. He realised that his was the lag House, and that masters whispered and watched. Sometimes, however, he picked up false scent.

Some days after Peter's adventure, Mr. Morley was late for Chambers. Dr. Warre was impressing his matutinal touch on the staff. It was in Chambers that House masters, Classical masters, Mathematical masters, French masters, Science masters thronged and pressed on their business. In the roar and rush and hustle, Warre sat majestical under the pictures of the Heads from the old time before him. Time was brief and conversation brisk. Except for a sally from Mr. Clinton, or an epigram from Mr. Broadpen, or a jest from Hua, the humorous French master, it was all business. In the ill-lighted gloom the untarnishable white spats of Herr Rudolph Blitz, the German teacher, were clearly visible. The Head was seen in serious converse with Mr. Munfort. It was being whispered that several of Munfort's sporting *bloods* had been reported for playing cards in Windsor by some over-energetic master. Munfort, being a keen whist player, was inclined to minimise the fault. The Head, though he often minimised in act, assumed the maximum of gravity in his speech. Some younger masters began talking among themselves. ' We pitched on a smoking party last week, but we have said nothing to the Head.' Approval of their leniency was added to disapproval of the master who, while on leave himself, had run in Munfort's boys. ' At least they were card-sharpers, weren't they ? ' laughed Robertson. ' Ours were only kids smoking from Morley's. You cannot be hard on kids there.' ' Cards are cards,' interposed an athletic master, ' and boys who play cards don't play games.' At this moment Mr. Morley entered. Overhearing what the last two speakers said, he picked up false scent with mathematical quickness. The speaker had perhaps a reason for wishing to

see Mr. Munfort's boys run in. He had had the misfortune to be run in himself for not carrying a light on his
bicycle, and the Magistral Board, which contained the
Lower Master and Mr. Munfort, had fined him without
looking to see who the prisoner was. The School had
been immensely amused, especially as the prisoner had
won the Cricket Cup a little too often. ' Cards are cards,'
he insisted, and Mr. Morley caught the words as well as the
mention of his name.

Mr. Morley was beginning to be troubled. Complaints
of his boys were reaching him from all quarters. He set
poenas with the frequency of a recurring decimal, but
boys had many devices for avoiding them. A list of lines
due was hung in his *puppy-hole*, and boys used to wait a
day or two before cautiously striking off their debts with
Morley's old blue pencil. A consummate actor like
Frencher was fond of bringing charred pieces of paper,
and explaining that he had finished the whole *poena*, but,
unfortunately, the destructive boys' maid had stuffed it into
his fire. Mr. Morley would nod suspiciously, but it was
a master's duty to accept a boy's word. No boy would
dream of cheating Jenkinson, on the ground that it would
be hard luck on ' Juggins,' but nobody hesitated to get
the better of a *beak* like Morley. Morley suffered a good
deal through not being an old Etonian. He did not realise
that matters between master and boy were regulated by
the unwritten rules of sport. If a master took a boy's
word, even if he doubted, it saved trouble in the end.
Morley never quite trusted his boys, and his love of accuracy made him a little over-zealous in his search for information. The more he hunted for contraband pipes,
cigarettes, and *cribs*, the more came into the House. If
a *crib* was dropped in school, or if left in front of a master's
eyes, it became fair game, but it was unsporting on Morley's part to search boys' *burries* when they were on leave.
It was like trapping game out of season. To complain of
a boy to the Head was within the rules, but to complain
of his own House was to call attention to his own incom-

petence. So the Head heard more buzz than truth about the Morleyites, and continued hoping that all was well within the walls of Jerusalem.

Mr. Morley relied on an internal purge, and meditating what he had overheard in Chambers, he asked Tudor to make sure the whole House were present at Prayers. That evening Peter and Socston were fagged round the House, summoning all to a House-row. There were many conjectures as to what was coming, and Lower Boys felt their tails grow delicate. In the previous half an insulting notice had been pencilled behind a door referring to the good repute of the Dame. Mr. Morley had insisted on a conviction and an execution. Nobody would give himself up, and everybody under Fifth Form had been caned by the Captain. After it was all over, Willum brought word that he had seen a grocer's boy write the scrawl. ' I bet Willum has written it up again to pay us off for being ragged,' was a theory raised. 'The Dame's got *hairy*, and wants blood ! ' ' Somebody has been ragging the Hag,' were other weighty suggestions heard in the passages.

Mid dead silence the Man announced after Prayers that he had had indirect word of a number of his boys breaking bounds and committing transgressions like smoking and card-playing. He had been accidentally informed, and so would not press for the offenders' names. A sigh of relief passed through the House. He obviously had no evidence, and was fishing in the dark. Only he insisted that before the half was older, all contraband such as cards and tobacco should be given up. He appealed to Tudor and the Captain of Games to carry out a search. There was a dead silence, and the Man hinted that he could find out the names of certain boys who had recently broken rules. A black look passed down the House. About half of them had broken bounds some time during the half, or smoked, or played cards. Each was calculating on how much the Man knew, and for how little the Man could be put off. It was bluff on both

sides. Frencher piped up, ' Please, sir, I brought back
some light cigarettes accidentally, but I have not smoked
them. I was keeping them for the holidays.'

There was a titter, for his taste in strong pipes was
rather well known. ' Very good. Go and fetch them.'
Then a Fifth Former remembered he had an uncut pack of
cards, which he produced, after a few minutes spent concealing four well-used packs. A few more rather innocent
offerings were laid on the table, and the House began to
see humour. The Man was being palpably ragged.
Titters bred daring. Frencher returned to the confessional. ' Please, sir, I keep a billiard ball in my *burry.*'
There was a shout of laughter, and the wicked ivory,
property of an honest hotel-keeper, was rolled across the
table not for the first time. But the Man was the only
one who did not recognise it. He could only take in one
thought at a time, and his present thought was that of a
lucky customs officer. Suddenly Peter was seized by a
qualm, and whispered to Socston, ' Haven't I got some
kind of cards of yours in my room ? ' ' Yes, but they
aren't the kind, you fool.' The House was looking at
them. Socston began to stammer, and then, rather than
appear to conceal anything, confessed he had lent Darley
some cards. ' I am sorry to hear it from a new boy,' said
Mr. Morley, and Socston went upstairs, and up also in the
estimation of the House. A minute later he left a pack
of cards in front of Tudor. The Captain of Games passed
his cane through them, revealing the portrait of Mrs.
Potts the painter's wife, Master Potts, and other well-
known characters in ' Happy Families.' There was a
convulsive laugh and a mild cheer. The Man handed
them back, and remarked they had better be sent to the
Eton Mission. The remainder he pocketed, and went
out. All eyes were on Socston. Either he was a March
hare or a bit of a sportsman, but for a new boy it was
far too cheeky. Something must be done. As soon as
Morley left, the Captain of Games, Dugannon, ordered
him to his room to be smacked. Socston followed him,

amid much dumb-crambo on the part of his friends. The Captain's door closed behind him. 'Would you mind smacking me to-morrow, after the Junior Steeplechase? I don't want to feel stiff,' said Socston, playing a trump. The Captain looked at him with a staggered expression. 'All right, if you're running, double or quits if you get placed,' and put back his cane.

The next day the whole House came down to the Timbralls to watch the finish of the School and Junior Steeplechases, and incidentally to see if Socston would win his wager. If he ended among the first six, the House scored a point in the Athletic Cup, and he escaped his caning. The School Steeplechase is the Eton Grand National, a stiff three-mile run from the Dorney Road round Butts across open country, with a cold finish at the School Jump, some eighteen feet across Jordan, under Fifteen Arch Bridge. Since Lawes cleared the jump at the Steeplechase of 1860, it had seldom been cleared without the icy splash, the certainty of which naturally drew the sympathetic presence of a large crowd.

The Junior event preceded the greater by a few minutes. Peter accompanied Socston to the start, and took his overcoat in the agonising silence before the pistol cracked, with a crack that pierced Peter's vitals. He cut back to the finish, praying and praying for Socston's success. He could do nothing but barter with the Almighty and offer penances and Lenten denial if only Socston could win. He found a huge crowd was assembled at the Jordan, where Socston was to be ducked to make an Eton holiday. *Pops* were holding the tape and flicking back the crowd with their canes as their forefathers once held back, with horsewhips, the seething spectators of prize-fights. Peter prayed steadily for Socston's second wind and Morley's glory. Suddenly, across Mesopotamia, the field between two rivers or drains, the white vests of the runners could be seen bobbing up and down. As they crossed

the farther stream a tall boy strode away. His face
swam into recognition, and as his friends shouted his
name he flung himself wearily into the icy calm of
Jordan. He was first! A second arrived, and fell
windless into the waters, which closed over his head, and
the crowd laughed well. Peter hung between two
pollarded willows with eyes on the horizon. Suddenly
he saw his friend struggling out of a bunch, and shrieked
encouragement, but his tiny squeak was drowned in the
good-hearted roar from the School as three boys fell into
the water, and Socston, scrambling out of the congealed
mud, passed in a bare third! The great *Pops* leaned
sympathetically over him as he shot like a water-be-
draggled rat past the line. Peter bundled him into his
dry overcoat, his shoes gulping mud, his mouth gasping
breath, his heart thumping through his thin envelope of
flesh. He looked piteous and exhausted to the spectator,
but his colour was still good. Under the great test his
guts had proved their mettle. Now a great athletic
career in running or rowing depends not on shapeliness or
science so much as guts. Form and knowledge cannot
procure athletic success, unless there are reposing within
many yards of clean white gut, unworn by overstrain,
untarnished by hereditary diseases. Upon his guts, the
most primitive and insensitive of his organs, an Etonian
depends to carry him through the lung-tearing ordeal
of rowing or steeplechasing. He must suffer all that a
racehorse must suffer, the nervous start, the fierce emula-
tion of others as nervous as he, the throbbing course, the
slow, drowning exhaustion, the struggle for breath, the
wrestle for speed, the hard agonising finish with only
the spur of shame or ardour to drive the failing, flagging
flesh.

Socston's position in the House was now settled. He
immediately became the coming Lower Boy. A slight
but perceptible gulf already separated him from Peter.
He had answered to the only test by which boy can judge
boy, that of public athletic contest against his peers.

G

From that moment a course opened before him which he would have been foolish to refuse. That night his caning was remitted by Dugannon after Prayers, amid a general murmur of approval from the Morleyites. A new boy had actually opened their score for the Athletic Cup. There had been nothing so plucky or unexpected since Baker minor won the School Steeplechase in jackets.

Socston celebrated his success by failing in every construe for a week, and collecting a fistful of ' yellow tickets,' which Mr. Morley cackled a good deal over signing. Mr. Lamb had seen the steeplechase, and signed without a word. In spite of the common emotion they had suffered, Peter dimly felt that Socston had set foot on a different plane. They still *messed* together, and combined chandlery stores to light each other's rooms in turn. They still shared tallow, ink, paper, and the most despised of commodities, books. At Eton books were treated like outlaws and vermin, something outside the Mosaic code. There was no protection for them, even though the College bookseller stamped owners' names in heavy gold lettering on the covers. Only *Pops* safeguarded their property by affixing heavy *Pop*-seals in coloured waxes to their volumes. Generally all articles of common use could be stolen or *bagged* under the owner's nose. The only redress lay in stealing in turn from a neighbour. But a loose sovereign would remain untouched for a half. *Bagging* was not stealing, merely a form of borrowing without asking and forgetting to return. By half-term Peter found half of his books gone, some of which he managed to steal back again before the half was over. There was some humour in helping to force Philips's bureau with a poker, and finding a number of books inside neatly stamped with Peter's name.

Whatever the two friends had in common, it was not love of study. Peter was already drudging his way towards Trials, a confirmed *sap*. He became despised, but tolerated. The position of *House-sap* had long been vacant in Morley's, and Peter showed distinct promise of filling it. He was enormously useful to other boys in Remove, who could depend on him to *spout* accurate translations a few minutes before they went to construe to their Tutors. He was better than a walking dictionary. He was a live *crib*.

CHAPTER VII

THE FIRST OF MARCH

PETER kept his *horarium* in his hat and his *diurnium* or School Calendar stuck with drawing-pins to the flap of his *burry*. Every day was conscientiously ticked off. There were always Saints' Days to watch approaching nearer and nearer until they passed into the limbo of dead holidays. St. David's Day was celebrated on the First of March. The celebration of St. Patrick's Day had been discontinued. St. Andrew of Scotland, however, remained high in the Eton Calendar, but the First of March marked only a half-hearted and generally sodden opening of the nautical year. In the old days an Irish or Welsh nobleman presented the Head with gold leeks or shamrocks in honour of their national saints. In Keate's day it had been once humorously suggested that the leading *wet-bob* of the School should present the Head with an umbrella on St. Swithin's Day.

On the First of March the patronage of the Captain of the Boats was dispensed and numbers of new oarsmen took part in a motley procession of boats from the Brocas Boathouse. Peter and Socston were down early on Windsor Bridge to watch proceedings. Crew after crew in their blue or red striped vests and socks came out on the rafts, shiveringly adjusted their oars, and after some adjuration from their captains and timid prompting from their tiny coxswains paddled to an uneven stroke up-stream. They were described in the *Chronicle* as 'novices in borrowed plumes,' provoking a critic to suggest they should develop '*feathers*' of their own the next year. 'Aren't they glorious?' moaned Socston, who had never

82

seen an eight-oar before. 'If I ever can get into Fifth Form
I will have a chance to get into a boat.' Peter was less
patriotically making up his mind that even a pressgang
should never hale him to the Brocas. 'If you 're in Fifth
next year,' said Socston, 'they might make you a cox for
the Fourth of June.' 'No, they won't,' snapped Peter,
'for I shall become a *dry-bob*.' 'You wouldn't be such
an ass as to miss getting a colour, would you ?' 'Well,
you know, I think I would rather get a Trials Prize than a
colour to begin with,' spoke Peter his thought. Socston
turned round, 'By Heavens, I believe you would rather
be a *Tug* than in the Eight ! ' Peter looked into his eyes
as boys rarely do, ' I wouldn't say that, but I would rather
get the Newcastle than make a century at Lord's.' Socston looked at him for a moment as a Mohammedan looks
at a Hindoo. A faint indefinable disgust as of caste swam
into his consciousness. Their friendship trembled in the
sudden balance. As a successful runner and a growing
favourite, he knew he had every right to despise and
relinquish this queer boy, who was not above confessing
such odious tastes on Windsor Bridge. The last splash
of the Eights, as they took the curve towards Brocas
Clump, whitened against the inky stream. Socston was
thinking aloud, ' Darley, I 'll stick to you though you are
an unhealthy *sap*, because I like you. But I wish you
would clean up a little. The fellows say so. They thought
you quite decent-looking when you came. Now they
think you are a hopeless *scug* with grease on your clothes
and inked string for a bootlace.' 'Does that make any
difference at Morley's ?' asked Peter inquiringly. 'Of
course it does ; if you are going to be no good at games,
you had better at least look clean.' 'But I am good at
something. I was the first boy at m'Tutor's to take
Remove.' 'The less you say about that the better.'
Peter thought Socston was right, and swallowed his rebuke
as well as he could. 'It 's awfully good of you not to
mind my being a *sap*.' Socston was not spoilt by his new
popularity. As he looked at Peter's wistful face he could

have thrown his arms round him with that genuine pity which is sister to love, but contented himself with inviting him that afternoon to tea at Layton's down Windsor. ' The Governor is coming down and wants to show us all the places where things happened to him at School.'

Mr. Socston senior was a fervent Old Etonian, a noisy patriot and a stickler for the least custom retained from antiquity. He had happened to be a great success at Eton. He had won his Field and his Eleven, a greatness he had never attempted to rival in after-life. Content with supreme achievement at Eton, he had let the larger non-Etonian world run by. He preferred to remain one of those Old Etonians who never grow old physically and snatch every chance to return to their haunts of former glory. To play in a football match or look up the sons of contemporaries was his perennial excuse for rushing from town. He was never happier than when wearing his blue and red quartered cap or lolling on the necks of young friends in whom he tried to relive his youth. The masters thought him a pest and suspected him of being a filter for racing news. The arrival of his own son, whom he entered at Morley's eight months before birth, brought him regularly to Eton on Saturdays. He was one of those who had watched Morley bowling against the Australians and had chosen accordingly. He had always hoped for a slow bowler in his family as some hope for Bishops or Chancellors in theirs.

Socston junior and Peter used to meet him at the station and accompany him on volubly conducted tours, until every brick and bypath lived with legend or escapade. There was no House about which he could not spin a tale out of the past, and the amused boys found the streets in his company peopled with all the queer characters of other days, forgotten Tutors and Dames forlorn. Mr. Socston was brimming with memories of his own Tutor, ' Billy ' Johnson, whom he insisted was the paragon of all Tutordom. He would point out the ' Mousetrap ' where Johnson lodged at No. 2 High Street, and, passing the Christopher, the pupil-room out of which Johnson used to emerge at the sound of soldiers with ' Brats, the British Army ! ' And in Common Lane he traced the spot where Johnson pursued a black hen in mistake for his hat, a feat equalled by the nerve-racked master who once set a hundred lines to an over-shrill canary.

For a quarter of a century Johnson was the most inspired and inspiring teacher in England. Poet and historian, the best writer of Horatian verse since Horace, his *Lucretilis* was on a par with the Greek version which Professor Cooke, another Etonian, gave to Gray's *Elegy*. In one case the critics cried Horace and in the other Moschus ! But Johnson was more than a Newcastle Scholar. He was a treasure-house of military anecdote and carried an exact knowledge of the Navy under his mortar-board. An ecstatic guide to youth, living for the intense and heroic in life or letters, he sowed Eton with that knowledge which is not acquired in examination-rooms, and left long flickering fires in the souls of past pupils and of teachers to come. He had exemplified how to be a poet though a pedagogue. Johnson's memory still persuaded many masters that a teacher could be a good conversationalist and a Tutor a man of letters. With him Virgil was a great Roman road and Homer a ramble through Greece, and he found time for wandering in the byways of English literature. Like a midwife of consummate skill, he knew how to deliver the boyish mind of its adolescent enthusiasms. He could touch the fragile and yet the faulty strings of boyhood. While he was a Tutor the Muses were not houseless in Eton.

It was on an ill day that he was driven away from the School he loved and made to suffer in exile and obscurity by the Philistines, who believed in cultivating boys' muscles rather than their tastes. But his memory had returned on the lips of Mr. Christopher and Jenkinson and Peter's Tutor, until Peter used to imagine Johnson's shade standing, as he used to stand in happy days, dreaming and dreaming in the old School Yard.

Mr. Socston had been at the Miss Gullivers', the first House on the left after crossing Barnes Pool, and his brain teemed with the memory of those ancient beldams. Incredible they would appear to modern Eton, those prim and sexless sisters, trying to keep order over the rowdy young gentlemen they penned for the night in their ramshackle hutch of a house, but Mr. Socston made the old House live again. There were the names of friends and *bloods* scratched on the brick entrance-way. There were the familiar rooms on the street once all devoted to the Miss Gullivers, save the one-eyed, box-shaped room over the arch, which boys had occupied when sick, moribund, or dying in the good days of old. The elder Miss Gulliver had been deaf, and, unfortunately, not only did not hear what was to be heard, but, like many deaf people, heard sounds when there were none. Angrily she would tear through the narrow passages, and lay imaginary riots to the peaceful. But when there was a real inferno, she slept the sleep of the just. Sometimes a boy was caught in the act, and she would hurl one terrible threat through the air. ' You shall go to Madam de Rosen's ! You are only fit for Madam de Rosen's ! ' and Miss Mary Gulliver, her sister, would shudder behind the green-shuttered windows, past which all Eton tramps down town daily, and immerse herself deeper than ever in the boys' accounts, which were written in a neat Victorian hand, with an accuracy no more to be challenged than the virginity of the writer.

Mr. Socston remembered Miss Gulliver as plump and Miss Mary as lean, so lean that she was hardly visible, only appearing at the commencement of the half to dull the anguish of returning boys with sherry negus. If one was Mary, the other should have been Martha, for she was busy with many boys. While Miss Mary purred at the fireside, the other in black bombazine, with white cap and streamers, prowled the House at night like some enormous puss, rushing into boys' rooms and snatching up playing-cards or blowing out forbidden lights with astounding speed. But they shared the one jealousy for Madam de Rosen. Now, Madam de Rosen was a lady and a Baroness in her right, and sat upright and queenly as she signed Praepostors' books or penned excuses for the sick and would-be sick. But the Baroness is now forgotten, and the name of Gulliver clings to Eton. The School has forgotten that Gullivers' once defeated the Field at football, and enjoyed the right to play on the Field themselves. Long dead are the giants who made the rest of the School look Lilliputian, dead the Baroness, and dead the whole race of Dames, but still there clings to the bricks of the old House the imperishable fragrance of the old maids Gulliver.

From the windows of Gullivers' Mr. Socston had witnessed the famous attempt to duck 'Stiggins' in Barnes Pool. Now 'Stiggins' was so nicknamed with all bearded clerics in the Dickensian era for the same proper reason that they were called Kruger in a later period. 'Stiggins' had been active in suppressing Election Saturday, an obsolete water carnival. Members of the Boats were demolishing the sign of a ship, which Runnicle, an unpopular tradesman, had decorated with the Harrow colours, when they were chided by 'Stiggins,' whereupon there arose a cry to duck 'Stiggins.' Husky oarsmen hustled him to the very edge of Barnes Pool, from which watery tomb he was only saved by another master, assisted by a good Evansite.

'Stiggins' and his red beard hanging over the Pool had become the principal legend in a generation of masters who included 'Badger' Hale, with his grey and black bristles; Johnny Yonge on his horse Gehazi, for it was as white as snow; 'Tolly' Waite, who lolled round with six chess games moving in his head, and was so called because he declined to 'tolly waite' snowballs; Oscar Browning the reformer, who reformed ahead of his day, and was stricken to limbo by Hornby.

Harry Tarver had sustained the thankless task of teaching French to an anti-French generation, but not all in

vain, for he had presented Swinburne with his copy of
Victor Hugo, and bred the lifelong adoration of a poet for
a poet. Swinburne's Tutor, ' Jimmy ' Joynes, had come
down the ages in *Vanity Fair* with a wicked-looking birch
in his hand. His greatest exploit had been to run round
the bevelled edges of an Eton fives court, jumping the
Pepperbox on the way. He was as forgotten as his pre-
decessor, ' Judy ' Durnford, whose nickname clung to
the passage leading to the Eton Wick Road. But Mr.
Socston enlivened the old palings by an imitation of
' Judy's ' nutcracker jaw muttering ' He ! he ! ' as he sped
homewards with his short trouser pulled over his white
sock. Joynes he mimicked with his trick of ever flicking
an imaginary fly off his sleeve. Mr. Socston remembered
all that was heroic among the boys of his time, and all
that was grotesque among the masters. His ideal bliss
still seemed to take the form of practical jokes on *beaks*.
He bored the boys when he solemnly paced College Field
to where the great elm stump had been where Keate
called Absence, or mourned the old Mrs. Lipscombe who
used to sit with an umbrella at the entrance to School
Yard. To his great delight he found the old blue-ribboned
octogenarian seller of tarts, who used to serve him at
the Wall, and introduced his son to Knock, a one-armed
vendor, the last of his race with the liberty of the College.

The younger Socston was bored with all these memories,
except when they touched athletic records, and Mr.
Socston knew the names and times of the winners of the
School Mile as well as some people know their Derby
winners. He had been enormously pleased by his son's
place in the Junior Steeplechase, and saluted him and
Peter vociferously at the station. ' Come along, and I 'll
sock you as much as you can hold, unless you 're still in
training.' Before they left the station, he pointed out
the historic spot where Wilson and Robertson, while yet
Etonians, arrested the insane Maclean, when he attempted
to shoot the Queen. His knowledge of Eton geography
and tradition never failed. ' Damnation Corner ! ' he

announced, as they turned to the Bridge under the
Hundred Steps, 'and many the times we ran into
masters there in the old days.'

The three stood on the Bridge while Mr. Socston
expounded. 'Here used to be the old wooden bridge
over which the rebels under Keate threw their school
books, all except Grenville, who would not part with
his Homer. He became a bibliophile or *sap*, and presented his famous library to the nation. The modern
Bridge was stormed by the boys during the Windsor
election of '74, in spite of the thin black line of *beaks* who
waited for them on their return. They caught most of
them, but not the hero, who swam like Horatius across
the River in his top-hat, against the current. Before the
Locks had tempered the waters, the current was stronger
than it is now. Bankes, who boarded at Okes's, swam
from the Bridge to Brocas Clump. Bankes, too, was the
first to wear silk stockings instead of pads at football.'
The boys swallowed all these yarns, and Socston humoured
him by always asking for more. 'What was the best
thing ever done on the River?' he now inquired. 'The
best thing ever done was in the days when all boating
was forbidden, and Lord Waterford rowed up the River
with an Eight of boys in masks. On their return they
changed places with hired watermen, who rowed on, and
only removed their masks under the eyes of Keate himself. Of course, we have all jumped off the Bridge in our
lives. Even Hallam, the hero of Tennyson's *In Memoriam*,
did that, and he must have been a soft youth.'

Peter looked over the iron railings and shivered. The
keen dark waters hurried foamlessly along, black, deep,
and strangling. Coils and eddies succeeded each other
endlessly. 'As soon as you can swim, you must both
pass the swimming test. Then you can go on the River,
and the last day of the half chuck yourself off the Bridge,'
continued Mr. Socston. For the second time that day
Peter made a mental resolve to avoid all enjoyments
associated with the River Thames. 'On the night

Charles Montagu was drowned off this Bridge Sam Evans
and Bishop Selwyn drew up the rules for Passing, but the
tradition used to be that a boy is drowned every three
years. Selwyn it was who performed the greatest running
dive in Eton history. He dived under the River at one
dive at Upper Hope,' continued Mr. Socston.

Peter interrupted to say that old Sam Evans was still
in the School, and that he was up to him in drawing. 'Oh,'
laughed Mr. Socston, ' we used to call him Mr. Turveydrop
because he reminded us of the old character in Dickens.
He must have been teaching the fine arts for fifty years.
I suppose he is now what is called an Old Master.' The
boys did not catch the subtlety. They strolled up the
High Street, Mr. Socston flowing with idle memories.
Here he had been served with tobacco by Kitty Fraser,
and here was ' Tap,' where he used to get his beer, and he
must needs rush in to greet Mrs. Thomas, who had
quenched his thirst aforetime. As they passed the old
Cemetery he traced the stone on the Long Wall where
Gladstone cut his long-erased name, and pointed out where
both Gladstone and Salisbury had boarded. Outside
Upper School he pointed out the window through which
Lord Waterford climbed when he stole the *swishing* Block
as a trophy, a feat which rang in Anglo-Irish annals with
the celebrated attempt on the Crown Jewels from the
Tower by the immortal Colonel Blood. In the School
Yard he called to their notice the window in Long Chamber
out of which an audacious Colleger had thought fit to
answer his name at Absence·to the ferocious Keate. The
object which interested him most in the Yard was the
well-known and colossal excavation by which a boy called
SHEPHARD had carved his name on the side of the Chapel.
Tradition asserted that he had been *swished* separately for
each letter.

' Now for Layton's,' suggested Socston, and the three
entered a fly and were driven through the icy wind back
to Windsor by the leering flyman Mr. Socston called
' Aaron.' At Barnes Pool Mr. Socston pointed out the

Shirking Stone with the battered College arms let into the brick. In the old days when High Street was out of bounds a boy below this Stone was expected to *shirk* or avoid a master by entering a shop or performing a purely ritual disappearance behind a lamp-post. The tradition had never died down, for still no Colleger was allowed to show his gown below the Pool, and after dark no Oppidan was allowed to attend a Tutor's room down town, on the presumption that it was still out of bounds. Collegers used to leave their gowns in the little shop called Clark's abutting the Stone. Both boys were feeling over-replete with traditions, but became indulgent during the meal of steaming scones and hot chocolate flecked with cream, by which Layton's is endeared to youth's sweet and tender stomach before it has become coated and crassed by the surfeit of the years. Mr. Socston had adjourned to the White Hart and came back demonstratively noisy. ' If you will always train during the half, I'll let you smoke in the hols.,' he informed his hopeful, ' and here is a tip for you both.' He pressed a gold sovereign into the hands of each. ' But my best tip to you both is to hurry up and get the College arms printed on you. You cannot be real Etonians until that happens. I mean it. If any boy of mine leaves Eton without being well *swished*, I shall cut him off with a shilling in my will.' ' Right you are ! ' cried Socston, ' I'll paint the Statue red or something. Somebody has already stolen the sceptre and somebody stole the Block. So there's nothing new left to do.' The father clapped his boy on the shoulders, ' Yes, you bring the whole glorious Block home with you or whisk off the Holy Poker, and I'll sing *Floreat Etona!* before you bring my grey hairs down into the grave.' Both boys felt a little shy at this exhibition of old-fashioned patriotism, and Socston remembered it was time for his father to catch his train. Peter, however, felt sufficient of a dare-devil by now to mention that he had already been caught with some other boys who were actually smoking. ' Yes, and you looked so good and innocent that they were all let off,' laughed Socston. Peter flushed and blurted out, 'Well, I jolly near got a " yellow ticket " for French yesterday.' The Socstons exploded with mirth at this bold tale, and did not fully recover themselves until the train was carrying away Socston's papa to London. ' You 'll have to do something braver than baiting a French master if you want to get *swished*,' remarked Socston as they hurried back for *lock-up*.

CHAPTER VIII

TRIALS

THE dull end of the dullest half was approaching. Trials cast a lurid apprehension upon the minds of all save the few who were prepared. Even those whom past experience had deadened to failure were dispirited. Peter devoted every minute to going over the construes of the half. Cuddled over his smoky fire in his *woolly-bear*, he blinked over Xenophon and Horace and worked up the odds and ends of notes which looked likely mark-getters. He filled his memory with a large amount of temporary rubbish to be dumped down on examination paper and then for ever forgotten. He was up to Mr. Robertson for Trials, and found himself dovetailed between boys of Block D or Lower Fifth, a system which was ingeniously devised to avoid temptations. *Cribbing* in Trials was a high offence and made impossible between neighbours.

The last Sunday of the half dawned in the middle of the Papers, and with cheerful vigour the School sang the hymn-line ' When trials come no more,' which Lloyd chose with tact a few days before he played the ever-popular ' Lord, dismiss us with thy blessing.' Peter was dashing through the Greek Testament and drawing maps of the Holy Land all that afternoon, when the riotously disposed of Morley's burst into his room. ' Stop stewing ! What a *fug* ! No more *sapping* ! ' Frencher opened his window, as he said, to let the smell of *sap* out. As he did so, his eye caught sight of something over Wise's Yard below which filled him with amusement. He turned round. ' I see a ballcock floating on a tank on the roof below.' Everybody thrust their heads out. It was a tempting mark, and Camdown suggested they should drop a piece of coal. 'And cause floods?' 'Yes, and go home to-morrow.' 'Sacked perhaps?' 'You might drown the Man in his den.' This afforded exquisite amusement until suddenly Frencher whistled a long, low whistle, 'Heads in, lie low.' Everybody ducked. 'There's a rat on the roof!' Excitement ran high. There was no doubt. An unfortunate stable rat was moving about on the roof eating the bread Peter used to throw to the birds. There must be a reward for killing such an appalling creature, and in the name of sport and zeal for the good of the School everybody armed himself with coal or lumps of wood. Even a brick was hacked out of Peter's chimney-place as a missile. Simultaneously everybody fired. Every shot struck the roof. The rat darted down the gutter, while with a gurgling sound the broken ballcock rose on its hinge and the tank overflowed. There was a scream of delight, and in feigned delirium they embraced each other or pretended to hide under the table behind the bed. Frencher rolled on the floor with laughter. Peter looked out of the window like Noah out of his ark. The roof was already a pool. The gutter was a torrent, and the inhabitants of Wise's Yard, to wit a flyman and two horses, were being rescued from several inches of water. Spectators were crowding to the windows of neighbouring Houses. Fascinated by the course of destruction, Peter leaned out of his window. His old friend the flyman caught sight of him and threatened the immediate summons of Mr. Wise, whereat as much laughter as though he had called for the Beadle. The minutes sped and the force of the waters was not abated. A comical suspense dawned on the boys. What would happen? Mr. Wise or a sub-stitute for Mr. Wise had appeared and led out the cab-cavalry amid jeers from three surrounding Houses. Willum had made a hasty inspection of the scene and threatened to send for the Fire Brigade on the homeopathic theory that a water-cure would arrest the waters. But no solu-tion came until the first trickle poured off the roof in front

of a window on the first floor. The window was immediately opened sufficiently to permit the egress of Mrs. Sowerby's head. One glance below sufficed to cover the cata-
strophe, one glance above to detect the culprit, and one
command to Willum to save the situation, ' Willum, fetch
the Dame.' Equally laconic was the Dame's reply when
Willum broke the news two minutes later. ' Willum, go
and tell Mrs. Sowerby,' which instruction on the part of
the Dame he did hurriedly convey to the latter, who, per-
ceiving there was no help in men or women, did succeed
by means of a broom-handle in adjusting the ballcock to
its proper level, whereat the waters were stayed and in
half an hour the inhabitants of the Yard trod on dry land.
Later, Mrs. Sowerby informed the Dame that the culprit
whose face she had observed was Darley and that the
damage could only have been done from his room.

After Prayers that evening Mr. Morley mentioned the
serious damage that had been done that afternoon.
While he kept to walls and plumbing the House were
disposed to accept his heavy figures of loss, but when he
referred to the damage done to valuable horses there was
an irresistible guffaw, and Frencher broke in, ' Please, sir,
don't let the stables do you. Those were the rottenest
old crocks. They are only kept alive till we go back
next week. Then they will be made into next half's
sausages.' This antique humour reduced the House to
unquenchable laughter, and not until Willum's chances
of an entry at Ascot with one of them had been referred to
could Mr. Morley continue. ' The serious matter, a very
serious matter, is that the damage was done by a boy of
this House. Darley, it was done from your window. Did
you do it ? ' ' No, sir.' Instead of leaving it in the
hands of the Captain to settle, Mr. Morley, still believing
Peter was guilty, grew excitable, and asked, ' Well, who
did do it then ? ' It was a fatal mistake, for it enabled
Peter to answer, ' I won't say.' That was ' check.'
Peter was ensconced behind the strongest tradition in the
School by simply refusing to give up the name of another.

H

Rather than finish the game and be mated, Morley asked the Captain to see to it, and left the room. There was a murmur of approval, and Peter knew that he had passed into the first degree of Eton Freemasonry. He had helped a brother at his own skin's cost, and henceforth there was nobody in the House who would not do him a good turn. The next morning, as he went downstairs, he noticed his name had been crossed off the fagging list, with a note to say, ' Excused fagging for the rest of half.' Mr. Morley was the only person in the House who did not realise why.

Trials dragged out their agonising length. Peter sat up late every night with a candle, and by day staggered exhaustedly from Paper to Paper. To save time he went to bed in his clothes in order to have an extra half-hour in which to run over a last list of dates or derivations. Examinations are seldom a real test. A certain type of mind can prepare itself against a stated examination in twenty-four hours. It is often the successful boy and not the dunce who really cheats the examiner. What with his carefully arranged store of tips and temporary information, Peter found himself finishing with time in hand to watch the unhappy struggles of others. He could see Frencher and Camdown minor making desperate efforts to save themselves from the ominous ' minus dash,' which denotes failure in the School List. They were employing all the well-known devices of *cribbing*. Their cuffs and watches were lined with reliable information, for they appeared to consult them every minute. Unfortunately for their system, the information they had so carefully provided was not the information required by the examiners, and both had begun to make signals of distress to their friends for notes or rough copies. Mr. Robertson was watching them curiously over the edge of the book he was reading. He was anxious to do his duty, and yet play the game. He had not inquired why their timepieces or laundry caused them such anxiety, but he did not intend to let papers pass over the desks. The

Fifth Former next to Peter had responded to Frencher's distress signal, and an annotated piece of Trials paper marked **D** was thrust over Peter's, while a gentle kick denoted the direction in which it was expected to travel. 'What is that paper, Darley?' shot Mr. Robertson, before it could be passed or destroyed. 'Nothing, sir.' But before Peter could mumble any excuse, Robertson had descended from his desk and intercepted it like a pass at football. 'Are you in Remove?' 'Yes, sir.' 'Then what are you doing with a piece of Fifth Form paper?' There was no answer, and no further question. There was no harm done, and nothing more needed to be said or done. Mr. Robertson was a sportsman. It pleased him to outwit boys without bringing down penalties on their heads.

By Wednesday the heavy burden of Trials was over. 'Reading over' took place on Thursday in Upper School. It was Peter's last day as a new boy, and he felt the exhilaration of coming promotion. The Head sat at his mighty desk, surrounded by his tired assistants, most of whom had spent the preceding night adding up marks. There had been the usual delay caused by some French master unable to finish his papers, but the last page had been corrected and the tale of multitudinous marks made complete. Peter breathed and looked round at the busts with satisfaction. His eye caught Gladstone's wiseacre mask, and he wondered if he had really been 'sent up' for good before he was out of Fourth Form, or whether it was a Liberal lie. It seemed a greater feat than being Prime Minister. He began dreaming. The Head had begun solemnly to read out the names in order. For Peter only Remove counted. At last it came, like the tickings of fate :—

'Lower Remove. First Class—
    Denman.
    Lord Charleston.
    Darley.
  Second Class . . . '

Oh, what a breathless minute, but another even more unexpected was to follow. 'Brinkman Divinity Prize—Darley.' As he learnt afterwards, he had scored nearly full marks, though the examiners were not sure whether it was a stroke of humour on his part to divide the Tabernacle into Holy of Holies, Holy Place, and Ladies' Cloak-Room, meaning the Women's Court! Except that Tudor had won a Distinction in Trials, these were the only scholastic honours reaped by Morley's House. The Morleyites failed by small figures, or passed by smaller still. When it was all over, the patient race of Tutors gathered up their gowns and mark-books, and followed the Head. Peter was swept out of Upper School like a buoyant cork on the gossiping, garrulous crowd, down the stairs, and once more through the mighty portico and the gates which he had entered with such trepidation only ten weeks before.

Peter looked back with young love at the old brick building. The dying sunlight was creeping into the diamond panes or lighting the long pilastered railing which ran the length of the roof. Between two leafless trees the open gates allowed a last glimpse of the Founder's Statue. More benevolently than ever, he seemed to hold out his sceptre like a candy stick and his orb like an apple, as though to say, ' Be ye good little boys, and learn good Latin, for such is spoken in the Kingdom of Heaven.' The glad gleam of the holidays was upon the crowd pouring through the gates. The tide of boyish life ebbed past the grey stone and purpling brick, dispersed, and disappeared. A month was to pass before it flowed back. Only one or two boys lingered to compare notes. Mr. Lamb came out with his eager stride, and made straight to Peter. ' Very good boy. Your Tutor approves of very good boys. Your Tutor has bought a prize for a very good boy. Will you come round and have supper with me ? ' Peter felt he had not worked in vain, and determined to work for further honours if it were only to please so good and appreciative a man.

The old portals were now deserted, as pupil and Tutor turned towards Weston's Yard. Generations had passed through them, and generations were yet to come. Under that crumbling masonry Etonians passed to Chapel, to Absence, and to Examination. The grey stones had seen them all, the masters rushing to Desks or Chambers, the boys to reward or punishment, the majestic succession of Head Masters, the daily gang of culprits attending after twelve, the prizemen returning with their emblazoned books, the boys 'sent up for good,' with their verses inscribed in copperplate on the glossy paper stamped with the Eton arms. They watched the new boy the first time he timorously knocked at the gates of promise, and the full-fledged Fifth Former leaving for the Army or the University, with his copy of Gray under his arm, leaving perhaps for ever and ever. They stood like the Alpha and Omega of Etonian life, the beginning and the end of each career. They were the Eton gates of Janus, which faced both ways, out of the unreturning past into the illimitable future.

CHAPTER IX

THE SUMMER HALF

PETER returned to Eton for his first Summer Half in a rhapsody of expectation. There is no better Summer Half in an Eton career except the last. On an early May afternoon he drove up the High Street, which was flowering with the season. Shop windows were already gay with the different cricket and boating colours to be won that half. The River had thrown off its grey drab for a blue ripple. The ugly, swirling, lead-coloured torrent had given way to a steady flow, moderated by sun and zephyr. The stream no longer assaulted the crumbling banks with winter's hatred and beleaguerment of earth, but poured and purred with youth's eagerness, coiling into every nook and backwater and turning back the moment it touched the spring-kissed margin, as though curiosity was instantly cancelled by hurry. Brooding swans sailed down the rivulet that feeds Barnes Pool. To the right beyond Baldwin's Shore a gigantic wistaria was beginning to out-lilac the lilac, and the lime-trees in front of Upper School were budding yellow and green. The Churchyard was indulging in what grammarians call oxymoron, and symbolising birth instead of death. Amid the rank grass and tombs the seed fallen from boys' bird-cages had caught root and flowered a little exotically, like the strange plants which were once sown over the Coliseum from the litter of the wild beasts brought to grace Roman holidays. Window-boxes were already bursting into colour at the conventional choice of Eton tradesmen. Mr. Morley had invested in several yards of marguerites.

Peter left his luggage with the engaging Willum and

went for a walk. There was not a boy in sight, for Morleyites would return angrily by the last train arriving
before midnight. He slipped into Weston's Yard and
glanced at his Holiday Task. He knew it so well he could
afford to dream. The old chestnut welcomed him like
some gigantic Christmas tree with the dark-green folds of
foliage lit by thousands of little white wax lights. The
hum of insects and scent of flowers arose behind his
Tutor's wall. The new College Buildings looked considerably less like a workhouse in the soft light of a May
afternoon. Even the facings of Caen stone, to which
Dr. Hawtrey had sacrificed fireplaces, looked ancient.
Beyond the tumbling old gabled house at the corner,
swathed with creepers and said to have sheltered Shelley,
lay the Playing Fields. Sward stretched beyond sward
and elm towered above elm. Far between the trees
Sheep's Bridge crossed Jordan. Peter ran under the
brick arch into the road up which only that august
trinity of Head, Provost, and Vice-Provost were allowed
to drive. The fresh young grass of College Field was yet
unworn by the pounding cricketers, and the College waterman slept in his punt. Peter mooned alongside of the
famous battered Wall, his thoughts carrying him back
to olden days. It was curious in the deserted silence
to look on that historic white stone, under which boys
of a sterner mould had fought their battles with the
ungloved fist.

Under this stone Sir John Coleridge fought Horace
Mann for an hour. Here Morell the Lexicographer fought
Butler the Physician. Here Shelley fought Style, and the
Duke of Wellington ' Bobus ' Smith. Here Bryant the
author of the *Mythology* broke General Conway's head and
Pascoe Grenfell displaced Lord Derby's nose. These were
the famous fights before the duel had been abolished for
men and the *mill* for boys. Here had Wood fought and
killed Ashley.

It was one of the heroic deaths treasured in the School
legend. It was on a par with that of Lloyd, of whom it

was only recorded that he 'died of a chill after beating Westminster off his own bat.' Peter pictured the famous fight when the two boys had fought to the death. Nearly eighty years had passed since a Sunday's quarrel between the two had been followed by a Monday's *mill*. He could still imagine the young combatants stripped to the waist, battling each other amid the frenzied cheers of their friends, while their seconds rested and brandied them on their knees between rounds, and the deadly minutes slipped by, followed by the quarter-hours and the half-hours from the warning but unheeded Clock, and they were still fighting. They began to fight at about half-three, and till five and half-five they still fought on, and the crowd grew and the cheering swelled while the sands of life ran thinner and thinner. They were in the third hour of their struggle when Wood fell upon Ashley's shoulder and hurt his neck. What a cry must have echoed through the old trees as the great fight was finished. What cheering awaited the victor and what consolation the loser, who was carried home and only gradually became insensible, dying without priest or physician about eleven that night. Then his brother ran out crying bitterly, and the shadow of horror must have swept that careless, excited School as the grisly Referee stepped through their ring and touched the little body consecrated to youth. Breaking into solemn groups they must have dispersed with a chill at heart when the dead boy was carried out of Weston's Yard. Peter imagined Ashley lying like the lithe and graceful body of Sarpedon in Flaxman's illustrations to Homer, carried by Death and Sleep. How glorious it was to have attained fame as an Eton boy and to be remembered from generation to generation. He turned sadly round in the direction of the Antechapel where he could gaze at the mute memorial above ' the body of the Hon. Anthony Francis Ashley Cooper, fifth son of Cropley, Earl of Shaftesbury, who died at this place on the 28th day of February, aged 14 years.'

Peter had learnt from Mr. Jenkinson the haunting

phrase that those whom the gods loved died young. He
too began to wish to die at Eton. Could there be a sweeter
fate than to die in battle under the Wall and be gathered
into the bosom of a mourning Mother ? Deep in reverie
he wandered back through the Cloisters. The sacred
green lawn with its confined but fruitless shrubs seemed
to defy the ugly iron railings by which it was closely imprisoned. The College Pump threw a trickle of icy water
upon the worn stone. The brass door-plates of Provost,
Vice-Provost, and Bursar had shared in the spring cleaning,
but he felt that the academic divinities they described
knew neither spring, summer, nor winter. Hornby the
Provost, with his imperious features and unchanging expression of cynical disdain for the race of boys and the
race of schoolmasters, who to him were only grown-up
boys and often harder to manage ; Warre-Cornish the
Vice-Provost, as frail and elegant as a Curate out of Jane
Austen, who had edited the Eton Horace, that perfection
of a school text ; the short-sighted Bursar, who was
always peering about for buildings to destroy or build—
to a Lower Boy these folk were sky-begotten, empyrean-
dwelling personages, unapproachable and unapproached.

In the buzzing city of life the Cloisters were sepulchral.
They seemed dedicated to motionless old age, piled with
priceless books that no eye read, hung with beautiful
pictures kept from the public gaze. The triune power,
Head, Provost, and Vice-Provost, sat within, guiding the
School and contemplating each other's majesty and
dignity. They had reached the heights of their ambition.
But the Head was a perpetual *memento mori* to the Provost,
for it was ordained that he should succeed him at his
death. Only once in a generation a Provost of Eton died,
and then the gates into the School Yard from the Cloisters
were closed, and the dead Provost was carried slowly
round the Cloisters, followed by his mourning family,
which was the whole Eton Foundation. From these
gloomy reflexions Peter turned into School Yard, and ran
into Jenkinson, who cheered him immensely.

' Why, Darley, you have come back early! How jolly
of you to come back so early! Nobody should miss a day
of the May Half. I wonder who you will be up to this
half? Perhaps it will be Mr. Clinton. How jolly being
up to Mr. Clinton!' Peter, who had heard otherwise,
suggested that Mr. Clinton was known to be cross. ' Clinton cross? Oh no, we found him very jolly in Greece.
I wish I could be as witty and good-humoured as Clinton.'
Peter's vocabulary had not yet acquired the word ' self-
depreciatory,' but his mind felt antennawise for some
such word. He could only smile sheepishly and murmur,
' Why Greece?' It then appeared that Jenkinson was
one of those sapient masters who, instead of playing
cricket for Middlesex or football for the Harlequins in
the holidays, led expeditions of tired Tutors to Classic
lands, where they conned their lessons again on a huge
kindergarten scale amid the actual Greek temples and
Roman ruins. Peter smiled at an enthusiasm which was
simpler than his own. ' By the way, are you going to be
a *dry-bob* or a *wet-bob*?' asked Jenkinson in the slow way
that questions from the Catechism are asked. Peter,
having decided that he would have enough to do to hold
his own in the class-room without wasting time on the
rafts or at the nets, neither knew nor cared. However,
with a memory of the First of March, he hazarded ' *dry-
bob*, sir.' Jenkinson looked serious, as though the boy
were deciding for or against taking Holy Orders. He
himself was strictly amphibian in his tastes, and believed
in the equal importance of athletics by land and water.
Though some masters stuck to the nets, or encouraged
purely *wet-bob* Houses, he had thought out his duty, and
such afternoons as he stole from work were spent encouraging his Lower Boys to bowl feebly at nets, while race
nights on the River saw him industriously following races
which were seldom won. Mr. Jenkinson seemed to be
meditating the great choice Peter had just made. ' Darley,
I think you have really done right to decide to be a *dry-
bob*. Mr. Morley was one of the best slow bowlers in

England. We all remember the Australian wickets he took when he was bowling at Cambridge.' Peter felt he was doomed to spend hours under the baking sun slogging at nets, hanging about in pads, fielding the inapprehensible, striking the unstrikable, and performing all the more dismal evolutions connected with the glorious game.

'Come this way,' suggested Jenkinson, who was an old Colleger, 'and have a look at College Hall.' They climbed up a dark flight of stone stairs, worn away by generations of hungry Collegers, passed under a low arch, and through outer darkness into a great baronial hall. A Gothic window of stained glass glowed with the early history of the College, and on either side long stone fireplaces had been recently revealed in the rich dark panelling, which had covered them for centuries. The beautifully tiled floor supported some half-dozen old tables, surrounded by benches for the Collegers of King Henry the Sixth. On the panelling was scratched the record of an Elizabethan school treat. Above the panelling enormous oil paintings of Bishops, Judges, and Scholars leaned out under the escutcheoned corbels, a slant that Jenkinson explained had proved tempting to generations of diners who had flicked pellets of bread into the voids behind the canvases. Under a bracket in a corner he pointed out the site of the old Latin Bible. On the right of the door was the servitors' desk, cut with the names of those who had kept the Mess book. Above all rose the noble arching roof of stained timber. It was more like a chantry than a dining-room, and Peter contrasted it in amaze with Mr. Morley's low-ceilinged, evil-smelling refreshment-room. 'Do the *Tugs* really eat here?' he asked Jenkinson. 'I thought they only had the remains of the food from the Oppidan Houses.' 'No, they are not the outcasts you think,' laughed Jenkinson; 'in fact, they are the real freemen of Eton. The Oppidans are only naturalised aliens, suburban inhabitants, what the Athenians would call the *Metoikoi*.' Peter gasped. The School, then, was founded for the Collegers, and it was only

a time-honoured courtesy that allowed Oppidans to be
called Etonians at all. The bitter myths and baleful
legends which Oppidans nourished against the *Tugs*
were due to that jealousy of higher position which is even
harder to bear than superior talent. It seemed on a par
with the distortions levelled at mediaeval Jews that the
Foundation, which was the very foundation of Eton,
should be shunned like a Ghetto, and oddly enough
Collegers in their first year were actually called ' Jews.'
A Jew founded Christianity, reflected Peter, and the gown
of the Eton Founder's Collegers had become the Eton
gaberdine. They strolled into School Yard, leaving the
buildings of College like some walled mediaeval city behind
them, a Carcassone in wine-coloured brick. At the
moment a young Colleger was hurriedly passing. Jenkinson stopped him, and recognising one of his pupils, told
the two boys they must be friends, as they were both in
Fifth Form. Peter was delighted to recognise Ullathorne,
of whom he had lost sight since their fortuitous arrival
in the same cab. Jenkinson had studied both their
minds, and began quietly enlarging on the new Classical
authors they would meet in Lower Fifth. As he knew
how to talk bat and boat to the athletic, he chose enlightened *saps* for occasional deliverances of his soul. It
was one of his rare intellectual pleasures, though talking
shop out of shop-hours was distinctly considered bad form,
and Eton masters take their idea of good or bad form
from the boys. Peter drank in the first words he ever
heard on Aristophanes, Euripides, and Thucydides. ' You
will be doing *The Frogs* of Aristophanes this half. It is a
mixture of Tory politics, poetry, and Christmas Pantomime. How you will like it ! Think of Lord Salisbury,
Swinburne, and Dan Leno all in one, and you get an
inkling of Aristophanes.' Peter gasped a second time.
This did not sound like lessons. Ullathorne was nodding
his head approvingly. He was famous even in College
for his precocity, and a special rule had been made limiting
his vocabulary to words of four syllables. Failure to

comply led to ducking under the School Pump. ' Is
Swinburne the right comparison ? ' he asked. ' Surely
Swinburne hated orthodoxy and Aristophanes loved it.'
' Well, they both jeered at the gods,' replied Jenkinson.
' But there are different ways of making fun of what you
love and what you hate,' insisted Ullathorne. ' Yes,
yes,' murmured Jenkinson, ' but it is not good taste to
laugh at what you love.' Peter could not help thinking
that Aristophanes' attitude of affectionate ridicule to the
stage gods was not unlike the Old Etonian view of famous
Eton masters. ' Euripides was always in exquisite
taste,' went on Jenkinson, ' but you have the feeling that
he is exposing and secretly stabbing the dear old gods
of his youth. There is something very horrible about
Euripides.' ' What a cynic's catechism you could
imagine him writing to-day ! ' added Ullathorne. ' Had he
been at Eton, he would have attacked the Classics in a
Shavian play.' Jenkinson laughed. ' Where do you get
your ideas, Ullathorne ? Promise me not to read Bernard
Shaw till you have reached the University.' ' I promise.
I never read a modern author twice.' ' You will both
like Thucydides. He was a jolly historian.' This
sounded banal to Ullathorne, who, with a look of elfish
innocence, remarked, ' That is not quite the term I would
apply to him. I agree that his historical record is incomparable, but those speeches only show a clever précis-
writer, a journalist trained in the Athenian Foreign
Office.' Mr. Jenkinson looked half-pleased, but a little
bewildered. Ullathorne, he realised, was a character, one
of those boy characters that even the mill of school life
cannot crush. His whole pose was laid in the form of a
grieved protest against the contemporary athletic worship.
Not content with deploring the hours spent at play, he
openly fingered an exquisite grief over the amount of
time he lost walking to and from School every day. In
order to rise to work, he had adopted the amazing ex-
pedient of going to sleep in a hot bath in order to be
roused by its chill in the very early morning. He was

fond of quizzing the masters, but his wonderful powers of Latin and English versification obtained him immunity. Incidentally he was an extremely High Churchman. As they entered the School Yard, he turned to the carving over the gateway, and removed his hat. 'It is the Assumption of our Blessed Lady of Eton,' he apologised. With another bow toward the Founder's Statue, he muttered, ' *Ora pro nobis, Sancte Henrice Rex.*' Peter felt attracted by this spiritual candour, but Jenkinson, who favoured the official Eton religion, pretended not to hear. ' Do you really pray to the Founder ? ' inquired Peter, who kept his religion hidden under a bureau. He was settling into the not uncommon habit of omitting his prayers save to entreat the Deity into giving special aid during Examinations. 'Yes,' answered the other, ' I have a true Colleger's devotion to him.' 'Then what do you pray for ? ' 'Oh, lots of things—*Sapientia*, first editions, the Newcastle Scholarship, chastity.'

Jenkinson led them dreamily into the Brewhouse Yard, the oldest remaining part of the College. The white stone buttresses of College Hall thrust themselves out under rectangular battlements of brick. The beautiful oriel window with its six stone-cased lights pressed down hoary crumbling roots into the cobbled yard. An irregular line ran both across and down the historic junction of Henry the Sixth's stones and Edward the Fourth's bricks. It seemed to petrify the Wars of the Roses and the symbolic division of England between Lancaster and York. The lantern cupola with its flag-shaped vane crowned the roof of the building, which was spick and span aloft and grew more rugged and ruinous towards its base. The tradition was that the Charter was threatened under Edward the Fourth, who preserved no love for his sainted rival, and to save the situation the unfinished building was hurriedly roofed and coped by the Provost with another material. Eventually Lupton's Tower and the main College buildings in brick flowered out of the haphazard stone. In days to come Peter decided it was symbolic of

Eton education. The Classical foundation was too often
trimmed and cut short that a soaring athletic career might
be superimposed.

In front of them stood the old Brewhouse, which, since
ordeal by fire in 1865, had fallen out of the life of the School.
Old doorways stood closed upon nowhere and diamond-
paned windows framed the opaque. There was no sign
of life. The iron bracket of a long-disused lamp was
rusting to powder. Boys' names, initials, dates, were
scratched upon the bricks, boys who had passed by twenty,
fifty, and a hundred years ago. The College had inscribed
the year 1714 on the water-pipes, and that date seemed to
mark the last human activity. The whole corner was
abandoned to the cooing pigeons. The ticking beat of
Eton's heart hardly seemed to reach this red-bricked trap
of sunshine at her very centre.

To their right rose the grand East window of Chapel.
On either side the buttressed wall shot up as sheer and
unscalable as a precipice. But the texture of the stone
seemed changed with the season and the grey winter
hardness had warmed to a mottled sunburn. Under the
bright blue it rose like a great rectangular pavilion, pitched
magnificently for the housing of the Graal and wrought as
though from some heavy silken fabric, which hung flaky
from the multi-arrow-headed pinnacles which pinned it
to unseen beams within.

' Isn't that jolly ? ' said Jenkinson. Again this was
not the word which would have occurred to Peter, but
Jenkinson was referring to the pretty timbered arch of
Tudor design at the exit of the yard to Barnes Pool. The
arch before them resembled a mediaeval Pullman car set
on a brick bridge between two buildings otherwise uncon-
nected. Beautifully carven and transparently glazed, it
was the only artistic addition to Eton in modern times.
It had been called the Eton Bridge of Sighs, and the
suggestion made to heighten the illusion by keeping the
Block and Birch in the farther building. Jenkinson was
full of appreciation as they passed. ' Like one of Mr. Chris-

topher's sonnets in timber,' he said feelingly. ' I never thought of Mr. Christopher's poetry as wooden before,' Ullathorne must needs gently remark, without drawing the least ire from Jenkinson. They were passing the series of Houses called Baldwin's End, Bec, and Shore. The Shore was the quaint old-fashioned building at the entrance to High Street. The End was a low, three-storied House of the rabbit-warren type but of incredible beauty. The outside wall had apparently been diverted into a flower garden. It was thick with a jungle of creepers which successfully took the place of blinds in averting the rays of the sun from various bow-windows. A gigantic wistaria, by whose boughs boys could reach their rooms, smothered and strangled the entire building. Baldwin's Bec, on the other hand, was a five-story sky-scraper of homely and ignoble ugliness. A mixed taste in chimney-pots only emphasised the horribly plain lineaments below. Compared with a modern workhouse, some Eton buildings could not have afforded to throw the first brick.

From the Shirking Stone to the Burning Bush stretched a strange series of buildings. Gullivers', an abandoned Inn, Morley's stucco-pretension, the College Bookseller, Little Brown's *sock*-shop, and a corner House, which might have passed in Bloomsbury Square, completed the line as far as Keate's Lane. The modern Houses with their Virginia creepers and heavy School arms opposite Upper School might be called edifices but no more, a term to which no respectable building could object, but temporarily without the hum of boy-life they looked as comfortably forlorn as well-made but empty beehives.

Facing the New Schools was the enormous quadrangular building associated during half a century with ' Hoppy ' Daman and Wolley Dod, who built it in symbolic relations to himself, uncompromising in exterior but homely within. In legend Wolley Dod's had been famous for *bloods*, and even for sheltering a boy of ducal family who became a father while at Eton. The old barrack was often held up to scorn, foursided as it stood to all Eton draughts that blew. But the lover of Palladian was fain to notice the decorative ribbon of stucco across its front. Two sets of steps behind iron railings led respectively to the abode of boys and Tutor. It was true that the five rows of windows were indistinguishably plain, but a single one over the Tutor's door burst into a protruding bow like a small conservatory which had been hoisted and somehow had stuck half-way. In comparison nothing could be meaner than the low white-washed fabric known as Drury's alongside. In appearance it was so straggling that the top story, having suffered a collapse of tiling, had been telescoped in turn into the first floor. Stray chimneys alone gave an impression of upright permanence, while no less than three doors had been prepared for the escape of the occupants in the probability of further subsidence. Yet this broken-down looking almshouse was Jenkinson's. Upon it he had based all his hopes, and within its walls were housed one butler, one Dame, and the twenty enthusiastic small boys whom he hoped to see grow up and carry his name and House-colours over field and flood. To Drury's was attached the splendid legend that with only thirteen boys in the House they had actually won the Football Cup.

' Remember you will have to pass in swimming before you go on the River,' had been Jenkinson's last word. Boys and masters combined to keep the rule forbidding a *non-nant* access to boating. Every summer the printed names of those who had not passed were placarded like an interdict in every House, and the individual stigma could only be removed after ordeal by water. There had been a tradition that a boy was drowned every three years from as far back as 1553, when Sacheverall had been drowned in Dead Man's Hole off the Playing Fields. All-good had been drowned in 1756 off Sixth Form Bench, Remmett a Colleger in 1701, Lord Waldegrave in 1794, Broderip in 1802, Shaw in 1807, Hope in 1816, Singleton in 1820, Booker in Barnes Pool in 1822, Dean off the oak-tree in the Lower Shooting Fields, and finally in 1840

Charles Montagu was dragged by a towing rope out of his boat and drowned under Windsor Bridge. From that time Passing was instituted. But even in 1882 a boy called Donaldson was drowned.

After a few days spent with fellow-*scugs* trying to catch dace off the Playing Fields, Peter determined to pass. There were pike in Fellows Pond and trout in the Thames, but fishing was slow according to all account. A Lower Boy once took a nine-pound trout out of Dead Man's Hole with a bleak, and a boatman once caught a huge trout by falling on it when it was foolish enough to maroon itself on Rafts. Thames trout were rare enough to be known by name. So Peter made his way daily to Cuckoo Weir, the shallow-running stream dedicated to Lower Boys. Two and three times a day he bathed behind the grassy earthworks, thrown up by Warre and crowned with little lime-trees. Bathing had ceased at Upper Hope, but farther up the river at Athens the Fifth Form could be seen bathing by hundreds. The best divers took their headers off the Acropolis, while the warm, lithe River, splashed by the waders, cut by the rowers, swum by Sixth Form at Boveney, by Fifth Form at Athens, and by *scug* and Lower Boy in Cuckoo Weir, ran winding to Windsor, waiting perchance for the boy it might surprise once in three or thirty years. Sinuous and sinister ran the River, whose sound lives in the blood of all who have ever swum or rowed against her unceasing strength, the River that plays and waits and in her time woos and swoops upon a Ganymede.

The great Eton industries during the Summer Half were Cricket and Rowing. River and Fields were invaded and infested by the two great armies, into which Etonians are as strictly classified as Guelph and Ghibelline, *wet-bobs* and *dry-bobs*. The green sod was slowly tramped, worn, and pounded into cinereous dust, while the live River renewed herself eternally under every stroke of the oars. Field and flood became gay with the colours which were distributed from those twin founts of authority, the

Captain of the Boats and the Captain of the Eleven.
The Hierarchy of colours was based on the heraldic
colours of the Eton arms. The blue azure of the Eton
lilies was divided between the Eleven and the Eight.
The Eight wore a blue blazer with white edge and cap,
the Eleven inversely a white blazer with blue edge and
cap. Upper and Lower Boats wore the blue and red of
the quarterings in stripes on a white ground, while Second Upper and Lower Cricket Clubs wore red and blue as
background to their white stripe. Pride and dignity,
position, popularity, power, and immunity accompanied
the wearing of colours. Obscurity accompanied their
lack. Peter decided he could remain obscure very
contentedly. He fell back on the ease which a *wet-bob*
can enjoy if he has not passed. It became possible to
keep up with the work which was imposed on him by
Tutors and other boys alike. If a boy takes to hard work
at Eton, he can work there as hard as anywhere. Con-
versely, if he decides to slack, he can do less work than
at any other school. But a *sap* is expected never to flag
or fail until his name is enrolled on the Newcastle select,
which to keen Tutors is like being placed for the Derby.
The *sap* has little time for the absorbing cares of practice
at nets and coaching on the River. He becomes amphibi-
ous, neither *wet* nor *dry-bob*, and with a little management
can avoid being dragged into either form of physical
slavery. He must endure, however, to remain incon-
spicuous, wholly ignored, or slightly tolerated. He is
expected to run with the herd, and not aim at the clique.
Romantic friendships or magnificence of dress are the
perquisite of the strong. *Saps* are required to club together, combining the harmlessness of doves with the
obscurity of bookworms. Socston, however, insisted that
Peter should accompany him in an early effort to pass at
swimming. Baptism is not more important to the
Baptist than Passing to the practising *wet-bob*. The boys
spent long afternoons learning at Cuckoo Weir, the Thames
artery dedicated to the gambols of *non-nants*, under the

eye of old Spong, the waterman-in-charge, who was a Crimean veteran resembling Mr. Herbert Spencer.

The dismal country beyond Arches on the way to the Weir had cheered up considerably with summer. A field of wheat had grown up, flecked red with poppies. In the hedgerows a parasite race of sweet-vendors or *Jobies* plied their trade, selling on tick to one generation and recovering with compound interest from the next. Knowing the hunger that follows bathing, they basketed their wares as cleverly as bird-catchers set lime. The *Joby* was the lowest grade of the community living on Eton. After the booksellers came the shopkeepers, after the College servants the House servants, after the *sock*-shop keepers came the *Jobies*. Only one of the *Jobies* was allowed within the precincts, old Knock, who referred all events sadly to the days of Dr. Goodford. Otherwise, the *Jobies* were the Ishmaels of Eton trade and supply.

As soon as a Passing was announced, Peter and Socston gave their names. Tests by water are always sufficiently harrowing to the tested to draw spectators. A sarcastic crowd lined the wooden ledges of Cuckoo Weir, while three solemn *wet-bob* masters, wearing pink Leander caps, sat on a bench with notebooks. The candidates were punted into midstream by Spong, who looked exactly like Charon ferrying a lighter packed with shivering naked souls across the Styx. The strong sunlight flickered through the leaves of the trees, painting a shimmering network of flesh tints against the thick olive-coloured water of Italy Hole, as it was called. Twenty yards away, across deep water, was the pole, which swimmers had to navigate in the proper Eton style of swimming, or hear the hated formula of failure monotoned from the bench, ' Swim to the steps ! ' The first name was called, and a boy at the head of Remove slipped into the water. ' Strike with the soles of your feet,' chanted Mr. Donaldson from the bank. ' Draw your hands up to your chest.' When the pole had been circumnavigated, the candidate was expected to swim on his back and tread water. Peter heard his name called, and with his heart beating engine-wise took the cool plunge. He remembered nothing till he found himself near the pole, resisting a fearful temptation to clutch it for a breather. The masters were shouting, but he heard not a word through his water-logged ears. Every time his mouth filled with water he managed to swallow it down rather than betray the least difficulty. Still he swam there and back, and imitated a cork bobbing on the water with tolerable likeness. He climbed out at the steps, and lay in his towel watching other entrants. The sport soon began, for the Lower Boys in two Houses, including Maxse's, had been fagged to enter whether they could swim or not. The first passed to the bottom of the weir by means of a *belly-flopper*, amid loud cheering, and was sent to the steps. The next swam half-way and sank till rescued by the wary Spong with a punting-pole. Socston was the next, and actually earned a word of praise, so correct was his Eton style. He joined Peter, and with currant bun in their teeth both became sensible of the pleasure which comes from watching the discomfort of friends. At the end Mr. Donaldson read out the litany of the successful. Both had passed, and threw their towels into the air with ejaculations Mr. Donaldson was constrained to suppress. As a *beak* he was not content with redressing grammar in class, but choice of expression as well. He was fond of challenging an oath, and once in a sermon recommended rapid counting as a means to exhaust wrath and prevent profanity. For some time later his school and pupil-room were shaken by the sound of falling books followed by the pious recitation of the numerals.

The wonderful days of May began to pass rapidly. Buds burst into brightness. The great elms drew their lustreless canopy of split-emerald over the Playing Fields. Every boy ordered a window-box of cheap blooms, masters' gardens lifted profusion and perfume to Heaven. The River swept like a green-hued snake, with rippling scales and shimmering coils, around Brocas and the Upper and

Lower Hopes, tempting and enticing boys to rush to the Rafts or the bathing-places after twelve, and after four, and again after six. The flow of sport was irresistible. It was a challenge to the daring, the ambitious, and the strong. The contest was often above a boy's strength, but the prizes were beyond rubies.

Socston gravitated toward the strong. He had developed enough strength to give him hopes of entering for the Lower Boy Sculling, and meantime his whole adoration went unto the athletic. Dugannon, his fag master, had attained Upper Boats. It was his last half at Eton, and he had encouraged his fag to expect a little coaching. The coaching never took place, but the few words dropped in careless suggestion kept Socston to a routine of punctilious watermanship. He learnt the Rules of the River, and committed every syllable to memory. Every day he sculled his whiff up to Boveney until every watermark sank into memory. No saying lesson was so well learnt. Before he reached the Railway Bridge, there was Deadwater Eyot on his right and the Brocas Clump on his left. The towpath continued on his left, crossing Cuckoo Weir Bridge and Bargeman's Bridge. Bargeman's Bush was opposite the egress of Cuckoo Weir. On the left came Hester's Shed and Cumberland Creek, a vain effort of the Butcher of Culloden to divert the River to a shorter course. Clewer Steeple was visible on the other side, the little Church whose river-aspect is sacred to all Etonians, but few of whom ever penetrate its portals. The great sweep of Lower Hope, faced by Lion's Leap and Swan Bay, almost doubled the River on her course, to which she returned out of Upper Hope and Athens Bay. From Athens Bay flowed the shallow entry of Cuckoo Weir, thickly hedged with alder and willow, to rejoin the main current half a mile farther back.

One 'after twelve' Socston found himself alone on Rafts. There were only a few minutes to get back in time for dinner. As he ran through the delicately cased outriggers, the stacked oars, and plump little dinghies, he

ran into Dugannon. He felt as awkward as a page who
has stepped on the royal train. Dugannon smiled at his
profuse apologies. ' You needn't say all that, you know.
By the way, what is your weight ? ' Socston had no idea.
' Well, come in here and I 'll weigh you.' He led Socston
into the Holy of Holies of the Eton boating world. 'There's
nobody here now, so sit there.' Socston climbed on to a
plush chair attached to a weighing machine, while Dugannon recorded the weight. Socston looked round in
puerile awe. A bow window picked out in light blue
bulged slightly toward the River. The walls of the cabin
were hung with brown mahogany-coloured boards, bearing
the names of the winners of the School Pulling and Sculling,
the names of Eton's racing Eights, the proud roll of the
Captains of the Boats, and the lists of Clubs and Colleges
they had rowed down to defeat at Henley. There were
drawings of some Eton Eights in the Forties of a primitive type, more resembling the war canoes of a South Sea
Chief than modern outrigged boats, before the days of
photography, for the thwarts were simply marked by the
names of the long dead oarsmen. It dated from the
heroic days when the records of the Eton River were kept
by Selwyn in detailed and unblemished Greek. In the
far corner was a faded photograph of Edmond Warre in
his prime as a rowing coach. There was the great brow,
the all-seeing eyes, and the lips whose commanding sound
seemed still to penetrate into every nook of the Eton
world. There was not a crevice in the River banks or a
stone or a brick in the School buildings which had not
echoed his word at some time. Time nor tide could
remove his mark on the River. Surely it was better to
rule over those Rafts than in the great Castle opposite.
' You are not eight stone,' remarked Dugannon. ' You 're
not near enough to Fifth Form to be a cox. So you had
better plug away rowing. Come on or we 'll be late for
dinner.' Socston prepared to trip back at his heels, but
with wonderful condescension his fag master allowed him
to keep pace beside him. They were late of course, and

the House preserved a silence of curiosity as Dugannon murmured excuses for himself and his fag, which Morley accepted. Socston, scarlet with blushes and exercise, made his way to his seat, pursued by the dissecting eyes of his fellows, who watched for favouritism with silent amusement or unforgiving scorn.

Socston was careless what they thought. Dugannon had treated him with the civility of one human being to another. He had been weighed by a member of the Upper Boats. Every fibre of his mind still thrilled with that exalted moment. Dugannon could have commanded him body and soul. As a matter of fact, Dugannon never spoke to him familiarly again, but Socston only smiled knowingly when the House chaffed him for being the great oarsman's favourite. It was enough to bring another imperceptible difference between him and Peter. Already he had set his heart on one day earning a colour. He gave himself two years to reach the Lower Boats, and began to practise assiduously for Lower Boy Sculling. The dingy little room he occupied down the turn of Peter's passage became endowed with a new importance, for the window at the back of the adjoining House had become the room of the new Captain of the Boats, and in senti- mental or ambitious moments he was content staring across on the chance of seeing that very great personage. As for Peter, he bought himself the straw hat which he was privileged to wear after Passing, and going to Rafts paid a shilling for a whiff, which he managed to swamp at the third stroke. It was most humiliating, for there on Rafts stood Sir John Edwards Moss, who with all his family had been Captains of the Boats. To Socston this grizzled old gentleman-mariner was the greatest of heroes, for he had presented the School with a new fleet of Eights.

CHAPTER X

THE Summer Half leaped into its stride and the sands of the Victorian era began to run out. For Peter all the apprehension of his first half had passed into sheer enjoyment. There was something new to do or see every day. The half had given him a new set of masters. In French he was up to the genial Hua, the only Frenchman who ever understood and mastered the British schoolboy. He was up to 'Friar' Tuck for Mathematics. Tuck was a famous football kick, and in off moments a parson. However, he was a fine old Colleger, one of the olden time, and was fond of telling a yarn of a boy who had come to College after him, and had been his junior, but had left early, gone to the University, and returned as a master before Tuck had left the School. The old types were dying out. But Peter had the privilege before the century passed to be taught drawing by old Sam Evans, who dated as a master from the Crimean War. Old Sam's drawing class had been kept up, and parents might be certain their boys would be only taught the most orthodox British school of art, without any indulgence in Impressionism. Sam was assisted by a tall and talented youth, Sidney Evans, who was also in charge of the smaller Evansites in the cottage adjoining Miss Evans's House. Old Sam gave instructions warranted to turn out a President of the Royal Academy, and Sidney walked up and down the line with his pencil. The chief ornament of the class-room was a life-size Dying Gladiator in plaster. It did not appeal as it should to the flannelled contestants of Eton. Peter had the bad taste to place his top-hat one

119

day on its head, whereat the nudity of the statue became ridiculous, and the class began to laugh and draw crooked. Old Sam looked around, and seeing the cause asked angrily whose hat it was. ' Yes, whose hat ? ' asked Sidney. Peter held up his hand. Sam asked his name. ' Yes, what is your name ? ' added Sidney. ' Darley at Mr. Morley's ! ' Sam entered it in a book, and Sidney made an additional note. But Peter never heard on the subject again. Perhaps old Sam was really old, or did not frequent Chambers. The threatened complaint never took place. Peter, of course, rushed off to prepare his Tutor for the awful possibility, and Mr. Lamb, always ardent to defend a pupil, went to the Head primed with Peter's brief. In the evenings, once a week, Peter read the *Iliad* with Mr. Lamb. On Sundays he read Milton with him, and as a result, though he concealed it to the day of his death, he was seized with a wild ambition to be a poet. He used to lie in corners by the River, amid the comfrey and loose-strife, and watch the kingfishers skirt the flowering rush with its purple and white flower appropriate to the colours of College, and try desperately hard to write blank verse, like hundreds who had been inspired by Eton before him.

He was curiously woken from the reverie in which he lived. Given up to his studies, and to pleasing the ever-pleasable Mr. Lamb, he had no time for the gossip or politics of the House. One morning at breakfast he was startled to see the whole House spring to their feet and hurl their small loaves of bread at the head of an unfortunate and unpopular youth in Fourth Form. Crack ! crack ! crack ! The wretch fled, a picture of terror, to the Dame, who issued several verbal proclamations on his behalf through Willum and Mrs. Sowerby. From Socston Peter learnt, however, that his offence had been dire. He was believed to have sneaked systematic-ally to the Man, and, moreover, not content with draw-ing up the rules of a *Pi-Club*, he had composed a list of members of the House whom he thought might be appro-

priately removed from the House for their own or the
House's good. This list, it was rumoured, he had sown
up for safety in the trousers of some other unhappy Lower
Boy, for whom both Mr. Morley and the House were
believed to be engaged in searching. It sounded too
ridiculous to be true, but true it was, and Peter was
severely questioned as to whether he was the recipient
or not. A number of trousers were destroyed during
the search, and then it was announced that the fatal list
had been secretly destroyed. But the rumour of its
existence gave some Morleyites a very unpleasant half-
hour. Mr. Morley addressed the House after Prayers
on the iniquity of throwing their loaves at the head of so
unoffending a youth, and delivered an ultimatum that
if it was a case of the boy or the rest of the House having
to leave, it would not be the boy—but it was. The House
made it so hot for the reputed sneak that he was glad
to move into a smaller House in the middle of the
half.

Being in Fifth Form, Peter drifted into a solitary
existence, but it appeared that he acquired sundry rights
such as going to 'Tap,' the only public-house open to
Etonians. Mr. Socston enlightened him as to this privilege, and after they had tea served by Phoebe in Little
Brown's, took him into the other hostelry, much to the
jealousy of Socston, who had to remain outside while
Mrs. Thomas served Mr. Socston and Peter with beer
through a slit. Peter glimpsed into the parlour and, to
his alarm, perceived the Captain of the Boats and another
Pop. If it had been the Archbishop of Canterbury hob-
nobbing with the Chancellor over a mug of beer, he could
not have been more impressed. Mr. Socston took them
down High Street, and pointed out where the Old Catherine
Wheel had been plastered into the Bridge Hotel, and the
Old Sun Hotel where George the Third used to *sock*, and
the old Cockpit where Etonians once matched their
roosters. Then he dragged them to South Meadow to
show them exactly where Walter Forbes, while a boy at

Eton, had thrown a cricket ball one hundred and thirty
yards ! And so the Summer Half began to run away.

Science in Fifth Form brought Peter up to Dr. Borcher,
who speedily established himself as a magician in Peter's
youthful mind. Borcher had perfected colour photography among other inventions, and alone of photographers he had photographed the Peak of Teneriffe
thrown on the air from the Peak itself. His adventures
lost little in the telling, and he held his boys in awed
wonder of himself and the elements he controlled. ' This
jar,' he began the first lecture attended by Peter, ' contains what is the most deadly explosive known to
man. One drop would shatter this laboratory. A table-
spoonful would damage Lower Chapel. If this jar was
dropped I could not answer for the safety of Windsor
Bridge. Now pass it round.' And all semblance of
ragging died down as the interested boys passed round
what was probably a jar of water. With buoyant
humour, Dr. Borcher proceeded to unveil in a series of
startling lectures, all of which Peter recorded word by
word, the amazing sub-stuff of the created universe, and
some of the more gruesome qualities of its elements. One
day the class was adjourned to South Meadow, and an
eclipse of the sun was watched and photographed. From
that day Peter became fired with zeal to be an astronomer.
Another day Dr. Borcher loosed hydro-balloons, and Peter
decided to become an aeronaut. Long before the science
of aviation was dreamed of, Fifth Form at Eton had learnt
how to test the upper currents of the air. At the end of
every half Dr. Borcher distributed tickets to good boys
for a free and easy variety entertainment in his Lab.,
where lantern slides were varied with tales of the eerie.
But he was remarkable among Science demonstrators.
His experiments did come off like magic !

In the old century the month of May was marked in the
Eton Calendar by the old Queen's birthday. Since the
famous occasion when an Eton boy saved her life from an
assassin at the station, the Queen was understood to

entertain a strong Eton sentiment. It was true that Prince Albert had not been an old Etonian, but he had laid the first stone of the new College Buildings, and his name was indissolubly connected with the Prize List. Two of his descendants were among contemporary Etonians, and the Queen enjoyed driving of an afternoon through the narrow Eton street. Once even she had called on Miss Evans. Often the boys were surprised by the galloping of an equerry, followed by the familiar landau, drawn by horses with postilion and trimmed with gillies taken from the Balmoral wilds. It was a tradition that the Queen bowed to the Eton boys, but not to the Eton tradesmen. Perhaps she remembered that William the Fourth was so Etonian in sympathy that he insisted on seeing the Eton Eight row against Westminster a few days before his death. It was a tradition that the Eton defeat had hastened his end. The long series of draws and failures against Harrow cricket might have had something to do with ageing the Widow of Windsor.

A diligent calculation by the Mathematical staff decided that Queen Victoria was about to celebrate her eightieth birthday, and the Head, at a hint from Windsor Castle, set about organising another of those remarkable manœuvres which at once edified the War Office and consoled the ancient Queen. His generalship at the second Jubilee had shown how great a Field Marshal had been sacrificed to pedagogy. At Spiers Corner were still the marks of the triumphal Arch which had been erected on that occasion, and as the older boys had taken part in the Jubilee Parade, the School as a whole could be trusted to perform another march to the Castle. The effort required from each boy was calculated at a set of Latin Verses, which accordingly was excused by proclamation. The Twenty-Fourth of May was an honoured feast in the Victorian Calendar, entailing whole holidays and gun-firing and cheering. There were not likely to be many more, and the eightieth of their sequence called forth the Head's fullest powers of organisation. After

Chapel the School assembled in School Yard, armed with umbrellas to meet the soft mulled rain which was falling. The Volunteers were arrayed more martially with rifles and bayonets. Dr. Lloyd had been summoned from his organ-loft as chief of staff, for it was expected that the manœuvre would be partly musical. Nobody had the faintest idea what they were expected to sing, but it was obvious from the semi-panic into which Lloyd had thrown himself that melody was on the programme. He was seen rushing to and fro in his beautiful musical degree hood, as though he had been practising to conduct a Grand Opera for weeks past, and was now about to risk his whole reputation at a royal command with rather faulty performers.

The Volunteers stood easy in their beehive helmets and grey tunics, while the divisions of the School were marshalled by their devoted masters. Lower Fifth proved remarkably obstreperous. ' What the hell is Lloyd loose for ? ' muttered Frencher, who was anxious to celebrate the day with practical joking in preference to musical theory. ' Looks as though he lost five minutes as an undergraduate, and has never caught up with them.'

' I bet we shall have to sing,' said Mouler. ' I knew they wouldn't let us off verses for nothing.' ' I suppose we 'll sing the " Carmen " with old Ainger prompting in the background.' ' Oh, no,' said Frencher, ' hasn't Christopher written some rot for us to yelp at the Castle ? ' But the phlegmatic placidity of Mr. Christopher's countenance at that moment forbade any suggestion of recent inspiration or fear that his verses might be momentarily torn on the ribald lips of a thousand boys. At this moment word was passed that they were to sing the National Anthem. ' And it 's all about the old Girl anyhow,' said Frencher, with an air of discovery, as the Volunteers began marching out of the School gates. The Head moved on, leaving his assistants to harry the file with umbrellas. A majestic and sphinx-like figure followed, concealed in a superannuated cab. It was understood to be the Provost.

By the time the School were tramping in fours down High Street the rain had cleared off. As they passed New and Lingwood's shop, one genius was seized with the idea of throwing his unrequired umbrella to Solomon and the assistant draper standing at the doors. Others saw the wisdom of marching unburdened, and cast theirs at the unfortunate pair, who must have collected fifty by the time Fourth Form were abreast. They also entered into their difficulties, and were irresistibly tempted to hurl more umbrellas like assegais through the air, to the total discomfiture of the recipients, the piercing of a plate-glass window, and the huge enjoyment of the umbrella-owners. Solomon was left looking ridiculously like a St. Sebastian clad in white paper, but stuck by a score of umbrellas instead of arrows. The incident added high spirits to the line, and they were prepared to enter into the musical programme. They reached the Castle like a long black serpent with a grey head under the anxious surveillance of the Head, who, accompanied by a brilliant staff, proceeded to marshal the loyal proceedings. The boys were fond and proud of the old man, and they gave him a friendly cheer as they passed. Napoleon could not have taken their salute more imperturbably. On entering the Court Yard, the Windsor Madrigal Society, under Sir Walter Parratt, was discovered under the window where the Queen was expected to appear, to the relief of the boys, who found their vocal power was to be sustained as in Chapel by outside help. However, the Volunteers, especially the recruits, were stiffening into impossible stiffness. But Lloyd was not to be done out of his treat, and he began to make energetic efforts to tune up the massed Madrigalists at the same time that he gave some belated musical instruction to the School. He had to take his chances when he could. He was popular, and everybody was anxious to help him with his impromptu programme. Word was passed to

sing up and drown the voices of the cads. Cad applied
to the Town and Borough merely meant non-Etonian
as the Greeks called the non-Greek world barbarian.
At this moment the Queen was announced to be on her
way from another part of the Castle, and amid intense
excitement the Madrigalists began to sing the National
Anthem in parts. The School joined in under Lloyd's
baton (how the dear man was enjoying himself), and
maintained a loyal roar a few beats behind to the end.
Meantime the Volunteers, under the guiding lead of their
devoted officers, stood to unquivering attention, and
presented arms to the empty windows. The Madrigalists
then sang the Jubilee Hymn, into the end of which Lloyd
loosed the whole School, much to the spring cleaning of
sundry disused echoes in the Royal Courts. The Queen,
whose musical sense had been completely destroyed
through listening to her unharmonious subjects for sixty
years, showed no sign of annoyance. The crumpled
little Figure came forward, and bobbed in gracious
appreciation, while Dr. Lloyd's features became cherubic
under his whiskers, and the Head's eyes gleamed with
loyalty. Meantime, Madrigals and Madrigalists having
been exhausted, the boys were allowed to relieve their
feelings by three hearty cheers. The whole School then
marched past in fours, while the Provost of Eton and
the Mayor of Windsor appeared like Moses and Elijah
on either side of the Sovereign, to add an awful and
unrehearsed dignity to the joyful day. The Provost's
ruffled hair stood erect, his features as unmoved as the
dusky Indian attendants behind the Queen. Doubtless
these Indians had been duly led, like the poor heathen
chieftain receiving a Bible from Queen Victoria in the
famous engraving, to a proper discovery of the reason
of England's greatness. But at that moment they must
have felt that Eton loyalty and the Eton Volunteers were
a possible reason as well.

After that summer the visits of Victoria to Eton became rarer and rarer until they ceased with the coming

of war clouds. It was nearly three-score years since she had watched the last *Montem* procession from the oriel window in Lupton's Tower, and longer even since Dr. Hawtrey had announced her accession to the School with the inspired quotation, ' Let us die for our King, Maria Theresa ! ' Amid bleak snows and burning dusts the sons of Eton had long since made good their whimsical old Head Master's allusion.

K

CHAPTER XI

THE EVE OF THE FOURTH

ONE red-letter day there is at Eton to which all other Feasts must yield. Even Founder's Day on the sixth of December is but a pale Sabbath compared to the royal rubric of the Fourth of June. King Henry's holy shade has withdrawn before the stolid memory of George the Third. As the pious founders of many a mediaeval college were supplanted by the more robust Reformers, as Henry the Eighth magniloquently refounded benefactions of the past by imposing his image and superscription, so by more popular acceptance and the personal affection of Etonians George the Third entered into the place due to Eton's Founder. What mattered the loss of America to a King who so completely won Eton?

For so many successive years Etonians celebrated his birthday that it remained chapleted in their calendar after his death, a day of feast and music, of rejoicing by field and flow, a blessed day entirely, beginning with empty schoolrooms and ending with blazing fireworks. Now even an Apostle's day has Early School! But the Fourth is a *dies-non*, a day that is no day, rather a chorus, an interlude wreathed with flowers. Twice only had it been postponed in tradition, once for the death of Lower Master Yonge and a second time for Mrs. Hornby, who memorably deceased on a Third of June.

The expectation which filled the eve of the Fourth was only broken by the serious controversy which had begun to rage round the question of the Old Etonian colour. Like all domestic politics, it had become intense and sarcastic. The Old Etonians had desired an Old Boy colour

128

to distinguish themselves from the Old Boys of other Schools. Both friends and foes pointed out that this was unnecessary.. There was a strong feeling as well against those who had passed through the School in *scug*-caps assuming anything like coloured distinction in after-life. Those who had passed colourless into the world deserved to die drab. However, the majority of Old Etonians were determined on a colour, and the next stage of the controversy was what colour ? The *Eton College Chronicle* seethed with letters from the indignant, the hopeful, the droll, and the suggestive. Some desired a light colour and some a dark one. Others wished to wear a peculiar button at the bottom of the waistcoat in order to stereotype the Eton custom of wearing it unbuttoned. The sacred light blue was out of the question. It was the glorious guerdon of the few or the more frequent mark of the Cockney who had once fancied Cambridge. The Old Etonian Association, however, in a sudden access of zeal, decided that it should be light blue and white, and the Shooting Eight, whose colour it was, decided that the Association ought to be shot. Then it was suggested that the Cricket Twenty-Two should give up their light blue and black, which they declined to do. Mr. Ainger, whose mind had become the engine of the Old Etonian Association, appeared much beset by the controversy which he had indirectly caused. It was understood that he even intended to give up his House in order to devote his attention wholly to kindréd questions. He had given Eton her *Carmen* and her Latin *Gradus*. It was possible that he might solve the greater question of the Old Etonian colour, which was a matter affecting the Empire.

Meantime the Fourth of June was approaching, and the Eton world was mobilising. During May the intent and preparation of Eton was concentrated on the Fourth. House masters prepared gelatinous banquots for parents, which might or might not raise their opinion of the Eton food supply. Tailors designed fancy dress, and haberdashers trimmed flowered hats for the crews. The Captain of the Oppidans invested a huge sum in fireworks. The Captain of the Boats filled up the vacant thwarts. The Captain of the Eleven selected the players to play the annual match against New College. The Eton tradition was stirred to its depths. The funeral games in honour of George the Third had more than taken the place of *Montem*. Only an inspired antiquarian could have recalled that famous spectacle, which only a few dimmed eyes left through the land had ever seen—the procession of the School through the Cloisters, the Fifth Form in red coats, with their fags attired as midshipmen, the Sixth in the gorgeous vesture of Grand Opera, the runners who penetrated the countryside demanding *Salt* or money from chaise and coach, after which the School then proceeded to Salt Hill, *ad montem*, where they witnessed the waving of the Flag and dined at the Captain's expense, marking his lack of popularity, if necessary, by damage with their swords. But the year 1844 found the Saltbearers jostling the ticket-collectors at Slough Station, and *Montem* perished as naturally as a hedgerow of flowers passes away in the approach of factory smoke. Mediaeval revelry could not survive the excursion train, and *Montem* was buried in the more sober glories of the Fourth of June.

Mr. Munfort, impersonating the old tradition, was making serious preparation for entertaining his visitors. He expected a Prime Minister and several of the Peers whose heirs were entrusted to his hands. His wine on these occasions was as excellent as Mr. Morley's was poor. He understood that good wine and good blood and, for the matter of that, a good House at Eton went together. Not that he was a snob, for he knew how to distinguish between a Peerage by purchase and a Peerage by inheritance. When necessary, he could apply a herald's discrimination, and he always had the wisdom to prefer a good old county name when borne by a parson's son to the strange exotic nomenclature, which would have been of more advantage to Mr. Maxse's House had it been a house in the city. He was critical of Houses like

Morley's and Maxse's. To colleagues of the old and
genuine Eton hall-mark he was loyal, but to Mathematical
parvenus, who had become House masters, he was radically
opposed. He had come to an excellent creed :—That
Eton was the most excellent of schools. That Eton
mastership was the most excellent of professions. That
the minute number of unsuccessful Houses at Eton were
seldom in the hands of Classics. That the successful
House masters were generally bachelors. Finally, that
Eton was founded for Etonians. Two interpretations
might be placed on the last phrase—that certain old
Eton families, with whom Mr. Munfort was connected,
might expect to appear on the Foundation from generation
to generation ; or that Eton was intended for those who
would be reasonably taken for Etonians in after-life.
Mr. Munfort had no room in his House for the nicest Jews
or the best-born cosmopolites. The millionaires of
Yankeedom left him unimpressed. An Indian Prince
he could just abide as an Imperial curiosity. On the whole,
he rejected aliens in religion or race.

In his day Mr. Munfort had seen reform very effectively
averted from Eton. He was a survivor of the great days
when Oscar Browning, the Eton master, whom George
Eliot described as Mr. Lydgate, set out to oppose the
Philistinism of Hornby and the athleticism of Warre.
Giants had clashed indeed. Oscar Browning had made
his House a refuge of culture. With alarming zeal he
had introduced Greek statuary, Italian literature, German
music, and, most unpractised of all, English history,
among his boys at the same time that Warre began to
supervise the boating and Mitchell the cricket. In their
conflict was modern Eton made and unmade. The great
intellectual days were no longer remembered, when boys
poured forth Homer between the rounds of a fist fight,
when Eton journalism was written in the stilted style of
the old Reviewers, when boys wrote English verse and
prose compared to which the modern School periodicals
were of a facetious and feeble vulgarity. Warre and

Hornby had made Eton the greatest athletic school since the nurseries of Sparta.

For a time Arnold's Rugby had tended to lead the van and mould the type of English School. Arnold's boys were interested in flowers and letters. Eton still afforded the leisure, if not the taste, for literature. A genius like Clark Kennedy could publish his work on the Birds of Berks and Bucks while still an Eton boy. The aimless and trivial frivolities of ' A Day of my Life at Eton ' painted the unintellectual side. It was perhaps the most damaging testimonial that had ever been offered to a School. By its tell-tale pages Hornby's Eton was classified in literature. Before the advent of Warre and Mitchell games were a side issue, and unorganised. The Jacob's coat of colours for games was not invented. Athletic caste and etiquette had not checked the originality of boys, nor had a taste for luxury corroded the old Spartanism. Out of school they were really free. But the new system imposed games, and even peculiar games that the player was never likely to meet again by land or sea. Voluntary they were a joy, but compulsory they could become a curse. When voluntary study clashed with compulsory games, the result was obvious. Hornby had been content that scholarship should shift for itself, and culture should not even be. He himself was one of England's mountaineers, and had been seen descending an Alpine glacier, roped to guides and axing every step. He had allowed the athletes their way, not that he was wholly wrong. In his slightly cynical way he always supposed that Eton taught her array of Viceroys and Premiers something which, however much of a handicap, did not prevent them attaining that rank. The great reform he had allowed had been the introduction of extra and varied studies for First Hundred and the creation of a chemical laboratory, which he cynically permitted to be built in the form of a permanent eyesore.

The various movements restoring beauty in Church and literature reached Eton in due course, and in due course

were repelled. Coleridge the Tractarian was prevented
from becoming Head Master. Rome seemed to underlie
the Oxford Movement, and immorality was associated
quite wrongly with the aesthetic revival. William Johnson and Oscar Browning had stood for the finer things.
Browning founded a Literary Society, and tried to break
down prejudice sufficiently for intellectual Collegers and
Oppidans to meet. Warre cared more if they rowed in
time together on the River. Mitchell judged every boy
by the straightness of his bat and the twist in his ball.
Warre and Mitchell went their triumphant way, while
Browning vainly tried to intellectualise Eton, not understanding that the spirit must come from among the boys
themselves. He was driven into the wilderness for his
pains, as William Johnson before him. Two of the best
teachers of youth were lost to the School they loved.
The mantle of Hornby, which had sheltered the Philathlete and the Philistine, fell eventually to Warre, in
whose latter days as Head Reform, cultural and aesthetic,
was voiced anew by Mr. Christopher, while the younger
men, teaching Science or Mathematics, had begun to
stand out for their rights and modernness of teaching.
The old tradition had vanquished the aesthetes in the
past, and Munfort looked to see the Classical tradition
defeat the insurgent Modernists in the present. He had
long given up the pretence that a boy came to Eton to
learn. If a boy took unto himself the ways of wisdom,
it was naturally the better for him. If a boy did not,
he could not see that it was the worse for him.

A great deal of the history of Eton was liable to run
through Mr. Munfort's brain on the eve of a Fourth of
June. He was the fine old Eton master, one of the olden
time, scrupulously polite to boys and colleagues, even if
they offended him. His attitude to parents was in studied
accordance with their manners. The bourgeois and the
wealthy he could smell out like a false quantity, and he
simply declined to enter their progeny in his book. They
could go to the less exacting Houses, of which the Head

Master was apparently tolerant. To the noble he could
be magnanimous. It was believed that one of his pupils,
a Russian Prince, had felled him to the ground with an
oil-lamp, when Munfort released a forbidden pet bird from
its cage. On recovering consciousness he never forgot
to address him as ' Prince,' while explaining the certain
obvious differences between an Eton master and a moujik.
Perhaps his politeness was based on that of Dr. Keate,
who, finding he had to flog a Duke twice in the same day,
observed, ' Your Grace is unfortunate to-day,' but did
not omit his duty. Many of the old men lived by some
such words of irony or wisdom. It was Dr. Heath who
laid down that no Etonian had the right to think until he
reached Upper Division, and Dr. Goodall who first discovered what every schoolmaster knows, that the best
boys do the very worst things. An implacable Tradition-
alist, Mr. Munfort spent the eve of the Fourth regretting
Hornby and Hornby's Star Chamber, when Hornby had
used his privilege to dismiss a master without reason given.
Warre seemed to him weak in comparison and hesitating.
Even when the truth was brought before Warre's eyes he
hesitated to remove a House master. The Fourth always
made Munfort feel patriotic for the School. This year
his patriotism took the form of wishing an untimely end
to Morley's and Maxse's Houses. That evening as he
walked round to Wise's Yard to order a cab for his distinguished guests, the proximity of both those Houses
confirmed him in his desire for their obliteration. As he
gave instructions to the obsequious ' Aarons,' he was
unaware that some of his own boys were concealing themselves within the stables. Nor was his vision caught by
the heads of Mrs. Sowerby and Peter, who were fond of
contemplating the Yard from their respective windows.

Peter's mind was filled with the sweet and harmless
wine of anticipation, as he watched Mr. Wise's horses
being feverishly groomed and curried for the gala of the
Fourth. The number of extra horses seemed called for
by the importance of the day. He had no parent or need

for cabs, but he had ordered his white waistcoat and
buttonhole and other perquisites of athletic divinity,
which were allowed to all boys on the Eton *Saturnalia*.
The Fourth meant morning sleep and evening excitement,
sunshine and ices, crowds and cricket, fire and water
harnessed to the triumph and pleasure of the day.   From
his happy anticipations Peter turned to a parcel on his
table, from which he drew and admired a waistcoat purely
white, except where it was speckled with flowers of a
bluish and sea-green variety.   His buttonhole was bought
to match.   It was a white rose dyed light blue on the
system of floral decoration practised in Alice's *Adventures*.
Peter was trying to keep it fresh with a toothbrush without
losing the dye, when Frencher and Socston burst into the
room.

'Great secret if you can keep it!' announced Socston.
'Yes,' said Frencher calmly, 'we shall be using your
window to-morrow morning.   Half a dozen of us are
rowing to Surley before breakfast.   We may think of
taking you as cox.'   'But isn't it a *dies-non*?'   asked
Peter.   'I thought we had to lie in bed.'   Frencher laughed
with exasperation, 'Bloody little goat!   did he think he
ought to lie tucked up in his little bed?'   Philips came
in and explained, though he himself had never done it
before, that this sort of thing was always done—in fact,
the authorities rather expected it, as they kept the door
locked.   'Well, what time do we start?'   asked Peter.
'About four in the morning, but we will call you all right,'
whispered Socston, 'so go to bed.   Your window is the
only safe one to climb out of.'   Peter replaced his gaudy
waistcoat and sprinkled his flower for the last time, though
under the chemical dye to which it had been subjected it
was turning a light brown.

CHAPTER XII

THE FOURTH OF JUNE

'Hush! get up and don't make a sound,' Peter heard. He had no inclination to make a sound. All present bliss seemed involved in the soundless. Surely there was no Early School if he remembered right. 'Get up, you young swine, before Mrs. Sowerby finds us.' This sounded worse than Early School, if it was earlier than even Mrs. Sowerby's coming. He turned sleepily over in his bed. 'Pull him out!' said somebody, and he found himself removed from his sheets by the insertion of a walking-stick, which was about as painless a process as the extraction of a winkle with a pin. The room was full of Uppers in their flannels. The window was being slowly raised and a short double ladder used by Willum was being thrust through the casement to the stable roof below. The only perilous direction was Mrs. Sowerby's window, which, heavily curtained and barred against serenade, opened immediately beneath Peter's. Each boy descending must have passed within a few feet of her hopedly unconscious head. Peter slipped into his flannels and descended mechanically. The ladder was safely stowed in the Yard, and the party of six tiptoed down the street to the Brocas where two *perfects*, light two-oars, were awaiting them. Peter, who had never coxed before in his life, found the rudder strings of one in his fingers. 'Start us!' shouted Frencher and Mouler. 'Are you ready? Go!' cried Peter, quite ignorant of the proper formula. 'Are you ready? Forward! Paddle!' shouted Mouler, and the oarsmen drove in their blades with an execration as a fresh start was made. Peter was however profoundly thankful that no one had witnessed his humiliation. The other *perfect* with Socston coxing Philips and Camdown major was well away, when suddenly, splash! and a small waterspout subsided under the central arch of Windsor Bridge. Both boats stopped rowing and the nervous coxes glanced behind their rudders. Some joker had dived off the Bridge in his flannels and was leisurely swimming to the Boathouses. This was one of the old-fashioned feats, which a generation accustomed to panelled motors and silken socks heard of with only languid concern. So they were not the only pebbles on the highway of adventure. The splash broke their tension nicely, and to a regular stroke they began rowing upstream.

The iron railway bridge moved jerkily over Peter's head. There was an Eton tradition, delightful to Lower Boys, that it was unsafe and would one day fall in the River-bed. Its gaunt ironmongery did not spoil the beauty of the sun, which shot upward like a hoop stretched with thin gold leaf. The Thames, not yet beaten with river traffic, flowed mirroring the virgin morning. No oar broke the water ahead, while warblers and kingfishers flitted in the scanty play-hour allowed to the feathered. Black-headed buntings hung among the willows and little grebes dived in the backwaters. No College watermen in their blue liveries watched the truants from their moored punts. No member of the Eight cursed them for disobeying the Rules of the River. Past Sandbanks and Cuckoo Weir they rowed, past the deserted Acropolis and green terraces of Athens, past Easy Bridge to Boveney Lock, where they ran their *perfects* over the rollers and brought a sleepy lock-keeper to the window of his island house.

'Going to Monkey Island, gentlemen?' he asked, and was told they were obviously rowing downstream to Staines. As Staines was in the opposite direction he took the hint in the spirit which accompanied it. They rowed on, leaving the gurgling weir on their right and a little, field-bound, deserted church on their left. It was

the old irregular post-driven weir, greened by the waters,
chipped and tanned by the sun, with a stronger appearance
of affording suitable fishing seats to the local kingfishers
than of impeding the power of the waterfloods, which
moved leisurely and foamlessly down to the brink, like
a careful athlete who moves up to a high jump, and then
bursts over with a sudden and furious effort, breaking into
sweat and a roar of I-told-you-so !

Straight ahead lay Surley, the haven of generations of
Eton rowers. Soon to pass away was that low-lying
hostelry of riparian delight where thirsts unpurchasable
were quenched in cheap beers and ciders. The smooth
grass ran down to the landing-stage. To the right of the
roof was an immense poplar bearing the legend SURLEY
HALL HOTEL. To the right again rose beech and more
poplars. Not a breeze touched the water. Every leaf
looked like fine enamel jewellery. Peter felt as though
he were landing with Captain Cook on some new island
in the Southern Seas. In spite of his dire need of bun and
coffee, he felt this was life. He clutched the wooden
landing-stage. ' Well coxed ! ' said somebody, and they
landed, carrying their oars with them, to breakfast. Of
Surley Hall it was said that the tea was of many and
wonderful colours. Boys ordered green tea and drank
chartreuse !

It was five o'clock, and it was necessary to be back in
bed before seven, the supposed hour of Mrs. Sowerby's
rising on a *dies-non*. It was too early for a hot drink, so
they all drank beer, which though easy for an oarsman to
absorb is inclined to stagnate in the coxcomb of a cox.
The chill Peter had felt coming up had left him, also
his slight powers of steering a boat. He took the bank
twice before reaching the Lock, and reprimand only made
him defiant and jocular. At Athens he began to swear a
little in return, much to the amusement of the company,
for the corruption of the professedly pious has always
appealed to human nature. ' Oh, Darley, what would
your Tutor say ? ' Peter had become careless what any-

body said, for at Sandbanks he ran the *perfect* into the shallows. Frencher stood up and punted her off, swayed, and with a landsman's clumsy heel opened the side of the shell. The *perfect* began to fill, and sank in two feet of water. A hasty council decided to abandon and conceal the boat in the shrubberies opposite. They swam across, towing their floating bark to the Berkshire side. The next lap was a run in squelching clothes through Clewer and toward the Great Park. Suddenly Mouler, who was leading, ducked under the palings and lay full length, shouting ' *Beaks!* ' Frencher and Peter fell over his legs in the rush for cover.

Two tall figures passed on the other side, followed by others. The lordly Eton drawl was unmistakable. They were followed by half a dozen horses led by stablemen. What could masters want riding at that hour ? Nobody dared peep till Peter, who was feeling cold and careless, stood up. ' Why, Munfort's House-colours,' he muttered. This was exciting. They were certainly not botanising for specimens for Gill's Museum, or searching for Dr. Borcher's hydro-balloons, which used to be excuses for wandering out of bounds. In fact, they were already mounting not floral but equine species. As the groom leading the last horse passed Peter caught his eye. It was the blear-eyed flyman from Wise's Yard, who let his old leer break into angry recognition, but, quickly realising that Peter had as little right to be out as his own patrons, he jogged on. ' All Munfort's *bloods* racing, by God ! ' muttered Mouler. Compared to their honest spree to Surley, this was a purple sin, an exploit of the first magnitude ! Each horseman was simultaneously breaking a School rule and the law of the land. The penalties of treason as well as expulsion hung over them, for horse racing was strictly forbidden by the Royal Ranger. Mr. Morley's boys felt about as heroic as stray curs who have crossed a pack of foxhounds in full cry, as they slunk back through Windsor and came home through the Brocas and South Meadow.

With a sigh of relief they turned into the Christopher entrance, only to find one of Wise's men and the grinning Willum holding the ladder under their arms. Mouler took command. 'Now, you convulsive clown, get clear of that ladder, and if you breathe a word to the Man, no tips.' 'You never 'ave tipped me,' quoth Willum. 'Well, here's a half-crown,' and Mouler seized the ladder. Willum laughed with purple scorn, and continued his hold on Mr. Morley's property. Mouler understood. 'Now, you blighter, when we get up we'll chuck you a sovereign.' Willum nodded, as though he had only been keeping the ladder safe till their return. But Wise's man scented blackmail, and moved across their road. 'Mr. Wise, I'm afraid, gentlemen, will 'ave to be told the uses 'is yard 'as been put to.' 'Then what the hell is Mr. Wise's flyman doing in the Park this morning?' flashed Mouler. 'I think Mr. Munfort will have to be told.' The cad flinched, with livid fear written on his face, and the way was left clear. As a matter of fact, Mr. Wise was as innocent as Mr. Munfort of what their boys or horses were doing that beautiful morn. The Morleyites then placed the ladder and climbed into Peter's room, to find the dry boatful waiting with faces of gloom. 'The Hag was waiting for us,' was all they said. In the silence which followed, Willum's purse was collected, and a sovereign in silver thrown down to him in a torn football scarf.

Breakfast proved that the Hag had done her work only too well. The Man sent for the guilty six, and informed them that Mrs. Sowerby had found their beds empty, and had reported the matter to the Dame, who had been much shocked, and had been sending for him and Willum alternately since an early hour. The Governing Body would require him, he thought, to add iron bars to windows so misused, and finally he referred to their thoughtlessness in awaking the good Mrs. Sowerby. Frencher tried chaff, and assured him that they had taken special pains not to disturb her; besides, Mrs. Sowerby was in the habit of waking them at rather absurd hours. This was a subtlety lost on Mr. Morley. They were each to write out a Georgic.

Though Pe*ter* was relieved in his heart at the future prospect of seeing his window barred, he spent a miserable Fourth wandering with Socston and Mr. Socston, who was not informed of his hopeful's earlier amusements in the day. They attended the time-honoured Speeches in Upper School, ceremonial recitations by the Sixth Form in court dress and languages equally impressive and unintelligible to their parents and friends, but carried off with a little light mumming which never failed to amuse. In the afternoon they read the Latin telegrams to the Head from Etonians all over the world, and attended the gala-Absence in School Yard, which was read by Warre in person, as posterity will always see him, thanks to Leslie Ward's cartoon in *Vanity Fair*. The crews of the Boats answered their names in fancy dress, white ducks, buckled shoes, and straw hats, with artificial wreaths over the coloured ribbons marked with the names and badges of their boats, *Monarch, Victory, Prince of Wales, St. George, Britannia, Thetis, Hibernia, Defiance, Dreadnought*. Mauve, red, blue, and green colours flashed in the sunlight, while minute coxes strutted about in Admiral's cocked hats with huge bouquets of flowers and tinsel swords hanging from their sides, the last ceremonial vestige of *Montem*.

The sight of Warre, standing in his dark robes, with the royal cipher emblazoned on his black stole, solemnly reading the names moved Socston senior considerably. ' By God, he was a man ! ' he muttered, and proceeded to tell how, as Assistant masters, Warre and Snow had rowed for the Silver Goblets at Henley, under assumed names, and the still greater tale of the Windsor Election, when old Hornby forbade boys to pass Barnes Pool till four on the day of the poll, and Windsor Bridge, farther down, till six. To carry out this instruction Warre alone was placed on Barnes Pool, while the rest of the staff were considered sufficient to hold Windsor Bridge. What happened was curious. No boy passed Barnes Pool till the clock struck four, when Warre returned quietly home according to his orders. Ten minutes later Windsor Bridge was carried by storm. Such was Warre comparatively.

Absence over, the crews went down to a landing-stage off South Meadow, followed by a mob of gaudy relations and gushing friends, who watched them paddle off leisurely towards Surley Hall, no doubt mistaking rowing for a very gentle and elegant art, and as good for delicate boys as Swedish drill. It was dark before the Eights returned. They dined opposite Surley and were timed to return by the light of fireworks off Fellows Eyot. Peter squeezed into the typical Fourth of June crowd that passed after dark through Weston's Yard into the Playing Fields, past the battered red wall of the Head's Garden, across a brook to a long peninsula alive with watchers. Against the magical rose of twilight the wall-flowers stood darkly on the wall, and a gigantic elm-tree clouded the very heavens. Across the Eyot at the water's edge rose one stark poplar, and at the Eyot's end rose a group of chestnut-trees, which turned to a silvery green under the sudden flash of a rocket. On the other side of the brook pressed the rag and bobtail of Eton and Windsor, the Joels and Jobies, the Aarons and 'Arries, the cads and the confectioners, the touts *et totum hoc genus*, amongst whom some Lower Boys were thought-fully throwing red lights. Such as were not extinguished in the water or trodden underfoot were thrown back with equal friendliness. By this time Romney Island was bursting with artificial fire, and the old elms stood clear in a form of ghastly sunlight. Star-shells, whistling lights, rocket after rocket culminating in the great set piece of the Eton arms and the *Floreat* lit up a sheet of the stream, across which shot the Eights, their crews rising in their seats, carrying their liquor like men, and passing into the darkness downstream with their oars at the salute. Trees and bricks were transfigured in the weird flashes.

False dawns and mock sunsets, hectic lightnings and sudden eclipses filled and refilled the Playing Fields as with wizardry. Each tree seemed mysterious and haunted. The grass lawns spread between like a deserted no-man's-land, untrod by living or dead. The old buildings, towers, and battlements might have been some magic creation of the evening, and in the luminous illusion Time itself seemed to stand still. The beauty and wonder of Eton surpassed the thought of the mind. Anyhow, it left Peter with an exhausted craving for bed, into which he fell by eleven o'clock.

But he could not sleep. He felt comfortless and worried. He had abandoned saying his prayers in this his second half. He felt he was a detected criminal already. It occurred to him that he might finish his Georgic, however. So, putting on his *woolly-bear*, and lighting a candle, he buried his nose in his bureau and began the soul-destroying task. A Georgic takes four hours. Writing lines of Latin poetry as a punishment has a number of points to commend it. It is injurious to handwriting. It fails to interest the mind or stir the brain. It has not the slightest educational value. It wastes sheets of clean Broad rule. It sets a premium on misspelling, for the master counts the lines without reading the words. When it takes the form of a Georgic, which is one of the few forms of Classical writing interesting to the sons of the landed gentry, it makes what might prove a valuable reminiscence a hateful memory. When it is written by candle after lights, it is injurious to the eyes as well as to the spirits. Yet there are educated men who have set such a penalty and not been penalised by the State themselves. One of the mitigations of Hornby's rule had been the receiving of lines by deputy in the person of his Butler, who, not being a scholar, used to accumulate old French exercises marked for the occasion as Homer with the accents !

CHAPTER XIII

AFTER THE FOURTH

THOUGH all Mr. Munfort's House knew before they retired to rest every detail connected with Mr. Munfort's Racing Club, their kind and admiring Tutor was left in happy ignorance. His spare moments had been fully occupied in entertaining Sir John Mumbles, a member of the Governing Body, who approved of his claret and deigned to visit him for the Fourth. Sir John Mumbles was an Old Etonian, who had attained a first-class at Oxford and translated the Psalms into Greek Iambics. His great learning had prevented him taking up a profession. His manner was commanding, for in the many committees he adorned he could only bear the position of chairman. Born to govern, he had never been taken into a Cabinet or offered a Proconsulship. Being a Conservative, he had attributed this to his friendship with Mr. Gladstone, with whom he had shared a number of Homeric heresies. For such a personage the Eton Governing Body offered a consoling field of influence. On the Fourth of June Sir John Mumbles became very important indeed, and under the influence of good claret he had asked Mr. Munfort's opinion on the delicate question of the Head Mastership. Believing that he was a lost diplomatist among other accomplishments, he had taken on himself to sound Mr. Christopher as to the expected vacancy, and to sound the older men as to Mr. Christopher. Mr. Munfort was generously in Mr. Christopher's favour. But he felt it was necessary to find out the extent that Mr. Christopher's reforms would lead to in practice. Mr. Christopher might easily stray from the Tradition, though

144

he was sound on the Church and the Classics. Would he be sound in dealing with the Mathematical 'Dames' who wished to usurp the place of the Classical Tutors? Sir John Mumbles became portentously grave, nodding and enjoying every detail of this weighty business. He valued the unseen power he felt he was wielding. Old Etonians filled English Cabinets. Eton Head Masters stamped the Old Etonians. He, Mumbles, personally selected the Head Master. It was a gorgeous satisfaction to Mumbles, who had been left out of two Cabinets.

On the Fifth of June Sir John Mumbles waited in vain for his fly. Mr. Munfort felt his importance sufficiently to accompany him to Wise's Yard to order the necessary vehicle to Slough Station. Entering the yard with the distinguished Mumbles, Mr. Munfort gave the Aarons a sound rating for the failure of the ordered fly, and refused to take the excuse that all the horses were lame. At this moment the flyman, who had acted as Clerk of a certain Course the previous day, arrived, and misjudging the panic of the other stablemen, concluded that all was up, and that his clients had been discovered. ''Ope you won't be too 'ard this time, sir. Fourth of June comes but once a year.' 'No reason why every horse should be lame, is it?' said Munfort, little knowing that he drew a bow at a venture. It was obvious that he surmised the real reason of their laming. ''Ope you won't be 'ard on the young gentlemen, sir. We only wanted to oblige them, seeing they intended to break bounds anyhow, and any 'oss dealer would 'ave charged them 'orrible.' 'What young gentlemen?' snapped Mr. Munfort. 'That is no reason why Sir John Mumbles should miss his train.' In a moment the flyman had seen his mistake and retrieved it. 'Oh, no young gentlemen of yours, sir, only some of Mr. Morley's as use this roof when they break out of bounds.'

Mr. Munfort and Sir John Mumbles both looked up to Peter's window, eyed the distance, and measured the spouting. Munfort looked at Mumbles, and Mumbles looked at Munfort, as though to say, ' What are we coming to with a House like Morley's ? ' ' Do they often come down that way ? ' asked Mumbles. ' Why, bless you, sir,' said the wary one, as he set his customers from Munfort's farther and farther into safety, and avenged a hundred personal wrongs, ' they come down there as regular as the rats.' It was not for Mr. Munfort to criticise a colleague, but he gave a portentous nod as he helped Mumbles into his fly with effusive farewell.

Sir John Mumbles drove away, full of the importance of his self-assumed duties. This was an unexpected discovery, and as he was now too late to catch his train at Slough, and as Dr. Warre had not paid the attention due to the importance of his suggestions lately, he suddenly told the man to drive into Weston's Yard, and round to the Cloisters. Mumbles decided to startle the Head. It was one of the functions of the Governing Body to keep their nominees up to their work.

Meantime, it was reported in Mr. Munfort's establishment that their Tutor had been seen walking into Wise's Yard, which he had never been known to do before. Furthermore, he was reported to have accompanied Sir John Mumbles there, and Sir John Mumbles had been seen driving instantly to the Cloisters. The Governing Body were regarded by Etonians much as the Council of the Ten were regarded by Venetians, as the unseen and uncontrolled controllers of their destinies. The Boy imagination is a scarlet runner, so swift, so brilliant, and so unsubstantial ! Inquiry at Wise's Yard assured them that the stablemen had not betrayed them. Mumbles must have received word from another quarter. The Governing Body was no doubt in touch with the Castle. The Royal Ranger must have informed Mumbles of their exploits in the Great Park. Nothing else would account for his visit to Wise's Yard in company with Mr. Munfort, or his driving post-haste to visit the Head. Everybody in the School seemed to know of their feat, but nevertheless, so strong is the non-conducting element between boys

and masters, that Mr. Munfort returned to his House with
the same ignorance in which he had set out. Easy-going
and conventional, he never worried or ferreted his boys.
Still, his silence at lunch, due to the fatigue of the Fourth,
was misconstrued. A number of *bloods* in the House had
come to the opinion that they were nearer expulsion than
they had ever been before. A council was held in the
Library with disquietening results. Munfort was bound
to look on their escapade as a form of high treason.
Tolerant as he was of most ragging, he was a stickler on
Church and State. To him Radicalism in politics was
what a false quantity was in Latin verses. It was un-
forgivable, and remained unforgiven. They concluded
he must be wild at finding lese-majesty actually committed by the boys of his House. There had been much
talk of lese-majesty in the papers recently over the
Kaiser's visit. Cases of German workmen had been discussed who had put out their tongues at Royalty, and
had been immured in a fortress for life. The boys felt
they had done worse. One suggested telegraphing for his
father's lawyer. Another, who read extra history with
Barten, referred to the Forest Law, and believed that
they were already outlaws and could only be freed by a
Royal Pardon. It was decided that in that case they
must get a Royal Pardon forthwith, and have it sent to
the Head. It was not impossible to get. The School
List contained a number of junior relations of the Queen.
The smallest of these was selected, and an urgent note
was sent to his fag master at an adjoining House to send
him round at all cost.

Royalty at Eton lived in a vacuum. Nobody had any
particular use for them, unless some rising House master
wished for a peculiar form of advertisement. They
seldom got credit even for their merits. Everybody was
so anxious not to be regarded as a snob that a Captain
would think twice before giving a colour and an examiner
would shrink from offering one of Prince Consort's Prizes
to them. So they were left in happy incognito, though a

furtive trade in royal autographs has been suspected as a means of paying confectioners' bills. But here was a distinct use for such, and the rulers of Mr. Munfort's House sat waiting in their blazers. The messenger returned, accompanied by a bright-eyed but nervous scion of the House of Saxe-Coburg-Gotha. To him it was explained what had happened, and how sorry they were for any damage done to the royal turf, and would he kindly go after school that evening and apologise for them and get the Ranger to send word to the Head that it was all right. The minor and semi-mediatised princeling, whose Eton life had been dismal hitherto, was delighted at an opportunity of serving really distinguished persons and acquiring a little respect and possibly popularity of his own. Immediately school was over, he started down town, and slipped from the Eton into the Windsor world. The deities and religion of these worlds being entirely different, he passed over the Bridge from despised anonymity into recognition. Policemen stood rigidly to attention, and Park-keepers removed their ornate hats. Half an hour later, and breathlessly he explained to the Ranger what had happened, and how the *bloods* at Munfort's were going to be hauled up by the Head, and how they included several choices for the Eleven, and how they were sure to be beaten by Harrow if they were *sacked*, and how unpopular the Royal Family would become if the Ranger insisted on them being *sacked*, and how they were decent enough to send him with an apology, and what an honour it was to be fagged by such *bloods* anyhow. The Ranger had had trouble with boys chasing the paddocked boars, and on the complaint of the royal keepers a Duke's son had been flogged, but this was the first he had heard of this escapade, and he was both amused and interested. He thoroughly agreed with his small relative's estimate of the slightness of the offence and the greatness of the offenders. He agreed it was more sporting than otherwise, and, in any case, racing was only forbidden in the Park to keep out Cockneys. It would be disastrous if the Royal Family were involved in the punishment of such great men as the Captain of Munfort's House, or in spoiling chances at Lord's Cricket Ground. He would do nothing to press for punishment, in fact he would immediately ask the Head to overlook the matter as a personal favour to himself. It was a very happy Lower Boy who skipped homeward. Once more the policemen stiffened and the big hats at the Park gates went into the air. A few minutes after *lock-up* he knocked at his fag master's door. ' I think it will be all right. The Ranger will send a pardon to the Head with the Big Seal.' ' Thanks, you are excused mess-fagging for a week,' was the gracious reply.

The day after the Fourth was always a quiet one at Eton. Dr. Warre had rested well after the celebrations of the Fourth, in which he had played a central and un-critical part. He had partaken of a glorified occasion to behold the Eton world, which he had largely created, and to enjoy the tributes of that world in appreciation of its chief. He was therefore much irritated by a visit from Sir John Mumbles, on whose opinions about Homer or rowing he set no value. Sir John, however, had not come to discuss either, but the state of Mr. Morley's House, which proved more irritating still. Dr. Warre had predetermined that his end should be peace, and that the School should remain as reformed by him in the Eighties. The athletics could be regarded as perfect, for no 'Varsity boat could win without a heavy Eton con-tingent. The teaching of cricket perhaps left something to be desired, and it was true he was responsible for bringing Mitchell to Eton. The calibre of the young masters left nothing to be desired, for they were hand-picked by himself. He was therefore much annoyed to hear Mumble's uncalled-for report, for he had become loath to dismiss any master who had grown up under his regime. He was aware of the intermittent war in the Eton heavens between Tutors and 'Dames,' and he dis-counted a good deal of the complaint he heard against

Morley from Classical lips. Before Sir John Mumbles had concluded his very disagreeable visit, he had decided to let Morley's House adjust itself by the law of surrounding excellences. Nevertheless, a scrupulous conscience fretted under that mighty torso, and Dr. Warre never ceased doing his duty. That afternoon he wrote a note inviting Mr. Morley to dinner.

Mr. Morley had never had the honour paid to him before, and hastily sent Willum to the Cloisters with a precise form of thanks. Willum's features glowed as red as the bricks as he passed the School Clerk and the Fusee and brandished the envelope. The Dame was equally pleased by what she regarded as an indirect honour paid to herself. At four minutes to eight, the hour of invitation, Mr. Morley set out, wondering pleasantly whom he was likely to meet and what possible reason there could be for the invitation. He rang and entered, but there was only the family at table. The Head had decided to break his complaints gently, and Mr. Morley was prepared by a good meal, out of which a patient decipherer of palimpsest could have probably reconstructed an exact menu as served for the Fourth. The Head showed good humour, and his little Latin quotations and old Somerset stories were received with reverential laughter by his family. For the benefit of Mr. Morley a new one was introduced. ' I was walking over Sheep's Bridge this afternoon,' said the Head, ' what you Mathematicians perhaps would prefer to call the *Pons Asinorum*.' There was a burst of amusement from the whole table except Mr. Morley, who observed that some boys were foolish enough to call a certain proposition of Euclid by that name. ' As I was crossing the *Pons Asinorum*,' emphasised the Head, and waited for Mr. Morley to catch the point, but Mr. Morley, not realising that the point had been made, threw himself into a listening attitude of painful anxiety. ' Sheep's Bridge,' suggested the Head, ' a loose rendering, I admit.' ' Yes, yes,' and Mr. Morley continued to wait for the joke. The Head tried a new tack. ' I understand that some effort

is being made to sweep Euclid into Limbo.' Mr. Morley
had never heard of Limbo, which he took to be some
Polynesian dialect, and made a shot into the conversation
accordingly. ' Yes, sir, the missionaries will find it good
practice in their schools.' There was again a subdued
laugh from all except Mr. Morley. The Head continued
to divulge his views about Euclid quite seriously, and Mr.
Morley, determined not to be left this time, greeted them
with a wild laugh which, unhappily, was shared by no
one else. The Head stared good-humouredly. He was
aware of the paralysing effect his mere presence caused
on masters as well as boys. ' Will you join me in some
port ? I call it old shoe.' Mr. Morley, who would have
eaten an old hat had it been handed him, bowed. The
family withdrew, and, left alone, the Head began very
kindly on the subject of his House, when the door bell
rang. ' Mr. Morley, you have been unfortunate in your
House. I attach no blame to you. There has generally
been an unfortunate House at Eton, and your case is
very unfortunate.' He paused. Mr. Morley flushed, and
his grizzly moustaches assumed Euclidean proportions.
The bell rang again. ' We shall not be interrupted,' continued the Head, ' for I have left word that——' The
anxious butler returned, and hurriedly whispered into
the Head's ears, first one and then the other. The Head
shot upright. ' Impossible, are you sure ? ' But the
butler dangled a visiting-card like a museum label giving
his date as a fossil. The Head read out the name as he
would intone a prayer, and since it was of that Family
for whom he had offered petitions all his clerical life, he
prayed to be excused. Mr. Morley bowed, and would
have left the house. The Head bade him sit and refresh
himself, while he made himself acquainted with the
object of the Royal Ranger's visit.

Dr. Warre stood on his own ground, and was not abashed
by his Royal visitor, to whom he offered a noble chair
and humbler refreshment in sepulchral tones. The former
was accepted. ' Dr. Warre, I have a favour to ask of you,

which I take the first opportunity of bringing to your notice.' The Head bowed. 'On the Fourth of June, a day, I believe, dedicated to my ancestor,'—the Head bowed—'some boys paid an early visit to Windsor, indeed trespassed on the royal demesne, the Park, you know.' The Head bowed and remembered Mumbles. He guessed now where the wind lay and, with a school-master's pride, interrupted, 'The matter has just been brought to my attention, sir, and you may be sure that the just penalty will be exacted. I only trust that no serious aspect of which I am unaware has made your visit necessary.' 'No, by Gad! only that, as they broke the rules of the Park by practising for the Derby, I called to say that, as it was the Fourth, I will take no action as Ranger, and I request you to do the same.' The Head was amazed at the first news of the racing, but continued, 'I have been considering the matter very carefully, sir, for some hours, and though I cannot entirely overlook the proceeding, I will not insist on more than a written apology being sent to you from each of the culprits.' His visitor was abundantly satisfied, and after a handshake, in which they would have made excellent models for Blücher and Wellington shaking hands after Waterloo, they parted.

The Head returned to Mr. Morley with a little unex-pected ammunition in his wallet. It appeared to be far more serious than Mumbles had allowed him to know, so serious that he immediately opened fire. 'Mr. Morley, the reason I felt anxious to see you privately was that a very serious complaint has been made referring to certain boys of your House, I believe, who broke bounds on the Fourth of June. The information has come to me indirectly, and from irreproachable sources, and I am bound to ask you first if you can confirm the report, for it is not really more than a report.' Mr. Morley replied that he was sorry that he could. The culprits had been discovered by the boys' maid returning from their excursion on the Fourth. The Head said he would be satisfied with their names, and that he wished the matter for a serious reason to be kept

quiet. Mr. Morley supplied the six names, including
Peter's, of all of whom the Head took a note in bright
blue ink. Mr. Morley was very precise, and disliked
mystery. Since the matter had come to the Head's ears,
he felt he had a right to know the source. At heart he
was annoyed and humiliated, because the Head had found
out for himself. 'I am sure, Dr. Warre, you will allow
me to know the source of your information since I have
to allow its truth.' The Head was not accustomed to
interrogation, and he hesitated. 'It comes from the
most exalted source you can imagine, and I must beg
you to leave it there, especially as the matter is not to
be pressed. The boys are not to be punished.' Mr.
Morley never imagined; but he made a clear deduction
that the Royalty, whose name had been so sonorously
impressed upon him, had something to do with it. 'I
trust that it was not serious enough for your distinguished
visitor to have been disturbed over the matter.' The
Head's loyalty was a passion, and he was truly anxious
that the Ranger's name should not enter into the discussion. His Royal Highness had asked for secrecy, and
he was entitled to it. 'No, far from disturbed,' he
assured Mr. Morley, 'and the information concerning
your boys I should say I received from a member of the
Governing Body. It was of a kind which it is essential
I should receive when the honour of the School is in
question. I am anxious that the matter should never
reach the papers, which have been devoting too much
time to Eton lately.' The Head continued that the boys
were not to be punished at the request of His Royal
Highness, but he would admonish them on the morrow.
Would Mr. Morley kindly leave their names with the
School Clerk? Mr. Morley withdrew. Fortunately he
was more susceptible to mixed fractions than to mixed
emotions, and he returned in time to utter formal Prayers
and make his nightly rounds.

He informed each of the excursionists that it had been
impossible to keep their prank from the all-seeing Head.

As the Head would deal with them on the morrow, they
were excused the Georgic he had imposed. Peter proved
to be the only one who had written his punishment, which,
however, he was able to sell to Frencher for a shilling, that
gentleman owing a number of linear debts to insatiable
autograph-collectors among the masters. 'Darley, I
placed you in this room,' said Morley, 'believing you
would never allow it to be put to purposes displeasing to
the Governing Body. You have deeply grieved your
Dame. In future iron bars will be placed across your view
at your guardian's expense.'

Peter felt a chill at heart. It seemed hopeless to try
and keep on the right side of the law in Morley's House.
Somebody dragged him into rows, somebody else caught
him, somebody reported him, and now he might expect
to meet the Head. He sat back and sulked while Mr. Morley diagnosed his heinousness, which for a new boy was
very bad—bad—bad, and he tweaked an ear at each
syllable.

On the morrow Peter waited full of fear and despair till
the crash came. 'Is Darley in this Division, sir?' asked the
Praepostor, suddenly swinging open the door of the class-
room in which Peter had been squirming in anticipation.
The Sixth Form Grandee addressed himself to the Division
master, employing the casual formula as though the object
of his search was so heinous that it was an insult to suggest
his presence. According to the ritual the Form master
always made a mental search, and finding that the accused
was under his jurisdiction, instantly confessed his presence.
'The Head Master wishes to see him after twelve.' Each
word fell like an executioner's knife, and without casting
an eye on the wretch he had summoned, the Praepostor
closed the door with a bang. The boys seized the opportunity of a little light relaxation. Some nodded sugges-
tively towards Peter, others enacted the mock pantomime
of a *swishing*, while at least one rehearsed the tearful effect
it was expected to have on the culprit. As the School
Clock boomed the penal hour, the master rose with, ' You

may go ! ' and out of the stream of minnows Peter darted
aside like one that has felt a hook. He found a small and
unhappy group waiting outside the Head's Chambers, of
whom the majority came from Morley's. The Sixth Form
Praepostor began to summon the guilty, one by one. The
six truants were left to the last and admitted in a batch.
It was a high trial indeed. Both Morley and Lamb were
officially present. The School Clerk was taking notes in
the corner. The Head in robes of office sat behind a table.
Beside him was his College cap like a Judge's death-cap,
ready for wear. On the walls were pictures of previous
Heads from Keate to Hornby. The Praepostor closed
the door and took up his place at the Head's right hand.
' I presume the boys I sent for are all here ? ' Dr. Warre
inquired. Then he read them out one by one. The
Praepostor scrutinised them, though he did not know
them from Adam, and assured the Head, ' They are here,
sir.' The Head then proceeded to deliver a charge on the
iniquity of horse racing and betting, which he described as
a ' familiar beast ' to man and boy, and moreover a matter
that came between him and his needful sleep. Consolingly
he alluded, however, to the well-known graciousness of the
Royal Family, to all of which the profound silence of the
boys added a profounder assent. The six were too impressed to be puzzled. Then the questioning began.
They confessed readily that they had broken bounds on
the Fourth, the hour and the means. ' I understand you
were seen in the Great Park ? ' They nodded. ' Are you
aware that racing is forbidden ? ' They believed so, and
Frencher piped up, ' But we were not racing.' ' You were
at least riding horses, which is strictly forbidden.' ' No,
sir ! ' burst out the six. Their unanimity at this point
was as surprising to the Head as his accusation had been
to them. ' What were you doing ? ' ' We were rowing
to Surley and back.' The Head proceeded, ' And you
found time to indulge in a little horse exercise ? ' Peter
knew in a moment that he was on a false track, and piped
a bold denial. The Head looked to the Tutors to support

him, but they had quickly realised the unlikelihood of boys in their first year like Peter and Socston hiring horses. Mr. Lamb, who was an adept at taking his pupils' part, suggested that they had not done more than break bounds. Nobody had seen them riding, and he felt they could not be punished for more than their Dame had discovered against them. Darley's school record was very good. He was in Fifth Form his second half. The Head, feeling a little confused, cut the matter short. He was prepared to waive all punishment, but they must sign an apology to the Ranger for their conduct in trespassing in the Park. A sigh of relief broke the atmosphere. The Head drafted an apology which all six signed without reading, for the three who had not been in the Park stood manfully by the others, especially as there was to be no penalty. In any case they all guessed whom they were shielding from blame.

The Document was as follows :—

'YOUR ROYAL HIGHNESS,—We, the undersigned, beg to express our deepest apology for our conduct in trespassing upon the Great Park on the morning of the Fourth of June, and for breaking the regulations of which you are the guardian. We are your Royal Highness' most humble and obedient servants.'

The signatures followed in gawky but careful lettering—

'JAMES DESMOND CAMDOWN.
'EDWARD FRENCHER.
'E. G. SOCSTON.
'PETER DARLEY.
'THOMAS MOULER.
'S. PHILIPS.'

That afternoon it was delivered by the School Clerk in person with the compliments of the Head Master and caused the greatest satisfaction and amusement to the Ranger, who had since received a belated report from the Park keepers as well as a few trophies of the race meeting. In returning thanks to the Head and assuring him that he hoped the matter would now be allowed to rest, he added that a printed card of the race meeting had been found which he had decided to keep for himself, but he begged to return a coloured cap which was similar to the colours printed on the race card and which he hoped would find its proper owner. The Head was more interested in the cap than in the letter. He remained several moments toying it. He was not only at fault, but he had come upon scent which was as puzzling as it was obvious. The cap was Mr. Munfort's House-colours !

CHAPTER XIV

WINCHESTER AND HARROW

THE great events of the Summer Half were the cricket matches against Winchester and Harrow. By sweet and mediaeval tradition Eton and Winchester were friends. The love of sisters or brothers, of David and Jonathan, of Francis and Dominic, lay between them. The victory of the one brought its own balm to the defeat of the other. It was only with Harrow that there was neither peace nor generosity. Defeat entailed smouldering hate, and victory savage exultation. The theory, no doubt wholly unproven, was that gentlemen went to Winchester, but not to Harrow. This was held to account for the priority of Eton in the expression ' Eton and Harrow,' corresponding to the verbal order of contrast between ' Gentlemen and Players.' The Winchester match could be played alternatively on the home grounds of the rival schools in the odour of chivalry and hospitality. But the Harrow match required the neutrality of Lord's Cricket Ground, where the partisans sometimes needed the stern disinterestedness of the Metropolitan Police to prevent open conflict. The Winchester match in June was of the nature of home manœuvres. The Harrow match in July was war.

The Winchester match of 1899 was the last but one played in the old Playing Fields and inaugurated by Dr. Lloyd, who skilfully intervolved the Eton *Carmen* and the Winchester *Dulce Domum* on the organ at Morning Chapel. There was a certain sadness in seeing the teams go out to do battle for almost the last time under the gigantic old elms, many of which were also seeing their last summer. The battered grass pitch and the tremorous boughs were to be exchanged for the bleak plain and toy saplings of Agar's Plough, which had been recently rescued by Etonian patriotism from the jerry-builders of Slough and the villa-dwellers of Windsor. Agar, like Barnes and Brocas, was a legend in Eton topography. It was said he was a Dutchman, but he was as mythical as his flying kinsman. Whoever he might be, it was decreed that he and his should plough no more. His farm became the precious possession of Eton. The legend that he was Dutch has never been solved by the antiquaries of Slough or the historians of Eton, either in separate research or working in collusion. The Pickwickian suggestion has been made that the origin lies in the phrase ' jogging to the Dutchman,' which used to describe the effort of crossing Agar's Plough in time to see the ' Flying Dutchman ' pass through Slough at speeds that have only since been paralleled by the motor traffic that passes through Eton itself. Before the turn of the century the Plough had been acquired, and avenues of young trees had begun their slow secular growth, storing up sunshine to give shade to the unborn, and building out of the elements affectionate associations for Etonian souls uncreated as yet out of the void.

Meantime, the old elms hung in gnarled disarray around the pitch of Upper Club, on which the Winchester batsmen in their dark blue caps faced the pick of the Eton bowling. For the first time in the year the whole Eton Eleven wore the light blue cap, which is more desirable in life than wigs of horse hair or any earthly aureoles of glory. The Winchester caps signified a prehistoric triumph over Harrow, who were condemned to wear no more than a blue stripe on theirs.

The Eton bowlers began exchanging balls—Martin, a long, loosely-knit fast bowler from Miss Evans's, and Bernard, a plump little *Tug*, with a curl in his slow left-handed balls. Behind the stumps bent Findlay, Captain and wicket-keeper, who let one bye pass in the innings

M

just to show it was possible. Martin bowled five overs, and the Winchester Captain was out for 5, leg before wicket. Then Bernard, with much trickiness, bowled two of Winchester's crack batsmen. The game seemed to go against Winchester, until Pawson and Mackenzie added 75 in the hour. Mackenzie had passed his 50, driving the ball again and again out of sunlight into shade, when he was missed in the deep field amid a groan of pain from the spectators. But with the next ball he was bowled by Lyttelton. An Eton Eleven without a Lyttelton was like a Cabinet without a Cecil, or a novel without a hero. The remainder were mostly bowled by Bernard, and the innings ended for 135. By lunch Eton had lost two wickets for a single under 50. Then Wormald, a thick-set smiter, and Gilliat stayed together for an hour and a half fighting for runs against the agile net that the Winchester fielding threw round them. Like the *Retiarius* in the Roman amphitheatre, closing and casting on the furiously darting spearsman, so were the fieldsmen. Closer and closer and more keenly they closed round the batsmen until the long-waited chances were offered and each was caught out with a spring of the wrist and a pounce of the fieldsman. Then the Eton wickets tumbled one by one, leaving Winchester 50 runs behind on the first innings and the first day's play. The next day Winchester batted again, and Martin and Bernard began dividing wickets until half the side were out for 56. But Darling, the Captain, turned the scales, and scored 65 off the Eton bowlers, while the Eton fielders missed him twice. Even so Winchester would have been down badly, had not Bruce and Comber each added 40 at the ninth wicket and left Eton 167 runs to get to win. Then the struggle began. Nearly a quarter of the score was made at the first wicket, yet six wickets were down before the 100. The tussle tightened, but Gilliat kept his wicket up, while Martin slogged for 20. By the time they were both out, there was one wicket to fall and 19 runs to make to win. Bernard, the bowler, and Lyttelton were playing for their lives. Amid agonising silence four leg byes were scored, thanks to a leak behind the wicket. Fifteen to make. A shout for leg before wicket was refused by the umpire, and Bernard, in his agile terror, snicked a single. More byes followed, and Lyttelton sent the ball to the boundary. Then he offered a catch, and the game quivered on a thread. It was missed! Another shrill appeal against Bernard's quaking legs broke the silence. ' Not out! ' Slowly Lyttelton made the runs, three to win! two to equal! one to equal! two to win! A stroke through the slips tied the match. Then Lyttelton hit the stroke of victory, which is vouchsafed to so few. The ball travelled to the fieldsman, and Bernard after calling turned back, but Lyttelton forced the run, and run it was. Winchester had still a chance of a tie by running him out, but the ball was thrown to the wrong end, and Eton had won. A cry of Etonian triumph mingled with love for Winchester broke the anguish. For a moment the Lyttelton myth had come true.

There was a rush to the Lodge, which the entry and exit of cricketing gods had raised to the dignity of a Pavilion. But the gods of Hellas, moving across ambrosia to be greeted by their peers and hailed by their adoring cup-bearers, could not have felt a more unearthly bliss than the Eton batsmen. The beat of a thousand hearts went out to them and eager hands struggled to lift them off the earth.

But all moments of astonishing fortune are paid for not less in the games of boyhood than in the struggles of after-life. When the Harrow match approached, Lyttelton was left out for the sake of an extra bowler and Bernard had to endure all the slow toil of bowling through an innings at Lord's without taking a wicket. But Bernard kept his light blue cap, which without service against Harrow is not a permanent decoration The only exception made is for the twelfth man in a year of dual victory against both Winchester and Harrow. Nearly a century had passed since the first Eton and Harrow match was played in Dorset Square with Stratford de Redcliffe on one side and Byron on the other. It was a tradition that the Eton victory had been drowned by Byron, who appeared that night drunk in a Haymarket box. 'Mike's' long rule was leaving Harrow with three victories ahead of Eton. No boy in the School had seen a victory. The oppression of defeat weighed on Eton.

The Eton and Harrow match remains in the Etonian mind like some memory of evergreen hanging over the empty tomb of youth. Socston's father remembered when the Captain of the Eleven wore a pink rose in his light blue cap at Lord's. Who does not remember the anticipations of the Thursday, the purveying of new and immaculate garments, the purchase of light blue ribbons, the adornment of umbrellas with light blue tassels, the resentment and impatience felt during the Chapel service on the Friday, with the Eleven already on their way and the match commencing at eleven? To attend Chapel and be at Lord's an hour and a half later made it essential to catch a train which left Windsor ten minutes after the best recorded time for the Litany in a canter. To catch the train even, it was necessary to leap from the Chapel steps into a fly. This Frencher had arranged to do, and was good enough to invite Peter and Socston to share the fly on condition they paid the net fees. But one obstacle remained. It was necessary to attend Chapel in everyday garb. Peter asked if they were to return to their House and change into holiday attire. Frencher's mind was equal to such an emergency. He had changed in the closed cab on the way to the station the year before. Of course it was not against the rules, he assured Peter. A fellow could drive stark naked through the street if he lay down on the floor of the fly. Before the last bar of the hymn was out of his ears Peter plunged down the stairs of the west entrance. The whole of Fifth Form was pouring out, running across the road to their Houses or jumping into moving cabs. Peter saw Socston tear up from Lower Chapel and leap into a fly, in which Peter, as in a dream, found his bag reposing while Frencher adjured him to choose between eternal damnation or causing them all to miss their train. The flyman was already cracking his whip and the wheels were revolving as Peter dropped ecstatically on the back seat. ' Get off my *bags*,' shrieked Frencher, and Peter found to his horror he was crushing Frencher's new pair of trousers.

By the time they had reached Windsor Bridge they had all three changed their trousers. At Layton's corner they were buttoning their white waistcoats, and had, at the station, time to thrust their old clothes into their bags and catch the first train. The majority of the School came by the next train, but there was a certain satisfaction in finishing their toilets, adjusting button-holes, and changing black ties for light blue as the crowded train slowly took the curve back past Eton, while agitated flys and figures could be seen hurrying between the trees this way and that through the Eton hive. The evacuation of a lighted wasp's nest is a quick business, but it does not equal the passionate scurry with which Eton leaves for the match against Harrow. It was different from the lazy and gentle anticipations of leaving for the holidays. It was fraught with fear and hatred and grim determination to see their champions sustained with watching anxiety and tumultuous cheering through the dust and sweat of two days of cricket. It was akin to mobilisation against an ancient enemy. It was as tense for old spectators as for new boys who sat watching and cheering for the first time, and Peter and Socston sat in the Eton Stand without missing a minute or a run. For two long days the outside world was forgotten. Eton had won the toss, and Longman and Grenfell were facing the dreaded Dowson, who with Hopley used to figure in the nightmares of Eton cricketers. But this year the Etonians seemed to master him, and 50 was scored for the second wicket. One by one the Etonian heroes, Longman, Wormald, and Lambert, made their forties, while Gilliat headed the score with 53. The three scorers of 40 fell to Black, the dark horse of Harrovian bowling. Eton made 274, but Harrow passed it by 9 runs. Peter felt he would have given his ten toes to give Eton as many runs and the lead. It was a gruelling afternoon for the Etonians, and only four wickets went down for 200, but those who sat with eyes glued on the pitch to the last moment were rewarded, for with the last two balls of the day Martin secured two more wickets and turned the scale again. The next day saw Dowson, the Harrow captain, carry out his bat for 87, while the Eton score was passed at the tenth wicket, which fell to an unbelievably brilliant catch by Bernard in consolation for the thirty-nine profitless overs he had bowled. But Mercury himself could not have performed a more speedy miracle on an Olympian pitch, and Bernard's catch at Lord's became legend. Eton returned to the wicket, and after Longman had been missed in the slips, he and Grenfell scored 167 runs for the first wicket. Lower and lower sank the Harrovian scale, until it sank into the very dust that the batsmen drove about them in clouds of slow-descending particles. But Castor and Pollux were insuperable until they met a twin fate, each being bowled by Wyld for 81. Twenty times they reached the boundaries, and twenty times the Eton Stand was lifted in minor ecstasy. So sinister was the Harrovian legend in the Eton mind that each run recorded against the Hill was cheered like a pin-prick given to the powers of darkness. A fourer to the boundary was like the flash of a sword-stroke. Harrow was visibly prostrate, wallowing in the dust, and Eton captainship was seeking to snatch victory within the limits of the day's play. The Eton innings was declared closed, and the bowlers were given a chance to get Harrow out in two hours. Not attempting to make the 256 runs needed for victory, the Harrovians played for a draw against time, which became certain when the century was made for the loss of only two wickets. Harrow was crawling out of the dust on her belly, squirming away from defeat, and the Harrow Stand squealed like rats dodging the terrier's teeth.

From the Etonians came silence, and only an occasional cheer for the fielding, which became better and better when the star of victory blinked and twinkled in the offing. When the score was 116, it shone out clear for a stupendous moment. Three Harrow wickets fell for nothing, and three roars of gorgeous satisfaction ascended, and the whole Eton Stand rose like the dead at an Archangel's trump, climbing over their benches and waving light blue handkerchiefs, hurling top-hats heavenward, dangling light blue acorns from their umbrellas, bellowing across the very short gangway that separated them from the sullen mob of Harrow. Play was extended for another quarter of an hour, while Dowson and Kaye tried to avert disaster and hold up their wickets in the shortening light. It was agony for the partisans of both sides, who cheered every runless stroke as though it was a boundary hit, and every piece of fielding as though it was a brilliant catch. But at the quarter of the hour the white-smocked ump'res picked the bails off the wickets, and Harrow, the hateful one, crawled unscotched out of the arena. The match was drawn !

Then the pent-up fury and excitement of the onlookers broke out. Eton ought to have won, thought some, and Harrow might have won, believed others. There was a wild rush across the level grass, and the surging mob, waving mixed colours, rolled up to the pavilion-fence, and then fell back upon itself. As their favourites appeared in the balconies of the dressing-room like Lucretian gods in the sky, clad in their aetherial vesture, and looked down on their sweltering, adoring devotees, school-sectarianism broke out, and not content with waving their own colours, each strove to cut down the handkerchiefs of a rival. Light and dark blue acorns were deftly slashed from umbrella handles. Handkerchiefs were torn and trodden underfoot. Eddies of boys swung against each other or melted away like foam. Then a shiny top-hat was tumbled, then another, and then fists were out, and a beautiful Harrovian boxer was clearing the ring, but Etonians closed on him, and he was hustled and tripped. Ponderous policemen were slowly clearing the ground, heartily assailed by both sides. Their equanimity contrasted with the excitement of a member of the Marylebone Cricket Club, who was trying to calm the heated boys with much more heated speech, and threatening that the match could not take place the next year at Lord's, whereat he was scoffingly reminded of gate-fees.

Peter and Socston found the mêlée a needed safety valve after two days spent on the stifling, sweltering benches. They darted toward the nearest dark blue, umbrella-brandished (to create a Homeric word) tassel, and cut it down with their sticks at the price of a sudden black eye for Socston. Like all symbolic incidents in life, it was worth while, for the sacrifice was only material. The rival Elevens could still be discerned sitting in the hanging balconies outside their changing-rooms, exhaustedly watching the cheering mobs, and only turning their heads in the direction of the chief diversion, the arrival of sundry low persons, understood to be Harrow cads, who were therefore promptly chivied by a ring of Eton Lower Boys. The cads wore the peculiar and unpleasant headgear associated with the Hill, straw hats like inverted and broad-lidded pans, but so flat that they had to be fastened with elastic round their ears. They were ugly-looking customers, and there was no challenge until an Eton *Joby* was produced, who had got into the Eton Stand with a ticket of last year, and was now urged to mincemeat his Harrovian equal. If he had closed and used his fists, he would have been surprised by the number of his patrons who would have probably paid him old debts on the spot, but in spite of his threatening offensive he flinched, which was made more possible by the slow verbal retreat of his rival. Prospects of a cad fight languished under these tactics, and the two passed off the ground under phalanxes of Eton and Harrow umbrellas, which each preferred to regard as a protecting *chevaux de frise* than as goads to action. Bending swathes of blue-coated police were passed through the crowd, until the ground was gradually abandoned to the neutrality of Law and Order. There remained a light turf-dressing of Cards of the Match, trodden tassels, and wrecked top-hats. Peter and Socston moved away, and suddenly ran into Jenkinson, bending to converse with Ullathorne. Jenkinson looked encouragingly for an opening. A boy's first Lord's should produce the healthy stolid enthusiasm loved of all Tutors. ' Wasn't it glorious ? ' murmured Peter. ' We ought to have licked them,' added Socston. ' Anyhow we drove the Harrow cads round the Pavy,' Peter aimlessly remarked. Jenkinson turned his face away. ' I really thought better of you, Darley.' Peter looked redly to Ullathorne. ' I incline to my Tutor's opinion,' said the *Tug*, ' that any barbaric display is out of date. Why fight the plebeian in the day of the plebs ? ' Jenkinson nodded approvingly. Ullathorne went on epigrammatically. ' This particular battle was lost at Marston Moor. The next battle of Waterloo will be lost on Lord's Cricket Ground.' Jenkinson was curiously tolerant of cleverness for an exact scholar. ' I am afraid, Ullathorne, you are not as fond of games as an admirer of the Greeks should be.' ' Well, sir, I cannot imagine Hector bowling " yorkers " at Lord's, or Achilles cutting him to the Scamander. A prize-fight would bring us nearer to the Olympian Games.' ' That's jolly, Ulla-thorne, but don't you think Greeks and Trojans might just as well have played the Wall game against the Walls of Troy ? ' ' No, sir. Neither could have understood the need of a referee, and he would have perished under their many-edged spears unless he placed himself in the Wooden Horse.' Jenkinson's big brow inclined. ' I am afraid you are right ; they had neither sport nor Christianity.' Peter was agog and aglow with this sort of conversation, and tried to discharge as much Virgilian learning as he could muster, ' I don't think *Pius Aeneas* would have kept the rules unless Pallas Athene was umpiring.'

' Of course,' rejoined Ullathorne, ' *Pius Aeneas* was not a gentleman, though he possessed certain qualities which would have made him a valuable member of the Eton Governing Body.' Jenkinson grew thoughtful, and they left the ground in silence. Polite-looking masters and vociferous boys were crowding out of the gates. Warre, as a *wet-bob* Head, did not honour Lord's, but Peter caught sight of the massive Harrow Head, a heavy loan from Eton. There was old Mike with an M.C.C. ribbon, with every over of the match stored in his mind, grimly appreciative of the scare into which Harrow had been flung. Jenkinson waved farewell, and slipped into the Underground for Hackney, the home of the Eton Mission.

Mr. Socston had kindly invited Peter to accompany his own boy on a spree to Earl's Court. Earl's Court on the Saturday of the Harrow Match was a function. Half the School were there, walking about and talking as though meeting in a dreamland, thought Peter. Mr. Socston gave him and his son a dinner at the Carlton. When Peter ordered iced lemonade, there was a laugh, and he was given his first sip of champagne. The garish dining-room swam for a moment. He forgot Mr. Morley's House and the coming of Trials, and an unfinished extra-work lying in his *burry*. It was time to go. They glided through the hot gaslit streets, three in a hansom, one of the lost pleasures of London. The entrance to Earl's Court was filled with Etonians beautifully dressed. The central thoroughfare was like a sublimated High Street. All the familiar faces passed in a dazzle of pleasure. The slouch and affected boredom of Eton was exchanged for the quick bearing and inquiring eyes of would-be men of the world peering through a door-chink into the world of sight and experience. It was a scene which held them interested for an evening, but they were like habitants of another world, the little world of Eton, which keeps its secrets and pleasures and desires to itself. Earl's Court was soon exhausted. There was a pretence of a mild rag at the water-shoot, which might have led to some horseplay in the water. At one moment Frencher was heard wagering he would take a dive in his top-hat, and Mr. Socston was offering him champagne if he did. But the arrival of non-Etonians and curious cockneys produced an atmosphere of frigid reserve. With an amused shrug Etonians moved out of the mixed crowd. They did not mind a roll with the police or with Harrovians at Lord's, but the line had to be drawn. True Etonians cannot, will not, show off before the crowd. And even at Eton itself showing off is a privilege, a closely guarded ritual almost, belonging to *Pops*. Practical jokes in public are their perquisite, and are such as produce admiration rather than mirth among their beholders.

Peter felt an iron clamp growing round his skull. A sweet sickness played in his gills. He felt as though he had overdived at Cuckoo Weir and swallowed mouthfuls of weedy water. Mr. Socston observed his failure in colour, and murmured something in favour of a brandy and soda. Peter was led to a bar and dosed. He could hear Mr. Socston telling an interminable yarn of his days at Eton.

'The first champagne I ever had, I had to run for. We used to run behind the coaches to the Ascot races— all the way through Windsor and down the Long Walk. We ran and hung on till we reached the course. Then we were given champagne and ran home again. All that is abolished. So much the worse for Eton. We were taught to make our heads young. We were never drunk. We ran it off. A boy who gets drunk over his liquor should be *swished*. A boy should learn to carry his wine.' But Peter had long ceased to care whether he had a head or not, preferably not. He could hear Mr. Socston talking all the way home in the cab. Every word soaked into his mind like ink on a wet jelly. The next morning he woke up with a start, and began repeating all he had heard like a saying lesson. 'By Gad, boys, I saw Thornton hit a sixer right over the Pavilion at Lord's. And, by Gad, it was with a bat that wouldn't drive. And I saw Buckland break the glass in the old tennis court with a sixer to leg off Harrow bowling. I believe I hit one myself . . . before old Mike . . . and his stand-pat forward system . . . they turned me out of the Eleven for swiping to leg . . . sixers all of them, by Gad ! '

CHAPTER XV

THE WINTER HALF

THE Winter Half found Mr. Morley as hopeful as the Mathematical mind could make him that his House would take a turn upward. Without any gift of sympathy or enthusiasm he began to look forward to a day when Peter would be Captain and Socston Captain of Games. Both boys had made their mark decidedly. His Fifth Formers seemed good for nothing, but he was convinced that new boys of good calibre would eventually take their place, and that reformation could be worked from below instead of from above. It never crossed his mind what might happen to new boys during the three years it would take them to reach the top of the House. However, taking the average run of boys, he did not see why Houses should differ so totally as they did. Boys were much the same. It was chance whether a House won a reputation. Change the boys, and another House would come into its place. He never thought of the effect of a change in House master. He was disappointed that his House never seemed able to pass the first round of the House Cup. Socston might augur a change, and anyhow, the House Cup was a sum in permutations. With Munfort's boys he could have won the Cup. Unfortunately a good House needed cultivation, and cultivation of any kind was not Mr. Morley's strong point. He had a new neighbour. 'Drury's' had been condemned, and Mr. Jenkinson moved farther down town. His small House hardly seemed a rival to Mr. Morley, who had no lack of applicants to choose from. There were firstly parents who had omitted putting their boys

down for the crack Houses before they were certain of
their sex. Besides, there were plenty of adventurers
late on the scene, American millionaires, foreign nota-
bilities, British Jews, and successful financiers who understood that a distinct social label could be purchased for
their sons by mere entry at Eton. Mr. Morley understood figures, and was often weak enough to take the
climbing class. Others, whom he refused, went to Maxse's,
derisively called 'the Synagogue.' As a result the
School List, once studded, not merely with the noble
names of England, but of the real and better-bred old
squirearchy, Pocklington, Micklethwaite, Bendyshe, Tre-
mayne, Ethelston, Dymoke, Aglionby, and the like,
became pitted with strange surnames, Semite or cos-
mopolitan. Parents were snobbish enough to avoid the
schools of their own tenets for the special glamour which
Eton incontestably confers on all her sons. The Unity
of the School became broken when boys could be excused
attending the Chapel ceremonial without which Eton is not
Eton. Members of the lost tribes are nowhere more lost
than at Eton. The luxury, which grew up in the background of the athleticism, gave wealth an advantage it
had never had before at Eton. Many a fine old Eton
name turned for reasons of poverty elsewhere unless
it could find a resting-place on the Foundation. And
certain Houses, weighed with undesirables, sank slowly
to the bottom of the pool.

The standing of a House is more affected by its place in
the Football Cup than by any other single event. The
Winter Half was an orgy of compulsory football. Peter
heard converse of nothing except of *pills* and *rouges*.
Five times a week he had to play the Eton game, which is
a variant of its own. Rugby was successful in imposing
its football use on the civilised world, but the Eton game,
with its *cornering* and *sneaking*, *rouges* and *rams*, is played
nowhere else. With its massed *bully* charging down the
field without forward passing and the conversion of
rouges into goals, it has been described as the Rugby game

without hands. Muddy fields, steaming *bullies*, and bruised shins were the order of the day from October to December. The House-colours at Morley's played up, inspired by the prospect of the first round of the Cup. They could defeat Maxse's, but they generally drew Miss Evans's and succumbed miserably. The Lower Boys played up, because they were caned if they shirked or slacked. The *sine* or House-team without colours played up in the lust to win House-colours. But, as a body, there was no spirit in Morley's. Their jealousy and dislike of Miss Evans's reached a high pitch, partly because they were neighbours, partly because Miss Evans's House numbered fifty instead of forty, and also because they set a tone. The Morleyites feared them for their prowess, and detested them for the aloofness and the superiority they felt and showed to other Houses. Peter's window opened on Miss Evans's back windows, and there was a brisk exchange of missiles during the half. Old fives balls and chunks of stale cake were hurled with unerring aim into Morleyite rooms, from which reply was made with catapulted lumps of sugar. The new bars on Peter's windows were noticed by the Evansites, and received with bitter chaff. 'Did the bears have to be barred in ? ' ' Would they like some stale bun in the bear pit ? ' and such neighbourly inquiry. ' Wait till the House Cup ' was always the unanswerable answer from Evans's.

Nothing disturbed the deadly intent each House nourished towards the House Cup. Even the outbreak of the Boer War in October did not worry footballers, to whom the Field was more important than many kopjes and visible Evansites more formidable than invisible Boers. It was generally concluded that the Boers would be finished by Christmas, especially as a rumour was current that the Eton Volunteers might be loaned for service during the holidays. ' Damned good job these Boers are pipped at last,' grunted Morley's House Library, who read their war news chiefly through the reliable medium of *Punch*. ' They never wash. They wear

elastic-sided boots and sing Psalms.' One night the
Queen's Schools were occupied with troops, and another
afternoon the Household troops marched from the Castle
to the station amid signs of delirious enthusiasm. Every
public-house in Windsor vomited the lower order of
Imperialists, shrieking 'Majuba! Majuba!' Tousled
women, loafers, cads, tourists, and Eton boys were swept
into the rush. Thenceforward there was only war and
rumour of war. The Black Week of December threw a
gloom over the School. Masters began to watch for the
names of past pupils on the lists of casualties. The boys
were better able to throw off the depression. They had
reached the Final of the House Cup, and besides, if the
war went on, there was a chance of older boys getting
out into the field. Anyhow, Buller was an Etonian, and
knew what he was about.

The half became one of misery for Peter, as soon as he
realised that he would never shine at the Eton game.
Socston showed promise, and they drifted a little farther
apart. Socston was promoted to the *sine* and the position
of Post in the House Eleven. It was not a pleasant position,
for Frencher as Back-up-Post believed it was his duty,
when not kicking the ball, to dig his knee into Post.
When a *rouge* was scored against the House, Socston had
the still more painful position of holding the ball, held up in
a framework of limbs to resist the running weight of their
opponents' *ram*. However, his pluck was appreciated,
and one evening the Captain told him he could wear shorts
instead of knickerbockers. Only those who played for
their House were allowed to play bare-kneed. Socston
joined the ranks of the keen, who played every day, never
figuring among the defaulters, who were encouragingly
smacked on Saturday nights in the Library, after which
the Lower Boys were allowed to play passage football in
their socks, while their Uppers and betters condescended
to supervise players so minute and unimportant. It was
a curious picture of past Eton, the long dark, filthy
passage, cramped and leaning slightly to one side, the

once whitened walls stained by the muddy impressions of balls, the low panelling hacked and chipped by a thousand boots, while two flaring gaslights in wire cages illuminated a heap of sodden boys wriggling like white worms at the bottom of a jar, while with sweat, smoke, and swearing the tiny ball was worked up and down the passage wall. At each rare appearance it was fiercely kicked, amid much subdued agony of stubbed toes, until one side had been driven through the Dame's door or the other pressed down the stairs.

One Monday the boys welcomed as a diversion the proposal which had been made by Dr. Borcher and other Science masters that some record should be made by the boys of the November meteors, of which a brilliant display had been cheaply promised in the newspapers. Mr. Morley's House decided generally that this would be an excellent excuse for Alpine climbing. Permission was obtained for those who wished to sit up an extra hour after lights-out on condition that they seriously took notes of the celestial phenomena. Peter armed himself with a clean notebook and pencils, and ascended to the top floor, where half the House had collected in what seemed fancy dress, some in blazers and overcoats, others in sweaters and beagling *bags*.

Mrs. Sowerby's historic step ladder had been raised to the sky-light amid some chaffing of the Fourth of June truants. The meteorologists climbed upon the roof, which seemed like a crazy quilt thrown down to cover this part of Eton. Here a strip of lead, here crooked tiles, here brick chimneys bandaged with iron bands. In one corner a decayed spouting, and in another a garret window choked with dust and the effluvia of cats. The outlines of other Houses could be discerned against the starlight, and laudable efforts were made to anticipate the morning duty of various boys' maids by rousing sleepers with sugar on their window-panes. The meteors showed no sign of appearance, and the watchers sat down to cocoa in the Library and guileless gossip concerning various

Science *beaks*. One of them had sent round a notice in the summer announcing the escape of some strange beast. ' It was a cat-eating lemur,' said Frencher; ' we could hear the squeals of the cats it killed for weeks in Miss Evans's garden.' ' Didn't Gill once dig up a pre-historic beast in a cave that wasn't quite dead ? ' inquired another. ' No, you 're thinking of Borcher. He raised a cat from the dead with a galvanic battery.' The statements of Science often reached weird proportions by the time they had been noted and discussed in Lower School. As it was, Dr. Borcher's lecture on the coming shower of meteors had left a vague apprehension that the planet might not survive until the Final of the House Cup was actually played. A display at least exceeding the Fourth of June fireworks was expected, and Borcher himself had described his means of photographing the meteors in spectroscope, and had promised to be able to announce in school whether they were made of dynamite or paving stones.

It had been announced that the best account written about the meteors would be sent to the French Exhibition with Jekyll's Latin Alcaics. ' The best Science notes are to go to Paris,' said Peter, explaining why he brought a notebook. The idea of an Etonian figuring in a French Exhibition was amusing enough to be repeated. Frencher imaginatively supposed the Man searching for his pupil's work in Paris, and finding the Dame at the Moulin Rouge. Another search was made in the heavens. ' Paris Exhibition forward ! ' called somebody, and Peter climbed to the roof. Philips was following him. They could hear the foot-tread and the hush ! hush ! of other climbers. Peter and Philips made their way gradually toward the other side of the Christopher Yard. They stood in places untrod save by sweep or cat. The giant shape of Upper Chapel rose over the road. They were climbing opposite somebody's passage. Suddenly they heard somebody moving within and shrank back into a recess. There was a half-open window a few feet from them, and a light could be seen approaching. With beating hearts the boys watched first the shadow dancing in front of the guttering candle, then the familiar bent form. 'Juggins!' whispered Peter. They could only watch, as he halted and began to finger the panelled wall, where the names of old boys had been cut in regular columns and slowly filled with dust, which he rubbed out with his fingers. Whatever Jenkinson was looking for he had found. He was holding a printed paper, which Peter recognised as the first printed list of Etonians killed in the war. For a moment a little dust fell like gold through his candle flame. Then he turned back into darkness.

The meteors, as Frencher later remarked amid groans, failed to meteoralise, and the Morleyites, having completed the perambulation of the roofs, returned to the Library, where more gallons of cocoa were brewed over a surreptitious fire. Caste was relaxed, and Lower Boys were allowed to listen open-mouthed to other than words of command from their masters. They hung round, feeling a dizzier elation than the social snob feels in the first moments at Court. The Captain of Games even spoke to Socston, and told him that he would propose him for ballot and election to the Debate, if he would hurry and get into Fifth Form like Darley. 'There's nothing in Darley's way except that his character is too good,' he added, at which there was a respectful laugh among the Uppers, while Socston's peers writhed with jealousy. Peter was happy to afford the great man a butt, and only blushed. Irreproachable and respectable masters were subjected to the most curious gossip, and the wildest stories were invented of their youthful scrapes. Towards midnight word came from the roof that a single meteor had been seen over the Chapel, but scientific interest had died down, and the boys separated for the night. Peter retired, forgetful of meteors and masters, with nothing but an acute sense of jealousy at heart. Just because Socston had his shorts . . . a Lower Boy talking to a House-colour . . . taking on airs as though his old friends were not good enough for him. He was realising that the divinest and most subtle of the goddesses ruling the school world was Popularity. Captaincy, athletic success, pocket-money, brilliance of mind, good looks can all bring a certain obvious favouritism, but neither colours nor position, cap nor purse can bring that divine touch which gives a boy charm among his fellows, the dangerous and lovely gift which can be turned to powerful good or per- verted to endless harm. That charm was abundantly Socston's. He was made for popularity. An Etonian father had bred him Etonian. His good looks were not seriously discounted by brains. His thick figure had grown into grace, and was likely to lengthen under Eton athleticism. His quickness with the ball reflected itself in tidiness of dress. Fellows liked to walk with him. His seniors liked to look at him, his juniors to look up to him. Peter clung to him, knowing that one day a colour would finally rend them apart.

With the arrival of the Football Ties, Socston actually played for the House in the Field. Henceforth he could look down on other Lower Boys, who had not the privilege of bare knees. There never were seen any *shorts* quite so short as Socston's. It was true that Morley's did not survive the First Ties for the Cup, being ignominiously trounced by Munfort's in the presence of a wholly un- sympathetic crowd. Mr. Morley had left his horrible *puppy-hole* littered with rotten extra-works, stale algebra, twisted compasses, and other signs of a deserted battle- field, and stood grimly watching from a corner of the ground. His eye never moved, nor did a bristle in his moustache relax as the cries of Munfort's friends rent the air, to be met with the shrill scream of his own Lower Boys passing into lament—' Morley's ! Morley's ! Maw-aw-aw-lays ! '

Peter was not enjoying the football Half. The Lower Boy matches against the assorted louts of other Houses he escaped, but the daily mixed refuse game, composed from four Houses, was a trial to the shins and a humilia- tion to the spirit. St. Andrew's Day came with welcome

relief and reverie. Thank heaven, he could moon and
dream all day without having to play in the Final of the
Lower Boy Cup or in the time-honoured Wall game
between Collegers and Oppidans. Peter was grateful
when Socston suggested they should sit together on the
top of the Wall and watch the steaming gladiators en-
meshed in each other's elbows below.

The Wall game is understood by few even at Eton.
The Wall was originally a boundary built early in the
eighteenth century, but a traditional game had grown up
against it in the same way that fives had developed
between the Chapel buttresses. The Wall ran for a
hundred yards from the corner house of Weston's Yard
along the Slough Road to Fifteen Arch Bridge. A stone
coping covered the thick bulging brick, which was ridged
on the side of the road. Climbing up iron-fitted footholes,
Peter and Socston crawled along the top, and sat with a
hundred boys tapping their heels for the game to begin.
The famous Wall was of a mellow red brick, much broken
and battered toward the base. It was chipped and
chapped all over. The surface was thickly bemudded
and plastered in places with patches of cement, but the
old red showed bright wherever it had been recently
broken. After Upper Chapel it was best loved of Eton
landmarks. Chalk lines at each end of the Wall, known
as Good and Bad *Calx*, offered meaning to the initiated
Latinist. The old studded wooden door in the adjutting
wall of Weston's was used as one goal, but so rarely was
a goal scored that initials had been cut to mark H. J.
Mordaunt's goal for College in 1885, Mordaunt, the last
Colleger to be Captain of the Eleven. A large elm-tree
in the distance towards Fellows' Pond was traditionally
used as the other goal. Fortunately no storm had blown
it down since the game was invented. As goals were
seldom scored, decisions were made in *shies*. Once the
ball has been worked within *calx* by either side and
touched against the Wall while off the ground to the
formula, ' Got it ! ' a *shy* may be said to have been *shied*

unless the opposing side *furk* or draw it out. There was considerable legend. Phillips, an Oppidan, had once kicked from *calx* to *calx*. Collegers still disputed the alleged goal of 1858.

Amid ringing cries of ' Collegers ' and ' Oppidans ' the two brightly apparelled Elevens filtered through the sombre and admiring crowd. The narrow space adjoining the Wall was sowed with sawdust, while the Wall itself was thick with spectators hanging over from the time-honoured coign of vantage. The Oppidans in their yellow and purple stripes, the Collegers in their white and royal purple took their places, the *bully* wadded with heavy sackcloth and clouts to shield their faces from the rasping of the bricks, the seconds pushing the *walls* and the *outsides* ready to pounce on the ball with lightning kicks. As the School Clock struck half-twelve, the traditional enemies buried themselves in each other, struggling and shoving in *bullies*, which lasted ten and twenty minutes before they broke up into swift scrim-mages, which finished the moment the ball could be kicked out, and wheresoever the ball was stayed the *bully* recommenced. Up and down the game slowly went with no result, for the Clock struck half-one, and the moment that the ball crossed the line after the half-hour the tournament of sack and leather was over. It was a draw.

Shy or no *shy*, the Oppidan spectators, little compre-hending the game few of their number ever played, howled down the cheers of the minute claque of Collegers, who at least had all played the game and showed some dim recognition of its points. True to their order, Peter and Socston waited for the chorus of small *Tugs* to shout ' Collegers ' in order to drown the same with a stentorian ' Oppidans,' regularly and scathingly repeated.

As they strolled back, they turned into Mr. Lamb's pupil-room. Peter had to fetch some verses, and Socston had to negotiate a ' yellow ticket.' Mr. Lamb had just come up from the Wall game, and sat with bowed head and gownless in his chair. 'Didn't you know St. Andrew's Day is a holiday for man and beast?' he sighed. 'I am sorry I forgot to fetch my verses yesterday,' muttered Peter. Mr. Lamb handed them to him from under a pile of blotting-paper, which had drunk his graceful signature a hundred times in blue and purple inks. As a rule he made some comment. They were a good set, even better than usual, for they were marked 'N. N.,' or 'need not make a fair copy.' And his Tutor had not a word to say! while Socston had as much difficulty in passing his 'yellow ticket' as a bad cheque. Both went out silent. 'What the deuce is the matter with m' Tutor?' murmured Socston, as soon as they were in Weston's Yard; 'perhaps his blessed *Tugs* were not playing on form.' Peter could not imagine a grown man feeling sore over a game, but Socston was right. Mr. Lamb was not only an Eton patriot. He was a Colleger enthusiast, and still deeply felt the issues of St. Andrew's Day. He had seen College mauled for an hour at the Wall without scoring, and he felt it would have been better taste for his Oppidan pupils not to have intruded while he felt sensitive. 'Polly, pretty Polly,' he said, turning to his beloved bird, 'say, "Well played, Collegers!" say, "Play up, Collegers!"' and the wise bird only laughed. 'Lamb, Lamb, play up, Lamb!' was all it would say, as the fond owner scratched his head feathers with the pen that had dissected innumerable Greek roots and tempered the unending flow of weekly Latin verses. 'Polly is right,' he sighed, and turned over a pile of Latin verses from half a dozen different divisions. With an eye as highly developed as a coin tester's at the Mint, he could pick out the one false quantity concealed in a thousand lines. They were rather more frequent in Fourth Form and Remove copies, but Fifth Form verses were more interesting, and sometimes showed traces of that real ingenuity to write Latin verse which lies somewhere between lexicography and music. Mr. Lamb's ear was filed to perfection. For a wager he could have turned a proposition of Euclid or an advertisement on the hoardings into correct elegiacs.

His pen moved here and there like the brush of some Old Master left alone with the canvases of his uninspired pupils, throwing in colour here, or altering a line there, so that some day their work might be feebly recognised as of his School.   Only the Old Master knew how many years of study and work preceded the shots and dashes he made with his brush, here a blob, here a soft shadow, here an obliteration.   But as nothing altogether unlovely left his studio, so no false quantity was allowed to leave Mr. Lamb's pupil-room.   It was his pride and his honour that it was so.   Thousands and thousands of verses passed his way to be shown up in school, or by a rare miracle to be perused by the Head as ' sent up for good,' but Mr. Lamb's neat little cipher was recognised as almost a hall-mark to silver Latin.   It was wonderful how he could change a single word and make a good line, or sometimes with a swift outpouring of minutely beautiful corrections add beauty where the form was stiffly correct.   It was like the lost mediaeval arts of ecclesiastical wood-carving or the illumining of missals.   And true to the old Eton traditions Mr. Lamb remained unmarried, giving all his meticulous mind and heart to the ungrateful pupils, who passed into the outer world and too often forgot their gracious Tutor and his precious art.

The School Clock kept him gentle pace as he slowly corrected paper after paper, sighing and signing in turn. Boom, boom ! and the Clock struck the double hexameter of midnight.   Mr. Lamb counted the beats, put aside his work, and thought over the day.   The muddy field and the red-brick Wall came back to him with the kaleidoscope of brightly-striped players.   Cries of ' Collegers ' and ' Oppidans ' still echoed in his ears.   The great cheering crowd came back like a Greek Chorus chanting around the splendid players, and the whole scene began to filter through his brain in metre.   With a weary smile and half-closed eyes he began writing beautiful verses :—

En stetit et stabit, duro stat robore murus.
En patet aequato levis arena solo.
Se nunc oppositis opponunt hostibus hostes;
Maxima de minimo proelia folle gerunt.
Hos Galeaeque tegunt tutos saccique trilices,
Hos vario vestis picta colore decet.
Volgus hiat plausuque fremit Martemque fatigat:
Inter tot voces arbiter iste silet.

And on and on, until the Clock struck again the hour.
Quickly he concluded :—

Aera sonant, dedit hora modum, de turribus altis;
Cuncta silent; fiunt foedera; volgus abit.
Urbanos, Pueri, vos tollite laude, Togati,
Et vos, Urbani, tollite laude Togam.

His zeal for College was swamped in his greater love for
Eton. Oppidans and Collegers, love one another! he
prayed. And there were liquid drops in his eyes, seemingly
from the long strain put on them, as he went to bed,
knowing that Eton shall be justified of all her children.

CHAPTER XVI

THE NEW CENTURY

No boy was present in the School when the old Clock boomed the change of the year and the beginning of the nineteen hundreds. Only dwellers in the Cloisters heard the solemn midnight of December 31, 1899, echo through the deserted School Yard. The last of the Eton Fellows, old Mr. Carter, had survived to usher Eton into the new century.

And the new century found a new Eton. The great historic Houses of Austen Leigh's and Mitchell's approached their last lap, making superb exits in the Final of the House Cup, and their last Elevens as Finalists enjoyed the privilege of all wearing their colours. These were the great Houses which had stood on the same level as Warre's and Evans's in the past.

The special significance of the hymn line, ' When war shall be no more,' though much appreciated in Chapel, was probably only revealed to old Miss Evans, whose House, after Homeric rivalry with Warre's, still survived three generations of Houses. A ten or twenty years' tenancy gradually produced association between a House master and the outward form of his hostelry. The mocking eyes of boys readily perceived a master's character in the shape of his House, until the Governing Body stereotyped the red-brick workhouse. The House, long known as Warre's, occupied in Peter's day by Austen Leigh, and flanked by Warre's yawning drill hall, was symbolic of the man who made it the most powerful and feared of Eton Houses. His only rival had been Miss Evans, one of whose Captains had laid as a last legacy on his

fellows the duty of blackballing the men of Warre
for *Pop*.

Had the great rivals forgiven each other as they faced
each other in Chapel every morning, like survivals from
another age ? The famous football Final in which their
Elevens had met and drawn three times without result
was a tradition. As last of the Dames, Miss Evans lived
on, determined to outlive as many as possible of the
impertinent Governing Body, who had classed her as an
anachronism and were going, at the first opportunity, to
make an end of her name and institution for ever. Yet
she lived on, haunting the square window seat which was
thrust like a lighthouse over Keate's Lane, or walking in
her quaint bonnet to her special stall in Chapel. Haply,
as she watched Dr. Warre she forgot the day when the
Field rang to their clashing names, for both had entered
into their beatitude, and would strive against each other
for the House Cup no more.

But the chronicler might wonder whether she had
forgiven Madam de Rosen, whose boys had once defeated
hers through the accident of the umpire not seeing that
the scorer of the winning goal had handled the ball. In
those days no amount of *rouges* scored by Miss Evans
could equal that stolen goal, and the memory lay bitter
in the hearts of all righteous Evansites. It was true the
rule was altered after the match, but the match was lost,
and eternity could not take the sprig out of the Baroness's
Cap. In her heart Miss Evans still heard the triumphant
rivals crying their war-cry, ' Play up, Mrs. de Rosen's !
Play up, Madam de Rosen's ! ! Play up, Baroness de
Rosen's ! ! ! '

Where was the Baroness now ? Where were the
Dominies ? Where were the Dames ? They had passed
away, each burying in the grave a little of the jealousy
they felt for the haughty Baroness. ' Honest Jonny '
had survived them all. The unique race was disappearing, which had included Dame Angelo, a noted beauty,
who wore patch and powder, and, as the boys had believed,

another who was a cast mistress of George the Fourth.
Between Dame Angelo being carried to Church in a
sedan chair and Miss Evans's homely bonnet nodding
under the high oaken canopy in Chapel there was a far
cry, yet they were sacredly one. They were both Eton
Dames, and would one day be classed as such in the
heavenly hierarchies amid Provosts and Powers—
Dominations and Dames !

Miss Evans entered the new century in solitary grandeur,
and the whole School watched for her boys' defeat. Alone
of Houses they wore a badge with their scarlet colour, a
cheerful black skull and crossbones. Since they won a
Cup three years in succession they had adopted black
shorts as a sign of further remoteness from the herd.
Perfect Evansites associated their colour of scarlet with
the constant scoring of *rouges*. Polite rivals referred to
' Bloody Evans ! ' And even with 1900 no one could tell
how much longer Evans's would last.

Warre and Hornby were in their last decade of work.
They sang their *nunc dimittis* regularly on Sundays in
Chapel, but otherwise showed no sign of retirement.
The old men who had made Eton under them were retired,
or about to retire. Ainger was moving from Keate's
Lane to a remote seclusion a few hundred yards down the
Eton Wick Road. With 1900 the world-wide question
of the Old Etonian colour was settled in favour of black
with a light blue line, and Ainger could piously turn his
attention to the Eton Register. The Eton historian will
record much else of 1900. In that year Lower Sixpenny
Colour was abolished, and the School Stores were established by the younger masters to the dismay and downfall
of the clan of *Jobies*. And the first of the new red work-
houses were occupied on the Eton Wick Road.

As the great Houses went their famous way to triumphant and belaurelled ends, the arena was cleared for younger
Houses. Here was their chance. Morley's and Jenkinson's began to look for place. But the tradition was
against Mr. Morley, and he struggled hard to keep his

Thoughts of you are roadside parks
on the highway
of my mind.

HAVE A
HAPPY BIRTHDAY!

Our very best wishes for
your birthday "Hubert".
also hoping you are
thoroughly enjoying your
holiday.
From Us Both,
Cliff & Etta.

Hallmark

House afloat. With the new year Dugannon and his
stalwarts were gone. The House fell into feebler hands
at the top, with stark growing wickedness in the Fifth
Form. He had made no effort to prune his boys, and it
was too late to arrange that choice characters should rule.
He had left his House to chance, and contented himself
with his hurried evening visit, correcting Mathematical
extra-works as a ticket-collector scans tickets, and
signing papers as with a rubber stamp. The House fell
to the Captain and the Debating Society, which was a
wise policy, provided he had the right boys at the top.
The Lower Boys suffered for his neglect. They were
fagged and caned out of spite, until there was no sense of
Justice left. Socston, from having been a favourite, lost
his protector, and found himself slashed on the least
excuse by Camdown major, the new Captain, until, as he
comically said, he found it necessary to grow a new skin
by rowing with redoubled energy. So was laid the
foundation of a great rowing career. He endured it
bitterly, only promising himself ample revenge should he
ever become Captain and find any of the Camdown clan
under his power. There is nothing absolute at Eton.
From the bully there is appeal to *Pop*, from the arbitrary
power of the fag master the desperate may apply for relief
to the Captain of the Oppidans. But the wise and the
patient prefer to wait their time. Eton is so many-sided,
and opens so many outlets, that no single character can
wholly dominate a House. And Socston waited. It
drove Socston to toil all summer on the River, where
he hardened his muscles and soldered his wind-pipes.
Peter was driven into the School Library, where, amid
his bursts of Classical work, he began to pick up the all-
consoling taste of literature.

The School Library had come into his life through
Ullathorne. There had been a snowfall that winter, and
the tradition of snowballing encounters at Eton had never
died down. There was some child's play at the New
Schools after Chambers. Late-comers, masters and boys,

were heavily pelted as they came through the Arch behind
the old Sebastopol cannon. The old feud between Collegers and Oppidans sprang to life, and Collegers found
their gowns a useful shield. Coming out of School again,
they were made to run the gauntlet. There is nothing
like the venom with which a Lower Boy will strike a
Tug in the back. Peter found himself joining in the
senseless mobbing of an imperturbable figure, which, with
gown tightly pulled over its head, and top-hat under arm,
stalked all the cooler for the snow towards College. Peter
had hurled a few assorted icicles at this grave object, when
it turned and curtly remarked, ' Come up to the School
Library.' It was Ullathorne, speaking without a trace
of rancour in his voice. No early Christian could have
addressed his persecutor more sweetly. ' Oh, I 'm damn
sorry ! ' burst out Peter, ' I never saw it was you.' ' That
makes it the worse,' replied Ullathorne, ' and you need
not swear. Oaths are the poorest substitute possible
for the work the Greeks preferred to get out of their
particles.' Peter loved swallowing wisdom of a kind,
which he felt was intended, and perhaps invented, to
puzzle masters, Ullathorne's only relaxation. Peter
followed him up the staircase, past the old embossed map
of the Holy Land, into a long room lined with bookshelves.
At the far end was a white marble Apollo Belvedere.
There were cases filled with Eton relics such as the original
manuscript of Gray's *Elegy*. From a corner hung a roll
of Porson's exquisite Latin verses. A gentle, though
bearded Librarian, looking like the disgowned spirit of
some deceased master, approached Peter to inquire, ' Are
you in Fifth Form, sir ? ' ' Of course he is,' grunted
Ullathorne. ' I beg your pardon, sir, is there any book
you would care to read ? ' Ullathorne took Peter from
case to case, summarising their contents. ' Sport ! ' he
sniffed. ' They have to cater for some of the masters.'
However, here was the History, and here the Poetry.
Ullathorne caressed the volumes of Swinburne. ' My
favourite Eton poet,' he murmured. ' Do you still read

English poems ? ' said Peter, who accounted escape from
Tennyson one of the benefits of a public school. ' Swinburne wrote as a Greek, not as a British writer. It
happened to be in English, but it was Greek,' was Ullathorne's reply, which sounded Greek enough to Peter.
' There are the *cribs*,' and Ullathorne stroked the best-
thumbed shelves in the Library; ' the local interest shown
in the Classics is tremendous. May I introduce a good
crib to you : Jebb's Sophocles. There is a foolish
prejudice among some of our official friends against the
use of translations. Personally I always use them.
When a scholar like Jebb spends a lifetime writing a
perfect version, it seems to me a reflexion on his scholarship not to read what he has to say.' Peter gasped a
little. ' You know I only look at a *crib* when I 'm fairly
stumped. There are more of Kelly's *Keys* knocking about
m' Tutor's than books by Nat Gould even. Surely you
don't ever want a *crib* ? ' ' It is so pleasant to find that a
writer like Jebb agrees with one. I cannot resist opening
him,' said Ullathorne. Peter nodded. He was learning.
He picked out a Lucretius from the shelves at random.
' Munro's ? ' asked Ullathorne, ' the finest translation of
Latin into English.' ' Wasn't he an atheist ? ' said Peter,
fumbling with a little knowledge. ' Lucretius invented
the atomic theory,' said Ullathorne, ' which certainly
reduced contemporary theology to atoms, but read
Cicero's answer to Lucretius. Cicero was an Anglican
Bishop born out of due time.'

Peter had enough to absorb, and began reading in the
suggestion book, which contained as many humorous as
serious entries, either calling for the purchase of some
rather improper book or the exclusion of some master
from the precincts. A request that a young classical
master might be barred the *cribs* was underscored with a
text which Peter recognised was in Robertson's handwriting, ' The ass knoweth his master's crib.' Even
Ullathorne approved.

' I 've got some Aristophanes to do,' said Peter, turning

to business. 'Yes, *The Frogs,* a very good Christmas pantomime if you read through Hookham Frere's translation,' said Ullathorne, ' but one needs both Drury Lane and a knowledge of the Daily Press in Athens to bring out the force of some of the passages.' ' I must say I don't think it very funny yet.' Ullathorne laughed. ' No, I suppose not ; an unmentionable editor has carefully taken out the unmentionable jokes.' ' Why, are there any ? ' queried Peter. ' Yes,' said the other. ' I 've read the Latin *crib.* There are things in it you could not whisper even on a dark night at Morley's.' Both laughed. ' He seems much more puzzling than Euripides,' said Peter. ' I never can do more than twenty lines an hour.' ' When I tell you that Euripides is the Greek Ibsen, you will kindly not place him amongst the less puzzling authors.' Peter was left silent. Feebly he tried to keep up to his brilliant pacer. ' Examiners think Euripides is rather easy.' ' Speak not to me of examiners ! ' cried Ullathorne. ' They are the fools who ask us the questions we are too wise to know how to answer. Not my remark, but you do not seem to have heard it before.' Peter shook his head. ' Whose remark is it ? Euripides' ? ' ' Well, it might have been. You 're getting bright. Nobody knows who says these things first. In College everything clever is attributed to J. K. Stephen. Just as in France everything clever is laid to Talleyrand. It is the same at Harrow and Winchester, except that at Winchester they are so clever that clever remarks are not noticed at all. Anything very stupid is claimed as out of the ordinary.'

Peter felt a little whirled in the head, but he was avid of information, and unfortunately became anxious to exhibit it. A few days later, finding himself in Drake's bookshop, he selected two large volumes of Plato, and tapping their covers, remarked audibly to Socston, ' Fine stuff really. If he had known a little more Greek, he might have been a Winchester *beak*.' ' What do you mean ? ' ' Plato.' ' You ungodly little beast ! ' And the conversation of epigram languished, as Socston walked out of the shop. Eton pride is not intellectual pride. It consists rather of a pride in contemning intellectual things.

With the departure of the splendid old stock new masters were arriving, some of whom had never been Etonians. Word began to be passed round the School in the Winter Half that there was a Mathematical master who suffered ragging. Peter found himself up to this Mr. Buttersby, and speedily abandoned doing any work either in or out of school. Maths. became a relaxation. On one occasion a pistol shot was fired, and the whole class fell groaning to the floor, where they remained in a dying state till the school was abandoned. Masters probably get the amount of ragging they deserve, for boys can gauge their ingenuousness to a nicety. In old days Mr. Cockshott could always be appeased by commenting on his likeness to the Prince of Wales, while Mr. O'Neill could only be induced to remit a *poena* by the sight of a poker being heated in the fire. The procedure up to Mr. Buttersby was always the same. *Saps* took in books to do work for less tolerant masters. Others devised means to pass the idle hour. Two or three crowded to the good Mr. Buttersby's desk with some impossible sum concocted for the occasion. While the unhappy Wrangler was dividing confusion or simplifying chaos on paper, the rest formed a *bully* against the wall and gave an exhibition of the Wall game. On one occasion it was arranged that a boy staying out was to practise a piano within hearing of Mr. Buttersby's class, bringing in the National Anthem once every five minutes like a recurring decimal. Each time, accordingly, that ' God Save the Queen ' was wafted through the air the whole division leaped to attention and remained standing in petrified loyalty. The most brilliant master could not make the idle work, and Mr. Buttersby was an instance of the incompetent master who could not prevent the *saps* from *sapping*. Peter worked steadily at Greek construe in the Mathematical hour against a racket which waxed with the half. Yet it was not all horse-play. Boys simulated ardour, and led Mr.

o

Buttersby into long and futile discussions. He was even induced to believe that his class was a great success. Again and again he was made to tell how he had won his Wranglership at Cambridge, and how the news had been cheered at his old School. One day a deputation approached his desk with the announcement that by a venerable Eton custom he was to be hoisted as the most popular master in the School. With pathetic simplicity he allowed the class to break up before the hour, while he was lifted from his desk and carried gently on the shoulders of the cheering lads from the school-room to the School Gate. It was just possible at that moment that he was the most popular master in the School. Unfortunately no such custom of expressing the boys' approval existed.

This final jest was almost too much for the mirth of the School. There had been no such goings on since the reign of Hornby. Rumour and suspicion passed through the magistral ranks. They were anxious to be loyal to a colleague, but when the good man reported his popularity among the boys the joke became apparent even to the masters. Some were pained. Some were amused. The old Classical men were perhaps grimly satisfied. But no one dared tell the Head. The School Clerk passed imperturbably by during school, though Mr. Buttersby's room, even on a Monday morning, sounded wilder than a Windsor public-house of a Saturday night. Mathematical neighbours were discreet. They left their colleague to be netted by that undesirable known as the external examiner. They became curiously absorbed when their learners pricked their ears at some burst of revelry from the entertaining Mr. Buttersby's school-room. The most humorous of them felt that their own jokes could not compete, and an amused expectation settled down on the New Schools. Something was bound to happen sooner or later. If it did, Mr. Buttersby retired. If it did not, Mr. Buttersby would become part of the Eton tradition. Who knew?

Rumour at last reached the Head.   After fifteen years of unparalleled success the shadows were beginning to fleck his career.   It reflected the sorrows of his Sovereign. The years of Jubilee were passed away, and the South African casualty lists were read with a growing despair in Windsor Castle and in the Eton Cloisters.   But a certain pride buoyed the Head.   The South African War was a gentleman's war, and no School had contributed more Generals of the old type, or more casualties, than the Eton he had formed and led.   He counted the names, and accepted Eton's sacrifice.   But tales of melting discipline within the School troubled him.   Strife was making itself heard between Classical and Mathematical masters.   Mr. Munfort and Mr. Morley were not on speaking terms.   Mr. Lamb was marshalling the head-strong young Greeks against the Mathematical Trojans, led by Mr. Winterstown, a quick-tempered Irishman, who thought Army Class I. more important than the New-castle Select.   Then came word, and even audible sounds, showing signs of the daily insubordination in the New Schools.   Nothing could bow those wide shoulders or lower that eagle head.   It was still Warre's Eton, and on a fateful day Dr. Warre set out to investigate.   One of the most striking institutions he made in his Headmaster-ship was his practice of inspecting his colleagues when least expected.   Like a thief in the night, so was the coming of the Head Master of Eton.   No master knew if he was safe.   At any moment the door might swing open . . . much to old Hornby's humour.   ' I am glad I was not inspected ' was his incorrigible remark.

Peter was one day indulging in a brown study in Mr. Buttersby's class, as it was perhaps the only kind of study possible under his auspices.   The boys had given them-selves to the possibilities of the hour.   The majority were doing nothing.   Several bright spirits were carrying on a conversation with Buttersby, their arms sprawling on his desk.   Frencher was asking questions about the famous Wranglership.   ' And did you really get it, sir ? '

and ' How did they illuminate the village when the good news came ? ' And the simple story was repeated. ' I am sure they rang the church bell for you, sir.' ' No, boys, they didn't.' ' Well, they ought to have.' The door opened at this moment with a sudden grinding sound, and Dr. Warre walked quietly up to the desk without turning to observe the Wall game in the corner.

Mr. Buttersby vacated his desk and rushed to meet him, crying out, ' Boys, the Head ! ' The class shuffled to their feet. Frencher retired slowly backwards from the front of the desk, his eyes suddenly fascinated by a Hall and Knight's Algebra, which he had deftly picked up. He resembled Keats opening Chapman's Homer for the first time in his ecstatic expression. As he turned over page after page, an almost rapt satisfaction came into his face. The Head waited grimly until the last boy in a horizontal position had assumed the perpendicular. Then the Head spoke. With a dulcet boom he inquired what work the boys were doing. There were several answers to such a question, but Buttersby saved the situation by gasping, ' Equations, please sir.' Frencher hastily turned up the chapter on Equations, the remarks of Messrs. Hall and Knight appearing to cause him one of the happiest moments of his life. The Head faced the petrified division with his untasselled cap still on his head. ' Open your books for me to see your work.' It proved a less fatiguing inspection than might have been supposed. Though each book was labelled, ' THIS BOOK WILL BE INSPECTED BY THE HEAD MASTER,' most of the boys dumbly turned over a white sheet. Some had designs to their credit which would have suited natural science notebooks. There was a tolerable collection of caricatures of Buttersby. Frencher made mute signs of his interest in equations, but no devotion to Hall and Knight seemed to explain his total indifference to them in his notebook. The Head made his farcical round, and drew himself up to deliver sentence. His cap was like the death cap of a hanging Judge. ' There appears

to have been no work done this half. What has been
done is not *quod Etona miratur*. Very unsatisfactory.
I will punish the whole Division.'

' I hope you will not be angry with the dear boys,'
broke in Buttersby. A titter broke the terrible suspense.
The Head motioned him to his desk and turned solemnly
on his heel. Without another word he turned the grinding handle and disappeared. His heavy regular tread
could be heard like that of a sentry pacing into the
distance. Then all was still in the Mathematical Schools,
and remained still for many days. A week later a Sixth
Form Praepostor sailed round with an edict suspending
all Leave for Middle Fifth, Short Leave or Long Leave.
It was an interdict against which only a dying parent or
a town dentist could prevail. The masters also were
gathered for admonition in Chambers, and received a
disquisition as to the use of a tight or a loose rein in their
dealings with the boys. Of this no word reached the
School, save a lurid rumour that the Head had advised
his staff to be tight in preference to being loose !

CHAPTER XVII

UPPER CHAPEL

PETER'S second year at Eton ran out of the hour glass to the slow drift of the Boer War. A generation grew up to whom the rumour of war became normal and casualties no accident. Mr. Daughan faithfully recorded the dead. Week by week Eton mourned her sons, for whom pathetic little obituaries appeared from tutorial pens in the *Chronicle*, rather like the reports of good boys leaving School. They would be missed. Their virtues were Etonian. Eton would remember them. *Etona haud immemor*, and in that phrase seemed to lie a hidden balm. Remembrance at Eton was sweeter than the world's acclaim. Boys waiting in the Antechapel scanned with renewed interest the fading arms of the Etonians killed in the Crimea, painted in days when all Etonians were armigerous.

There was a perfect moment to be passed every day by arriving early for Chapel, while Yard and Antechapel were still empty and the entrances were only guarded by William of Waynflete in his canopied niche and old Porter Blake waiting with his slate and hand-barrow for orders. For a moment the Yard lay deserted, save for the pigeons whose cooing mingled with the sound of the bellows pumping up steam for the magic hand of Lloyd to transmute into melody.

Peter felt as though he stood on a spring-board before the plunge into another Eton day. As the bell clanged and the School poured out of street and alley, lane and passage, he felt the joyous unity which the Chapel imposed on all by the very power of its bulk and beauty. He never climbed the spacious stone stairs without feeling as much crushed as sustained at heart. But it was the note of the organ that gave him courage and wonder and peace. He could have waited listening to Lloyd's voluntaries for ever. Sometimes he played a memory of the mediaeval past, and the forgotten Mass and long-hushed Gregorian floated back, and in a dream Our Lady's Scholars of Eton swung their censers and the chantry priests appeared on the well-worn altar steps in Lupton's Chapel, praying for the holy dead. Sometimes he improvised from the stately music of the eighteenth century, and the old bewigged Fellows and Provosts of the past nodded in their pews, and boys in blue swallowtails and brass buttons with lace collars lolled below them or, by an old custom, passed round church-*sock*. And for royal anniversaries and Head Masters' birthdays Lloyd had appropriate tunes, and how decorously he used to play ' Tom Bowling ' on Trafalgar Day, and how the School rejoiced when a modified version of the Eton Boating Song pealed through the Chapel to announce to Heaven yet another victory at Henley.

Against the west wall, all swathed in modern times with Bath stone, were the brass mementoes of Etonian lives cut short abroad or in their bud at School. In the corner, oppressed by the gigantic figure of Dr. Goodall, scraps of mediaeval figuring and inscription had been saved from the wear of time. Opposite was the font with its soaring font-cover of carved wood, and in the midst of the Antechapel, facing the altar, was the marble effigy of the Holy Founder, a white dream of purity and piety, fondling the model of the Chapel, in which the youths of England were to pray centuries after the dynasties of York and Lancaster had passed away. He who had been despised had outlived his despisers. He who had lost his only son in war had been given an endless stream of sons. All the turmoil and intrigue against which he had raised his nerveless hands had perished, and though he had been stripped, he had builded better than any of his contemporaries dreamed. Only a part of the great building he had designed had been completed, but it was the most famous Chapel in England. In the saintly perspective it had been intended to fill Cathedralwise all the area covered by Keate's Lane. As it was, only the Choir had been completed, to receive the wonder and love of generations less inspired. Morning after morning Peter glanced at the marble statue, which seemed like some angelic being playing with a toy of his fancy, a fancy for which he had suffered himself to lose the kingdom of this world. Ullathorne often told him of his devotion to the Sixth Henry, for whom the Seventh Henry had asked canonisation from Alexander VI., Pope of Rome, and implored him never to pass his images at Eton without making proper reverence. Only the accident of the Reformation and the stinginess of Henry the Seventh had prevented his final canonisation. The prayers of the Church were beginning to lift his name in orison, ' *Ora pro nobis, devote Henrice*,' when changes in religion swept his cult away. Save at his twin foundations of Eton and Cambridge, he had fallen out of England's love and memory. When his holy bones began to miraculise on behalf of the discarded claims of the House of Lancaster, they were dug up at Chertsey Abbey and buried under a nameless slab in St. George's Chapel, Windsor, whither Ullathorne took Peter to kneel on Sunday afternoons. The House of York, the arrows of the world, the murderers in the Tower, and even the Devil's advocate, had done their worst. Amid the crash of wars and the fall of thrones Henry had preserved that exquisite mediaeval chastity which would not suffer him to look on dancing girls or on the naked bathers at Bath. Swear he would not, save by the word ' Forsoothe,' and in the fragrance of martyred sanctity he died. There he stood in frozen ecstasy above the black stream of laughing careless boys, saying for ever his recorded words to the first Eton boys, ' *Sitis boni pueri, mites et docibiles et servi Domini !* ' Though England and Rome forgot him,

those who ate Henry's bread remembered him across the
ages. Eton was his shrine for ever, and the Eton *Carmen*
was sung of thousands in his honour :—

> ' *Sonent voces omnium*   *liliorum florem*
> *Digna prosequentium*   *laude Fundatorem*
> *Benefacti memores*   *concinamus qualis*
> *In alumnos indoles*   *fuerit regalis.*'

The Chapel was separated from Antechapel by a stone
screen and mountainous organ-loft. Sheaves of musical
piping filled the intervening space, cut off a few feet from
the arch, like stalks of Brobdingnagian mare's tail. Idols
of St. George and King Henry were balanced on columns
on each side of the organ. On the other side the pipes
were strangely embellished with what were variously
described as centipedes or moulting angels. Passing
under this melodious leaden herbage, the long aisle led
through the centre of the Chapel altarwards between rows
and rows of polished seats facing each other. The rows
nearest to the aisle were known as the *knifeboard*, owing
to their bleak and limited comfort. The rest reached
back to the double sets of top-heavy stalls and carved
canopies that rose like petrified cypress-trees, trained
against the walls, and completely covering the beautiful
mediaeval frescoes of Our Lady's miracles, which it had
been thought fit to conceal for ever from Protestant eyes.
Above them was set a mighty acreage of modern glass,
like strips of garish bunting, ordered by the square yard,
and stretched between the old grey pillars. As a climax
of clashing colour, the great East window dominated the
whole building with a rush of crude and glaring light.
It had only been achieved by a window tax mercilessly
plied on the boys of a previous generation. Gigantic
Apostles, Gargantuan Evangelists filled whole lights in
the window, wearing, as the boys thought, straw hats
rather than the nimbus and brandishing well-bound
leaving books to show that, though rejected by the world,
they had at least not been expelled from Eton. They
were figures that a Rubens might have painted, had he

been armed with a mop and assorted pails of distemper. In the top-centre was depicted an Ascension which some boys, judging by the ring of Apostles with stretched arms and upward faces, had mistaken for an early case of blanket-tossing. Below stood a Calvary, stark and white against appalling clouds of sepia gloom, pleading, perhaps not always in vain, against the gods of the Palaestra and the Playing Fields.

Within ten minutes every morning the Upper School poured in to the fane before the slow swinging Chapel bell wound up with a few hurried and frantic notes, as a signal to all within hearing to run, for it meant the organ was booming and a strange procession was proceeding up the aisle. First came two Sixth-Form files of Oppidans and Collegers in their stick-up collars, advancing neither at a stroll nor at a stride, but with a rhythmical precision, as though preparing to step an altar dance, until they suddenly seemed to think better of it, and passed discreetly aside to right and left to immerse themselves in prayer, while the rest of the School stood bolt upright. Dr. Warre had objected to this prayer as ' bastard ritualism,' but it went on. There was no variation in the *ram*, as it was called by a football metaphor, unless the older hands allowed a new arrival in the Sixth to pace solemnly ahead of the line to the amused gaze of the onlookers. Immediately behind the Sixth stalked the Head, and switched to his desk to the right. Behind him again came the Holy Poker, the white-whiskered bedesman carrying a silver bauble over his shoulder with the air of a nonchalant cricketer carrying his bat. His duty consisted of letting the Provost and Vice-Provost into their high canopied box seats, where their boots were liturgically screened from public view. At Eton boots, for some reason, are carefully scrutinised in public. A boy's standing in the School can be summed up by hasty glances at the colour of his cap and the elegance of his boots. Buttoned footwear are the first step in social success. Patent leathers denote, of course, that

glittering peaks have been reached. Only *Pops* wore
pumps in the street. Chapel was always pleasantly
devoted to social scrutiny, which had the effect of
ensuring a toilet that Early School could not evoke from
her unwilling patrons. Hair was generally brushed and
pomaded, and a few *Pops* shaved away the down, which
they alluded to as their damned bristles.

The Provost and Vice-Provost faced East, while the
School sat facing North and South. A few unhappy
wights sat on the bare altar steps facing to the West.
Only when the Creed was intoned did the whole School
luff to the East upon the sudden organ breeze. The
religion of Eton was High and Dry, remote from the waters
of strife, pompous and dignified. The choir gave it the
stamp of Cathedral service. In doctrine it was heavily
surcharged with the orthodoxy of Hornby and Warre,
who lived in a cloistered world, where neither sceptic
nor nonconformist was considered. The real religion of
Eton is an ethos, an atmosphere, a memory. Sheer
beauty of surroundings can affect the soul and endow it
with some sense and craving for the beautiful. Words
or sermons cannot mould the Etonian. It was something
more subtle than intellect or heart that the organ-song
touched within, as it swept daily over seven hundred
heads, like a summer wind dragging prayers and preach-
ments like unheeded dust in its wake.

Peter felt the organ move under his soul. So intense
was the effect made upon him that he had to recall that
the effect was due to Lloyd in the organ-loft and the
ludicrous figure he often watched working the gas-engine
bellows under the stairway, reminding him of some
ghastly loon on the point of inventing perpetual motion.
There were days when the organ grew husky and had to
' stay out.' Lloyd, not to be outdone, led the choir with
a pitch pipe below. Peter's eyes would loll round the
mighty building till every stall and window, every detail,
every personage became part of the furniture of his mind—
the tall gas chandeliers inscribed with ' ESTO PERPETUA,'

the gigantic roof poised on corbels, and jutting with pendants like short, rounded stalactites in mid-air. And his eye would wander through the stalls until it lit on Provost and Vice-Provost, whom he imagined to be the older deities of the place, set aside like the Titans, while the brighter gods of Sixth Form and *Pop* held the real sway. Nothing looked sturdier than Hornby or frailer than Cornish. Cornish was the hero of a famous book sale, where he had been twitted with wishing to buy a Mazarin Bible, the most valuable of books. ' Oh, dear me, no,' he answered humbly, ' I have two better copies at home.' His reference to the College treasures was correct.

The Provost is generally a departed Head Master who lingers awhile instead of joining the heavenly circle immediately. His ghostly duties are shared by the Vice-Provost, also a retired master in the intermediate stage of bliss. Peter could not help looking sympathetically at the Vice-Provost when they chanted the Psalm concerning the burden of years after the three-score and ten. He would never have been surprised to find him one morning translated to one of the stained windows, caught like a haloed transparency upon the spectral rays that flooded the Chapel. Yet in the days when he had lived, his name had been great on the lips of the boys, and his House had fought many a fierce fight for the House Cup, insomuch that one of the hymns—' Lift up your heart, lift up your voice '—had been adapted to his use, and in the middle of the words the School used to chant his football cry to the organ, ' Cornishes ! Cornishes ! ' And the day had come when Cornish alone, in Upper Chapel, recognised the hymn for his own.

As the Head swung into his place, the whole School swung to attention, and the two Conducts, so called from the Latin for hirelings, followed to their desks. They made another odd-assorted pair, one very like a fine old purple-faced Renaissance prelate, the other a little pale, prim-looking curate of Victorian caricature. None knew

whence they came or whither they went. Day by day
they monotoned the services. Day by day they read the
Lessons, and twice a week chanted the Litany, not
without some timing on the stop-watches of their young
friends. Their familiar features thrown upon youth's
vision left a negative which few Etonians could not
develop in memory to a lifelike sketch. Their duties
were recitative, not spiritual. So far was the moral
life of the boys out of their keeping or ken that for
confession or ghostly advice a boy would have as
gladly confided in a *Joby*. Like the choir, they were
hired.

On Hornby's face no boy could read what was written.
He had been a Fellow of Brasenose with Pater, and never
tired telling of Newman and the Oxford Movement. For
forty years he had lived apart from the human race,
unquestioned and beyond appeal. As Head Master he
had ruled from the seclusion of Black Potts, a fishing
lodge once loved of Isaac Walton down the River, and
his rare appearances in the street had been occasion for
local excitement. In him there could be no alteration
or shadow of turning. He had attained. What more
could he require ? He had played in the Eton Eleven
and rowed in the Oxford Eight. He had been the greatest
of mountaineers. He had been seen during holidays
arrayed in Alpine rig, hacking glaciers with a climbing
axe, and shinning the most perilous pinnacles of Mt.
Blanc. He was possibly the only person in the Chapel
who, in his prime, could have scaled its outer wall. He
was a perfect Thucydidean scholar. He had attained all
that the power of his body and mind could attain, and now
he had fallen back into a kind of brooding contemplation.
He sat there watching what ? waiting for what ? Was
he a wasted force ? Was there an unfulfilled ambition
beating behind that capacious gown, niched beneath that
soaring canopy ? Had those piercing eyes ever looked
farther afar than the glaring East window ? Had ambition lain behind that stony satisfaction ? Peter might

well ask himself, but it is given to no boy to read the soul of a Provost.

All the School saw Sunday by Sunday was the solemn boxing and unboxing of old Hornby by Holy Poker, and his portentous advance to the Communion Table, his grey hair upright, and his red hood slung loosely over his giant shoulders like a rowing scarf adjusted after a brisk row. All they heard was the far-off mumbling of the Ten Commandments, with that quiet pomp and decency which Englishmen associate with the messages of Heaven. That he had flogged their fathers was all that most boys knew. Perhaps he had mistaken his vocation, and, as Warre should have commanded in the field, Hornby, the son and brother of Admirals, should have gone to sea instead of to seed. Ships were still his great interest, and his invariable query of the nautical was whether there would be another Trafalgar. He was ever wrestling with the great problem, whether iron ships could close with an enemy as in the brave wooden days of old, when Hornbies rode the sea. Was this the secret of his brooding at Black Potts ? When the School were dreaming of coloured caps during service, did he see himself in a cocked hat on a quarter-deck ? He would have been a great man in any commanding profession, had he not loved his ease. He had been too courteous to be a disciplinarian. Only with an effort of will could he screw himself to the pitch of dismissing a master. He had had a lazy man's affection for flogging as a remedy, and the amount of flogging under his régime was in fair proportion to the lack of discipline. In a sudden emergency he liked to strike home. When the boys made a scene in Chapel by trying to drown a new-fangled chant with the more familiar melody, Hornby gave prompt directions for them to be overpowered by the organ. In a sea battle he would not have hesitated to flood his magazines. On another occasion, when the boys were reported to be trooping across the river to the Windsor Races, he descended on Masters' field and, by hastily mobilising forces, held the vital points along the bank. He passed as a reformer through the accident of having become Head a few years before the old Statutes were repealed. He was credited with a humorous cynicism, the revenge of the great upon the littleness of the world. He had refused leave to Upper Boys to wear white top-hats lest, as he explained, they should be mistaken for bookmakers. The awkward and incoherent preacher was the most subtle after-dinner speaker in England. How felicitously he had referred in a Fourth of June speech to Lord Rosebery's Derby victory. Etons reckons her Bishops by the half-dozen and her Premiers by the couple, but most precious in her sight are those of her sons who have made the blue riband of the turf an Eton blue. Rosebery had done it with Ladas. Once, unconsciously, Hornby had given a sure racing tip to the School. A certain noble Duke had asked special leave for his son to go to Ascot to witness what the Duke confided to Hornby was a certainty. This fact Hornby had to explain to another boy, to whom he refused leave, with the result that the ducal tip spread rapidly through the School, and enabled many an honest shilling to be turned at the expense of the bookmakers.

To such as Peter Hornby was beyond the clouds, almost Jovelike when he uttered the curses of the Commination Service in Chapel. Ullathorne had once approached him in the course of a deputation which a few pious masters and boys arranged to petition for an Early Communion in the College Chapel. Owing to the rule of fasting, they mentioned that boys otherwise were compelled to go to the parish church down town. ' You do not expect me to prevent them,' was the crushing reply with which Hornby slaked their High Church zeal.

Besides Warre and Hornby and Miss Evans, there sat in the stalls two venerable relics of bygone Eton—old William Carter, ' Billy the Bursar,' the last of the Eton Fellows elected on the old Foundation, and Henry Luxmoore. Carter had been a really efficient Tutor, but so stern that boys often left early to avoid being up to him. He was Lower Master in the Fifties, and was the last living witness of the famous fight in the Playing Fields when Ashley had fought to the death.

Luxmoore, whose initials were H. E. L., had been known as ' Satan ' among the boys, and to Peter he did not seem unlike Milton's hero as he sat with long snowy locks and outstretched, ring-emblazoned hand and faraway eyes in his stall, listening to the weary round of preachers, or contemplating the gorgeous Burne-Jones tapestry of the Magian Adoration, which he had presented to Chapel. He had come to Eton, bringing the aestheticism of Oxford. He was a devoted follower of Ruskin. That he was at heart a pre-Raphaelite had been successfully concealed from Hornby, but he stood against the claims of the exact sciences and Teutonic aspects of life. Ainger used to say that he himself kept one foot in Philistia and one out. But Luxmoore planted both his out, unlike Arthur James, who long strove to accompany Oscar Browning's tastes until one evening, when Brahms was played in Browning's rooms, and James moved to the corner where Munfort sat grimly inattentive, and said, ' Philistia, be thou glad of me ! '

Luxmoore had approached Watts for the Sir Galahad, which Watts himself preferred to give the School, but the Burne-Jones tapestry was his own gift. Luxmoore's shyness kept his great aesthetic powers in the background, and even the pupils he most influenced were reached by correspondence, not by interviews. He was an artist to his finger-tips, but with a sense of order and discipline and promptitude. He disliked the Balliol cult of success, which appealed so strongly to Warre and Hornby. His works included lay sermons on the Resurrection and personal chastity. Hard toil and fine perceptions were his cure and consolation in a wayward and Philistine world. Humour and good sense militated in him against the intolerance of the gouty, and left him one of the few Tutors who influenced his pupils in after-life. As he went his peaceful way, inveighing against the ugliness of modern Eton builders, or sketching in exquisite colours amid the miniature gardens of Tangier Island, a slight aroma of romance blew through the ink and paper memories of his life. That he was different to other Tutors was all the School perceived, but to those who knew he was the noblest epitome of Eton.

The younger masters sat in stalls, or when on duty in desks. Though there was some bartering of work in desks for so much correcting, few absented themselves from voluntary attendance, for the Head watched for sceptical as well as aesthetic tendency. Doubt in one article of the itemised faith was to him doubt in all. He was credited with preventing a Unitarian relative of Matthew Arnold from becoming Captain of the School. Any unorthodoxy in the Sixth he met with studied sarcasm. It was true he had come to accept Shelley as an Eton institution, but he still held out against Swinburne, whose tardiness in School he remembered, and attributed to French novels. He spoke of him to the Sixth as old Butler used to speak of Byron to Harrow boys, like old mother hens who found the School had hatched wicked and far-soaring merlins, a danger to all subsequent chicks. Swinburne was long rebuffed at Eton, where his old teacher, Mr. Cooksley, ventured to criticise the mock Greek choruses of his *Atalanta in Calydon*. He was allowed in the total absence of any other Etonian poet to write the great Ode celebrating the four hundred and fiftieth anniversary of the College. Often his lines figured as versions for Greek Iambics, but, like Fielding, greatest of Etonian novelists, Swinburne was not admitted to the School Library.

So was orthodoxy notably preserved. Neither Ritualism nor Scepticism found any encouragement, and the Services gave rise neither to thought nor enthusiasm. To Peter Upper Chapel became a refuge and a sanctuary, a cooling choral oasis in summer and a joyous warmth of the soul in winter. The more unhappy he became in the

P

narrows of Mr. Morley's warren, the more consolation he
found in the majestic spaces of St. Mary of Eton. The
breath of the organ was balsam to his mind, and he could
forget the daily round and dulness of life in the throb of
worship which sometimes stirred through the whole
School. There were only two disadvantages, the sermons
and the hired ' canaries ' who, with some muscular
assistance from Mr. ' Thunderguts,' rendered the Sunday
anthem, while the languid School stood to attention or
thumbed their watches. The length of most anthems
was known to a second. A little diversion was sometimes
obtained by loudly singing a hymn like ' Conquering
Kings ' in the unauthorised form of ' Kinquering Congs ! '
And the familiar trap in the lines ' Can a woman's tender
care cease toward the child she bare ? ' was invariably found to contain the feminine of bruin. Masters
whose names or nicknames occurred in the Psalms were
closely scrutinised to see if they turned an eyelash. One
unfortunate youth, who was subject to blushing, or
smoking, as it was called, was always made a cynosure at
the words, ' He shall but touch the mountains and they
shall smoke,' with the happy result of reducing him to
instant crimson.

The tradition of ludicrous sermons was maintained, and
any very egregious utterance was liable to softly pedalled
irony. Compliments to the School sandwiched between
moralisings were received with time-honoured appreciation. From the Head's country came a preacher, who
lived long in Eton memory as the preacher of the worst
sermon remembered. The ordinary sermon is forgotten,
but a certain distinction belongs to the worst under any
heading. The worst novel, the worst sermon, or the
worst poem in the language survive. The School had
acquired an ear for the absurd in metaphor, and laughed
when they were told they could not scrape away the rock
of eternity with their finger-nails, as their fathers had
laughed before them when the old Fellow, preaching at
Dr. Hawtrey's funeral, remarked, ' My young friends, you

would have laughed if you had seen the maps we had to use in those days,' and laugh they did. And they laughed again when the Reverend ' Jumps ' Jones began a sermon, ' My dear brethren, last Sunday I told you all about the Seraphim. This Sunday I will tell you all about the Cherubim.'

It was seldom that moralities were pressed from the pulpit, a form of interference which Lord Melbourne once resented on behalf of English gentlemen. Peter listened to a worthy master nicknamed the ' Pi ' preaching on the rather unpopular and unsporting text which to Englishmen covers the most respectable and least respected of the commandments. The School listened good naturedly to all that voice and sincerity could say on the matter. However well and nobly put, adjuration to chastity comes against the British grain. No Semitic formula of domestic hygiene, though sanctified by the holy mediaeval Church, has yet availed against the Aryan or English code, which will not allow the sinning male to be excommunicated or cut. On the contrary, he will always be admired or tolerated. Nevertheless, Eton is far from the dark spot imagined by the low-bred Press, or by Nonconformist hypocrisy. Athletes, to be successful, have to be ascetic of their bodily powers and scholars have plenty to absorb the glow of their youth. Etonians allow liberty of morals among themselves, and the boy who wishes to be *pi* is supported by the code. But he must not infringe another's view-point. The majority pass through the School tolerant of others, amused by the exaggerations of gossip and, however bored by the pious, unattracted by evil. If a boy is forewarned by experience of the stronger temptations which will meet him in the outside world, the experience is cheaply bought.

An Etonian may take his own line provided he does not assert piety in public. Peter made the curious mistake of expressing approval of the sermon just mentioned, and found that he had immediately placed himself in a new category. He joined Socston the following day in front of the College Bookseller. Socston, whose life was above reproach, immediately cut him dead, for the prig is kicked in Fourth and shunned in Fifth Form. Half an hour later Peter burst angrily into his old friend's room and demanded an explanation. Socston was friendly. ' You mustn't lose your hair. Come in here when you like, but I can't be seen with you outside. I might as well walk the street with a parson.' ' But you 're *pi* too,' stammered Peter. ' But I don't say so,' was the answer, ' and I have to keep in with the *bloods* if I am ever to get my boats. They don't want Noah himself in the Ark if he 's going to talk *pi*.' ' But I never did. I only said I liked the sermon,' said Peter. ' Well, that was bad enough,' said Socston, ' but Frencher says that nobody can pass your room after Prayers without being offered a tract, and that you begged him for his mother's sake not to drink beer in " Tap." ' Peter broke into angry repudiation, but he could see that Socston's look of scorn augured ill for their companionship. ' Why, I often drink in " Tap " myself,' he insisted, and by way of dissociating himself with piety he added desperately, ' And I know a fellow well at Evans's who says he doesn't believe there can be a God.' The effect on Socston was simple. ' That 's just the sort of thing an ass in Miss Evans's would say. Don't be a barnyard jackass.'

In his puzzled religious state Peter used to stare at the picture of Sir Galahad presented by Watts to Upper Chapel, which hung between the pulpit and Lupton's Chantry. A beautiful white cloud broke like a puff of incense over the knight's head. The gentle feminine face and the clasped hands of the knight seemed remote from the hearty Eton ideal. The white carthorse, with bowed head and plodding gait, symbolised a humble drudgery surrounded by life's tangled mysteries. Perhaps it conveyed this world's sadness with wistfulness of the next. Perhaps it was only a Tennysonian poster.

Peter studied it long, but failed to gather any religious impression from the masterpiece. He came to the conclusion that Sir Galahad, had he been at Eton, would have been a *Tug* something like Ullathorne, but not in armour —perhaps in padding and playing for College at the Wall.

CHAPTER XVIII

WAR AND WORK

THE wearisome Boer War had become continuous with Eton life. Existence at Eton without the far-thrown shadow of the veldt seemed remote, though Eton's relation to an outside world became clearer. There was a life, then, beyond the Playing Fields, an encounter fiercer than the Football Cup, and foes more important than Harrow. Nevertheless, these were nearer to the eye and more vivid to the senses. And Eton was going down in defeat to Harrow year after year. Would the Boer War ever end ? Would Eton ever win at Lord's ? The strife beyond seas became as unreal as the spiritual warfare the boys were assured was always being fought in their midst.

To Peter the novelty of school life and the war had soon disappeared. The course of both continued without respite, dull and arduous with perhaps an occasional red-letter day to break the monotone. As in war, so at School, the red days are as rare as the pitchy black, for routine and the slow advance of event are grey. But early in the new Summer Half one of life's brilliant memories swam into Peter's ken. Early School and breakfast despatched, he was on his way, with a carefully concocted map of Asia Minor, on which, in view of ever travelling beyond Troy, the places were marked by their classical, not modern names. Constantinople was labelled Byzantium, and the Black Sea Euxine. Nothing counted better in examination than such fossil knowledge. Besides, he had in mind a page of Euripides, which Ullathorne told him was simple only to the simple. If the wise saw a problem in it, it was certainly lost on Peter, who was also trying to mutter over a few tags of his saying lesson, of which three were run through their minds weekly like old-fashioned drenches. As he emerged from Judy's Passage a cheerful yell smote his ears, and he perceived a growing circle of boys engaged in the forcible assault of Mr. Broadpen's House, from which flags were waving and missiles descending. Socston was running past, his books tumbling from under his elbow, the conventional niche for carrying them at Eton. ' What is it all for ? ' cried Peter. ' Mafeking has been relieved ! ' shouted the other, ' and the fellows are going to smash "Broader's" for hoisting a Boer flag.' Peter looked in vain for the offending flag amid the Union Jacks and coloured shirts hoisted to the windows. Before his patriotic susceptibilities could be shocked, he found himself in the firing-line, exchanging handfuls of gravel and armfuls of books for volleys of sugar, which whizzed through the broken windows from within. Pane by pane was cracked amid uproarious cheers. The crowd grew, and the defence, not knowing why they were attacked, waxed fiercer. Whitewash, mortar, chips of brick and stone riddled the air or fell in chunks from the devoted mansion. As the besiegers approached nearer, cold water, cheap crockery, and enamelled tubs were dropped on them amid excitement which was unquenchable. In vain a few masters walked through the riot, dissuading, pleading, or threatening. The boys had seen red, and the pent furies of youth were not relaxed until the last pane had been smashed and the Boer flag had disappeared, leaving no trace as to its origin.

Cheer rose upon cheer, and the enthusiasm for destruction spread, for the windows of Mr. Christopher's House began to vomit books round the next corner until there was a heap several feet high of Eton Latin Grammars, blue *Poetae Graeci*, red *Scriptores Romani*, brown *Sertums*, green Latin Verse *Gradus*, Liddell and Scott's Lexicons, and the sombre Latin Dictionaries of Sir William Smith.

When all was over the bowed and philosophic figure of the 'Broader' himself was seen advancing from his lair behind some miserable cropped shrubs and surveying the destruction without a word. With one grim glance over his shoulder, as though he was looking at a particularly filthy piece of exercise, he turned and disappeared. His phlegm received an ironical cheer, which was drowned in the sudden thunder which greeted the announcement from the direction of School Yard that a whole holiday had been granted in honour of the greatest siege since the relief of Gibraltar. It was maddening to think that Baden Powell was not an Etonian. At this moment an Archdeacon who had been preaching at Eton drove past, waving his hand under the delighted impression that the cheering was for him.

Mafeking Day was bright in Eton annals. Who can forget the spontaneous outburst of colour, the great red flags with their black skulls and crossbones hanging from Miss Evans's, the general exhibition of bright-hued football shirts like a harlequin's laundry, the white and purple scarves round the windows of College extending to the island lamp-post which stood in Weston's Yard? With the casting aside of books there was a rush to the River. The new Club on Queen's Eyot was auspiciously sampled. The days of Surley Hall had been numbered, and as the pull to Monkey Island was beyond the rowing reach of untrained boys, Queen's Eyot between the two had been acquired. Temporary landing-places and refreshment rooms were erected. It was to become the great River mark dating from the Warre dispensation. It was a cheap Club to which all *wet-bobs* were expected to subscribe their half-crown. The Eton College Boating Club went up in a mass to inaugurate the new island. The lordly choices in the Eight pulled out in pair oars. The host of Upper and Lower Boats in outriggers and gigs followed, while the River loafers and rag and bobtail of the bathing sheds forewent the pleasures of munching buns in the tepid shallows and made an effort to get up the River. Peter found himself squeezed into a gig with Socston and Frencher, coxing for them to Sandbanks, after which he was made to row.

Peter rowed like a galley-slave under the whips of chaff and scorn. He felt sore and blistered in thigh and finger-joint by the time they landed at Queen's Eyot. His arms were aching in their sockets, and his wind was coming and going like a leaky donkey engine. Hundreds were disembarking and crowding the hot wooden shanty, in which two servants of the newly-floated School Stores were slowly handing out the *sock*. They became slower and more confused with a hundred orders shouted at their head. It was no day for dawdling, and boys began to help themselves. The store was quickly overrun, and whatsoever things are buttered, whatsoever things are fruity or of good report among boy epicures were carried off, payment being deferred. The old *Jobies* had always given *tick*, the School Stores must be taught likewise. ' I don't think the shop will pay to-day,' murmured Socston. Frencher appeared with a huge seed cake, which they divided and nibbled in the grass. Socston collared six bottles of stone ginger-beer. Peter felt his exhausted frame rising pleasantly under cake-chunk and ginger-froth. He lay back as though slumbering in asphodel. With the muscles tired, the thirst roused and quenched, and the digestive juices as absorbent as cotton, what could be sweeter than well-won bodily rest ? And the evening was full of expectations.

Heavily and joyously they paddled back. Orders had come for the whole School to parade in the School Yard after dusk. In the green haze of summer darkness the boys crowded to this strange nocturnal Absence, where the masters were chivying the wobbling ranks of the School into some approach to military order. The streets were crowded with processions of bicyclists clad in lanterns and ready-made fancy dress. As the School followed to Windsor, the spectators lining the pavements increased in number and decreased in gravity. Soldiers were beating wildly on tin trays on which was gummed Baden Powell's portrait. Over the bridge there was a bellowing crowd, whose vulgarity caused a chill of reserve even amongst Lower Boys. The disgustingness of the plebs was not lost on the patricians. Up Windsor Hill to the Castle gates the drunken jubilation never ceased. It seemed curious that the relief of an unbeleaguered city, a few dead Boers, and an issue of private postage stamps could drive so many people into an ecstasy, beyond a combination of Booth and beer. When not howling obscene references to Mr. Kruger's family life, some of the spectators devoted their remarks to compliment the silent boys marching through the streets. ' Three cheers for Florit Etona ! Look at the rising generation, young 'eroes all o' them. Gawd bless them ! ' ' Cads all be damned ! ' was young Eton's comment.

By slowly struggling against the wallowing mob, shepherded by grunting policemen and ushers, whose ears were automatically closed to the unpleasant dialect of the Windsor slums, the boys were squeezed into the Castle Yard and given their last opportunity to serenade the gracious nominator of the Victorian era. She was waiting for them, and as mildly pleased to be serenaded as sixty years ago. Peter enjoyed the evening enormously, but there were members of Morley's House to whom an outing after *lock-up* under the supervision of masters was a tame proceeding. On his return, he found the staircase crowded with immature *bloods* discussing the day's event with some contempt. ' We might as well have been a charity school going down town in twos,' declared Frencher. ' It's bloody being shown off to a heap of cads as though we were taken to a school treat,' spoke Camdown major. ' I wonder they didn't give us each a bun and a souvenir mug.' ' I should like to see Windsor for myself after dark,' added Frencher. 'Then I vote we take the first chance we get of climbing out by the Library window,' suggested Mouler. ' I believe Paris by night doesn't compare with the royal borough,' whereat there was a general adjournment into the Library.

There were no signs of high literary interest or intellectual attainment in Mr. Morley's Library. On the walls hung sundry football groups in frames and the ribboned rules of Mr. Morley's Debating Society. The literary provender consisted entirely of novels and bound *Strand Magazines* in states of decreasing repair. The only recent addition to the room was a soiled testimonial, which the Debating Society had patriotically forwarded to Mr. Kruger at the outbreak of war, and which had been returned by the military censors for the supposed reason of an unnotified change of address. It could not be described as a choice or a chaste document, but it was pinned up as an appropriate decoration for Mafeking Day, for a red-letter day, when the immortal words of Albert Chevalier, delightful entertainer of a generation of Eton youth, seemed transferable to the nation as a whole :—

> 'The moke on his back wore a Union Jack,
> And Pa had his whiskers shaved !'

Chevalier at the Queen's Hall, Dan Leno at Drury Lane, the Egyptian Hall mysteries, and the diving at the Aquarium, all these past delights made Long and Short Leave pleasurable to Etonians.

School life in summer was pleasurable monotony. The River became to Peter nurse, mother, and mistress. Turning *wet-bob*, he passed every spare minute walking by her side, fondling her, or breasting her with his arms. Under the strong summer sun the current grew to a green transparency. The ribboned weeds moved like endless antennae along the River bottom. Flights of silver dace pierced the shallows like watery meteors, while an occasional and almost legendary Thames trout moved like a solitary Cyclops round his cavern. The Playing Fields became alive and white with cricketers, serious or dilettanti. There was a good deal of ragging till Mike's arrival or presence was heralded by his dogs. Every evening Mike made Mat Wright the pro. bowl at nets while he eliminated all play unbecoming to a gentleman.

Bathing became Peter's passion, and Athens was a perfect bathing-place. During the long afternoons he would swim up stream from the Acropolis with a few friends, and lie under the farther banks, where no water-men could see them, waiting for steamers or house-boats to pass by. A barge being towed or house-boats with broad bases pushing through the water afforded wonder-ful opportunities for being dragged through the foam. The race of bargees was an indignant and boy-hating race always, and it did them good to be splashed with water and selected taunts. In the evenings crowds came down to bathe, and the red glow of the sun dwindled into the hot brown dusk. Stag beetles came out of the decaying oaks and elms, filling the soft air with their whirlings. At Athens the chafers became almost a plague, and the bathers lined up with knotted towels in their hands and knocked them down by scores with broken wings. More and more chafers seemed to rise out of the very ground and fly towards the distant trees. Faster and more furious waxed the sport. A line of naked boys with towels round the loins sweated and struck through the air, bringing a chafer down at one blow, or cracking a neighbour's shoulders with another. It was good sport, and the red-hot sun turned in for *lock-up* like any boy keeping hours.

Queen's Eyot was always an effort to reach, but on half-holidays Absence was called there by a rowing master. The Club became popular, and began to be used by a number of Morleyites who had not paid their subscriptions, small as they were. This was noted by the Captain of the Boats, who bided his time, and one fell Monday every boy who had been to the Eyot on the Saturday without being a subscriber received a polite note requesting him to visit the Captain of the Boats between schools. It was soon rumoured what this meant, and Morley's supplied no less than a dozen candidates,

including the son and heir of a famous London store.
As this youth was broad in the beam, his fellow-convicts
eased their own apprehensions by remarking how much
the magnitude of his sufferings would surpass theirs.
' You 'll be like a giraffe with a sore throat, acres of pain,
and it will be a *pop-cane* too,' suggested Frencher, who
was one of the delinquents. Peter and Socston had both
paid their subscriptions, and naturally enjoyed the
moment. The guilty ones were leaving in a body for the
ordeal, all except the heir of much Empire trade, who was
still trying to get sick leave out of the Dame. ' He won't
know me. I 'll shirk,' he wailed to his mates. ' You 'll
get it double to-morrow,' smiled Frencher. ' Will nobody take my place ? I 'd give a sovereign to any one.'
' Make it two ! ' shot Socston, who was short of cash.
' Thirty shillings anyhow ! ' ' Then have the dirt tanned
out of your hide ! ' ' All right, two *quid*.' ' Pay in
advance, and I 'll go and take your place. He 'll not know
me from Adam.' The fat one sighed, and placed two gold
pieces in Socston's palm. Without a word Socston
joined the others. Half an hour later they came back
with six mighty welts each across their legs. Their faces
looked very blank, and the tale they told on their return
was a sore one indeed. Socston tried in vain to make
his bravado equal the sting he felt every time he
stretched his legs. ' My God, we did catch it,' and he
decided that in future his price would be five guineas
inclusive. For the vengeance of the gods has to be felt
to be appreciated.

Punishment from a *Pop* was feared far more than the
official flogging from the aged Head, which was more a
rite of degradation than an infliction of pain. Such pain
as was exhibited appeared principally in the Head's
grieved surprise at the wickedness of the culprits, but the
Lower Master seemed perfectly aware of so well established
a fact, and only sought to transfer any pain he might feel
as quickly as possible to the boy. Among Old Etonians
swishing remained a staple joke and an honourable memory.

At Eton it was regarded as a joke by the spectators. Only the very youthful trembled or wept. Peter often felt ashamed that he had not figured on the Block, and almost envied Cheener, a small, much-chaffed youth, whom he found mourning the appalling prospect of facing the Lower Master on the morrow. Cheener was a pure *scug* who spent his afternoons like Shelley trying to set fire to old stumps in South Meadow with a magnifying lens. One afternoon he had been so unfortunate as to flash the canary of a neighbouring Dame into fits in the course of his experiments with light, and a complaint had been made to the Lower Master. His friends rendered him inconsolable by their first-hand narratives of encounters on the Block, which, taken down in black and white, read like scenes on the guillotine. Cheener, having been wrought to the necessary pitch, agreed to submit to any process they thought likely to save him pain during the inevitable *swishing*.

After twelve the following day Peter witnessed for the first time the noble feat of arms, which can only be performed decorously and dexterously on the Eton Block. Passing from pupil-room, he met Ullathorne hurrying out of College. ' *Swishing*,' remarked that sapient youth. ' I have had to get two College fags to hold down. Look through that window and see what it is to be *swished* to make an Eton holiday.' Peter joined the excited throngs who were peering into Lower School, exultant over the fate of others. The window was opened, and the monosyllables of the Flea could be heard as he harangued evildoers. The first boys he ordered to sit on the Block and go, the second to kiss the Block, but with a rich twang which convulsed the spectators with laughter. A small boy was summoned for incorrigible idleness, and the Flea decided on a victim. ' You naughty, naughty little boy ! ' and he called for a birch, which was handed to him in the form of a huge bouquet of plaited twigs by a Praepostor. Meantime two grinning helpers solemnly lowered the boy's trousers and held up his crumpled shirt as acolytes

hold up the edge of a vestment. Sighting his mark, the
Flea let go the birch with a motion similar to a cut in
cricket. The birch fell with the sound of many waters.
In fact, a *swishing* is onomatopœic, for the act and the word
sound alike. Peter felt more and more sick as the Flea
laid in again and again, until the floor was covered with
pieces of birch, and the victim's skin became minutely
but harmlessly lacerated. As for the victim, whom Peter
had expected to see carried out on a stretcher, he was seen
holding up his unbraced trousers in a hurried effort to
collect souvenirs of the birch from the littered floor. The
Flea, noticing this signal lack of decency, only inquired,
' Can it be that you glory in your shame ? '

It was a historic scene in the most historic schoolroom
in England, the oldest still in daily use in the world. The
dates on the pillars, and the still earlier ones on the shutters,
gave some colour to the tradition that the pillars were
taken from the Spanish Armada. The names cut on the
wood were centuries old. On one shutter was the erased
name of John Greenhall, a convicted highwayman. In
the pillars were hacked enormous holes and slits, while a
wooden partition divided the room into two class-rooms.
Peter was leaving the scene, when a young *Tug* ran out
to announce to the Fifth Form offenders waiting outside
Chambers that the Head was away, but the Flea had very
kindly consented to take his place. A groan of amused
horror arose from several large gentlemen, who were
waiting with no severer prospect than of being brushed
by the majestic Head. To be bloodied by the Flea was
a very different experience. Unfortunately it was true.
There was the Flea waiting for them in his Lower Master's
cap, with black rosette and crossed bands instead of the
ordinary tasselled mortar-board. The white rudiments of
whiskers did not conceal the stern lines of his mouth and
jaw, and his twinkling eyes did not counteract his itching
fingers. After expressing horror at the crimes for which
they were mulcted, he invited them to follow him to the
Head's Room, the panelled sanctuary set with Greek

reliefs and the glorious names of those who had won the
Newcastle Scholarship and Medal. The Praepostor
of the day and the holders-down followed, the former
handing out the birches like a loader, for the law of
hygiene did not permit the same birch to be used twice.
One by one the Fifth Formers were sent squirming about
their business. The last to be dealt with was several
inches taller than his executioner, and was nervously
brushing an immaculate silk hat. Though on the verge
of *Pop* and the Eleven, he had been detected smoking,
and appeared thoroughly displeased with the situation.
' Mind you stand well up to me,' the tall gentleman
whispered to the *Tugs*, for it was customary for compas-
sionate holders-down to catch the stinging tail of the
birch on their knees before it twisted round the bare
thigh. Both *Tugs* obeyed, but a little obviously, for the
Flea ordered them both to take a pace to the rear, and
proceeded to throw in some prodigious *swiping*. Every
blow broke like a wave on the beach, swish! swash!
swaush!!! The birch broke! It was a famous *swishing*,
and the Flea came down quite warm and panting, with
the veins protruded on his hands. But the grim butchery
was not over for the day. The School Clerk reported a
tiny delinquent waiting in the antechamber of pain
below. It was Cheener, looking very minute and miserable compared to the lordly gentleman who, pale with
fury, was picking his way out as delicately as Agag of old.
The Flea inquired the nature of his offence, and was told
that he had frightened his Dame's canary with a mirror.
' Naughty, naughty boy,' quoth the Flea, ' take down your
trousers.' The trembling child was not, however, unprepared for the emergency. As he bent over the Block,
it was noticed that his body skin was not the same colour
as his hands and face. ' What have you been doing to
your posteriors ? ' and the terrible Flea stayed his shot.
The holders-down relaxed, and the victim resumed the
vertical. There was no doubt. A square foot of his
periphery had been carefully coated with a thick liquid

mahogany-coloured shock-absorber. The Flea shook internally, and the Praepostor laughed aloud. ' You naughty boy, go home and be washed.' And the guilty fled, marvelling at his great escape. *Solvuntur tabulae risu*, as Ullathorne remarked when telling the tale in College later. The Flea's boys could always tell when there had been a *swishing* by the good humour of their Tutor at lunch. But this day he seemed almost radiantly disposed.

CHAPTER XIX

CHANGE UPON CHANGE

DURING the Christmas holidays of 1900 the old Queen, worried by a succession of British disasters in the field, and possibly by repeated Eton failures against Harrow, gave up her most gracious ghost. The Easter Half was imminent, and there was a wild but unrealised hope that the holidays might be prolonged by the national mourning.

The gloom which brooded upon the Castle was reflected in the College. Like funeral mutes the members of that loyal Foundation proceeded to Chapel. Like pontifical undertakers the Provost and Head entered to the sad notes with which Lloyd marked the grief peculiar to the Royal School. With bowed heads the two great Victorian Head Masters mourned their neighbour and patron. Warre's whole career had run parallel to hers. Born in the year of her accession, he had become Head not long before the first Jubilee, since when each had reigned in uncontested popularity. On that occasion his famous dream-composition in her honour had been revealed to him in sleep when he heard the chorus ' Victoria, Victoria ' beating in his ear. Already his military mind was seeking some striking manœuvre in which to express the grief of the boys. As the day of the royal funeral approached, he launched a broad strategic plan to enable the Volunteers to be brought into dignified action with the un-uniformed part of the School. A rehearsal was ordered on Agar's Plough. The Volunteers paraded and marched in their light blue and grey, followed by the whole School in double file across the Playing Fields, cutting up a muddy path in their trail. The pomps of death were symbolised by an empty cab and the Volunteer Band proceeding slowly down the line. Expectation that the Volunteers would fire three volleys was disappointed, but the cab, with Wise's grinning flyman on the box, was received with all the funeral evolutions. Volunteers presented rigid arms, while the School removed their hats with as pious a presentation of grief as seemed consistent with the general idea of the manœuvres.

On the solemn day when the time drew near to bury the Victorian era the Volunteers paraded in the School Yard. Their grey uniforms had appeared at no funeral since Mr. Gladstone's. The undrilled civilians made long black, irregular lines, division by division. The order for march was given, and the School tramped out slowly in silence, broken only by the thud of boots on the cobbles, through the School gates and down High Street, past the familiar shops each set with the mourning shutter Eton shopkeepers display for a death at the Castle or in the Cloisters, or among their own restricted number. Across the Bridge they marched, and by the South Western Station round the Castle, until they emerged at the top of the Long Walk and were posted between the gates of the Park and entrance of the Castle. For two hours the loyal cohort of Etonians waited until the first boom of the eighty-one guns announced the arrival of the dead Queen. Minute by minute the guns marked the sands of her life, while the raucous bells of Windsor tolled in medley. The time still delayed and delayed. The Dead March broke with relief on their ears, and from the gates the Life Guards advanced in ironic guardianship of the dead. The tiny coffin weighted with Crown and Sceptre toiled slowly up the hill, drawn on a gun-carriage by sailors with improvised ropes and wearing their straw hats. Immediately behind the coffin strode the new, weary-faced King, the Duke of Connaught, and the Duke of Albany, recently an Eton boy, and all the male members of the Royal House, for whose spiritual welfare Eton doth ever pray. Many vari-fated Kings had come to pay their last tribute to the Queen—Kings like George of Greece and Carlos of Portugal, whose assassins waited the hour, Kings like the shabbily satanic Leopold of Belgium and the dapper Kaiser, for both of whom was reserved the world's loathing hate. Nearer and nearer the coffin approached, and the last lap home commenced. With short hoarse cries the officers of the Eton Volunteers ordered arms to be presented, but not hearing the word 'reversed,' many presented arms as for an ordinary salute. With some stage whispering from behind, and some prompting from Generals in the procession, rifles were turned to the proper angle. Five minutes later the coffin had disappeared into the Castle. Doubtless, had she seen the confusion that befell the Etonian ranks, the old Queen would only have smiled. It would have sufficed her that Eton's love closed her public life. *Fuit Regina!*

The gates of the Castle closed, and only the Royal Standard at half-mast fluttered over that pile of heavy gloom. From the Windsor Cloisters arose the bitter sweet aroma of ten thousand dying flowers. The mourning visitors retired into silences as deep as the silence of the vaults under St. George's Chapel. In the great Mausoleum the ashes of the Prince Consort never moved.

Etonians marched solemnly home to tea. They were all glad to have seen a historic scene. It was something to have lived under two sovereigns. Their fathers and grandfathers had known nothing but Victoria, and now it was over. It was a pity the old lady had not waited another month before dying, for they lost the holiday for her accession, and the new King had acceded in the holidays. It was a real pity!

So was Victoria carried away, and a new cog clanked in the rusty wheel of time. And Eton too, Mother Eton was revolving, changing before her own bewildered eyes. Mike had been succeeded by Mr. Quills as instructor to the Cricket Eleven. In a way it was a key position to the life of the School, and Quills's caricature appeared duly in *Vanity Fair*, the last of 'Spy's' gallery of Eton masters. As an organiser of victory, a cricket Carnot, he promised well, though there was a blot on his sporting escutcheon, of which boys only spoke in whispers. Was he not the bowler who, at his Captain's bidding, had bowled five wides to the boundary to prevent Oxford following on in a celebrated 'Varsity match? Were not the two scandals of late Victorian cricket Mold's unfair bowling and Quills's wides to the boundary? Old Eton cricketers looked serious when they read the name. He must not teach the boys tricks. Eton must win on the straight bat that Mike had slavishly taught. Quills himself was an enigma. He coached the Cricket Eleven, and he was capable of taking the Sixth in Greek grammar. Yet he was the least literary of the Classical masters—a great Classic in flannels, a Philistine under his gown, the perfect exponent of the Cambridge School. Whether at Sapphics or cricket, he knew every stroke in the game.

Boys noticed other changes. Spottiswoode succeeded Ingalton Drake, the bookseller. The old system of division Praepostors was eliminated, the masters and School Office doing the work previously done by the boys in turn. The historic and original rooms of *Pop* were destroyed, and the Eton Society migrated into the Old Christopher, which, at the same time, was abandoned as a boarding-house. Ullathorne cherished a belief that the name of the Christopher descended from Catholic days, and that once a symbol showing Christopher carrying the Christ-child had been hung as a lesson to the teachers of lessons, until the Reformation had reduced its status to that of a Pub. The new century, however, had wonderfully restored its splendour. With the advent of *Pop* the old inn became the Eton Downing Street. There was a scholastic change, and the morning schools were prolonged from three-quarters of an hour to the full hour. Hitherto twelve o'clock school had been so overlapped by Chambers that it was often reduced to a half-hour.

Change followed change. Electric light was introduced

into the older Houses, and the candle-light, which had figured in Eton bills from the sixteenth century, flickered out for ever. Magnificent new Houses of stone and red brick began to arise, as sanitary and rectangular as inspectors could wish. A ' Ritz ' in red brick was even threatened upon the sacred site of the Timbralls. Parents and the Governing Body were loud in their admiration of the new Houses, which were certainly as sumptuous as second-rate family hotels. There were hot baths on each floor, and the passages were masterpieces of indirect ventilation. Except at the corners the rooms inclined to be identical in size and absence of character. The Bursar was looked upon as a rising authority in architecture, and was encouraged to crown the space between Miss Evans and Upper Chapel with an immense single chimney of brick, which for long was mercifully mistaken for the Eton steam laundry.

But the boys loved and preferred the old warrens, old fashioned and insanitary as they were, though the landings were dark in winter and stuffy in summer, though the tiny rooms slanted into each other, and the bricks crumbled in their fireplaces, and the knots in the old flooring had been carefully excavated with red-hot pokers, which had long since gone to dust themselves. As dwelling-places they were cramped, crooked, crazy, crumbling, curious, and almost incurable, but generations of boy-life had made them cosy, and each room remained familiar because it was different from its neighbour. Rooms which could be cheerfully nicknamed the ' Black Hole ' or the ' Coffin ' could be loved like home.

Though more reforms came under Hornby than in the whole period since the foundation, the School had settled to the tradition of doing the minimum of work. Hornby was content with carrying off a few University Fellowships and Prizes every year with well-trained *Tugs*, who could be afterwards added to the staff or paddocked in College livings. For the idle he invented ' yellow tickets,' but he had no desire to send Etonians to face the

world with an exhausted brain power. He was famous
for his own lateness in school, his boredom with his own
teaching, and his readiness in translation. As he said in
one of his after-dinner speeches, ' We didn't teach golf
or metaphysics. I don't know what we did, but we did
teach something.' As to the fate of Newcastle Scholars,
he was inclined to shrug his shoulders. As long as India,
Canada, and Ireland were under the beneficent sway of
Etonians, as long as Foreign Policy, come Tory or Radical
Government, was subject to his old pupils, he felt assured
of the world's peace. But Warre, in spite of his love of
athletics, was struggling against the contented languor
of Hornby's régime. The maximum of work could not
be attained, but the minimum might be discouraged as
a thing *quod Etona non miratur*. Warrę's conscience
still haunted the curriculum. Classical masters were
made to bear the burden of reform. Slowly they were
becoming educational Jacks-of-all-trade. Not the
Classics alone, but Geography, English History, and
French construe were added to their tasks. They were,
it is true, producing more variable wits among the boys,
but not the solid brain which the Classical mill had ground
in its undiverted course. To communicate so many
subjects was beyond perfect mastership, for a master
tied to a schedule of many subjects becomes a correcting
machine. Teachers are born, not trained. There is a wider
gulf than imagined between learning to teach and teaching
to learn, and it is harder to catch the ear of a class at Eton
than the ear of the House of Commons. Mr. Lamb taught
by suggestion rather than reprimand. Peter found appreciation for all his work. False inflexions were marked with
a smile, false quantities with a sigh. But he was never
hurried or vexed. He came to find in his Tutor the partner
of his hard work and the originator of all his success.

Though no Oppidan could be made to work hard unless
he was willing, a number like Peter worked to relieve the
tedium of games. A lure of constant School Prizes was
held out to them, and grateful Tutors repaid the least

signs of industry by richly bound selections from Mr. Ingalton Drake's expurgated shelves. Peter had accumulated Stevenson, Matthew Arnold (the Head would not have liked this, his favourite book for boys being the *Last of the Barons*!), Kingsley, and Lucas's *Open Road*. In College boys were professional *saps* and, as the price of their gowns and scholarships, were kept with inky noses to their desks. A King's Scholar low on a Trials list was as rare as an Oppidan leading one. To the Oppidan *Tugs* were dolefully identical and industrious. But two exceptions to the level average passed through College at this time, causing huge amusement in different ways. There was the ' Slack *Tug* ' and the ' Fat *Tug*.' The former was a scholar who had to be reprimanded for the Oppidan privilege of idling. The ' Fat *Tug* ' was a character who fell with a mirth-giving splash into the Eton pond. He must have been the fattest boy who ever went to School. Of him the prophets had written that he would be the first that ever burst the try-your-weight machine! Peter was one of the large admiring crowd who watched him attend his first Absence in a specially designed gown, which legend said had given Tom Brown sleepless nights to make. Good-humoured, vivacious, and scholarly, he broke Eton's monotonies and conventions whenever he appeared. In an Eton fives court he rolled about, Peter thought, like an elephant hunting a marble. A huge, cheering crowd came down to Cuckoo Weir to see him pass the swimming test. His success was a foregone conclusion, for not even a decuman or tidal wave, remarked Ullathorne, could have submerged him. He died young, leaving only the memory of his wit and good cheer with a generation who also were destined to die young.

The Winter Half came again, and Eton, ever-changing, sped to her changeless goal. The idleness and semi-suppressed mutiny in a house like Morley's were not typical of the School, which at least was never lazy. It was keenly and absorbedly occupied in itself. Boys had a choice of too many occupations. Masters were over-whelmed by the interlapping of the tutorial system. The School was not interested in Morley's, and as Morley's did not appear very interested in the School the inevit-able found its issue as surely as the rivulet finds the sea. Peter had been drawn into a literary group who fre-quented the School Library and read the *Spectator*. This affectation of *Tugs* and *saps* led to his complete ostracism at Morley's. Once as he came into lunch on a day of Transvaal disaster, somebody called out ' Pro-Boer ! ' which was generally taken up. ' I 'm not ! ' said Peter fiercely, for his father had been a soldier in Egypt. ' You must be. Don't you go and read the *Spectator* in the Library every week ? ' was the unanswerable reply. Peter tried to follow the reasoning. To be a *sap* was to be intellectual. Some Pro-Boers were intellectual. Some intellectuals read the *Spectator*. It seemed inconclusive.

Henceforward Peter took refuge in his new friends. Reaction was bound to come against the Philistine spirit prevailing. It was on its way, as a matter of fact, not through the masters but from the boys themselves. The old school of masters were impatient of religious or literary novelty. Warre and Hornby had suppressed anything connected with the Oxford Renaissance. The Head's idea of Heaven was based on a good military band transferred from the walls of Windsor to the celestial Jerusalem. To Ullathorne's fury, Hornby had forbidden the *Dies Irae* to be sung even in translation in the Chapel. Hornby's only spiritual moments, he insisted, had been at glacier tops. They had banished Oscar Browning for his art's sake. Joynes had to leave for his sympathy with the Irish cause. Salt had left as a Humanitarian. ' It was the vegetarianism that did it,' had been Hornby's grim farewell. Reaction was certain.

Meantime, individual boys or cliques, despised by their fellows, and not encouraged by the masters, desired and sought better things. There was solid reading of Ruskin and surreptitious talk of Omar. Charleston used to lend his copy of the *Yellow Book*, which had been kept out of the Library as decadent. When the initiated discovered Mr. Christopher was a contributor, their excitement knew no bounds. ' I bet Warre doesn't know,' said Ullathorne. ' The *Yellow Book*,' gasped Peter. ' M' Dame told me that a man got two years in Reading Gaol for writing one of the sonnets in it.' ' I wonder which,' said Ullathorne. ' Christopher deserves to go to prison for that last royal ode of his. He must have hopes of succeeding Alfred the Damned.' Charleston laughed. ' If we must have a hell, by all means let it be useful and include bad poets like other bad people.'

Charleston was an Eton type, the cultured son of a cultured father who might have been a Cabinet Minister for the asking, but preferred to give literary breakfasts to *littérateurs*, and collect *Etoniana* all his life. His boy had been brought up amongst the dilettanti, and, though he had avoided their decadence, he had become a gracious sceptic at fifteen, for he had read Gibbon in his holidays. Without any obvious effort, he won Distinction in Trials, and was being groomed by his Tutor for the Captainship of the Oppidans. Miss Evans had already marked him with her second sight into boys as a rising glory of her House. Though she was no more than a plain-minded woman, without the least instinct for books, she knew that books counted more than caps in the long run, though not in the short Eton canter. And though with her own farm and cows she brought up and fed fine fighting Elevens, she protected the *sap*. Once her House won the Newcastle. She was the matrix of the Lyttelton tradition, through whom she had overcome her conservative feelings and invited Mr. Gladstone on occasions to meet her boys at breakfasts. What Mrs. Yonge had been in the eighteenth, Miss Evans was in the nineteenth century. Both had borne down and survived all rivalry in the Eton matriarchy, and if any weakness could be found in their armour, it was a weakness for Bishops. Dame Yonge took the direct course of marrying her son

Edward to the natural daughter of the good Lord Holland, who obtained for his Etonian son-in-law the two Irish Bishoprics of Dromore and Ferns. Miss Evans took a milder interest in Colonial Bishops, and a brass plate was erected to commemorate the days when Bishop Selwyn trod her passages. The touch of sentiment she once allowed herself was kneeling for the blessing of a Bishop from her own House. Miss Evans had a fancy for unusual boys, and she rather enjoyed the cynic. Boys who were being over-actively disliked she used to send to the cottage over the way, whence she brought them back a year later strong enough to hold their own. She knew enough of human nature not to remain impartial. She disliked the weak evil-doer on sight, while she rather approved of the rowdy good-humoured type in whom might lurk an incipient Colonial Bishop. When her bell was muffled with socks and the curfew failed to ring one night, she was the most amused. When she introduced the common breakfast and a leading boy by way of protest poured the teapot up and down her table, she took no notice. Belonging to a less athletic era, she used to amuse the boys by speaking without proper reverence or exact knowledge of the leading champions. She had seen too many Captains of the Boats rise to splendour and pass into outer nonentity. Belonging to a less formal and less organised Eton, she allowed her boys to loiter outside her door after *lock-up*, to the furious envy of opposite Houses. She was distinctly pre-Warre, and Warre noticed her fossilised survival into a world which he had moulded afresh.

It was a great day for Peter the first time that Charleston invited him to have tea with Miss Evans herself. Charleston insisted that she was the sole Dame. 'There is one Dame, and her name is Jane Evans,' he muttered to Peter when Peter's Dame was mentioned. They entered by the familiar ever-open door in the whitewashed wall opposite the wistaria-clad cottage in Keate's Lane, the famous door entered and loved by generations of Evansites. Bishops and Statesmen, Captains of the Eleven, and winners of the Victoria Cross, have passed over that boy-worn threshold. Past the open stairs, and under panelled landings, Charleston led him through a long passage into a great timbered hall with a high gable-shaped roof set upon walls decked with the trophies of war and the chase. Antlers, spears, flags, and armour composed a fitter setting for the last of the Barons than for the last of the Dames.

A few guests sat with some boys at the large mahogany table. At the head sat Miss Evans, looking as though she had stepped out of the Sargent portrait, which hung behind her on the wall. Peter recognised her and her picture from each other. She had a slightly drawn, masculine mouth, and a straight short nose, but Job's patience, and humour besides were housed in her gleeful eyes. Over her whitening hair was set a whiter cap. She stretched out her strong hand to Peter, with a touch of the same easy power which was etched in the lines of her stately face. She was obviously worth any two House masters put together. 'Darley, come and sit next to me. Charleston has told me all about you, and some of my boys served with your father in Egypt. You had an uncle at this House. He came to Eton very young, because his parents went to India. He came very young. I remember him standing in petticoats at the bottom of the stairs. I was a strong young girl, and I carried him up under my arm.' Everybody laughed, and Peter felt as though he had found a mother in Israel indeed. Her boys showed a curious mixture of reverence and familiarity. She controlled them better than most Tutors, and naturally declined to be controlled in turn. When Warre issued an edict against the custom of calling ' Boy,' in order to economise the time of Lower Boys throughout the School, Miss Evans allowed her boys to keep the custom, which died out in most parts of the School. In vain the new-fangled Governing Body directed her numbers to be reduced. She wisely declined correspondence, but offered to interview them, which the Governing Body were also wise enough to decline. When necessary, she proved a match for her own boys. When a particular rowdy and scatter-brained boy was approaching the stage and stature of a swell, she would send for him and rather pathetically confide in him as the last friend of her declining years and the only hope of good order in her House. The astonished youth left her presence, and generally began kicking the first boy he found in the passage speaking above a whisper. This old lady held sensual boys in check, who were liable to go to the dogs when her influence was lost. She was the last Dame to have been *brosiered*, the Eton form of a strike against food conditions. To bring a Dame to her senses, boys used to eat steadily through her larder, calling steadily for more. When the larder was emptied, the *brosier* was complete. Miss Evans broke *brosiering* by producing unlimited quantities of salt beef !

Charleston, who would have been bullied into a prig at Morley's, had become quite sociable under her friendship without ceasing to be a scholar. ·It was understood that he might one day shed honour on the House, and he was left alone. He had decided not to communicate his misgivings as to Christianity to the Dame until he actually had to read prayers as Captain. He kept up a brilliant friendship with Ullathorne, with whom he was fond of discussing theology on lines that would have proved distressing to Warre and puzzling to Hornby, and to which Miss Evans would have decidedly said ' Rubbish ! ' He was fond of surprising Ullathorne and Peter, when he found them reading the ritual notes in the *Church Times* or discussing Lambeth Judgments, by dropping some naïve scepticism.

The three friends began to meet in Charleston's rooms, for Miss Evans allowed boys whom she trusted to dispense hospitality, in spite of a general rule that only fag masters and grandees could wander at will into other Houses. On these occasions Ullathorne sometimes did

a difficult Latin verse for them. Latin elegiacs, he
insisted, were so much easier than Limericks, in which
he pretended it was his highest ambition to win a competition. Masters at that time were competing for the
guinea prizes offered by the *Westminster Gazette* for Latin
verse. Ullathorne's sense of mockery compelled him
to enter solemnly for the rewards of doggerel. ' Do
finish this pentameter for me,' moaned Charleston, ' the
English runs—

    ' after wars peace is best, after strife tranquillity.'

' Try *ultima palma quies* as your ending,' said Ullathorne at a shot. So Charleston finished off a copy which
was eventually ' sent up for good,' containing, as Jenkinson announced in school, the best pentameter he had ever
known from the pen of a boy. Ullathorne was explaining
to Peter that the Rosary was a very appropriate devotion
for Etonians, as their Chapel had been dedicated to the
Blessed Virgin by the House of the Red Rose. ' Our
precious Founder would be particularly distressed, I
suppose, if he noticed the modern precautions taken
for the souls of Eton boys,' said Charleston mockingly.
Ullathorne's queer-shaped head drooped. ' I am afraid
the Governing Body think that Eton boys, like niggers,
have no souls.' ' Or that the soul is acquired with a
University degree,' suggested Charleston. Ullathorne
was not riled, but continued sadly, ' I dare say, though,
that the Head thinks an Eton leaving book sufficeth unto
Eternity.' Peter and Charleston were fond of bringing
out Ullathorne's mediaeval humour, one as the foil and
the other as the disciple. They went on to ask him what
would happen to the Eton masters in Purgatory. ' Purgatory,' said Ullathorne, ' is a spiritual steam-laundry
run with a sense of humour. Mike, for instance, will
have to bowl lobs to deceased Harrow batsmen. Morley
will have to write Odes in mediaeval macaronics.
Christopher will have to coach Charon's Eight up and
down the Styx. The Flea will be set the impossible

task of birching the Cherubs. The Reverend Dr. Borcher will be made to study theology. Gill will be given a dead imp to stuff and mount in a glass case. Maxse will have to learn Hebrew.'

There was a wild burst of laughter, and Peter threw himself on the floor, wriggling with glee. Ullathorne was too priceless. ' What will happēn to Jenkinson ? ' asked Charleston. ' Oh, saints don't go to Purgatory,' answered Ullathorne quietly.

The friends edited a little paper called the *Insider*, which was not printed, but hectographed and distributed to the initiated. They wrote it as a private protest against the dulness of the *Chronicle* and the vulgarity of the *X Magazine*, the flashy portent in Eton journalism at the time. Though endorsed by the high literary name of Gilbert Frankau, the *X Magazine* was suppressed by Warre on account of its approximation to American ideals. Though the *Insider* was the reverse of the *X*, its promoters felt that it would be suppressed if published. The sceptic Charleston and the orthodox Ullathorne agreed in their dislike of Sunday Questions, of which comic versions appeared from time to time in the *Insider*. Charleston reduced the story of Elisha, the mocking children, and the avenging bears to the form of an inquest on the bodies of the children. A quotation from *The Jerusalem Times* described how a gentleman of prophetic appearance gave evidence. Under cross-examination it was proven that he was the last to have seen the children alive. Yes, they had referred to his baldness. He may have used intemperate language. He had cursed, but he had not sworn. He had never owned a bear. He had no idea there were any in the neighbourhood. He believed they may have escaped from a travelling circus. No, he was no relation of Lord George Sanger, etc. It was clearly Charleston's concoction.

Another number carried some interesting notes from ' our sporting correspondent in Palestine,' wherein various Old Testament stories were reduced to terms of

Eton athleticism. In preparation for the Jericho mile, Elijah, ' that promising young Tishbite,' was credited with a record time when paced by his trainer Ahab in his chariot ! Peter felt shocked until he saw Ullathorne laugh, and he asked him whether it was right to laugh at holy things. ' Lord bless you, there 's not much holiness among Prophets and Patriarchs. As for the chosen Kings and Judges of Israel, no Y.M.C.A. could have held Solomon, and Samson was not a very edifying type of muscular Christianity, was he ? ' ' My dear boy,' drawled Charleston, ' the end of the matter is that some of them might have qualified for *Pop*, but none for the Eton Governing Body.' ' Oh, dear ! ' said Peter, ' I never think of things in that way.' Ullathorne saw he was worried. ' Friend,' he said, ' keep your tears for the New Testament, and get what jokes you can out of the Old. It is certainly no joke the way it is taught. And remember that there was no holiness till the Catholic Church came.' ' Then oughtn't we to go and belong to the Catholic Church ? ' Ullathorne looked at him radiantly. ' Peter, Peter, thou art in the Catholic Church.' Peter was quite content to think so. ' Am I ? ' ' Yes, Peter, henceforth thy name shall be Simon, Simple Simon,' concluded Ullathorne.

The next number of the *Insider* contained a fable of Æsop by Charleston, describing the visit of the Church Mouse and the Country Mouse to each other. Peter, as Country Mouse, visited Ullathorne, the Church Mouse, in College, and was handsomely entertained on dregs of *Bever* and the parings of altar candles. The return visit of Ullathorne to Morley's was broken up by the riotous return of the Morleyites from the races. However, Ullathorne replied by writing a satiric Decline and Fall of Miss Evans's House in the style of Gibbon, attributing the decline to the impious opinions of a certain atheistic Peer, who succeeded to the seat of the Lytteltons.

Subsequent numbers contained a brilliant Pageant set

forth in a series of historic scenes between Eton and
Windsor, illustrating :—

(a) Mediaeval Piety—

    1. King Henry the Sixth setting the first Sunday
       Questions.

(b) Tudor Magnanimity—

    2. King Henry the Eighth offering Anne of Cleves
       as a Dame to the College.

    3. Queen Elizabeth opening a new Boat House
       on the plea that the Armada had been
       defeated on the Eton reaches of the River.

(c) Stuart Despotism—

    4. King Charles the Second endeavouring to
       impose his illegitimate boys against Statute
       on the Foundation.

(d) Guelph Familiarity—

    5. King George the First addressing the School
       in German.

    6. King George the Third being *hoisted* on his
       birthday.

    7. King William the Fourth collapsing after
       Eton's defeat by Westminster.

    8. Queen Victoria, in the year of her succession,
       seeing for the first time the infant Edmond
       Warre in his perambulator among the
       rushes of the River.

The *Insider* was risky, and the proprietors kept it close
among themselves, but they supplied that touch of pure
satire without which any community or society becomes
stale. Masters' books were gently parodied, and bump-
tious boys were given hints how to behave when they
were entertained by masters. Two golden rules were laid
down for their behaviour. They were never to criticise
the wines on such occasions, or to refer to another master
by his nickname.

A copy of the *Insider* containing the Eton Pageant

R

fell into the hands of the authorities, and an apology was required for the mere mention of the Head's name in a comic sheet. Some masters succeed by the sense of ridicule they inspire. Others cannot afford to be ridiculous for a moment. Dr. Warre was one of these.

The same number contained an amusing masters' bibliography from the pen of Ullathorne, in which the fecund Mr. Christopher was credited with an increasing list of works, including *The Chalvey Papers*, in which he sketched some duller colleagues; *Fast Etonians*, a study in Beaus and Bucks of the eighteenth century; *Out of a Slough Window*, an Eton master's broodings during holiday; and *The Hill of Trouble*, which was believed to be a shot at Harrow.

The *Chronicle*, which was liable to be 'dry, didactory, dull,' was the only official paper, though in the summer months the booksellers swarmed with *Gnats*, *Amphibians*, and other ephemerals, which supplied little more than illustrated supplements to the *Chronicle*. The *Bantling* alone, edited by Christopher Stone, made some effort to meet a non-existent literary demand, and died in consequence before it was weaned. Literary rivalry took the exasperating form of search and counter-search for misprints. In the end the *Chronicle* always survived with its sapient but unenthusiastic leader, its minor poetry, its correspondence devoted to Old Etonian protests (Mr. Socston wrote regularly, and sometimes advertised for early numbers of the paper, which he kept bound in many volumes), and its endless lists of Elevens and matches and scores which sooner or later were as dead as last year's trigonometry papers. The *Chronicle* was subservient to athleticism, and while athleticism ruled the *Insider* kept inside its own inkhorn.

CHAPTER XX

NOCTURNAL

THE Winter Half came round again with its compulsory tax of five games a week, and its plague of bobbing, bounding, resounding balls. Streets, passages, yards, fields became infested with balls. From the Playing Fields, which in summer could be heard echoing a mile away with the crack of bat and ball, could now be heard on a clear dry day of kickabout ' bup ! bup ! bup ! ' It was a sweet sound to Socston's father, who came rushing down in an old Field shirt of red and blue quartering to play for Old Etonians, or any Scratch that needed an extra man against the School. Among the patriots he was tremendously popular, chiefly because he had forfeited his blue at Cambridge by insisting on playing for Old Etonians in preference to University matches. It was, of course, sheer folly, for he would have shed far more honour on Eton had he joined the few Etonians who had played for Cambridge. But he was a Don Quixote in these matters, and thought that a fellow with his Eton Field should not really care whether he played for his Planet even. Boys from other public schools adore the University, sampling the freedom of life for the first time, often disparaging their old schools, whereas Etonians at the University are often miserable, and sigh for the days that were. Freedom is no novelty. Socston's father had always thought the 'Varsity a poor place compared to Eton, and only endurable on account of the Old Etonians to be found in select and disgusted groups. ' Wait till you go there,' he informed his son, ' and have to herd with Harrow and Old Slops and Bedford Grammar.'

Socston nodded carelessly. He did not belong to so
enthusiastic a generation. He and Peter were secretly
amused watching the *Pater* rush madly about the Field
playing a little more stiffly and feebly every time. He had
lost his wind power, and when he headed the ball he shed
his cap and disclosed advanced calvities, which provoked
unfeeling laughter from the slouching watchers. One
day, after a bustling match, during which he had detected
unfilial laughter more than once, he turned to his son,
' It 's all very well. Why don't you get your Field ?
You haven't even got your Boats.' ' Well, I know I am
going to next First of March,' replied his son. ' You 're
a disgrace to the family, you haven't even been *swished*
yet.' Socston closed his lip.

Mr. Morley's Debating Society had several times de-
bated the propriety and possibility of visiting Windsor
after dark since the excursion on Mafeking Day. The
Library window had never been barred, and could be
opened at night. By dropping to the wall round the
Dame's garden, it was possible to reach the yard beside
Miss Evans's and emerge on Keate's Lane. When an
expedition to the Windsor Theatre was proposed that
evening, Socston thought he would teach his father that
the modern Etonian had other relaxations besides chasing
pills round the Field. As a member of the Debate he
volunteered, and was admitted into the flash crew, who
crept into the Library that Saturday night, after the
Man had said Prayers (more like a recitation of saying
lesson than ever) and had performed his smileless round.

' Anyhow, the Hag won't be able to catch us this time,'
remarked Frencher, who had a real love of melodrama.
The Hag's lair looked out on the other side of the House
to the Library. To slim athletic boys it was nothing to
drop from a window-sill by the finger-tips. From Keate's
Lane they passed unchallenged into South Meadow, and
by the Brocas over Windsor Bridge. The theatre was
only a hundred yards on. It was not the Play that
interested them. It was getting there and back, and their

chief thought was not to catch the eye of the heroine but to avoid that of the Dame.

Peter was unaware of Socston's escapade, partly because he was not in the Debate, and partly because Ullathorne had devised a different programme for him that evening. He was not in the Debate because *saps* were always blackballed. Socston had been admitted, thanks to the trick of a friend who, after dropping a white ball himself, asked the President's leave to change the black ball he had dropped by mistake!

There was always a serious side to Ullathorne's religion. His Tutor, Jenkinson, had impressed him with the importance of the Eton Mission, to which he told Peter it was his duty to subscribe a tithe of his pocket money. They had both promised to go down to that lugubrious haunt on Hackney Downs with Jenkinson, as Ullathorne put it, to see an expensive way of showing the poor how the rich lived. Peter suspected that Ullathorne must disapprove of it liturgically. The altar candles were probably not of the right colour. Meantime, Peter had fallen entirely under Ullathorne's influence. Peter admired his amazing powers to construe at sight, or write Latin verses almost by second sight. He acquired the habit of believing Ullathorne could not make a mistake in his exercises. By a curious logic he went on to believe Ullathorne must be right in religion. Religion and lessons were so much the same. When Ullathorne proposed that he should go to Confession he made no fight. The Protestant in him had ceased to function, partly because nothing Evangelical was taught, and partly because Ullathorne was always dropping an attractive counter-religion into his ears. Eton official religion was, of course, bound to teach nothing doctrinally, especially as the sons of Lord Halifax and Lord Kinnaird, Presidents of violently rival religious societies, were at that time joined in common worship under the roof of our Lady of Eton. Certain wholly unliturgical changes were being made in Upper Chapel, and the *Insider* published some amusing letters supposedly written by Lords Halifax and Kinnaird to the Provost, the former protesting that the alterations were being made an excuse for ceasing to turn to the East during the Creed, and the latter scarcely crediting the rumour that the spare planking was to be made into a Confessional in Lupton's Chapel!

As a matter of fact, Ullathorne's form of vengeance on the Provost for refusing High Church practice took the form of inveigling as many Etonians as he could to Confession in the High Church at Windsor, which was out of bounds. Peter agreed, not quite certain that he was not contravening some dreadful by-law of the Governing Body. 'Rubbish,' said Ullathorne, 'our Holy Founder was of the Catholic Faith, and would like nothing better than a few more Confessionals and less cricket nets.' 'But,' said Peter, 'was not the Battle of Waterloo won with bat and ball on the Playing Fields?' 'Bury that stale chestnut,' broke in Charleston. 'The Duke never played cricket at Eton. My father says that tag is the most fatuous one sung even by the cricket-crazy. What the Duke really meant was that, if he had not milled in the corner of the Playing Fields and learnt the lesson of holding on till both eyes were bunged up, he would never have held on at Waterloo till Blucher came to his rescue. What he said was not, "Up, Guards, and at them!" but "Pound away, gentlemen, and we shall see who can pound the hardest!"'

Ullathorne used to obtain leave from the Master in College to go on an evening for spiritual advice from Canon Carter of Clewer. It would be necessary for Peter to do the same, so Peter went to Mr. Morley's pupil-room, where he found him striving in semi-darkness to let mathematical light upon members of Army Class I. 'Please, sir, may I speak to you alone?' Mr. Morley was not accustomed to confidences, but he ushered him across the darker passage to a dreary drawing-room, in which the *Encyclopaedia Britannica* tempered the crude athleticism of golf sticks and cricket groups. 'No trouble with the Head Master, I hope ? ' ' No, sir, I only want leave of absence to go down to Windsor on Saturday night.' Mr. Morley pricked his ears. ' Why should you go to Windsor on Saturday night ? ' ' Because it is on Saturday that Canon Carter hears Confessions.' Mr. Morley was puzzled, and referred him to the Dame. ' I think you must ask Mr. Lamb as well.' Peter had no difficulty with the Dame, who hoped it was the first step to becoming a Cowley Father. ' Guid laddie, guid laddie,' she murmured, and wrote him a ticket to take to Mr. Lamb.

On Saturday evening Mr. Lamb was leaning back in his beautiful rooms. Shelves of morocco-bound Classics were varied by more exciting books to read to big little boys. Little big boys, he had discovered, disdain healthy fiction. Naked candles glowed in wooden candelabra, throwing the shadows of Mr. Christopher and Mr. Robertson on the wall. Christopher, who was a model House master, had reached the stage of open criticism and secret disgust with the athleticism of the School, which he vented in Lamb's rooms amid silences only broken by the parrot. Few masters dared to show any outward enthusiasm for art as against games. Luxmoore had uttered Jeremiads against the unsightly architecture of modern Eton, and his voice had been as the unavailing chirp of the sparrow on the housetops. But Christopher's rancour against the Philistines was beginning to echo in the School. Moreover, his House was socially the best House at Eton, and parents competed madly to place their boys at Christopher's. Mr. Lamb was wise in his generation, which was the rising one. He had a furtive love of the arts which made him listen to Christopher, though, as a sop to the athletes, he used to appear in flannels and compile small but graceful scores at cricket. He enjoyed discussing modern poets like Henley and Le Gallienne with Christopher, who seemed to know such writers personally. His ear for Latin verse had been transferred to English prose. He thought Henley's

'Sunset' the climax of English poetry, but his taste was moulded with Classicism, and he did not approve of the yellow writers of the *Yellow Book*. Mr. Christopher was in an uncertain position. He was the leader of the *literati*, and being approached, he believed, as to his policy should he be made Head Master of Eton, he had let it be known that he was a reformer. Whether he was also an aesthete they could guess. A verbal discussion had taken place between him and Austen Leigh, who was anxious that no reforms should ever cause him to turn in his grave. 'There is no need to change anything,' the Flea had ended by saying. 'And if I were Head I should make changes to-morrow,' replied Christopher, thereby qualifying his chances of so doing, for word was reported to Sir John Mumbles.

Robertson was inclined to be Christopher's chief supporter. He read the moderns, the symbolists, and was fond of Latinising verses of the Celtic School. It was his ambition to restart the Literary Society and renew the boys' Debates, which, he said, had once made *Pop* a nursery of Statesmen instead of a paddock for prospective Blues. 'I think an Essay Society is about as far as you will get,' said Lamb. 'I thought of inviting a few promising boys to tea to show them books.' 'Well, what sort of books?' 'Would it be wrong to explain Beardsley's pictures to boys?' 'It would be thought wrong,' drawled Christopher. 'Yes,' chimed Lamb, 'and to incur being thought wrong is wrong in our position.' 'It is not a cheerful outlook,' said Christopher, 'that any taste for modern literature is construed as sowing incipient immorality, or as slighting the tradition of the School.' 'There is scope for development,' added the pacific Mr. Lamb, 'but we must not infringe tradition, which in an ever-changing school is good simply because it is tradition.' 'Well, if it is tradition to discuss the choice of a bat or batting-pads with boys,' snorted Robertson, 'rather than the pictures and books in their rooms, I am done with tradition.' 'The Eton tradition

aims at a particular freedom, but not at general variety,'
suggested Lamb. 'But we need variety, and a system
which will land boys in more than three or four professions,' said Robertson. 'Read Stapylton's *School Lists*,
with the boys' fates appended after twenty years.'
'Nevertheless, those Lists inspired the best school song
ever written,' said Lamb, quoting J. K. Stephen's poem :—

> 'There are some who did nothing at school, much since,
> And others much then, since naught :
> They are middle-aged men, grown bald since then,
> Some have travelled and some have fought,
> And some have written, and some are bitten
> With strange new faiths : desist
> From tracking them : broker or priest or prince,
> They are all in the Old School List!'

'It is difficult to suggest or argue on an Eton question,'
smiled Robertson, 'without J. K. S. being thrown at
one's head.' Christopher looked pained. He had regarded J. K. S. as a splendid example of the Muse breaking through the School system. 'He was a poet whom
School tradition had recognised,' he pointed out. 'Yes,
they recognised him before they recognised Swinburne,'
said Robertson a little bitterly. 'These are the three
Eton poets, Shelley, Swinburne, and Stephen, and to
Eton the greatest of these is Stephen.' 'It is true, however,' remarked Christopher, 'that Eton failed to stifle
Shelley or to dry-nurse Swinburne.' 'That was left to
Watts-Dunton,' said Robertson, 'who presumably wrote
most of his Eton Ode for him. When Swinburne wrote
officially for Eton, he only showed how little Eton had
done to inspire him. His Ode will be forgotten when
Stephen's and Billy Johnson's live on the lips of the boys.'
'They are the two essentially Eton poets, because they
were true to Eton ; one sang the Wall and the other the
River,' said Lamb. 'The Eton Boating Song,' said
Christopher slowly, 'I am inclined to regard as a true
inspiration. It was not written to order, but during the
half-conscious sleeplessness of a summer night. Apart
from the unhappy attack on Rugby and Harrow, it is

everything which a school chorus should be.' 'Surely,' muttered Robertson, 'you don't see any real poetry in—

> "Jolly boating weather, and a hay harvest breeze:
> Blades on the feather, shade off the trees"?

That beginning always gives me hay fever.'

'I do not say it is poetry,' said Christopher, 'but it throws the Eton spirit into song, all her athletic grace and speed, social contempt, self-centred freemasonry,' and he quoted further :—

> 'Twenty years hence this weather may tempt us from office stools,
> We may be slow on the feather and seem to the boys old fools,
> But we will still row together and swear by the best of schools.'

'Bravo !' cried Mr. Lamb. 'Twenty years hence,' said Robertson, 'should be a motto over the room of every school master. He only thinks of three years hence. What will his pupil do at Cambridge, Oxford ? Will he pass Greats or Little Go ? Will he win a rowing cap ?' 'Stapylton's *Lists* show where Etonians are in twenty years,' Lamb struck in, a little proudly. 'I find the *Lists* very disappointing,' said Robertson. 'Sixth Form produces blameless and fameless Bishops. Third Form rears her famous Diplomatists and Generals. An occasional actor, artist, or stockbroker shows individuality, but I cannot read patiently through the noble army devoted to the duties of J.P.'s, and slight military careers varied by conservative membership in the House of Commons.' 'You forget Labouchere,' said Lamb. 'No, I do not,' caught up Robertson, 'It was his fellow-Etonians, Gladstone and Rosebery, who forgot him, because he was a real Radical.'

'There is more variety in Etonian deaths than lives,' went on Robertson. 'Etonians die deer-stalking in Scotland, or lion-hunting in Abyssinia. They are drowned in Hawaii, or murdered by Zulus, Afghans, or Matabele. They have died riding in Portman Square, steeplechasing, or playing polo in the ends of the world. But all this variety points to one type. If only an Old

Etonian sometimes died of absinthe in the Latin Quarter of Paris, or was poisoned as he entered a Papal Conclave, I should feel happier in my pupil-room.'

' But these sporting deaths,' cried Mr. Lamb, ' are the glory of our School. They are second only to the deaths of boys killed in action.' ' I have no doubt that the life of adventure has its scholastic value,' replied Robertson, ' but what minute tributes Eton has made to literature, music, or science.' ' The School produced Parry and a President of the Royal Society,' said Lamb tentatively, ' as well as the founder of the Geological Society.' ' And the air of " Rule, Britannia ! " was composed by an Etonian, Arne,' said Christopher. ' They were brought up under the old régime, which did a good deal for literature, I admit,' said Robertson. ' There was Hallam, Kinglake, and we only just missed Thackeray, who was of an Eton family.' ' What hard luck ! ' repeated Lamb. ' We had Thackeray's father, Tennyson's brother, and Dickens's son.' ' And Lady Morgan's husband,' added Robertson, ' as well as Caleb Colton, the eccentric author of *Lacon*, who became one of our distinguished suicides. There are too many self-slayers in the *Lists*.' ' The outside world must often prove disappointing to Etonians,' murmured Lamb, ' but that would account as well for our fine record in travel and exploration. Etonians were not contented with the Grand Tour, but plunged afield like Harcourt, the first Englishman to visit the tomb of Confucius.' ' To return to letters, we produced, as far as I know, nobody else.' ' Well,' interrupted Christopher, ' I have been searching the *Lists* for my little book of *Eton Annals*, and I noted Manning, who wrote the *Lives of the Speakers* ; Rose, the translator of *Ariosto* ; Leslie Stephen and Rowland Williams, who contributed to *Essays and Reviews*.' ' Do not forget Henry Bradshaw, greatest librarian, Celticist, and liturgist of our time,' said Lamb. ' There was a greater variety in the pre-athletic era, which will interest you, Robertson,' went on Christopher. ' There was a dandy in " Beau "

Brummell, as the world called him. He was called
"Buck" at Eton. There was Kean, the tragedian;
Signor Borroni, the singer; Christie, the auctioneer;
Blaquiere, who served as a Middy on the *Bounty* and
ended as Chancellor of Toronto University; Smyth minor,
who became stationmaster at Reading, must always be
distinguished from the Smith minor who represented
Eton at Trafalgar. There was Heald, whose only fame,
according to Stapylton, was that he married Lola Montes.'
' It is not difficult to imagine Brummell and Heald coming
from modern Eton,' said Robertson bitterly, ' but our
Tory Towers have always bred some redeeming Radicals
since the day of Fox and Whitbread and the Friends of
the People. I fear there are few sympathisers with the
Boers at Eton except myself.' ' Eton has some striking
characters in the advanced ranks,' said Christopher,
from his knowledge of research. ' Horne Tooke, the
friend of Wilkes; Pigott, the friend of Voltaire; Grieve,
the friend of Marat; and Julian Hibbert, the friend of Owen
the Socialist, were all Etonians, and were probably well
abused by their fellows, though the great Whig tradition
once permitted Englishmen to be Radicals and yet remain
gentlemen.' ' Do not forget Lynch, who signed America's
Declaration of Independence,' said Robertson. ' I wish
our pro-Boers were as numerous as the pro-French and
pro-Americans must have been.' ' I have no doubt,'
said Christopher, ' there are some amongst Old Etonians,
and that even John Burns has votaries in the School.
But the Head should not be told if there are.' ' The
Head cannot understand being on the side of any except
one's own class, country, and School,' remarked Lamb,
' and I think he is probably right.' ' Yes,' said Robertson,
' Conservative patriotism is probably right, but Christianity happens to be the negation of both. You remember
what trouble Christ had for being a pro-Samaritan. I am
proud at Eton to be a pro-Boer and a pro-Harrovian.'
' We have some difficulty in keeping your views from the
Head, especially the last,' concluded Lamb, with a generous

smile. ' It is so difficult, that I think it may be wrong
to bring new views to Eton,' declared Christopher. ' Both
Ruskin and Morris have been brought through my advice
to lecture, and I no longer feel I can fight the Philistines.'
' Never mind,' said Robertson admiringly. ' If you
are not among the fighting Judges, you will one day be
reckoned among our Prophets.'

' Well, it would be interesting to know what you would
do, if you were Head,' said Lamb kindly. ' I should
change the Service in Chapel,' said Christopher ; ' as we
cannot appeal to boys by liturgies or litanies, we should
appeal to their emotions. The worst boys have faint
and faltering dreams.' ' Dreams ! ' laughed Robertson.
' Boys don't dream. If they do, Mat Wright and Dan
Leno and Edna May fulfil their dreaming. And yet the
Gaiety Chorus ought to lead them to some chorus-ending
of Euripides.' ' Yes, all beauty of form returns to the
one Ideal,' murmured Lamb platonically. ' But the only
beauty of form prized here is cricket form,' went on
Robertson. ' Mike has cleared the Muses out of the
Playing Fields. Where is the old Eton intellectualism ?
Compare the *Microcosm* and the *Etonian* under the editor-
ship of Praed and Canning with modern productions.
The *Chronicle* combines the dulness of a Chapel Sermon
with the meagre results published in the *Sportsman*. Can
you imagine Gladstone in *Pop* to-day ? ' ' No,' said
Christopher, with a melancholy look, ' he would
certainly be blackballed.' ' How can you reach boys
who will neither read nor write literature ? ' ' Orally,'
said Christopher. ' Sermons should be preached by laymen
appealing to the humorous, the human, and even the
biographical side of boys.' ' The Lives of the Lower
Masters might be edited for that purpose,' suggested
Robertson, ' instead of the Sunday Sermon which remains
a mental treadmill, though in honour of what gods I
know not.' ' Mumbo Jumbo for one,' replied Christopher,
with sudden stress, ' Mumbo in whose honour children are
sacrificed in dark academic groves.' ' Whose school-room

exactly are you thinking of ? ' queried Lamb. ' Alas !
my own,' sighed Christopher, ' and yet these quick,
lively, bird-like creatures called boys——' ' Call them
sparrows in Fourth and geese in Fifth Form,' interrupted
Robertson. ' Parrots, but not always so wise,' chimed
Lamb. ' Yet these caged bird-like creatures,' continued
Christopher, ' never fail to appreciate every straw of
humour, every seed of anecdote that I offer them. The
other day our ridiculous editor of Thucydides described
the speech of Brasidas as brief and soldierly. I pointed
out it was neither, and the whole class were the better for
the merry peal of laughter which followed. The boys
now look on me as a humorist, which they prefer to a
punster. I believe they would groan at Russell Day's
laconic shot at a boy giving his name as Cole—" Well,
Cole, scuttle ! " ' ' They enjoy a gentle sarcasm, especially if it is directed against their natural enemies,' said
Robertson. ' You should try your darts on the Governing Body.' ' No doubt they still regard them, as
Gerald Balfour in his youth assured one of them, with
unmitigated contempt.'

There came a sudden knock on the door, and Mr. Lamb
left the room. ' Well, what was it ? ' asked Robertson,
when he returned. ' One of my pupils has made a novel
request. He wished me to sign a ticket to go to Windsor
to-night.' The others pricked their ears. ' In order to
make his auricular Confession. I could not refuse.'
' Well, Ritualism is better than conventionality,' said
Robertson. ' It is curious,' said Christopher, ' that it is
always those boys who need confession least who most
wish to go.'

As soon as Peter had obtained Mr. Lamb's signature,
he hurried to join Ullathorne at the portals to School
Yard. The small door was opened by the School Clerk
for Ullathorne to come out. They both wore *scug*-caps
instead of top-hats. ' Isn't it glorious ? ' said Ullathorne, as they raced down town. It was certainly
Ullathorne's idea of an adventure. ' The most glorious

thing of all is a Retreat at Cowley. But I have never
been able to make one fit with Long Leave. Just think.
All the Canonical Hours of the Church and total silence.
It is like living in the tomb with our Lord.' Peter thought
this a very wonderful saying, and on Ullathorne's advice
decided to go to Oxford to be near Cowley, instead of
Cambridge, which Ullathorne had heard was very poorly
furnished with Confessors of the Church of England.

They passed through the by-streets of Windsor and
turned suddenly into a dark little church, shot by fumes
partly of spirits, partly of incense. Sinners had preceded them. Ullathorne drew Peter to a corner, where
there was a curtain on rings. An old man, not unlike
an old Eton master, sat there motionless, save that he
wore a biretta instead of a mortar-board. His long
white hair and ascetic, thin, drawn features showed him
to be a scholar. His head was bowed, but his eyes carried
that sparkle of defiance which really good men acquire
through being at grips with naked evil. Ullathorne knelt
and began in a low voice, ' I confess to God Almighty, and
before all the company of Heaven, to our Blessed Lady
of Eton, to our Holy Founder King Henry the Sixth, and
to you, my father, that I have sinned exceedingly in deed,
word, and thought.' Then followed hushed whisperings,
questionings, and ghostly admonitions. Ullathorne
withdrew, and Peter took his place to make his first
confession. With blinding tears he poured forth the
sins of his childhood, raking his memory till head and
heart ached together. They were possibly not so serious
as he imagined. The old man's face never moved, but
his raised hand trembled, as though absolution lay in
their finger-tips.

' Yes, yes, all that is past. You are at school, my son ? '
' Yes, father, I am at Eton.' The confessor had also
been at Eton, and his painted portrait hung in the Provost's Lodge, a study in youthful and radiant beauty.
' What have you to reproach yourself with since you
were at School ? ' ' Oh, I broke bounds once, and I

went on the roof once, and I have sworn, and I have used the *cribs* in the School Library, but I looked out the words in the Dictionary afterwards.' 'Leave excuses to your Confessor. You have no evil to confess, no temptation not resisted ? ' ' No.' ' May God keep you innocent always, but when the great temptation comes, remember, whether you are at Eton or in the world, to pray to the Lady who loves Eton, for Eton is hers,' and he slowly uttered the Absolution. Peter felt that the peccadilloes of fifteen years were as though they were not. He trod on air. The two boys walked away in silence holding hands. A soldier arm-in-arm with two frowsy girls passed their path. A chorus of foul revel met their ears from each corner, but they felt strong enough to have stood for the faith in the Roman Arena. They came down Castle Hill, and took the cross-cut to the Bridge at the back of the theatre. ' *Laudate Dominum omnes gentes,*' chanted Ullathorne.

Suddenly the figure of a boy appeared on the wall in front of them, and dropped. Another followed, and both slipped into some stables. A third followed right in front of them. It was Philips ! Philips, the parson's son. Peter cried his name. ' Good God, Darley,' came the answer, ' were you at the Play too ? There were three *beaks* in the gallery all the time we were in the stalls. We never saw them till the end. Cut as fast as you can over Windsor Bridge. We are getting down to the River,' and he disappeared. Peter and Ullathorne quickened step, and promptly ran into the trap laid by three masters, and surrendered at discretion. ' Here are two of them,' announced an athletic gentleman, who had recently exchanged a thwart in the Oxford boat for a less laborious position at an Eton desk, ' but where are the other three ? We saw five in the theatre. What are your names anyhow ? ' ' Ullathorne, sir, and I am in College.' ' Darley at Morley's, please, sir.' ' You should not let bigger boys take you to the theatre.' ' Please, sir, we weren't there at all.' ' Nonsense, don't tell lies. Come along, we must catch the others at the Bridge.'

Peter's immediate instinct was to save the others, and he forewent the pleasure of showing his pass. ' Please sir,' he stammered, ' we can tell you everything.' The masters delayed, and Peter clung to the arm of one. ' Please, sir, we were not with the others.' ' Nonsense, we saw five of you, we followed you into the theatre.' ' Oh, no, sir,' said Ullathorne, playing up to Peter's lead, ' you couldn't have seen us. We never went near the theatre. We went somewhere far different.' ' Well, where do you go at this hour of the night ? ' Both boys did their best to retard the pursuit by engaging in naïve conversation. ' To tell you the truth,' said Ullathorne in confidential tones, ' we were out of our rooms in order to attend a little—' and he paused while the masters looked suspicious, ' a little extra Divinity.' ' And here,' chimed Peter, ' is my ticket signed by my Tutor to be out to-night.'

The masters began to look bewildered, and, imagining they had struck some form of confirmation class, took their names down and hurried ahead to catch the others at the Bridge. Peter and Ullathorne fell behind, and when the *beaks* were out of sight whistled. There was a whistle in reply, and the guilty Morleyites rushed out of a yard. ' Have you been caught ? Where are the *beaks* ? ' ' Hush ! ' whispered Peter, full of self-importance, ' we 've saved you, but don't cross by the Bridge. We 're out with leave.' There was nothing for them but to swim or row, and the Brocas boat-house was on the other side. Peter agreed to try and get a boat across, while the theatre party climbed into the garden of the old deserted-looking house. Sure enough, there on the Bridge looking at the stars were two masters, to whom Peter and Ullathorne wished a conscientious good night. Ullathorne went on to College, while Peter had the luck to run into one of the boatmen known from generation to generation as ' Brocas Bill.' Slipping five shillings

S

into his hand, he besought him to get a gig to the steps
opposite if he wanted more. 'There are half a dozen
of m'Tutor's fellows waiting,' and he fled, leaving a
puzzled, but fortunately avaricious, boatman in the
Brocas Lane.

Meantime the Morleyites were scouting in the old
garden. 'Well, here's the River all right if we can ever
cross it,' muttered Frencher. 'Isn't this house always
empty?' said Philips. 'We might climb in and see
whether there is anybody waiting on the Bridge.' 'This
is the house my father always calls haunted,' said
Socston, 'and, by Jove, there's the door this side ajar.
Let's go in anyhow.' Socston and Philips went in,
while the others scoured the bank for a stray punt.
They found themselves in a pitch dark hall. 'Good God,
what a dungeon!' cried Socston. They tried an empty
room, with old carving on the wall. As they came out
they heard footsteps cross the hall, and both stood with
chilled hearts against the wall. The silhouette of a man
crossed against the glass garden door. They scrambled
up the stairs in terror, and took refuge in the first bedroom.
It was as empty and deserted as the rest of the house.
Through a fan window they could make out the River
and the Bridge. They listened, and the footsteps began
to follow them up the stairs. There was a large open
cupboard, and they flattened themselves into it. It
was a passage! and they followed it through the house,
climbing and crawling. They found themselves in
another room, and climbed out of the window. Catching
hold of the water-pipe, they slid down to the ground
in time to hear their comrades whistling from the water's
edge. They ran towards the sound, and found them
trying to punt a boat with muffled oars. 'Look sharp,
there's a ghost walking about that house. Nobody lives
there, and we could hear steps in every corner walking
out at us.' Philips and Socston went home, feeling
that more terrible things than masters moved in the
darkness. Once in the *whiff gig*, they rowed upstream

and, landing softly above Rafts, sent 'Brocas Bill' a rich man to bed.

They never turned to look behind them, or they would have seen a silent figure standing motionless at the open garden door, the figure of a man watching them without the slightest trace of approval or disapproval in his placid features, but with a reserve and an intensity which only an expert brings to bear in studying the species of boy. He himself was perfectly recognisable. He was Herr Rudolf Blitz, Instructor in German to Eton College!

Herr Blitz was a lonely yet intellectual figure in the School. Boys were often rude to him in class, and Tutors were ruder still in ignoring his complaints with consistent disloyalty to their Teutonic colleague, a situation he met by wearing spats and resigning himself to his hobbies. He happened to be a great intellectual, and he consoled himself with being the last court of appeal, when a passage in the Classics was disputed among the masters. He had the Classics at his finger-ends, and on his shelves was the best private library collected at Eton since Hawtrey's. With his usual contempt for English opinion, he occupied rooms in the haunted house. By day he taught his somewhat barbarous native tongue to barbarians. By night, and this was the advantage of a house that was shunned after nightfall, he often went to town to gamble, which was the continental form of sport. He thought nothing of throwing away a week's salary at a throw. There was a reason why he looked indulgently at the Morleyites scrambling through his back garden. For different reasons the Head heard nothing from the different masters who had seen them—from Herr Blitz nothing, because he did not consider it was his business, and from the others nothing, because they had made a mess of theirs.

CHAPTER XXI

UPPER DIVISION

THREE more successful Trials had brought Peter to the top of Middle Fifth. One more shunt, and he could enjoy the privileges of Upper Division. The Easter Half brought some sensation in the form of floods. In spite of the Thames Conservancy, the River unconcernedly overflowed, and laid South Meadow and the Playing Fields under water. Lower Chapel developed cracks which were healed by patches of plaster. The whole building threatened to split. As the waters stole slowly towards Keate's Lane, an elm-tree was confidently pointed out as the high-water mark for the School to be sent home. There were no boys left who remembered the blessed deluge of 1894, when the waters prevailed against the prayers of the Chaplains and the whole School was sent away. The tradition was that the flood reached Keate's Lane, and that the last inch in the water was caused by the patriotism of Miss Evans's boys, who sacrificed their books to choke the drain opposite their House.

Floods left their dates in Eton history. A flood swept away the original Fifteen Arch Bridge, and there was a great flood in the year the Great Duke died. In the College Buttery, over the old binns, there was record of the Flood of 1774, when the water was two feet and four inches in the great cellar under the College Hall. And in November 1894 it was one foot and ten and a half inches.

Once more hopes ran high, and verses in the Psalms referring to the presence of the water floods were hugely appreciated in Chapel. A punt was necessitated in the Eton Wick Road, and the overcrowding of the ferry became a novel and delightful excuse for lateness in School. However, to the dismay of the boys, the waters were enfeebled and, beyond creating a cataract in Barnes Pool, and leaving the corpse of a cow in South Meadow, refrained from penetrating farther. As games became hindered, attention in school became more difficult. Deprived of the fierce channel of sports, the boys brewed mischief and the masters conflict among themselves. College Field became a shallow lake, and as the Head glanced Noah-like over the face of the waters, he was surprised to see some small Collegers floating behind the tinplate security of a bath-tub, whereat he withdrew into the recesses of the Cloisters and issued an edict worthy of the brethren of Trinity House, solemnly forbidding the use of vessels of any description upon the floods. But whether it entailed humour or seriousness on his part no master or boy could say. All they knew was that the Head occasionally perpetrated an act of grim humour. When the stolen Block was returned, after one of its several rapes, Warre took care that the first victim should be a scion of the very family which had removed it. And there was humour in estimating Chapel shirking at five hundred lines of *Paradise Lost*!

Peter had sampled all the masters in Middle Fifth by now. He spent two halves up to Christopher and one to Edwards. They were laborious days for masters and *saps*. They made the best of the system, while the rank and file contributed no more than their tithe. A few professional duffers or cricketers were allowed to perform nil. Steadily they read Thucydides on the Peloponnesian War, which became as great a nuisance as the Boer War. Latin took the form of chunks of Cicero, which was as easy as uncut macaroni for boys to chew. The light humour of Martial and the grim satire of Juvenal were unfortunately outside the programme. Mr. Christopher could not disguise his dislike of prose

writers. The sad, phlegmatic man only came to life
when a gleam of poetry came under his eye. As bribes
for attention, he told and retold his slender stock of
stories. Sometimes he told a mild ghost story, and
sometimes he described the habits of the birds living in
his garden. Once he set some lines he had written about
a carrier pigeon he had had the misfortune to shoot
while bearing a message between lovers.

Mr. Edwards was less literary, but more efficient. He
induced as many boys as possible to struggle grimly
through the more uninspiring Classics which were chosen
as their portion. Both Edwards and Christopher looked
on the half as one long obstacle race, but while Christopher
advised climbing obstacles, Edwards urged breaking
them down. He was by way of being a sportsman and
a martinet. He was fond of threatening to read the
Riot Act, and at the least provocation would shout
' Mutiny ! ' The first time Peter heard this he was much
frightened, but, as the second occasion also passed in-
nocuously, the third time he heard him he laughed.
Edwards adopted the terms of sport to the subjects.
' Gentlemen,' he used to announce with ironical effect,
' the Greek iambic season has set in ! ' ' Close time for
Latin Prose has arrived ! ' No subject was more cordially
disliked than Latin Prose, for which a printed piece of
English was given to the whole Block on Mondays.
Ullathorne had once noticed, what his division master
had not, that it was the English of a paragraph of Cicero,
and he essayed a subtle trap. He did not show up his
version, and by the next school, when it was called for,
he had copied out the original Cicero with a few cautious
mistakes inserted. Next day the weary master returned
the thirty Latin Proses he had corrected between midnight
and Early School. ' Ullathorne, yours is first-rate. I only
had three real corrections to make.' Ullathorne glanced
at his paper with a thrill. One was a correction of himself,
but two were corrections of Cicero. ' Your sentences are
clever, but they don't quite meet the version at those

points.' 'Not quite Ciceronian, I am afraid?' asked
Ullathorne, without turning an eyelash. 'Not quite,
why should it be?' said the kind but tired teacher.
Ullathorne told Peter, but no one else.

Edwards was the energetic treasurer of the Eton
Mission, a hobby he pressed in school by minute collections of halfpence. Every House carried out a terminal
collection, but with very varying response. Morley's
House was about as interested as the Rationalist Society
in Christian Missions. Edwards's constant advertising
of the Eton Mission led Peter to join a party of boys
whom Jenkinson invited on a specially conducted visit
to Hackney Wick, the suburban slum which had been
adopted by our Lady of Eton. The chance of leave was
never to be lost, and Peter found Charleston in the party
of Jenkinson's boys who arrived at Victoria Park Station,
beyond the East End, on a muggy winter afternoon.
Jenkinson's keenness was like an epidemic. He gave it
to his boys, and their friends caught it in turn. In high
spirits they passed into Wick Road under a railway
bridge, and sought the Mission into which pour the Eton
pennies formerly diverted to the East End of Chapel.
Amid the appalling ugliness of the slum, they found an
Eton colony and quadrangle of Hall, House, and Church.
Cut off from the green sward, the hospitable missioners
kept in touch with civilisation through the medium of a
racquet court. After tea the company of Etonians,
young and old, visited a boys' club, where Peter had his
nose blooded in a boxing bout, and Charleston defeated
a champion at chess. Mr. Jenkinson was the success
of the evening, entering with such seriousness into the
tastes and conversation of the natives as to be acclaimed
one of themselves. Returning by a late train through
the dismal vista of what resembled a shabby inferno
pawned by some disconsolate fiend, conversation turned,
as Jenkinson intended, to the lives of the poor. Statistics
of the housing question were mentioned, which Peter
could not help suggesting would apply to some Eton

Houses. There was a general agreement that more money and more parsons must somehow be sent into the East End, except on the part of Charleston, who showed himself so contemptuous that Jenkinson remonstrated with his heartlessness. ' It 's not that,' said Charleston, ' but I have long come to a conclusion as to these matters.' ' What 's that ? ' ' Socialism pure and simple ! ' Mr. Jenkinson was tolerant, but doubted whether the poor would find Socialism so jolly as they expected. Charleston said he had set himself the Holiday Task of organising his father's employees to assert their rights. He had even thoughts of collecting the College servants and watermen into a Trade Union, and made the suggestion in the train. ' Why don't the masters have a union ? ' he asked Mr. Jenkinson. Jenkinson laughed. ' The Governing Body is far too intangible to fight, and besides, we are rather divided I believe.' ' Well, then, we ought to start a Trade Union of *saps*,' said Charleston, and Peter immediately volunteered for the post of secretary. As a matter of fact, a *saps*' union was really needed until Warre introduced a Relief Act on their behalf.

Tugs and *saps* were henceforth classed together under one master according to their place in Trials. Divisions were no longer composed of a few *saps*, whose work was held back by the slowness of the mediocre and the deliberately lazy. The dunces were herded under a driver and the élite under a trainer. Donkeys and racehorses no longer kicked each other in the same traces. The change came in Peter's time. It was the most beneficial in the history of the School. For the first time a number of Oppidans received a good chance to acquire learning in congenial company. To his delight, Peter found himself moved to the Select Division of Upper Fifth. Ullathorne and Charleston joined him in a corner school-room of the New Schools. To his greater delight, he found the experiment had been placed under Jenkinson, who had been promoted and eased of dufferdom for ever. The golden age had set in for Jenkinson. His House, tended like a sensitive plant, had become a hardy annual in School athletics. The Lower Boys, with whom he had started, were struggling in Lower or Upper Boats by now. The flower of his boys were being tried for the Eight. Jenkinson, who had never lifted an oar in his life, lived up to the reputation his boys had won for him, and appeared almost every night on the River with his white tie and old change coat, walking up the tow-path half an hour before a race was in sight. The bent shoulders, the grey curls, and the enthusiastic blue eyes were as familiar as Warre's had been in his boating days. Race by race, and heat by heat, his House began the conquest of the River.

At the head of Fifth Form Juggins came into his Classical heritage once more. Xenophon and Virgil were left buried in Remove. He began to teach Plato and Sophocles to boys who realised that there was a glory in Greek. He loved to read the *Antigone*, the play which Sophocles had died while reading aloud. But the mystery of the play, the stumbling-block in the character of Antigone, which had even puzzled the Greeks, he had solved. He announced his wonderful discovery one day to his boys. The troublesome passage must be an interpolation by the poet's son acting as literary executor. It was brilliant! As he left, he overheard Ullathorne saying to another boy, 'But Juggins was quite wrong over that,' and secretly he was filled with delight. There were many consolations in a Select Division.

Saying lessons were no longer a stuttering drag to his ears, for the boys in Select had their lines running pat. Every boy took Extra Books voluntarily, and few failed of a class in Trials. Jenkinson took courage, and forgot he was an Eton teacher. He talked of Socrates as he might of another House master, and took sides in the *Dialogues* of Plato. They were reading the *Phaedo*, and the tears came to Peter as he read how Socrates discoursed during his last night on earth. The wonderful alternatives he proposed struck Peter like a voice crying in the desert of grammar. Why should a man fear death, for either there is immortality or there is not. If there is not, then death is a timeless sleep. If there is immortality, how wonderful to meet all the famous and clever men of the past. Both Socratic alternatives seemed better than life. Peter had never thought of death as an absolute good before.

Jenkinson really showed signs of working himself to death over his unwieldy but promising class. Every piece of written work, even their notebooks in school, were minutely examined and little comments added late, far too late at night. At last Jenkinson took unto him Stone, an old Newcastle scholar of the Fifties, to correct the Greek Iambics. Peter had always written Iambics according to three or four rules. Whether they made poetry or sense did not seem material. Stone's standard was high, for in a copy of twenty lines there were seldom twenty words left without their accents being scalped with slashes of red ink. Jenkinson loved Sophocles, and the boys were reading *Electra*. When they met Ismene, he told them how, during his last visit to Greece, as he approached Athens, he had heard a child call Ismene's name, which showed that the Sophoclean names lived on. He wrote a little poem about it. ' I am positive it was only Clinton hiding behind a tree,' whispered Ullathorne to Peter.

One day the door creaked open, and the Head strode in. The Select Division turned to stone. Jenkinson struggled against lumbago to leave his chair, but the older and suppler Head, with true courtesy, bade him remain seated, and stood listening to the lesson. So suddenly he entered that one boy was too sleepy to notice. As he woke up, he caught the eye of the Head, who remarked, ' Do you oppose the umbrella of indifference to the rain of knowledge ? ' He was obviously in good humour, for the translating was good. They were construing the famous chariot race in *Electra*, and no boy had to ask, as on a historic occasion, to be excused on the ground that he could not do justice to the passage. The Head stood noting their performance in a big note-book. As a climax, Jenkinson called out, 'Ullathorne, go on!'

Ullathorne rose, adjusted his gown, and holding his book at arm's distance began slowly reading out the Greek and the English. It was too good for a boy's version. The Head's eagle eye fell on the cover of the book. It was not the same as the red interleaved texts of the others. 'Thank you,' said Jenkinson, with the trainer's relief as the favourite wins. 'Hand me that book,' growled the terrible Head. The others watched in an agony of expectation. Jenkinson nervously broke in, 'I hope it is not Jebb's translation.' The Head was puzzled, puzzled as he had not been for years. 'No,' he said, 'it is an unusual book for Upper Fifth. It is apparently a Hebrew Grammar.' And he turned to the title-page as though he were not quite sure. The boys whistled under their breath. 'Where was the page you were reading from?' the Head tried again. 'I was reading by heart, sir. I have always liked this play.' The boys burst into subdued applause. This was great even for Ullathorne. The Head actually bowed to Jenkinson as he left the room. Then he halted, and addressed Ullathorne. 'Most unusual, but Eton used to admire a good memory. I remember a boy who knew Homer by heart—poor Walker. What profession are you going to follow?' Perhaps he had spotted a future assistant. Ullathorne, pale as a candle, bowed, 'A priest, sir.' 'Excellent,' continued the Head. 'Eton has sent out the best of clergymen.' 'A priest of a religious order, I mean,' added Ullathorne. The Head looked puzzled again, but only for a moment. Then smelling, as it were, a rat from the English Church, he suggested, 'You must always beware of *a priori* reasoning, or you will end in a visit to Rome.' It had proved an exhausting inspection, and he no longer felt young mentally.

However, the Head was not one to appear worsted, and before the end of the half he returned to Jenkinson's class-room. They were construing Greek Epigrams this time, those exquisite little tear-bottles of pagan grief. A shy Colleger was put on, and apparently gave the correct version of a rare word. 'Very bad, you may sit down,' thundered the Head. Then he explained. It was so rare a word that it was *hapax legomenon*, only once recorded, and for this word Messrs Liddell and Scott gave one meaning, and the well-read Mr. Bohn another. It was unfortunate that the construer had taken the same view as Mr. Bohn. There fell a stern silence.

The strife of Greeks and Trojans, of Classics and Modernists, had loomed afresh in the School, but the Head kept himself apart. That would all devolve on his successor. Masters took to discussion in groups in the privacy of each other's rooms. Christopher and Robertson had dropped into Lamb's rooms one evening. Christopher was a Greek with poetical Trojan leanings, while Robertson was a non-Classical master with Greek enthusiasms. Betwixt them the smiling Mr. Lamb kept the peace and registered the arguments, at least those in Greek favour. Christopher was afraid the way Classics were taught developed a cynicism for all intellectual things. 'For the majority of boys the Classics are a failure. They go away without more Latin and often with less Greek than they could pick up of French in a Long Vacation.' 'Our University results are striking,' urged Lamb. 'I don't know,' resumed Christopher. 'Only one Oppidan in twenty takes an Honours degree. If Greek is to be taught it must be made easier.' 'Cut the grammar!' cried Robertson. 'But Greek has such a noble grammar,' insisted Lamb, 'and it makes a good gymnastic.' 'Damn the gymnastic!' said Robertson. 'We must have the Classics, but hand out *cribs* and dash through Homer and Virgil like the serial parts of new novels, explaining how inferior Guy Boothby is to Homer, and what a sorry mess Hall Caine, Corelli, and

Conan Doyle would have made with the plot of the
Æneid.' Mr. Lamb seemed doubtful. 'You must not
vulgarise the Classics.' 'Of course you must,' insisted
Robertson. 'The boy taste is vulgar, and you must cut
and sauce the Classics to suit it.' 'It looks,' said Christopher, 'as though the boys get so disgusted with the Classics
that afterwards they reject the Classics of all languages
including their own.' 'Yes, what has any Etonian ever
done for the English Classics?' asked Robertson. 'Some
were written by Etonians,' suggested Lamb. 'I know
they were,' replied Robertson, 'but the School Library
does not admit Fielding's novels or Swinburne's poems.
I am on the side of the Classics, if you will teach them in
a modern way. Trojanise Greek. Teach Latin on the
Berlitz system. Teach English Grammar before Greek.
Encourage Latin conversation. Instead of Greek
Iambics, let them write the *Eton Chronicle* in Greek.
Did not one of the Selwyns keep Eton's Boating Diary in
pure Attic at the beginning of the century? Otherwise
I will join the enemy. I will go and see Winterstown
to-morrow.'

'Mr. Winterstown, I am afraid,' said Lamb, 'portends
disaster to the School. He represents the Irish type at
Eton.' Christopher laughed. 'I suppose he wants the
same rights for mathematical masters as Parnell wanted
for the Irish, or at least the same fees as the Classical.'
'Well,' said Lamb, 'we must fight it out for their
sake as well as for ours. It was their defeat that made
the Trojans live in history.' 'I have always wanted to
hear the Trojans' point of view,' said Robertson. 'They
must have thought of the Greeks as the Boers think of
us.' 'Except, to be accurate,' said Lamb, 'it was the
Trojans who made the raid which led to the Ilian War.'

'What it comes to is that we must encourage originality,' said Christopher. 'Our general type is not
sufficient, though it is generous, genial, unembarrassed,
courageous, sensible, and active, but it is too level.' 'It
is the level type that smooths the road of Empire. If we

had professors among the masters, doubtless we might rear prodigies among the boys,' said Lamb. 'Don't we neglect the intellectual and moral levels altogether?' asked Christopher. 'The full Classical course contains both,' laid down Lamb. 'It is supposed the higher mathematics must always be associated with low morals,' added Robertson mischievously. 'The code of morals among the boys,' insisted Christopher, 'is wrong. Vicious tendencies are no bar to social success. It is not actively corrupting, but it is undeniably low. There is no appeal for the young and weak, who are often puzzled as to the moral line.' 'Boys should be told that the line lies strictly between the Beautiful and the non-Beautiful,' suggested Robertson. 'Mathematical masters should not be allowed to prepare their boys for Confirmation,' was Lamb's solution.

'I don't believe in Confirmation at all,' said Robertson. 'My standards are all Greek. Boys can only be influenced by a man's friendship, by something given in return for the adoration they feel for the strong. We masters should acquire what lapses to *Pop*. Almond of Loretto and even Thring of Uppingham won it. They were the heroes of their boys, and their friendship became the strongest thing in the boys' lives. Their Schools were Christian echoes of the Sacred Band. We do not dare approach boys from a point of mysticism. That is why Confirmation is a failure, both from a religious and a personal side. Rather than parade the boys before a Bishop they will never see again I would initiate them into Eleusinian Mysteries.' 'It certainly does not impress the boys,' said Christopher, with a sad pontifical smile. 'Too often a Tutor is the last person to whom a boy will breathe his moral condition. Their first Communion is too often their last, and Confirmation is forgotten with the rest of the School Routine.' 'It might almost be better to hand the boys over to a Committee of Games,' broke in Robertson. 'Our colleague upstairs is playing for Middlesex.' 'No, a Committee of Old

Etonians whom the boys would admire and respect,'
said Christopher, ' men as different as Quintin Hogg
and Lord Halifax, who have given as laymen their lives
to religion.' 'That sounds better than parsons,' said
Robertson. 'At present examinations kill originality,
and Confirmations stunt religion.' 'All we get from the
boys,' said Christopher, ' is a courteous respect for the
formalities of religion.' ' I know,' said Robertson, ' and
it gives me a sympathy for the scoundrel who drives his
chariot along the abyss of expulsion.'

Meantime the Confirmation season had returned, and
a number of boys needed special preparation to meet the
Bishop of Oxford for the first and last time in their lives.
The principal requisite for candidates was age. Of the
tribe of Munfort were sealed a dozen, of the tribe of
Jenkinson were sealed a dozen, and of the tribe of Morley
were sealed a dozen, including Peter, Socston, Frencher,
and Mouler. Mr. Morley collected them in his dreary
drawing-room for a preliminary address. They stood
with the sheepish grin which boys instantly drop like a
torpedo-net to meet *pi-jaw*. Willum stood grinning with
satisfaction at the door. Rumour had it that the Dame
had had him confirmed twice, because, like vaccination,
it had failed to take in the first instance. The Man was
punctilious about public religion. In Desks he was
rumoured to say his initiary prayer by burying his head
in his hands and counting twenty. Five would have
been irreverent, fifty Pharisaic. The Man eyed them
suspiciously, and referred to the interest the Dame
took in their candidacy. There was a suspicion of coming
examination in his words, and looks fell to zero. Once a
week they were to attend lectures from one of the Conducts
in Chambers after *lock-up*. They were to bring a notebook each and a pencil. This he repeated several times.
The pencil was important. That evening the bored
Morleyites went to the Dame for tickets. She received
them with spare pencils, and begged them to ' keep pure
for the Bishop.' Peter was the last to leave, and of him

she attempted a query. 'Laddie, how many Sacraments are there?' 'Seven, ma'am; at least a *Tug* told me there were seven.' 'Guid laddie, don't let the auld Conduct persuade ye there is one less.' And Willum stood at the door like the ripe fruit of her sacramental training.

Under the dark, but no longer forbidding, gates the Morleyites entered the School Yard. The urbane School Clerk was there to usher them into Chambers, where they sat down in awed silence, for the mildness of the Conduct was tempered by painful associations recalled by the room. The Conduct began reading long extracts out of the Catechism, as soon as he had entered their names. Then he asked some questions which apparently had no answers. He urged the boys to take his own answers down in pencil. By this time reverence, the supply being thin at any time, had worn off, and there was a concerted move to invent answers for the next question. 'How many Sacraments are there?' asked the good man. 'Seven,' asserted Peter. 'Rubbish!' snorted the Conduct. 'Six!' 'Five!' 'Four!' 'Three!' came from different parts of the room, like soldiers answering to number. Mouler made the winning shot with 'Two!' and treated himself to considerable self-congratulation.

'What are they?' asked the Conduct, not suspecting he was being slightly ragged by the eager lads. Philips, the parson's son, held up his hand. 'Please, sir, bread and wine!' This looked obviously right, but it wasn't. 'Next.' 'Bread and water!' shouted Mouler, anxious to repeat his success. 'Rubbish!' and he was silenced in general laughter. 'My duty to God and my duty to my neighbour,' ventured Frencher, on a new tack, which also proved rubbish to the general glee. And so an hour was passed.

Through Ullathorne, however, Peter received a considerable amount of careful preparation in these days. On half-holidays Ullathorne took him to visit his Confessor, and Peter sucked in all that was proffered him, even promising to say his prayers again. He became scrupulous, and wrote down his faults in a notebook, which Ullathorne tore up, substituting a rosary, which he warned him to hide as he might hide a catapult. Ullathorne was a little intolerant of the happy-go-lucky, unmystical religion of the English. The *Insider* produced an imaginary account of the perfect Etonian that might be produced on principles of sentimental but unsupernatural theology. He read it aloud for Peter's benefit. 'The perfect Etonian must be athletic from baptism. He must be keen, but not a *pot-hunter*. He must get his House-colours before Confirmation, and possibly his Mixed Wall before he leaves. He must work somehow without appearing to *sap*. He must get into the Newcastle Select and congratulate his junior for winning the Scholarship. He must be twelfth man for the Eleven and not sulk at Lord's. He must visit the Eton Mission and play cards with the working men. He must be a sportsman, but never bet. When he is very old, he may become Bursar, and finally he will be translated to heaven in Dr. Keate's old chariot.' Peter burst into simple laughter. 'I never knew religion could be so funny.' 'It's the funniest thing there is,' said Ullathorne, 'that is, if you really think you are in the Ark. You can either laugh at the funny animals in the Ark or at the foolish people outside. Whosoever will be saved, it is necessary that he develop a slight sense of humour.' 'Well, that is certainly what we do at Confirmation class,' said Peter thoughtfully, but after studying Doré's illustrations to Dante in the School Library, he added a sense of fear.

The work for Confirmation proceeded steadily through the School. Mr. Christopher succeeded in bringing his boys to the mystical stage. Mr. Edwards made a good impression by reading to his, and ordering them to conform to the standards of decency or the Riot Act. On one occasion he was disturbed by the row in Morley's, where, for natural reasons, the House master had not felt

T

equal to undertaking a Confirmation class himself.
Edwards hurried over into Morley's passage. 'Stand
where you are,' he shouted to the raggers. 'Don't
move! Don't move! Read the Riot Act!' And they
stood still, subdued by his outburst, but no Morley
appeared, and Edwards retreated like a poacher to his
own demesne. Mr. Munfort enjoyed a decided success.
Some of his parents had desired their boys to be prepared
by a clergyman, whereat their hopefuls waxed indignant
at the stigma placed on Mr. Munfort, and announced,
whether they meant it or not, that they would be damned
if they were confirmed through any means except Mr.
Munfort, who knew considerably more about it than
parsons anyhow. Mr. Jenkinson left his boys with something of the best that was in Sparta and Athens and
Galilee for ever mingled in their minds. Only Jenkinson
could have combined the Attic and the Christian grace.

Confirmation arrived duly in lawn sleeves and a Doctor
of Divinity's hood. Two hundred boys in very different
stages of preparation were marshalled. Crowds of friends
and parents came down as for a very solemn form of
Speeches. There was a gala service in Chapel. The Head
surveyed the candidates with unruffled clemency, and
Peter began to wonder whether at last he would have a
chance of speaking with him personally. He had so much
to say to him, and he had never had the opportunity.
Perhaps it was coming. He felt that his School record all
these years had been untarnished, and he longed to feel
that strong arm on his shoulder and to hear, 'Well done,
thou good and faithful servant!' But the Head proved
more distant than ever on Confirmation day. It was true
that he constantly looked down the anxious lines, but his
eyes seemed only to dwell upon one or two old offenders.

The Bishop performed his work with ease and grace.
There was a tradition at Morley's that a boy had once
greased his head so thickly with bear's grease that the
Bishop's hands had been limed like a bird to a branch.
Accordingly a good deal of extra grease was rubbed in

on the chance, but nothing happened. The service was magnificently decorous. The Provost was desirably pompous. The Head was graciously inclined. The Conducts were faithfully efficient. The parents were rapturously edified and the dear boys were submissively confirmed.

Peter met Ullathorne on the Chapel steps. Not knowing what was appropriate to say, Peter uttered, ' *Gratters !* ' the stock felicitation on winning a new colour. ' Don't *gratters* me,' said Ullathorne. ' I am taking a week's retreat at Cowley St. John to recover from the effects.' ' What do you think of this ? ' and Peter showed him a High Church manual which his Dame had presented to him in the morning. Ullathorne looked and sniffed, ' Old Sarum. Try this,' and he handed him Father Stanton's Catholic Prayers for Church of England People.

Peter took it to his room and hid it as some boys hid their *cribs*. He was, of course, allowed to use *cribs* for his Extra Books and often devised what Philips called Man-traps, which consisted of leaving the blue-coloured *crib* half-hidden on the table for the eye of Mr. Morley, who invariably pounced and found he was wrong. This would have made a curious Man-trap, but Peter decided to keep the book strictly to himself and to read it only after lights. He opened it that night. There was a little inscription from Ullathorne with a Latin hymn to King Henry the Sixth in his handwriting. As he read, he felt his soul creeping into a cranny where it could not be seen. It was like reading Homer or the *Arabian Nights* for the first time. He read on and on. Suddenly he noticed a dull glow under his door. He quenched his candle with a wet thumb and assumed slumber. The glow grew brighter. He crawled out of bed and opened the door an inch. To his surprise he saw a Lower Boy, Cheener, burning up papers on the lead carpet. Nor did Cheener seem to notice Peter's approach. ' What on earth are you doing here, at this hour ? ' and Peter felt that a mild kick under his nightshirt was not out of place. Cheener moved away in a kind of stupor. Peter put out the burning paper, wondering why he should burn old exercise books in the dead of night. The School Clock boomed and then struck one. It was very curious, but it had been a curious day. He was not a Captain so he decided not to report the matter. There was no harm done and perhaps Cheener had his form of religion like Ullathorne. He had heard of fire worship. Anyhow he preferred to fall asleep and think no more about it.

CHAPTER XXII

THE LAG HOUSE

FORETHOUGHT and afterthought had not prevented Mr. Morley's House passing to the lag of the School. The Uppers who ran the House wasted their time and their sustenance at roulette, while Lower Boys picked up mischief. Peter and his friends made the best of it. They mostly became hermits or individualists, careless of the pulsating or applauding influences in the School outside. Having reached Fifth Form they escaped the mesh and devoted themselves to their hobbies, hobbies which might surprise the outsider. Postage stamps and guinea pigs were left to Fourth Form. Among Peter's Fifth Form cronies was Ormton, who had picked up a taste for Egyptian hieroglyphics in the Museum and could find his way more easily about a remote dynasty of the Pharaohs than a football medley. He was quite sincere in preferring the Sacred Book of the Dead to the novels of Guy Boothby. Ormton was at Morley's and was fond of contributing sham hieroglyphic tablets supposedly dug up on the future ruins of Eton to the *Insider*. Outside Morley's there were other originals, who swam into Peter's backwater, all intellectual and retiring. There was a quaint youth who took snuff and wrote the best hexameters in Fifth Form. There was one of the best amateur photographers in England, who exhibited landscapes and clouds of almost Japanese effect in the pioneer exhibitions which Dr. Borcher used to organise in Upper School. There were advanced naturalists, who used to wash mammoth bones out of Thames gravel and collect the eggs of all the reed and river birds between Brocas and

Oxford. Peter had once joined a moth and butterfly brigade, who obtained occasional leave to treacle the elms in the Playing Fields. There were Marbled Whites to be found in the Great Park, Red Admirals round the decaying mulberries in College, and Death's Head Moths in the potato beds towards Philippi. The Camberwell Beauty was reported in the Thames willows. Boys with such pursuits were utterly ignored and the collections of local Flora they made for the Museum were received with the scorn reserved by English boys for kindergarten. The School was really unaware of their existence, but if they were not encouraged, they were not persecuted. Keeping away from the main stream and the fiercely contested prizes tossing on its congested current, they crept under the shady bank into the haven where they would be. Eton afforded them the rarest boon in youth. They were left alone and they paid the price in unpopularity, but contempt is the nurse of the talents.

Once more the football half returned and Morley's House showed signs of dissolution. Mouler and Frencher ran the games and the Debating Society. Camdown major was Captain of the House on school seniority alone, for Peter not only defeated him in Trials but did a good deal of his classical work for him. However it was good to purchase an ally when Mouler and Frencher were in the offing. Socston's interests were entirely with the River and out of the House. The Football Cup roused little concern at Morley's. The House was divided into groups who kept to themselves. Conversation at meals languished except when a rise could be taken out of the Man.

Mouler issued an order for others to start training for the Cup, but his own after-breakfast pipe was a little too public to bring home the force of example. Every Sunday the *sine* was made to forgo the sweetness of a long lie in order to run to Boveney Lock before breakfast. In the afternoon the Lower Boy Eleven were ordered to walk to Half-way Gates down the Long Walk, where Mouler appeared once and read an Absence of an unauthorised nature. Delinquents were smacked in a mass every Saturday, but still nobody could be induced to feel keen for the House. As match after match was lost by the *sine*, Mouler put up a notice to say that in future *sine* were expected to do a training walk as well as their morning run on Sundays. During prayers a notice was added in a forged hand to say that House-colours were expected to answer their names to Willum at Boveney Lock in future. It was signed in large scrawling capitals, ' Willum,' but it was attributed to Ormton or Peter. As it bore the sign of a revolt in the Fifth no inquiry was made.

Peter and Socston gave Ormton credit and one evening, after an infernal *sine*-match in which Morley's had lost by a dozen *rouges* to nothing, the disgust was so general that *saps* and athletes joined in revolt. ' We shall never get that House Cup—why train at all ? ' remarked Peter. ' We may as well try to pass the first round of the Cup, which the House has never done yet,' suggested Socston. ' I 'm so sick of the whole thing I never want to see a football *pill* again.' Ormton came in at that moment to join in Extra Books, a peculiar task for *saps* who wished to win Distinction in Trials. They dived into their Homer unconscious of the fret and clamour of the House. The spell of the *Odyssey* came upon them as Ormton read aloud the translation while the others followed in the Greek. Homer, the distant Mycenaean ancestor of all boys' books from *Crusoe* to *Treasure Island*, is the first of the Classics to arrest the boy-mind. It is extraordinary how quickly Fifth Form boys working in trio, one with *crib*, one with notes, and the third with the Lexicon, can cover a book of the *Odyssey*. In one day *saps* can prepare a book of that Mediterranean novel by working after twelve, after four and all evening till lights are out.

With a sigh of relief Peter closed the Lexicon, but Ormton shut the *crib* with a sense of appreciation. ' They were fine fellows, those Greeks, but the Egyptians were

more wonderful. I wish we had an *Odyssey* in Hiero-
glyph.' This was a little too much even for *saps*, and
Ormton was told so. ' By the way, did you put up that
notice ? ' asked Peter. Ormton nodded. There was a
general laugh of approval. ' That taught the House-
colours to mind their own business. How can you expect
anybody to train when they see the Debate smoke pipes
every morning after breakfast ? ' remarked Socston. Peter
had been thinking on a train of thought remote from
Morley's House politics. Suddenly he said, ' Ormton,
my *pater* used to travel a lot. He died in Egypt, and I
remember the mummies' heads he found being sent up
to the lumber-room at home. Would they be of any use
to you ? ' Ormton's eyes dilated with excitement. ' Why
of course they would,' and he began drawing Hieroglyphics
with the red-hot poker on the wooden fireplace, explaining
them the while, until Peter's mantel resembled the outer
coffin of a mummy. He promised to send for them forthwith and Ormton agreed to arrange the specimens so that
they could make a joint presentation to the Museum.
' Won't the Custodian be excited ! He has just got all
the Egyptian things poor Myers gave Eton before he was
killed in South Africa, but heads, real mummy heads, will
be gorgeous.'

That night Morley came in as usual and seeing the
decorations of Peter's fireplace gave way to a furious
cackle, promising to send in a handsome bill on the part
of the Governing Body, whose property it was. Mr. Morley had not the knowledge to realise, what an expert in
the British Museum could have told him, that every
figure drawn with the poker was as correct as though it
were drawn in Egypt four thousand years before Christ.
Mr. Morley's Egyptian knowledge was confined to the
diagrams Euclid once drew on the Nile mud, but he was
not more accurate with the chalk on the blackboard than
Ormton with the hot poker illustrating Peter's lintel.

Meantime Jenkinson's House had become ambitious to
win their House-colours, which could only be done by

defeating a House already emblazoned. The challenge
has to be made through the Captain of the Boats, who
selects a House of mediocre calibre as antagonist and the
match is played in public. One day after twelve Socston
rushed into Peter's room. ' We 're down to play Juggins's
for their House-colours ! ' The news spread through the
House and the various passages and boy-runs trembled,
while everybody who had a chance of playing for the
House stampeded to Ingalton Drake's window next door.
There was no doubt, the gods had chosen Morley's as the
lag House for Juggins's to win their colours from. At
lunch the coming match was the one topic. Mouler and
Frencher were genuinely alarmed. Jenkinson's were
known to have trained and practised like prize-fighters.
They had a House-colour or two, the remnants of extinct
Houses. There was general execration at their imperti-
ence, and members of Morley's Eleven grimly counted the
casualties they proposed to make in Mr. Jenkinson's
academy. Lower Boys hummed with the prospect of
watching their Uppers in the arena. The match was to
be played as soon as Saturday, and that evening the names
of Mr. Morley's prospective Eleven were placed on the
notice-board. Socston was in the responsible position
of *short*. Mouler was *long*. Frencher went *fly*, with Peter,
Ormton, and the rest of the *sine* in the bully. It was not
a formidable side and only a half-hearted cheer rose from
their Lower Boys as they took the Field. Peter had
never before played on the sacred Field itself, which was
reserved for School Matches and encounters for the Football Cup. Jenkinson's Eleven received continual cheering
from the crowd and even a lordly ' play-up Jugginses '
from the brilliant-breasted *Pops*, who moved up and down
with locked arms, swinging canes between the players and
the plebs. Whenever a *rouge* was scored they moved
towards the goal and cleared the space necessary for the
curious process of conversion. Morley's versus Jenkinson's was a squalid match between inferior players on a
muddy day, and drew no interest except the keen desire

of the School to see Morley's well beaten. Jenkinson's and the public assembled in force and kept up a steady cheering for the favourites. In their midst stood the benignant and buoyant Jenkinson, who had read ' Sohrab and Rustum ' to his team the previous evening, and refused to hoist an umbrella against the drizzle, that he might share the discomforts of his players. At the further end of the ground stood the silent Morley wearing an old discoloured cricket straw. The Morleyites were moving round him and raising his war cry like a disheartened jeer, ' Mah-Mah-Mah-leys ! Play up, Morleys ! '

. Both teams were thoroughly nervous and wild. Kicks were missed, and swearing and confusion were general. Badly played, there is no less entertaining game than the Eton game. Jenkinson's touched a *rouge* and though they were unable to force it through the goal, they held their own until the last five minutes, when the Morleyites amid cries of derision began to press. Mouler and Frencher's oaths and counter-oaths were audible above the grunts and thuds. The school were amused and even delighted when Mr. Morley, venturing to request Frencher to play a less selfish game, was rewarded with a request to mind his own business. While an argument was developing between Mr. Morley and his hopefuls, there was a sudden break up in the bully and Socston suddenly seeing nothing between himself and the enemy's goal except the ball made a dash and scored a goal, leaving Morley's unexpected victors. There was an inhuman yell from the Morleyites and Morley's straw hat was lifted, apparently from behind, into the air. In view of the victory Mr. Morley took no notice of the assault. By the time his hat was replaced and his spectacles adjusted, the Morleyites were scrambling through the crowd at the ever-obstructive stile over which every spectator had to climb in and out of the Field. The stile was a landmark that generations of indignant letters in the *Chronicle* had failed to remove. Through this time-honoured congestion the Morleyites shoved their way, shouting their

rare shout of victory and swelling with disdain for the
defeated. ' Poor old Juggins ! Did they want their
colours ? Well, they just have to wait and feed up on
pap.' On the other side of the stile stood Jenkinson,
showing a cheery front to his inward misery. As each
member of his team came through, he cast him a faithful
look or a winged word. ' Well played ! You deserved
to win, and you will win next time.' He stood there
seeing his boys through the bitterness of a defeat which
had hit himself hardest. Spectators passed him sympathetically. Morleyites seeing the symbol of the vanquished nudged each other and began rubbing in the
defeat. ' Well played, Morley's ! Morley's ! Morley's ! a
goal to a *rouge*.' There was a curiosity to see the visible
effect. But nothing was there revealed, except the well-
known accent of Jenkinson saying to the dishevelled
players, ' Well played, Mr. Morley's, very well played
indeed ! ' Peter felt the shaft and the Morleyite crowd
bent their heads with shame. Peter turned aside : ' Oh,
I 'm so sorry you did not get your colours, sir,' he blurted
out. ' Sorry, are you ? ' said Jenkinson, bending his
massive brow, ' I 'm as glad of that nearly as of a win.'
Peter hardly caught what this strange man meant but
untouched chords moved in his heart and he felt overwhelming sympathy. A sharp pity stung him almost to
unendurance. A win would have meant so much for
Juggins, whereas no success in the field would ever re-
habilitate Morley's House. The players had all passed,
and it was safe to try a quotation which came to his
muddy lips. ' Sir, don't you remember Lucan's line :

' *Victrix causa deis placuit sed victa Catoni !* '

Peter had learnt it by accident at ' private business '
the previous night, and it seemed to fit the occasion.
' Yes, Peter,' answered Jenkinson, ' one of the greatest
things ever said of a man, and I think Cato would have
been on our side.'

Though the match had been won, Mr. Morley brooded

long over his brawl with his Captain of Games in public.
It had been widely commented on in the School, and Mr.
Morley felt his House would stand no chance if in the
coming half Mouler became Captain of the House as well.
With his spectacles astride his nose, he read and reread
the House list. If only Mouler could be deprived of his
last year, Darley would become Captain, and with Socston
as Captain of Games he foresaw happier times. Logically,
but unwisely, he calculated, and in the evening he wrote
to Mouler's father retailing the unpleasantness which
had occurred on the football field as the climax of dis-
respect to his authority. He requested Mr. Mouler to
remove his boy at the end of the half. There would rest
no stain on his character. He was unfitted to be Captain
of such a House as Mr. Morley's. That was all.

Twenty-four hours later, Mr. Mouler descended upon
Morley's, and was ushered by the ever-jubilant Willum
into the master's presence. Mr. Mouler was a dry little
stick, and equally unaccustomed to use the ordinary
intonations of the human voice. For a half-hour their
voices rose against each other in a crescendo of cackles,
until Mr. Mouler, aiming at a weak spot, declared that
Mr. Morley was not playing cricket, and Mr. Morley
replied that it was not playing football either to insult
one's House master in public. As Mr. Mouler repeatedly
declined to withdraw his hopeful, Mr. Morley thought
an explanation from the Dame would be in order, and
Willum was sent to prepare the way for an interview, but
returned with a burning face, and so stout a refusal that
neither of the male disputants thought fit to press the
matter. Willum's boiling condition was alleviated at
that moment like a red poker dropped into cold water
by the arrival of Mrs. Sowerby, who, with icy scorn,
announced that the sins of Master Mouler had been sufficient to bring the Dame to bed, and hinted that there
was not enough sal volatile in the house to enable
her to face Mr. Mouler senior with any prospect of
composure.

That being that, Mr. Morley attempted compromise, and promised that if Mouler was removed quietly at the end of the half, he would ask the Head Master not to refuse him his leaving book. Mr. Mouler saw the game was up, and consented, but not without assuring Mr. Morley that he would regret to the end of his life that he had not retained the best and only sporting Captain his House was ever likely to obtain. Mr. Morley assured him perkily that he had a very good Captain up his sleeve, and that the House was not so bad as Mr. Mouler insinuated, and indeed, with Mouler's departure, was likely to improve rapidly. Willum, his jubilancy succeeded by the signs of terror, showed Mr. Mouler out, and Mr. Morley retired, feeling he had solved a very difficult mathematical problem.

Soon after these events, Peter found a great intellectual relief to the life at Morley's. Ullathorne offered to take him to the Cloisters to visit his friends, Mr. and Mrs. Thackeray, who had long made that corner of the Eton world a quaint delight to those who were lucky enough to find entry. Peter had heard of Mrs. Thackeray's genius, and was delighted at the idea. With reverent feelings, the two boys entered the Cloisters from the Playing Fields, and rang an inaudible peal on a long iron rod, which seemed to be related to the brass plate engraved with their names. The silence of mildew was unbroken from within, and they passed questingly from door to door. They were of oak and iron, studded with huge rusty handles to match the scabby stonework. They opened, if they ever did open, on a square shrubby iron-railed enclosure, whose omphalos was a pump. A little less daring, the boys tried a bell marked 'PROVOST'S SERVANTS,' and were advised to try the opposite corner. It was mysteriously ajar, and they passed up the stairs into a corner suite of rooms, out of which was visible Romney Island, and, close at hand, the drooping boughs of an enormous plane-tree. The rooms were pleasantly furnished with Early Victorian wares. A little bric-a-brac tempered the severer atmosphere of books. In the midst Mrs. Thackeray offered tea and epigrams to the appreciative.

'Dear Mr. Ullathorne,' she began, 'let me immediately congratulate you on being "sent up for good" again, for the tenth time, I believe.' 'No, the sixth time,' laughed Ullathorne. 'This is my friend Darley, who has also been sent up.' His hostess's hand was extended in benediction. 'Dear Mr. Darley, let me congratulate you then on being "sent up for good" for the sixth time.' 'No, it is for the first time,' and Peter's scarlet became purple. 'Mr. Darley, it is necessary for you to state whether you require tea or coffee or cocoa.' 'Cocoa,' said Peter, thinking it was quickest to make. 'There is no cocoa; ring the bell.' And Peter rang a bell which, like most of the bells in the Cloisters, was out of gear. 'Perhaps you would prefer to recite the "Bells" by Tennyson,' said Mrs. Thackeray, to save the situation, and, on second thoughts, Peter asked for tea. By this time Mr. Thackeray had made an entrance as noiseless as the bell, and carried Peter into the next room, where he inquired his literary tastes, and filled Peter with a sense of ease. It was delightful to listen to this quiet and learned scholar among his books. Peter could overhear Ullathorne and Mrs. Thackeray in the next room talking in choice and sometimes elliptic speech. They were too serious to cause each other amusement. When they ceased to be oracular, they became coherent to the general. Of all subjects, they were discussing Joan of Arc. 'The Provost is too nautical to care for the Saints,' declared Mrs. Thackeray. 'But on reading of Joan's burning, he distinctly said, "Poor thing, poor thing!"' 'Perhaps,' said Ullathorne, 'he thought reserve necessary in his position. I believe our holy Founder was present at her trial.' 'You don't mean to say so?' 'Yes,' continued Ullathorne, 'the Saints are not recognisable to the Saints. In their humility they mistake each other for ordinary people.' 'Then we can

only hope he did not see her burn.' 'It is most devoutly
to be hoped, but we do not know,' laid down Ullathorne.
'Most devoutly to be hoped,' chimed Mrs. Thackeray,
and, with a sigh, as though the possibility might be
reported as a fact in *The Times* of Monday, ' we can only
hope.'

'I am glad you like Miss Austen,' Mr. Thackeray said
to Peter. 'Do you remember Mr. Woodhouse's Christian
name ? It is my test question, as it can only be known
by inference.' Peter knew it not, but Ullathorne threw
it off as easily as a smoker throws a smoke-ring from his
lips. 'I should like you to read this,' said Mr. Thackeray,
placing a signed copy of William Johnson's *Ionica* in
Peter's hands. 'What passage are you opening ? ' asked
Mrs. Thackeray. 'Is it Mimnermus in Church ? It
would be an unsettling poem if it were not so beautiful.'
'Did you really know Johnson,' asked Peter, 'when
he was a master here ? ' 'Yes,' said Mrs. Thackeray,
closing her eyes very gently. 'He was very much with
us in those days. He was here and there and everywhere
in Eton. One day he was no longer with us, and we have
missed him for forty years.'

'And where do you board, Mr. Darley ? ' asked Mrs.
Thackeray, gently breaking the lavender quiet. 'Mr.
Morley's,' replied Peter, and the silence was renewed.
'Your Dame seems familiar to us,' she continued. 'Forgive me for recalling what must be a personal matter
with you. Here in the Cloisters, we can do nothing,
nothing. Since the other Dames decline to call on her,
she has appealed to the Head Master, but nothing can
be done for her. It must be so comforting for her.'

'Why ? ' asked Peter, a little bewildered. 'She can
now devote herself wholly to good works,' Mrs. Thackeray
pointed out. 'And what book of poems are you next
bringing out, Mr. Ullathorne ? I hear all the masters
are quoting parodies from the last. Mr. Jenkinson read
your skit on the Eton Society with a Homeric roll.' 'How
can I publish more,' groaned Ullathorne, 'when the

ushers fail to recognise parodies of their own poetry? Christopher, Jenkinson, Robertson are delighted instead of furious. It is most disheartening.' 'Since the evergreen J. K. S., the parody of Browning and Whitman has gone out of fashion,' said Mrs. Thackeray. 'How startling he seemed to us in word and verse. I feel my curtains are still impregnated with the wise things he used to say, and which we, alas, have forgotten.' 'Is it true that he once used his hostess's teapot to warm his bare feet before breakfast?' asked Ullathorne. 'Would he had! Would that my teapot had ever been a step to Parnassus! Would that Mazawattee tea might recall the delicious sayings of fifty years ago!'

Mr. Thackeray had flitted in and out several times. As he was making a last diaphanous appearance from the next room, Ullathorne told him that Mr. Robertson and his Tutor were bringing out an edition of Lucian between them. 'How very clever Mr. Robertson must be,' said Mrs. Thackeray unaffectedly. 'But do not be disappointed about your book, Mr. Ullathorne. I once had a success with a first book, a most remarkable success. But that was all. We need never allude to it.' And she sat back, like some mute Milton, some cloistered Brontë.

Peter looked round the unique apartment, which seemed transported from some Cathedral Close in a novel of Trollope, and felt deliciously at home. Apart from the fragrance of the tea urn, here was mental comfort, here was real conversation, here were people who talked about something besides football. Their anecdote, epigram, and repartee hummed as deliciously in his brain as the water in the kettle. He hated to return to his Dame's and the small talk of Mr. Morley's Library.

By this time Mr. Thackeray was ready to show them through the Provost's Lodge and Election Room. The Provost had been seen going out, which made a good reason. Peter was not prepared for what followed. The Provost's Lodge was no drab sepulchral lodging, as he imagined. It was ablaze with colour and beauty. In one room were vivid mediaeval pictures of Richard the Third, Henry the Seventh. On the walls hung a galaxy of portraits by Reynolds, Gainsborough, Hoppner, and Romney. Portraits of Eton boys on the threshold of life, with one hand pushing aside boyish things, and with the other grasping the first hazards of life. Many were but Dukes and Earls in gold brocade and lace collars, of whom nothing was afterwards recorded, save that they were nobly begot, and in time nobly succeeded their begetters. There was Reynolds's foxy little Duke of Gordon, whose brother History describes as sometime riotous, and Charles James Fox as a schoolboy, with dark lustrous locks over his ears, large black eyebrows, and a prominent nose above lips that curled with the dream of some coming speech. Too wicked and witty for school, he was already Eton's prodigy and darling, and well aware that impudence covers a multitude of mistakes. There was Gainsborough's young Lord Granby, but, above all, Romney's incomparable studies of the ringleted, half-serious, half-exuberant boys in whose features his mystic brush seemed to limn their future, pictures of such as Grenville, Grey, and Wellesley in their morning prime. Wellesley, the future Indian Viceroy, with deep-set eyes and Roman features, the typical and perfect *amator Etonae*, whose own epitaph was written in her praise, and whose body was buried in her Chapel :

> ' *Si qua meum vitae decursu gloria nomen*
> *auxerit, aut si quis nobilitarit honos,*
> *muneris, Alma, tui est, Altrix; da terra sepulchrum*
> *supremam lacrimam da memoremque mei.*'

Grenville, orator and statesman, leaving Eton in blue coat, with carefully powdered hair and pigtail, already inclined towards the great future, of which he and his friends could have little doubt. Grey, the carrier of the great Reform Bill, also with his hair powdered, and blue eyes contrasting with his clenched fist and the reserves of graceful power underlying his young face. What a

u

difference lay between this picture and Grey's mature bust in Upper School! It was almost the contrast between a Venusberg and a Morgue to see the two different rooms dedicated to the dead. The most beautiful of the Romneys was a portrait of Mr. Woodcock, whose Miltonic beauty peered under the dark hair surrounding the oval masculine face. It was perhaps the most haunting picture ever painted of youth, a Narcissus without a touch of vanity.

It was curious to dwell on the fates of these wonderfully pictured Etonians, all painted, not as pictures generally are, at the weary or fierce climax of life, or in the rheumy ebb of old age, but in the dew of fresh youth. Failure and tragedy there was among them as well as trumpet-lifted success. There were Edward Chamberlayne, once Captain of the School ; Samuel Whitbread, the reformer ; and John Damer in gold brocade, who all committed suicide. There was the vital and compelling Lord Holland, who carried off Lady Webster. There were two Captains of the Oppidans, Thomas Plumer and Sir John Mordaunt, who were accidentally killed. There was the second Earl of Powis, also killed, and the Lord Walsingham, who was burnt to death. And there was the hero of Tennyson's *In Memoriam*, with thick underlip and mischievous eyes, who of all was most fortunate in his early dying. Towards recenter times there were portraits of Chief Justice Coleridge, Bishop Ryle, Stafford Northcote, Goldwin Smith, and Lord Rosebery, all Eton's favourite and successful sons, and then the gallery had been presumably cut short by photography and the price of painting. It was a dazzling sight, like so many votive offerings hung up in the Temple of Youth, by the exquisite thoroughbreds of the past. Whether they were Tories or Whigs, they were all aristocrats, and to be led or ridden by such a race of godlike young creatures can only have been satisfactory to the British people in the extreme.

As they passed through Election Room, with its carved

roof, with windows set with broken mediaeval glass, with the Picture of Venice given by the Council of the Ten to Provost Wotton, and saw where the Provost formally ripped the gowns of Collegers leaving the Foundation. Peter wondered whether women of equal beauty and culture could have ever been found to satisfy such splendid embodiment of the other sex, little dreaming that any of those bright, eager faces had faded under disease and dissipation. What indeed was the percentage of unfulfilled promise to astounding success? That Eton might bear one Grey or one Rosebery, how many disappeared who had bloomed as fair on the spring path of youth?

It would have been interesting to set the contemporary girlhood side by side with Eton portraits if they had come under the same brush, but there was curiously only one female portrait in the Provost's Lodge. Mr. Thackeray delicately indicated the naked form of a beautiful woman, preserved in gratitude by the Foundation. It was Jane Shore, the leman of Edward the Fourth, who of her beauty and charity prevailed on the King to spare King Henry's foundations at Eton and Cambridge. Little was known of her save the tradition that in those white arms had rested the Majesty of England, and that she had saved Eton. She had known misery as well as splendour. She had passed to the Tower, and she had helped to strew flowers at the funeral of Henry the Seventh. Then she disappeared. But the College kept her in everlasting memory as the Magdalen of the Eton Calendar. Much was forgiven her, because she had loved Eton much. It seemed strange to Peter that her naked beauty should be preserved and guarded through the centuries by a succession of strange oia fossilised Fellows and Provosts, moving about like mummies, peeping out of the black cerecloths in which they were wrapped, and the more so when he reflected that any boy keeping such a picture in his room would probably have to leave the School.

But there was more to be seen yet, a roomful of Keate's old pupils, and in a corner a drawing by Richmond of

Edmond Warre, as Newcastle Scholar. It was a soberer creation than the Romneys and Gainsboroughs. The strength of the subject seemed to surpass the power of the artist. It was not without the beauty of strength, but it showed character rather than manhood triumphant, athletic rather than intellectual pride. There was no taste of pleasure, as with so many of the other portraits, on those well-shaped lips, no shadow of desire in the frank, keen eyes, lit by the glow of Classical appreciation, and as yet all undimmed by study. And the thick locks of hair fell like a brown nimbus round the future ruler of Eton. Ambition hardly shone in the countenance of the young eagle. Life's great prizes were in his reach already. The Newcastle was his, and a thwart was waiting him at Oxford. The Head Mastership he can hardly have visioned. It was a tradition that he only came back to Eton as an assistant in order to pay off an honourable debt incurred at Oxford, which his father found impossible to pay. It was not an ordinary debt, but one incurred in raising Volunteers, and it was a debt which had a vast influence in Eton history, for Warre came and stayed for his half century.

In the following week Peter began to look forward intensely to his coming appearance before the Head. He felt certain that at last the Head would lay a friendly arm on his shoulder and say some encouraging words. So auspicious an occasion as being 'sent up for good' could hardly be passed over. To make certain of attracting his special attention, Peter sat up late copying out his verses in the most perfect copperplate on the vellum with the College arms, which he proudly purchased from Ingalton Drake's. Every letter was formed separately and the pencilled lines were carefully removed with rubber. It filled Mr. Lamb with admiration and Mr. Morley noted that there was not a blot. Tutor and House master signed the accompanying card, and with his folio wrapped in tissue paper he presented himself with thirty others at Chambers. The School Clerk motioned them all to enter,

Oppidans and Collegers in their common glory. Ullathorne of course was there, and expectant of the prize
which was given for every third appearance. The visitors
were requested to seat themselves honourably and not
to stand as though they were summoned for offences.
There was a confused silence, and everybody attempted
to sink gracefully on the limited seating area without
also destroying his neighbour's hat. It was like the
drawing-room game of musical chairs, for one shy youth
was left sitting on the floor. There was a titter and the
Head looked up. This apparently amused him, for he
made the proper proverbial allusion to the difficulty of
sitting between two stools. As this was the only remark
he made, it became embedded in Peter's memory. In
order the Head received exercise after exercise as though
they were *poenas de luxe*, signed the tickets as though
they were cheques, and dismissed the writers in freezing
silence. Peter, who had hoped for a minute or two of
winged converse, was again disappointed.

He was consoled, however, that afternoon by tea in the
Cloisters. ' Dear Mr. Darley,' said his appreciative
hostess, ' this must be a proud day for your Dame to see
you break the spell and present the rare sight of a pupil of
Mr. Morley's bringing his sheaves to the Head.' Peter
leaned back feeling he was understood at last. ' The
Head never said whether he thought them good or bad.
He shovelled them into a drawer.' Mrs. Thackeray
looked toward Mr. Thackeray, who very kindly asked for
Peter's rough copy. To submit Latin lyrics to the greatest
authority on Horace was like showing a school-room water-
colour to Turner. Mr. Thackeray nodded approvingly.
Peter felt blissful. ' I am afraid you must scorn our
platitudinous teas,' Mrs. Thackeray suddenly suggested
to Peter, whose vocabulary did not yet contain the word
platitudinous, for he smiled and insisted they were quite
digestible. His solecism was politely unheeded. ' I will
show you my scrap book. You will find it lighter,' and
she thrust a ragged old volume upon him. Peter opened

the pages and was riveted by pen and pencil caricatures of all the Eton characters he had ever heard from tradition. Here were facsimiles or ghosts of Mr. Socston's Eton. Here was ' Stiggins ' with his pale straw-coloured beard, perhaps meditating the one famous moment of his life, when the waters of Barnes Pool all but touched the aforesaid beard. Here was the Baroness de Rosen fishing in her cellar for empty bottles during a severe flood. And of those still in the flesh, there was Hornby in his prime descending the edge of a glacier, roped to guides and armed with axe as he surprised a gentle colleague in the valley below. Here was Warre coaching the Eight, standing up and bawling from coxswain's seat. This seemed incredible to Peter, but Mrs. Thackeray reassured him, ' Dr. Warre used to sing and make fun when he first came to Eton.' But Peter could not conceive Warre young, any more than his Tutor old.

That evening, feeling rather pleased with himself, Peter attended the rather gloomy function known as Supper. Its necessity had long been superseded by the lavish hot teas provided by parents in addition to the House fare. Theoretically Supper was a relic of the past, as its substance was a relic of lunch, for it consisted of cold meat, cold beer, and cheese. Mr. Morley rather tactlessly announced what Peter would have preferred to keep a secret from those present, that he had been ' sent up for good.' Conversation died under the strain of appreciating this new honour to the House. Without waiting for the cheese, Peter rose to go, thinking no more about it, when a sudden and distinct hiss broke the air. Apparently the conservatives did not enjoy new precedents being set for the House. However, Peter no longer cared what the House thought of him, though he had a strong suspicion that the direction from which the hiss had come had often been assisted by his industry.

CHAPTER XXIII

THE GREAT KEYHOLE MYSTERY

MR. MORLEY'S House reassembled the next half without
Frencher or Mouler. Mr. Morley, deciding on a purge,
had had Frencher detained in his home circles. Frencher's
case had presented no difficulties. He had not passed
Trials for three halves and could be honourably superannuated. Mr. Morley returned from the golf links in
better form for the losing battle he was waging against
the odds. He was doomed to lose the game because he
had never learnt its unwritten rules. Not by calculation
can an Eton master add a cubit to the standing of his
House. He must inspire his own boys. It was puzzling
rather than painful to Morley that Jenkinson's should
already be considered a better House and that parents
should shun his list as much as Maxse's. He had hoped
that after Camdown's captaincy came to an end in the
summer Socston and Darley would bring the House into
stride with the School.

It was true that he knew how to prune, but he had
neglected to water or cultivate his garden. He had
lopped strong branches which seemed crooked, but he
was leaving the undeveloped to carry the burden of the
House before they were strong enough to command the
undergrowth. Nothing could alter the School opinion of
the House. In vain the Dame praised Morley for showing
strength of character, though as a woman she must have
been aware that it could hardly be said to exist. And
what a woman knows is sometimes revealed to babes.
Morley's House knew Morley better than he dreamed.
They could size him to a nicety, for he never varied in

mood or manner. Day by day he appeared at his open door three minutes before each School and symbolically looking neither to right nor left walked parallel to the Long Walk, took an angle of 45 degrees across the road past the Sebastopol cannon, and at one minute to the hour disappeared under the Gothic arch with its thin heraldry and mottoes, gummed like pasteboard to the battlemented brick, which marked the entrance to the New Schools. As the hour struck like a metal gong through the slow arteries of the School, Mr. Morley placed his heavy key in his keyhole and entered, followed by his division. His was a precise soul. He was made in a geometrical mould and hardly deserved the slings and arrows of his Eton career. Even so, Destiny was playing with the very lock which he turned every hour he took school.

Frencher and Mouler were not to disappear from Mr. Morley's horizon yet. To soothe their parents and keep the legal peace, they had each received a leaving book, the heavily bound, yellow-leathered poems of Gray, stamped with the gilt arms of the College, the time-honoured and ornate certificate that they had not been expelled. Gray was the poet *quem Etona miratur*, without a copy of whom no Etonian gentleman's library or character is complete. Much to their families' distress they both preferred to boast they had been *sacked* and had acquired no little standing at their Army Coach in consequence. Expulsion from Eton was no impediment in London Clubs. There were certain regiments where the expelled were welcome without questions and minor colleges at the 'Varsity where they could comfortably reside. In a historic case, the Duke of York sympathising with one of Keate's victims had commissioned him in the Guards forthwith. There was the astounding case of a President of the Royal Society, whom Hawtrey had expelled for experimenting with chemicals in the first week of November, a time when the growing darkness of winter seems to demand new possibilities in lighting. Expulsion was generally reserved for conduct unbefitting a gentleman, but in the eyes of the boys it entailed no disgrace. Once an Etonian always an Etonian, *Etonensis in aeternum.* What the world could not give, its opinion could not take away, and no name could be struck from the old School Lists. Many a fine fellow has had to leave, and Frencher and Mouler finding themselves enjoying a prestige they did not deserve, quietly encouraged the legend that they had made Eton too hot for themselves, and meantime plotted to get even with the Man for docking their Eton careers.

Towards the end of the half they made a surreptitious visit to their old School and were hailed as heroes at Morley's. Their account of their doings at the Army Coach was proportionate to the stories that were believed at the Coach's of their Eton doings. Their entrance into Morley's was not unnoticed by Willum, who duly reported their arrival, and received cross-directions from both the Man and the Dame to usher the unwelcome visitors from the House at each other's request. Willum delivered his disagreeable tidings in Camdown's rooms. ' Mr. Morley, 'e says that the Dame says, if you don't leave the 'Ouse, 'e will 'ave to speak to the 'Ead Master.' A derisive jeer cut Willum short. ' Willum,' said Frencher, ' in future when you speak to an Army Candidate you will stand at attention. Willum, tell the Dame that the Man can go to Hell ! ' A convulsive shudder passed through Willum, not without an avaricious gleam, as Mouler added, ' Ten shillings if you do, Willum.' Willum withdrew on tiptoe as though the flooring might be expected to give way under such studied blasphemy. Half an hour after *lock-up*, having impeded as much *sap* as was then flowing in the House, the terrible pair of Army Candidates swaggered out and began walking toward the Slough Road, after lighting pipes of a size and virulence to apprise others how ancient they were, even for old boys. ' What rotten baccy Camdown keeps,' said Frencher. ' They don't seem to rag the Man as we did in the old days.' ' By Gad, let 's rag the Man again,' said Mouler as they passed the New Schools; 'let's climb the gates and muck his school-room. Isn't it the first day of Trials to-morrow?' Frencher hugged himself and emptied his pipe of a glowing wad. They found the door of course locked. 'Well I vote we come back and fill it up with putty.' The idea was not to be lost. It was a unique chance if it could be done then and there. Delay would be the same as failure. While the School was engaged in Trial *sap*, the *saps* working sappily, the moderate workers moderately, and the lazy desperately, the two conspirators stole back through Eton and by hazard encountered the old *Joby*, in whose debt they haply remembered they were deepest.

The *Joby* was much interested by their unsolicited confession of unpaid debts and not unagreeably surprised by their offer to liquidate it on the spot. They were in need of putty, they could not forbear to mention, perhaps as much as he was in need of cash. The *Joby* scratched his head. He could not provide putty, but if they accompanied him to Tangier Lane he could dispose of some plaster of Paris. Since the School Stores had come, he had had to give up the provision business. He disposed of plaster casts of the School arms to visitors in the holidays. Times were not what they were. Boys weren't so generous as might be expected.

Under the *Joby's* directions they poured the plaster into a jar and departed, wishing him good-night. He had better understand that their generosity was to be accompanied by intense secrecy on his part. The *Joby* nodded and made no attempt even to guess why they needed plaster of Paris in the night. They could do what they liked with it. His soul was aggrieved by the School Stores. His thoughts fell back on generous patrons in the past. Life was not all joy to *Joby*-kind.

Meantime the conspirators had climbed back into the New Schools and, having mixed and poured the plaster into Mr. Morley's keyhole, discovered in their generous state of mind that there was enough to go round the buildings. Rapidly they passed from room to room, plastering the vital points. It was a piece of splendid sabotage. It was like taking out the linch-pins from a row of cabs or soaping a slide for the whole School to fall on. They threw the rest of the plaster over Fifteen Arch Bridge and started for a late train from Slough. It would be delightful to wake up the next morning and think what would have occurred at Eton before breakfast. Mr. Morley struggling with his key. . . . Boys kept out of school. . . . Trials disorganised. . . . The Head sent for. . . . It might teach the Governing Body a lesson. It would have been interesting to record their great thoughts as they hurried past the indistinct plain of Agar's Plough. Far behind, the great looming elms were visible in the Playing Fields. Behind the unleafed trees lay the low, night-clad battle-ments of the College and above them stood the twin towers carrying the School Clock, like two giant carriers. Beyond were the pinnacles of Chapel. The moon came out and all became silver and lucid. A mysterious transformation played upon the colour and material of the College. The grey stone silvered and the purple brick glistened to argent. The wind gently displaced masses of thin cloud drift, which floated over the School like the long weed-tresses which summer released in the River. Under the slow movement of the moon-dappled clouds the little world of Eton slept.

The School Clock struck the hour of one, first the four solemn quarters and then the single clang. The bell spoke not less vibrantly or compelling, when it spoke to a thousand or when it was only heard of the sleepless. A thousand boys slept the numbing sleep of exhausted youth. Tutors and House masters enjoyed the reward of anxious toil. Perhaps only Mr. Christopher among their number stirred in metrical inspiration and wrote lines which sleeping boys would yet have to Latinise with much clawing of *Gradus*. Swells and athletes roosted like fighting cocks, their rooms piled with trophy and cap, cup and oar, their walls honoured by sacred photographs of the Eleven arm-in-arm or of the Eight balanced on a ladder or of *Pop* grouped, where they and College alone had the right to be taken, on the steps of Chapel.

Perchance Eton was dreaming. The Provost dreamed that Oscar Browning was still at Eton and felt troubled. The Head dreamed he was dead and stroking Charon's boat across the Styx and felt morally sure that the Provost, who was bow, was not doing his fair share. The Vice-Provost dreamed he was showing Horace round the Chapel and trying to quote from the *Odes*. Miss Evans dreamed of Paradise the Blest, from whose walls she could see Bishop Selwyn gently waving her House-colours. The Lower Master dreamed he had seen the Derby won by a jockey in his House-colours and was wondering how to break it to the Governing Body. Dr. Blitz dreamed he had broken Lloyds' Bank. Mr. Munfort dreamed he had been knighted by the King for winning the House Cup a third time. Dr. Borcher dreamed that by a reflex photograph from the light of a star he had at last taken a picture of the other side of the moon. Mr. Jenkinson dreamed that by some extraordinary slip he had become Vice-Provost and was making a list in his mind of worthier candidates. Mr. Morley never dreamed, but his Dame dreamed that the Queen had returned her call.

Boys dream little, except under pressure of strawberry jam or lobster. Overwork kept few minds restless. The majority, like a pack of tired hounds, who bay after a hare in their sleep, followed their athletic hobbies. Goals were kicked under the sheets, and wiry wrists stretched against Harrow's phantom bowlers. Ullathorne dreamed he was saying his thanksgiving Mass for winning the Newcastle. Charleston, that Gibbon had been introduced as an external examiner, and had ploughed everybody for the Wilder Divinity prize except himself. Peter suffered from an ever-recurring dream of an unprepared construe. He dreamed, too, that he was late for Trials, and was running to the New Schools. He was beating

on the door of his school-room, but in vain. Something
kept the door immovable . . .

The moon sank behind the old elms, but the cloud-rack
never ceased to hurry across the sky. Like legions, the
mists took shapes and died away, like spirits gathering
in deserted places. From the ends of the world spirits
in pain or weariness, or at peace, swept towards Eton.
Lonely graves of forgotten pioneers or unrecorded missionaries in the South Seas were opened. From American
ranches, from African jungles, from the Austral bush,
from all the lone lost lands the close-bound army of
Eton found their way home. From the African veldt
passed the long line of dead, old and scarred some, and
some, who had been at the School but a few months
previously, bringing their young wounds to add to that
fearful wreath of blood which Eton was to lay on the
sarcophagus at Frogmore.

Spirits passed back into the common brotherhood,
forgetful of the wounds of war and the chase. Spirits,
forgetful of the squalor and fever of their bodies, returned
to where boyhood had been happiest. Life's delusion
and illusion, tragedy and routine, bitterness and weariness were well forgotten, and the first stage of the released
spirits must be the reminiscence of boyhood's days. Eton
had given them contentment of old, power and glamour,
their first taste of triumph or romance. So while Eton
slept, her dead came home. Who knows ?

The next morning was one of the most famous in Eton
history. At an early hour the School Clerk and his
assistants were carrying out their multitudinous labours.
While boys and masters still slept, one great mind was
astir. As nobody had ever seen a dead donkey or a
Provost without his cassock, nobody will see a School
Clerk asleep. Otherwise, *quis custodiet custodes* ? Ubiquitous and amphibian must a *custos* be in all places and
weathers. He must be the eye of the resting Head and
of the invisible Provost. He must be the first to meet
accidents, or to stave disaster, guardian of the School

Office, auditor of Absence lists, editor of Tardy Book, dread Acolyte of *swishing*, polisher of the Block, and binder of birches. Who indeed could deceive or corrupt thee, though he were a Greek or a Croesus? Who could persuade thee to forget one defaulter, who could induce thee to leave out one twig from the Birch in which the majesty and justice of Eton is enshrined? Who could be beforehand with thee at the keyholes of Eton? . . . In the early morn the School Clerk had marshalled his assistants, and was arranging the printed papers, which were to distress a thousand boys, planting ten thousand new quills, and piling fifty thousand sheets of Trial paper, marked Block by Block, and finally preparing the thirty different school-rooms for the ordeal by written examination, known as Trials.

It was at this stage that one of his assistants gave the alarm, and he hurried to the New Schools. There the portentous truth flashed upon him. Room after room was reported to be plastered. No keyhole would open, and disaster seemed imminent. But plaster of Paris is not cement, and there was just time enough to save the situation by some forty minutes. A gimlet was borrowed from a passing workman. With dripping brows and aching fingers, they succeeded in throwing the last door open before the hour struck. The majority of the boys heard nothing till School was over. The Clerk was able to report the outrage and his successful counter-action to the Head at the same time.

The Head was profoundly moved, for it appeared to be more than a practical joke. It was an act of rebellion. It was a defiance of his authority, and almost a personal attack. Disconcerting accounts were appearing in the Press. The Press of the outside world was particularly resented at Eton, when it touched the Eton world, which kept its news and its standards unto itself. Hawtrey had once bitterly protested against Higgins's Eton articles in the *Cornhill*, and the Head's soul sickened when the *Daily Mail* and *Daily Graphic* printed cheap Eton news.

Unfortunately, there was a demand in the Press for snippets and snapshots, of which advantage was often taken among the boys to supply items of quite misleading information. On the other hand, there was a steady leak of School news and reliable hints to the Press, which caused the School Clerk and the 'Fusee' to look with suspicious eye even among the College servants. They themselves kept many secrets of the School in their bosom, secrets which they did not reveal to boy or master. Did they ever discover who filled up the keyholes? Strictly, it was only their business to discover and repair the harm. But the culprits? The School Office was not a detective office. And the mystery was buried in the grave of Moses.

The Head immediately invited the guilty to surrender themselves, and when there was no response, stopped Leave in the coming half. It was always a Head Master's last card, but it was not popular, for it caught the innocent for certain, and the guilty only by accident. There was naturally some resentment against the culprits in the School, but it afforded an absorbing topic of conversation. It was such a magnificent crime. Historically, it was on a level with the theft of the Block from Sixth Form room, or the abstraction of the sceptre from the Founder's statue. If it had been successful, it would have been even paralysing. The Press became open to clues and suggestions. The Head waited, and the interdict of Leave remained. He felt that a misunderstanding had arisen between him and the Eton world, which he so greatly ruled and finally judged. As he came across the School Yard by the familiar diagonal path, through the cobbles, his brows were seen to be more knitted, and the shoulders stooped by just a finger's breadth. Sixth Form could afford him no consolation, and the Eton Society no help. Only his great popularity in the School could stand the strain. At last a hint, a rumour, was noised through *Pop*, and brought to the ears of Sixth Form, but it was only a rumour, that the outrage had been committed by old boys,

and by nobody actually in the School. And the Head
heard the rumour gladly, and summoned the whole of Fifth
Form one 'after-twelve,' to meet him in Upper School.
The old man stood upright in the battered desk, and his
brows were knitted no longer. The School were watching
intently, and when the doors were closed, he arose and
spoke. It was not very clear what his heavy tones
intended to convey. But at that booming, the awed
and interested School were held. They listened with
pricked ears. He had reconsidered his judgment. He
had received intimation as to where the crime lay. He
was glad to excuse the School. He was glad to restore
Leave. As his halting sonority ceased, a mighty burst
of applause shook the old room. The love and confidence
of the School came back to the old man, and he was
pleased again. He shot bolt upright, and faced them
as an old general looks at the troops he had disciplined
and loved. It was a great moment, one of the moments
when the School is at one with itself and with its Head.
All that occurred only served to confirm the popularity
which he could always summon from the misty deep of
the School sentiment.

The Summer Half was further marked by the sudden
declaration of Peace in the Transvaal. It was time
enough, for Peter and Socston, who had been fags themselves when the war commenced, were now fag masters
in turn. Peace was naturally occasion for a holiday.
Red flags, with skull and cross-bones, adorned Miss
Evans's. Red and blue shirts marked Hare's House at
the corner of Keate's Lane, and down the road the
motto, 'Peace with Honour' was displayed, that time-
honoured formula of escape from a bad business. The
lists of Etonian casualties were totalled, the last Old
Etonian being killed only two days before the end. As
a result of the holiday, from May 28 to June 6 there
was not a single whole school-day, and the School began
to look forward to even longer leisure in honour of the
new King's coronation. A Coronation Ode was composed

by the ever-gifted Mr. Christopher, and rehearsed in School Yard, with the band of the Scots Guards playing Lloyd's music, but the great day never came. At the Winchester Match the disastrous news spread that the Coronation must be postponed owing to the Royal sickness, and all fresh holidays were left doubtful.

However an unexpected visit by Indian princes in gala dress gave the School some opportunity to loose their enthusiasm. Their arrival during Absence caused a sudden rush through the School gates. Peter found himself lifted from his feet, carried forward and crushed in the narrow exit without knowing the cause. In the street the Indians were being tumultuously serenaded by the children of their conquerors and possibly by their future rulers, though for how long into the future perhaps neither East nor West could say.

Rumour and gossip of the keyholes simmered in the London Press. Mr. Socston was much excited by what he read, and came down to retail the stories which collected round Hunt, the most famous character of his days, who had pinioned gamekeepers while poaching in Ditton Park, catapulted a Royal Train passing over Arches, and finally broken into the Mausoleum at Frogmore. Mr. Socston was glad to think the old spirit lived, and Socston felt the cockles of his heart warm toward the first adventure likely to come his way.

CHAPTER XXIV

THE PRIZES OF YOUTH

THE Summer Half sped fast and Peter, Socston, Charleston, Ullathorne were in their fourth year. Only the fifth and last remained before they passed to University or Army, but it should prove the most glorious of their Eton lives, when prestige covered a multitude of enjoyments. Peter realised that he must brace himself to face the Captaincy of his House as soon as Camdown went. He knew his success would depend entirely on Socston's co-operation. Socston was the coming oarsman. The First of March had seen him rowing in the *Victory*, an Upper Boat. There was a chance of his winning the School Pulling and being tried for the Eight. Peter had been reading modern history and compared himself to a weak Avignon Pope whose influence was honorary compared to the French Sovereign, terrible with armies. It was quite possible that Socston might become a School swell as well as a *blood* in the House before the holidays. It required deep thought. He must either make terms with Socston, probably Socston's terms, or he had better leave the School.

A boy's thought may or may not be deep, but it is short, and in a flash Peter decided to leave. His Guardians had told him he could, whenever he felt able to compete for a Scholarship at Cambridge. A Classical Scholarship was out of the question at his age, but he felt that Barten, the History *beak*, could get him a History Scholarship and also his deliverance from Morley's. He threw himself with frantic energy into Extra Studies. Mr. Barten was surprised, but began to set him essays and to discuss the result. A master will not be outdone in keenness by a boy. Mr. Barten had a most interesting acquaintance with all History, which both he and his terrier Sandy seemed agreeably surprised to think any boy wished to share. Peter decided on a surprise, and spent an afternoon with the aid of the School Librarian consulting the most recondite authors. The result was prodigious. He showed it to Ullathorne, who suggested one or two topical epigrams. ' It 's a good thing to bring home history to our worthy masters, who live too much in the present, just as I think it is a good thing to inflict a little theology on our pastors. If I were you, I should compare Frederick the Great to Keate. Maria Theresa was in the position of a Dame succeeding a Tutor at the head of a House. Compare the Grand Electors to the Governing Body electing a Head instead of an Emperor. Say that their invisible inutilities sometimes combined to produce one visible Utility ! ' Peter scratched it all in. ' Write the sort of things that Macaulay would have written if he had been an Etonian instead of an unkicked prig. Begin in this style : " Every Fourth Form boy knows who wrote the *Letters of Junius,* and the veriest tyro in Third Form would scorn to consult Gibbon on an uncertain Sunday Question." ... That is what fetches them.' Evidently, for it fetched a sigh from Barten, and Peter ventured to ask him if he could try for a History Scholarship. When Barten assented, Peter went straight to inform Morley that he would not be able to remain as Captain of the House next half. Mr. Morley raised his voice in expostulatory falsetto. He was angry, a rare emotion. The Man pleaded what a wonderful turn the House was going to take. Peter bent his head to the squall. He enjoyed the situation. ' No, sir, if I had to stay at Eton I should prefer to go to Mr. Jenkinson's.' Many a bitterness, cast on him by Morleyites, he was avenging on Morley himself. ' I think it is better Soeston should be Captain. The discipline of the House would suffer if I were " sent up for good " again.' And yet in his heart he pitied this good

man, who would have been so happy had he never come
to Eton.

Morley was troubled. He had lopped two unhealthy
boughs and now a healthy one broke of itself. He had
hoped against hope. ' I don't want Socston to be Captain
of the House,' he said. ' Rowing men are rowdy. I want
a Captain like Tudor.' Peter smiled bitterly at the proposal and his pity melted in anger. He had no wish to
be a second Tudor.

That evening he sauntered into Socston's room and
surrendered any rivalry. ' You know I am going up for
a *schol.* at Cambridge. Barten thinks I can get one,
though I am the youngest to try.' As he relinquished all
possible temporal power, Peter anchored himself a little
proudly to the intellectual. Socston could afford to be
generous. ' I wish I were half as clever as you, Peter. It
must be wonderful being able to do your construes in
your sleep. I don't know what the House will do without
you. We shall all fail regularly in Trials.' Peter was
half pleased at the compliment. ' I hope you win the
School Pulling. That will do more to please the Man
than anything I can do with scholarships.' ' Oh damn
the Man ! what has that got to do with him ? He never
watches a race on the River.' ' Well,' said Peter, ' his
boys do not give him much excuse for hugging the winning
Post, do they ? ' Socston laughed. ' That's true, but
now I am paired with Crake from Juggins's in the Pulling,
perhaps. . . . Come to *Parade*, won't you ? ' And Peter
was grateful to attend that curious resort of Eton fashion.

Parade had become an extraordinary function in ordinary life. The School could be socially divided into those
who paraded during the last twenty minutes before *lock-up*
and those who did not feel smart enough. Every decent
chap paraded. Only the indecent, the *scug* and the *sap*,
skulked in their houses. The proceeding was rather in
the manner of Noah's Ark. *Pop* paired with *pop*, *blood*
with *blood*, and the swells went by two and two, down to
the lesser breeds, who were on the borders of swelldom.

Between New and Lingwood's shop and the old brick-encased horse pond called Barnes Pool, the paraders walked rapidly up and down every night, passing each other again and again. Into this eddy of glowing chat and laughing gossip Peter stepped with his old friend. As they passed each other the swells nodded ' good-night.' No small boy dared join the entertainment unless he was taken by a swell. Peter had been more than three years in the School and had never spoken to a *Pop* yet. His ambition had been the less exalted one of exchanging confidences one day with the Head. Past Barnes Pool an organ was grinding Italian Opera and the little Eton world was gossiping inanely and feverishly about itself, its tiny scandals and its petty intrigues. Though *Parade* was denounced by various masters as sheer advertisement or effeminacy, it was here that all the School news could be picked up. Who was going to get a colour ? Who was in the graces of the Captain of the Boats ? Who were friends, and who had fallen out ? How were the masters behaving themselves ? In fact, it was a living Eton's *Who 's Who*.

As they passed down the line, the Captain of the Boats passed into view, wearing creamy white trousers below his glossy black coat. His boots would not have disgraced the ankles of Hermes. His shining broad-brimmed hat would have lent respectability to an Archdeacon, and an orchid which might have won a prize in a garden-vegetable show, reposed on his bosom. Across his white waistcoat hung a gold chain, with two Shields, commemorating victories in School events. On his arm was Crake, Socston's fellow for the Pulling. Crake called out ' Good-night,' and Socston answered. The next time they passed, the Captain of the Boats condescended to nod to Socston, and lo ! when a third time they passed, the white-trousered god wished Socston good-night ! Socston stammered a reply. Peter immediately felt it was incongruous walking with him, and offered to move on. ' Yes,' said Socston, ' suppose you move on.

I want to see Crake about the Pulling.' Peter left him, and a minute later watched Socston chatting to the Captain of the Boats. The great man slowly wheeled with one arm in Crake's and the other in Socston's. Peter felt how important it was in life to have had an Old Etonian father.

Peter hung about the door of Morley's till Socston returned, flushed with pride. The swell School had seen his social rise, and he took care that everybody in Morley's found out by the simple process of eschewing all conversation for forty-eight hours. 'Gratters,' murmured Peter. Absorbed in his future, Socston nodded and walked past. Even at meals he disdained to converse with the Man, which the House interpreted as the natural coolness rising between an oarsman and a golfer. As a matter of fact, Peter, abandoning all hope of friendship, had mentioned to Socston in the Library that the Man was not anxious for Socston to be Captain. There had been no reply. Mr. Morley's tactlessness had nettled Peter, and in turn he nettled Socston. It was fatal to the House, for Socston was becoming the paramount influence, and to show his latent power, he promptly encouraged disorder. He was in the dangerous position of semi-authority. He was in the Upper Boats, but not a *Pop*. He was a *blood* in the House without responsibility. Peter and Philips found their slight authority undermined. They were both waiting for the result of the Pulling. They would then know for certain whether it would be worth while staying on at Eton.

Meantime the House drifted. Camdown tried to infuse keenness into the Cricket Eleven, but half the House turned *wet-bob* in order to follow their own pursuits. Ormton consulted British Museum Catalogues, and transcribed the Book of the Dead between old exercise covers. Peter had procured a hamper of the mummy heads his father had brought from Egypt, and Ormton was perfectly happy mounting them for the Museum. Peter himself became a hermit in the School Library, rushing down to Athens for a cool dip twice a day, while he flung himself into Universal History. A good deal of betting was carried on in the Fifth Form ranks through the medium of Wise's stableyard, and as turf losses were the rule rather than the exception at Morley's, a certain importance accrued to wealthy members of the House. Weak House masters made the mistake of allowing themselves to be dazzled by vulgar parents. Mr. Morley's contained its quota of heirs to great tradesmen and financiers. As a result boys, whose fathers had been involved in shady transactions on the Stock Exchange, assumed an undue importance when favourites on the turf failed to win. There came this year a black Derby Day in the history of the House, when every shilling that could be raised in or out of the House had been placed on a great unplaced. Peter long remembered the cry of disappointment that went up, as Willum produced the evening paper, and the white faces that gathered in the Library afterwards. Financial stability was only restored by the sons of an Indian Prince and of a Jewish Alderman then in the running for the London Mayoralty, whose mother's accent was large enough to attract an admiring crowd of Eton minnows during her visits to her son. The Alderman provided viands which were insultingly accepted by his son's fag masters. The Indian was a good-looking, silky youth, known as the Baboo, or Babs for short. He was believed to have been a married man at twelve, and the tales he told of oriental dissipation always admitted him a hearing among his elders. Babs was a character, and must have brought back strange tales of English life as well as Old Etonian ribbons to deck his eastern harem. Sweetly devoid of the moral sense, and a most amusing companion, he became a ringleader, not in sports so much as in amusements, and the flagging spirits of the House were invigorated by his efforts to please. Unfortunately, Socston became charmed by him, and placed him under his protection. It was not estimated at its historical importance at the time, but it was to mark the end of Socston's career as well as the last phase in Morley's House.

Meantime, Socston was approaching his zenith. His whole time had been spent practising for the School Pulling, and some admirable coaching from Flinders, a *wet-bob* master, as well as Crake's form, made victory a possibility. They soon hit their stroke together, and became fashioned to a perfect pair. They were light in weight compared with the members of the Eight, but they rowed cleanly and together. They learnt to row as Warre would have them row, to practise the swing which is the glory of the Eton system, instead of relying blindly on the slide. Warre had laid down that the body should swing like the pendulum of a clock, and never sit still for an instant. Warre had laid down there were twenty-seven distinct points about the stroke of the oar, and Socston believed he had mastered twenty of them. In the school of Warre he learnt that he must feel feet, loins, and hands simultaneously, as he drove the oar through the churning water. Had not Warre laid down from the Classics that the way to pull was *rem ad umbilicum adducere*? The hollow belly, the quavering arm, the hoicked pull, the unquiet feet on the stretcher were all condemnable. As for *bum-shoving* it was not *quod Etona miratur*. No, the pull must be unwavering, uniform, undeviating, relentless! And though Warre no longer haunted the River banks, the great tradition was passed on by de Havilland and Donaldson, and there were other oarsmen that Warre could approve among the very young masters. Flinders was simply a Roman legionary, severe to boys and severer to himself. His motto at the desk or on the tow-path, was the same —har-r-r-d! Jenkinson thought he was the finest man on earth.

The heats of the School Pulling were announced in Drake's window. Crake and Socston drew against an unwieldy pair, and with ease and confidence gave them the slip. Great crowds followed the races, masters on wheel or horse, partisans in running shorts, spectators in half change. Jenkinson had taken up a position at the Railway Bridge, and as Crake rowed past he cried, ' Well rowed ! well rowed ! ' Crake heard the familiar voice, and lengthened out. It was an easy win. Socston found himself in the Final of the School Pulling.

Most of the School attended this event. The favourites were a pair out of the Eight, and very serene and powerful they looked, as they paddled to the start in their light blue socks. They were the stronger, not the more graceful pair. They took the Windsor side. A pair containing a Colleger and an Eightsman took the Eton side. Socston and Crake were in the centre. They were both well lined with raw eggs in brandy, to dull the agonising moment when they took station. On the right loomed the gigantic Castle glowing white in the hot sun. Far behind were Rafts and rest. Ahead was the gruelling struggle, the long, cruel laps, the ghastly pursuit and heart-tearing finish. The bank was lined with excited boys. All Jenkinson's and Morley's Houses were there. Socston looked to the coach with a clicking heart for a few last words which came through a megaphone. ' Don't worry about the start. Get it long, and keep it long. When I call " Row ! " I expect you to row har-r-r-d.' Socston never heard the preliminary words of the starter. There was a crack, and he saw the water churning to right and left. Mechanically he dug in his oar. He felt Crake swinging behind him. They were soon together and the water rushed past. The Railway Bridge shot overhead. He knew the River as well as an engine-driver knows his track. He knew without looking ahead exactly where he was, and he could tell by the eddies on either side that the other pairs were a little ahead. He took the middle of the river up to Sandbanks. He came in a little, and as the crowd thinned, he could hear the grating voice of Flinders encouraging him. ' Lengthen out, lengthen out, and keep steady.' They swept into Athens Bay, and there a shout greeted them.

The crowd had taken a short cut across the bend, and were waiting to catch their wind. Jenkinson stood by the little bridge leaning on Peter's arm. Both screamed together, ' Crake ! Socston ! ' They shot past, a close third. The race was developing into a tussle between the bigger pairs. No one could say who was leading till they turned the Ryepeck. The mighty twain in light blue socks were ahead, and the homeward pull had begun, when cometh a time causing rowers to echo the plaint of the unfortunate residents of Cape Horn who wished they had never been born. In close procession the three pairs followed in each other's wash. But it was no funeral procession. The second pair were challenging the leader with quick thrusts. At Sandbanks faulty steering lost the lead to the leaders, and the second pair took their place. Socston stole a look ahead, and seeing, spurted. Crake kept pace gallantly. Socston heard a wild scream from the bank and Flinders crying, ' Now you 're level ! Hard ! hard ! har-r-r-d ! ' He turned an eye, and saw the great blue-socked leviathans rolling away to his left. He had cut them off, and only needed to finish his spurt to get ahead. He could feel the boat shooting under him. But no eddies to right or left showed him how far the leaders were. He fell into dogged pursuit. The sweat rolled down his face and his back ached. The shouting and cheering stung him to row faster and faster strokes. Crake was never late on his stroking by a hairsbreadth. They were swinging the better for being tired. But his tongue was parched, and a rower's agony came upon him. He felt his stomach turn and turn. Then his heart began to burn, and his lungs became full of painful breath. The cramp peculiar to oarsmen is something between sea-sickness and a woman's travail. It can only be met by rowing oneself clean out, and finishing the rest of the race like a machine. Socston decided on a last spurt, and they brought their nose level to the leader's stern by the Railway Bridge. They could see the other's wash ! It was something to discover that their rival existed, and that they were not pursuing a phantom in nightmare. For a few strokes they fell back. In front of Brocas Clump Socston decided, out of sheer carelessness whether he lived or died, to make one more spurt before dropping out of the race. A howl rose from the bank. 'Level! level! level!' He glanced round and saw the first Pair well over on the Berks side. He had the inside station, and driving close in to the Bucks bank, gave spurt. Under the force of pitiful adjurations from their friends, the others spurted too, but Socston noticed that they remained level. His mind was moving with clearness. He remembered there could not be more than seventy yards to the Brocas Rails. Why not spurt the whole way, and get rid of the tearing agony at his heart? Anything to escape the pain, and he cut the water furiously, again and again! There was pandemonium on the bank, shrieks that they were leading. Socston did not care. His lungs were splitting. He gasped for breath. What did he care what the fools shouted on the bank? He longed to damn them from his thwart. What did he care for Crake? He could row his guts out of his mouth for all he cared. What did he care who won the infernal Pulling? His only desire was to get to Rafts and lie still for weeks. A few last strokes were needed, and he gave them with his last breath of wind, and Crake, the uncomplaining, unsighing Crake, gamely gave of his ebbing strength stroke upon stroke. . . . It was a famous victory. Socston lay back in the boat. The Castle rose out of the sky like the walls of Heaven. Soon he would drink nectar.

Peter had seen all, and he was glad, but he did not suffer as he had suffered years back when Socston was running in the Junior Steeplechase. He felt gladder for Jenkinson than for Socston as he walked back and took up a position at a top window of Morley's, looking over the Long Walk, to see the *hoisting* which always followed a great race. He thought of Socston at that moment partaking of *brew*, a boating euphemism for champagne, before being brought up the street in triumph. Already a crowd was collecting between the Chapel cemetery and Barnes Pool. Traffic was impeded, and each tradesman's cart allowed through was hailed with groans and ironic cheers. A diversion was created by the old ' Pecker,' who was invariably drawn from his house by the sound of cheering, and unwisely walked up and down, pretending to keep the order in which his long defunct House had always been lacking. For thirty years the ' Pecker ' had been ragged, and his appearances at *hoisting* always caused preliminary excitement. Scores of voices chirped, ' Peck ! Peck ! Pecker ! ' with the most amusing effect on the Pecker. The amusement was, of course, that ' the Pecker ' was not amused. He poked aimlessly through the throng, speechless with pent fury against the boys, until his straw hat was tilted over his eyes, and he himself was gently jostled home.

As the remonstrant ' Pecker ' was bundled off, the *Pops* could be seen sweeping up the street from ' Tap,' where many a manly thirst had been quenched on the way from the River. The long line of flower-decked grandees, arm-in-arm with swinging canes, advanced mid a welcoming shout from the School. In their midst were Socston and Crake, restored from the effects of their parching struggle by flagons of champagne. Before the victors could collect themselves, enormous men, led by the same blue-socked pair they had vanquished, lifted them off their feet. Six seized them in turn, and ran with them violently down the street, the School dividing to let them pass and screaming their applause, while *Pops* and Upper Boats ran like gorgeous footmen in the dust behind. Right up to the Chapel they sped and turned, dashed down again, and then made a run with them to their House-doors. Followed by the deliriously cheering School, Crake was dragged into Jenkinson's. A minute later a top window was opened, and his head was thrust over the crowd, while jugs of water were poured from above. A minute later Socston was dragged into Morley's, the narrow passage was filled with bellowing *Pops*, Willum was hurled into a dust-bin, two Lower Boys were swept off the stairs, and the room in which Peter was sitting was forcibly entered. Socston was gasping with pride and wriggling with mock modesty in powerful hands. As his red face and closed eyes were thrust out of the window, a shriek of laughter went up from the street, and torrents of water descended from above. Finally, a large white jug was thrown into the street, breaking itself into a hundred pieces. Like the glasses which the Jacobites used to break after drinking the King's health, lest another might be toasted in them, so the Jug, which had baptized the winner of the School Pulling, was spared any meaner use. It symbolised the Eton sacrament of *hoisting*.

Henceforth Socston was a School swell, a probability for the Eight, and a certainty for *Pop*. Whatever leadership and authority there was at Morley's fell instantly under his careless feet. A School Shield, with the Eton arms, appeared on his watch chain. His importance was immeasurable. He never spoke to Peter again in this world.

It was a great misfortune for Socston that he was not yet in *Pop*, for he became the lonely and idle master of himself and his House. There was a thought of trying him for the vacant place in the Eight, but the Captain told him that his weight was not yet sufficient, though he was a certainty for next year. The House was not good enough to produce a House Four, and Socston found himself without any event to train for. His eager mind turned from rowing to horse races. There were always the races at Ascot and Windsor to attract adventurous hearts, and the number of boys who claimed to have attended one or other of those race meetings was considerable, perhaps because such deeds were as difficult to prove as disprove. As Ascot week approached, the editors of the *Insider* brought out a special comic number, satirising the betting craze, by describing horses running from the imaginary studs kept by Eton masters, and advising boys where to lay money. An essay in the style of Bacon appeared :—

'ON HORSES

' Horses serve for delight, for ornament and for ability. For delight in the Windsor and Ascot races ; for ornament to Head Masters and Provosts and for ability in conveying cabs to the station. Some horses are to be ridden, others to be wagered upon and some few to be chewed and digested. Some very few of a fiery disposition may serve Mr. Daughan. But horses are best ridden by deputy. Of the three means by which racing may be visited from Eton College, the wise means is to assume disguise at some trusty tailor and to drive discreetly thither after asking a friend to answer at calling of roll. The frolicsome means is to go with visages darkened unto ebony as is the custom of minstrels, and the means perilous is to go and return upon a motor bicycle between the calling of two rolls. *Magnum periculum magnum gaudium*, the Latin adage meeteth with it a little.'

It was not difficult to recognise Charleston's touch.

Socston meantime had made up his mind to go to Ascot races. Provided he did not bet he felt he had nothing to lose. His father would be delighted if he succeeded. He could imagine him boasting in the London Clubs how his boy had kept up the old tradition and gone to Ascot, though he had come to look on his father as rather a fool. If he were caught and *swished*, he would be mentioned in his father's will. As he had no friend to answer his name for him, he decided to use the novel motor bicycle. Ascot week is always celebrated at Eton by a subdivision of Schools and extra Absences in the afternoon at 2.45 and 6, with School thrown in between, but it was just possible to visit the racecourse within an hour. To bring back a race card was about as much as there was ever time to

attempt. No year passed without the School being
represented on the course, though few who succeeded
felt it was worth doing a second time. It offered a safety-
valve for the first escape of youth's assertation. It was
thought necessary either to go to the races, or to dive off
the Bridge, or to edit a comic paper before leaving Eton
in style. *Saps* preferred journalism, sporting men the
turf.

Socston left Afternoon School briskly, but not so rapidly
as to attract a master's attention, passed down High
Street, and slipping into a yard below the Bridge, emerged
on a pre-arranged machine, crossed the Royal Borough
and shot down Windsor Great Park. Ascot was at the
other end. Socston gave himself ten minutes on the
course. He had time to see one race finish and the horses
for another go to the post before he turned on his heel.
He wheeled his way through the throng of gipsies, toffs,
touts and bookies and then his blood chilled as he heard
his name deliberately uttered. ' Socston ! I declare ! '
It was Mouler. ' Let me introduce you to my *Pater*.'
' *Pater*, here 's a fellow from Morley's.' Mr. Mouler became
interested. ' And this is not my sister,' and Mouler
laughingly pushed forward a pretty girl with an inquiring
face and a tinge of rouge on her lips. Her eyes caught
Socston in one of those minutely divided moments of time,
when recollection from the past swamps the present. He
knew her and yet he could not place her, those blue,
rather wistful eyes and the serious, painstaking little
mouth. ' Are there many Eton boys here ? ' she asked.
' No, it 's against rules,' answered Socston. (By this
time he had decided he liked her.) ' Aren't you very
brave to come, if it isn't allowed ? ' she asked. ' Oh
no, lots of fellows do it.' ' From Mr. Morley's ? ' asked
Mr. Mouler. ' Yes, I suppose,' said Socston, instinctively
lowering his voice. By this time he was sure it was time
to start back. (He was also sure he was in love.) ' By
the way,' said Mouler, ' can't you get up to the Subscription Dance at Clarence's next week. We shall all be

there. The Baboo, I know, has taken two tickets. I saw him at a ball last week. Well, good-bye, old man, and don't let the Hag catch you.' Socston was off, bringing back something less tangible and more precious than a race card.

'Socston!' called the master, reading second Absence. 'Here, sir!' shouted Socston, panting twenty yards away. The Master looked at him and let him approach humbly with his hat in hand. 'I suppose you 've just saved your skin. Ascot week is not a wise time to fall asleep in your room, you know.' And the Praepostors laughed. Socston did not laugh, but the Master only wanted to have his little joke.

Once the peril was passed, Socston felt a growing fancy trouble him. He went to the Baboo's rooms that evening and asked him if it was true that he had seen Mouler at a dance last week. The Baboo was dumb. 'Oh never mind telling me. I 'm not Captain of the House yet. I met Mouler to-day at Ascot.' As Socston placed himself within the Baboo's sneaking power, the latter confessed he had been to town several nights. So had other members of the House. There was nothing to prevent them, and there was the four o'clock train to Slough on which to return. Socston laughed. 'Babs, I never knew you were a sportsman. But tell me, who is Mouler's sister? I mean the girl with him.' 'Oh, that 's no sister of his,' said the Baboo, 'she joined the ship at Alexandria when I came from India. Some officers adopted her, as she is supposed to be an English officer's daughter, but her mama is not known.' 'Is Mouler gone on her?' 'Yes, but why do you ask?' and with an Oriental's quick vision the Baboo added, 'Oh, I see. Well you could cut out a paralytic fool like him any day.' 'Will you see her at the Subscription Ball next week?' 'I will; and why don't you come with me? I have two tickets.' Socston sat down and threw his head into his hands. He was ready to go for the sake of breaking a rule that deserved breaking. But this was more than a rag. It

was a real temptation. He was not training for anything,
so he could afford to lose a night's sleep. But the risk
he ran was the risk of expulsion. He had never really
dared that before. At the same time he knew how easy
it was to climb out at night. House masters trusted their
boys over well and resented acting as policemen. In the
days that followed he made up his mind again and again
to consult Peter, but something failed him. He would
come right up to Peter's door and then slink back to the
Baboo's luxurious room to discuss their chances of getting
to London and back. ' Well, we 've never been caught
yet and I expect you can do what I can.' Pride settled
it for Socston, the pride that would not let him talk it
over with a despised *sap* like Peter would not allow him
to refuse a risk that an Indian cheerfully took once a
week. And then there was the girl. The Baboo was very
mysterious about her. He wouldn't even divulge her
name. Socston was determined to see her again. When
the night of the ball came, he was waiting in the Baboo's
room at eleven. ' Is anybody else coming ? ' ' No ! '
They slipped out of the Library window and turned down
Keate's Lane across South Meadow to the station with
their collars turned up and tweed caps on their heads.
Train and time dragged, and it was not till one o'clock
that they reached the dance at Clarence's.

They brought their stick-up collars and dancing pumps
in their pockets, adjusted them in the cloak-room, and
took the floor. Socston, being country bred, knew the
barn dance, and no more. Babs immediately found a
girl he knew, and began moving lithely and rhythmically
before her like a smiling brown cobra, thought Socston,
who was feeling jealous. Suddenly he perceived Mouler,
resplendently dressed, with his father and the girl Socston
loved. His heart was in greater danger of snapping than
during the School Pulling. He made straight and
blushingly for the couple, and was wildly welcomed.
Mouler, with Etonian courtesy, explained to the girl
what a hazardous thing it was for Socston to have come

Y

at all, and left her with an impression that he had climbed
chevaux de frise at least to get out of Eton, and would
receive a stroke of the birch for every minute he spent in
her company, that was to say, if he were caught. ' Oh,
how I have loved Eton,' the girl murmured in approved
style, and her fingers played with a light blue sash, which
Socston felt sure was worn in his honour. ' I have always
longed to dance with an Eton boy.' Socston blushed.
' I can't dance, but may I talk to you behind the ferns ?
I have so much to tell you. I am sure to be caught, and
they will *sack* me if they find out I am in love with you.'
She was of the sex that is always younger in years but
older in wisdom, and knowing a love-sick innocent at
sight, she trusted herself to him in the shadowy corner.
He talked about his rowing, about the House, the School,
about the Eton Eight. It was so different to what she
usually heard from men. When the protestation of love
came, she accepted it with a little sigh. It was like
picking a fresh wild flower in a heated conservatory. He
sat shyly by her side, uttering abrupt sentences. His only
thought was to plan another meeting. Meantime, he
offered her oarage on the Thames, and protection in any
part of the Universe. She smiled, perhaps with pity
rather than love, and promised to watch his next race at
Eton, and come with him to Henley. ' We mustn't
stay here too long,' she said. ' Well, give me something
if you really would care for me. You haven't even told
me your name yet, and I can't take you in a punt at
Henley if I don't know who you are,' Socston blurted, in
desperation to make hay while the sun shone.

She stood up in her slim beauty. ' Well, Mr. Socston,
if you will forgive me not telling you my name, I will
give you a charm from my bracelet. My father found it
in a tomb in Egypt, and I have always worn it, but it
has brought me no luck. Do you want it ? ' Socston
quivered with the joy of thinking she cared for him. ' Oh,
you ripping girl ! I will wear it, but isn't it broken ? '
' Yes, the other half is missing, but it is real jade and more

valuable than you would think.' 'Oh, of course it's valuable. I know all broken things are,' he blustered in apology, and as her eyes fell on his watch chain, he fumbled furiously at it. By Heaven, he would give her something really worth having. 'Here's my Shield for the School Pulling, with my name and the date. I can win another.' She clasped it to her bracelet as they joined the Moulers.

'Had a good time?' asked Mouler junior. 'Oh, wonderful! Wish to God I hadn't got to get back for Early School.' 'Mr. Morley's must be a very quiet House since Tommy had to leave,' suggested Mouler senior. 'Oh no, I mean yes,' said Socston. 'We miss him in the House a good deal. Some of the fellows think he would make a better captain than Darley next half.' This was a sore point. 'You can tell the Man,' broke in Mouler junior, 'that I wouldn't rule his swine-roost for anything.' Babs swept past at this moment on a lady's arm. 'Is that gentleman at Mr. Morley's too? I often see him at dances,' asked Mr. Mouler. 'Yes, he's just got into the Debate. We generally call him the Baboo.' Mr. Mouler nodded his head disagreeably. 'A real sporting House, eh? Much too sporting a House for my son to have captained, eh?'

Socston was ready to return, but the Baboo whispered to him that roulette was being played for stakes in a room upstairs, and it would be well worth watching, even if they hadn't a penny to stake. As the unknown beauty was also anxious to see the game, Socston consented to delay, though he did not like taking direction from the Baboo. Still, he couldn't help admiring the grace and dignity with which he held himself in the ballroom. He must have had gentlemen among his ancestors, and with what an easy smile he gave his arm to Beauty and took her upstairs. She beckoned Socston, and at the top disengaged herself for his arm. Oh bliss! Oh rapture! This was sweeter than even *hoisting*. The whole party slipped into a crowded room in the middle of which a wheel was revolving, while young women and old men slipped gold and notes into numbered squares. It was fascinating to watch for the winner, and Socston was vividly reminded of the Race-Horse Game he used to play with counters at home. 'Let's plunge,' whispered the Baboo. 'Haven't a cent,' said Socston. A soft hand touched his. 'Put that on for me on the square that old gentleman puts his on. He is the luckiest gambler here.' 'Right you are !' And Socston, with his left hand still fairy-held, reached forward with his right, and when the old gentleman with his bowed head next staked a note on red, Socston dropped a sovereign. As he did so, the old gentleman looked up, and their eyes caught. Socston's hard-worked heart was given another fearful bout, for the eyes were eyes which had last met his over *Wallensteins Tod* at extra German ! The red won, and Herr Blitz drew in his winnings. Petrified, Socston forgot to take the two sovereigns which were his. With wonderful cool-bloodedness Herr Blitz pushed them over to him, and without a gleam of recognition returned to the play. It was a great night, and Herr Blitz made more in an hour than any of his slumbering colleagues could have earned in a week.

It was nearly five in the morning when Socston and the Baboo, strange conjunction of East and West, crawled out of the train at Slough, and crept back through the Library window in time to be roused by the Hag for Early School an hour later. They exchanged not a word till they felt safe. 'In Heaven's name, did you see old Blitz ?' whispered Socston. 'Why, I'm up to the fellow at Early School.' 'I have noticed him there before,' said the Baboo. 'He is the greatest sport in the room. He sometimes drops a couple of hundred.' Socston whistled.

They attended Early School, but returned to breakfast without adding an iota to their knowledge. The Baboo made such a hash of geometry that he was complained of in Chambers, but saved himself with a written excuse from his Dame to the effect that he had not been sleeping very well owing to the well-known difference in the climate with India. Socston came utterly to grief at German, but was not complained of.

CHAPTER XXV

THE DOWNFALL

THE gamut of emotions experienced at the dance at Clarence's must be extended to include the extreme interest, almost pleasurable, which Mr. Mouler felt at finding any of Mr. Morley's boys absent without leave, coupled to an illogical wrath that they should return safely to Eton, while his hopeful had, as he considered, been removed on a lesser count. His first intention was to write to the *Daily Mail*, which he knew would be more disliked by the Head than anything in Heaven or earth. His second decision was to call on Sir John Mumbles, his old chief in Colonial matters. Mumbles had given him no satisfaction when he appealed to him to prevent his boy being *sacked*, and he was anxious to get home with a little dig as though to say, now what is your old Governing Body about, when boys can come up every night to London ? Sir John Mumbles he did succeed in making very uncomfortable for a quarter of an hour, and having thoroughly enjoyed the effect, and disregarded Mumbles' advice to refer the matter to the Governing Body, and not to the Head, who the Governing Body believed was showing signs of strain, he wrote a sarcastic letter to the Cloisters, warranted to disestablish Morley completely.

'CLARENCE'S HOTEL.

' DEAR DR. WARRE,—I hope you will not mind my bringing a slight matter of school discipline before you. As long as Eton contains so many as a thousand boys, it must be difficult to control, and the removal of boys on slight or unfounded charges is bound to occur. May I suggest that a closer watch be kept on the railway stations at night ? It was my curious experience to be present at a ball here last night, at which several members of Mr. Morley's House were present, for I overheard them making their usual arrangements to return by the four o'clock train to Slough. I must apologise for intruding, but I feel that it is only right that Mr. Morley should be aware of these facts, when engaged in the responsible task of choosing next half's Captain.'

It was a bitter letter, but Mr. Mouler had once been a minor Colonial Administrator, and knew well the use of those shafts by which a supine or mismanaging Colonial Secretary could be stung into action or reversal of policy. For the Head it was a bombshell, when he opened it on his breakfast-table the next morning. For the moment he decided to defer sending to Mr. Morley for an explanation. Most of Mr. Morley's boys were unknown to him, and besides, he understood that the more dangerous characters had been removed at the end of the previous half. Could they have corrupted others and left them more wicked than themselves ? He heaved an Odyssean sigh, and passed to the next letter. It was also displeasing. It was a complaint from the owner of a house-boat down the River, that the wooden partitions of his dwelling were made the target of stones and missiles by Eton boys on Sunday afternoons. The Head felt his withers unwrung on that score. It was quite impossible, and he replied that no Eton boy could possibly indulge in such cowardly behaviour. His correspondent must have mistaken the miscreant. He passed to the next communication, which was a notice of scholarships awarded at Cambridge to Etonians for Physical Science and History. A Minor Exhibition was awarded to Darley for History. It was not a Sixth Form name, nor particularly familiar to him for any reason. He noted it in bright blue ink. Then it passed from his mind, and he began the painful mental digestion of the other letters. It was a Saturday, and he decided to wait till Monday. Meantime, he spoke to no one of his staff, but the King sent for his Confessor. He sent for the faithful and intelligent School Clerk. The Head was regarded by his admiring and loyal staff as the soundest but stupidest man they knew, but the intelligence of the School Clerk had never been questioned. Unhampered by dates or Greek roots, he could always bring a clear unbiased mind to a problem. Since the affair of the plastered keyholes he had risen to a position almost of Grand Vizier. The Head already foresaw a useful link to knit his régime with his unknown successors. The sands of his own administration were running out, and he was always wise enough to uphold his Clerk against a Master. He felt he was slowing into his last terminus, and that his grip on the School was not what it had been. He ruled out of the prestige of the past by the unchallenged influence of his name. Like a dying Pope he noted candidates for the succession trying their hand in other head masterships like the cardinals who watch the papacy from archbishoprics far from Rome.

All Sunday the Head turned counsel in his thought-devouring mind, summoning wisdom and decision to his part. The Homeric anthem passed through his sorely revolving brain, ' Endure, O my soul, who hast endured so much.' Uncomforted by a particularly bad sermon on behalf of Foreign Missions, he walked through the Playing Fields very slowly, with the School Clerk at his side, whom he questioned whether it was possible for boys to go to London for a night dance and return in time for School. A slight knowledge of the railway time-table enabled the Clerk to demonstrate that this was exceedingly possible. So much for that. He then turned to the complaint made by the owner of the house-boat, and asked the School Clerk to walk sometime in that direction, and inform him whether such un-Etonian conduct could possibly be. He returned alone.

The afternoon was passing, and the Head had come to no decision about Mr. Mouler's letter. The School Clerk

was waiting for him, and to him he listened. He was very
sorry to have to tell the Head Master what he had seen,
but he had approached the house-boat through the willows
and heard distinct sounds of stones rattling on the roof.
On turning, he had caught sight of a boy with uplifted arm.
' A boy from the School ? ' queried the Head. ' Yes, sir.'
' Did he see you ? ' ' Yes, sir, he saw me full.' ' Then
I can take no action against him, or he would attribute
his punishment to you.' ' Yes, sir, the gentlemen have
always trusted the School Office.' ' You may tell me
the name of his House, but no more.' ' Mr. Morley's,
sir.' ' Thank you, you may go.'

The Head sat down and ate his words in a letter of
apology to the owner of the house-boat. Then he walked
into the Playing Fields and gave the letter to the first
College servant he met to deliver by hand. He was only
desirous to perform his duty to all men. With weighty
thought upon him, he strode through Upper Club and
emerged in Agar's Plough. He was beginning to glimpse
duty, and duty once conceived would be tenaciously
carried out. He was coming to the conclusion that
perhaps it was more important for the School that
Mr. Morley should cease to hold a House than that
the dancing truants or stone-throwers should be
punished.

As he walked homeward he felt relieved in his mighty
mind. He no longer ignored the salutes of the boys.
He made slight signs of recognition, though as Head he
never lifted his hat. In his fields he was King. It was
a great and responsible thing to be Head Master of Eton.
The very elms seemed to stand to attention as he passed.
Watermen on duty at the River watched him from afar.
Lower Boys followed him with the fascinated stare with
which young birds contemplate a full-grown snake.
Oblivious of any coming doom, the more or less innocent
victims of Mr. Morley's House were playing Bridge in
their rooms for small stakes. Several Morleyites, however, walked abroad, though not together. Peter and

Socston were loitering under the trees with different
companions when the familiar form of the Head loomed
in the distance. As he passed, they removed their hats
and stood still. The Head looked through his spectacles
in their direction for a moment. Oh, Heavens merciful!
he had left the path for the grass. He was making
straight for them. For twenty-four hours Peter had had
only one thought in his mind, and that was his success
at Cambridge. His Tutor had announced it triumphantly,
and Barten had spoken to him with praise which he
thought more generous than true. The felicitations of
Mr. Lamb had been really overwhelming. Mr. Jenkinson had crossed the street to say how sorry he was that he
was leaving Eton. Peter naturally guessed that the
Head was making for him, and his heart swelled. The
greatest moment of his Eton life was approaching. The
Head himself was going to congratulate him before his
fellows on winning the Exhibition. All his years of *sap*,
he felt, were worth the bother and trouble for this priceless minute. He did not mind never having won a colour
now. The words for which he had waited during all his
Eton career were coming at last. As a new boy taking
Remove, and again when he won Distinction in Trials
his first half in Fifth Form, again when he was 'sent
up for good,' when the Head visited Jenkinson's division,
and when he was confirmed, he had braced himself to
meet his Head, to hear his words as a man to a
boy. . . . Well, it was coming at last. . . . The great
man was drawing nigh. The Head, with a benevolent
smile on his firm, fine-featured face, however, passed
Peter by. He drew himself up to Socston. 'I saw you
win the School Pulling, and I enjoyed the race. I am
sorry they cannot try you for the Eight till next year.
You finished in the way we used to row at Eton.' And
he passed on toward Cloisters. Boys resumed their
top-hats. Watermen relaxed, and the zephyr breezes
played once more through the enamelled green of the
elms, and dipped upon the unoared River. Clang, clang,

clang, . . . the great bell was summoning all to Evening Chapel.

The Head answered Mr. Mouler's letter on Monday, discreetly and politely. He regretted that it was true that Mr. Morley's House was lacking in discipline. He intended to look closely into the matter, as he had received complaints from several quarters. He could not believe that it was possible for Eton boys to act so disgracefully as to frequent night dances in London. It was possible Mr. Mouler overheard some past members of the House talking among themselves. Though he was grateful for Mr. Mouler's kind warning, he could not act on what was only a vague rumour. The Head was anxious to let Mr. Mouler understand that he did not approve of gratuitous tale-bearing, as well as his preference to make discoveries for himself. Mr. Mouler, on receipt of the letter, danced with rage, and sat down to write a screed to the *Daily Mail*, bringing his boy's enforced dismissal before the British public, and asking whether attendance at dances was not a far worse misdemeanour. It was a furiously funny concoction, and he closed it in fine Old Etonian style with ' *O tempora O mores !* ' a phrase that the *Eton College Chronicle* always kept in stock for veteran correspondents.

But vengeance is a dish best taken cool and again the wise Colonial Administrator let second thoughts change his purpose. He was nettled by the Head's letter, and at any cost he would teach him a lesson. If the Head thought that no Etonians attended night dances in London he would easily show him otherwise. He went upstairs to the room occupied by his son. As he expected, there was a bracelet on the table, which he had several times examined with interest since the dance. His son had told him laughingly that his best friend had fallen in love with his best girl, for he had found his School Shield on her bracelet, and had confiscated it accordingly. He had not the heart to tear it off the bracelet which had been his own gift, but his father had no weakness for

sentiment and snapped off the golden souvenir. Hatred
made him blind to the callous cruelty of his next act.
He was only burning for revenge on Morley, whom he
believed was an unjust master. He enclosed the trinket
in a piece of hotel notepaper and sent it by registered
post to the Head with the cryptic note 'Found on the
floor of Clarence's after the dance of last week. Please
to return to the owner.'

The later years of the Head were not as peaceful or
happy as he might have desired or deserved. To drive
a flock of a thousand untamed boys even with the aid of
forty wondrous-assorted assistants was not a euphonious
process. Letters from parents, reformers, religious
societies, humanitarians assailed him. They were of the
futile, the polite, the imprudent or the impertinent.
The enclosures from Mr. Mouler he classed amongst the
impertinent. It went to the Head's heart to see the
sacred School Shield returned from what was for all he
knew a den of infamy. And the name! He read with
keen anguish the name of the handsome boy whom he
had congratulated in public for the very winning of that
Shield. *Sunt lacrimae rerum!*

He had already come to a great decision and this only
showed that his determination was right. He decided
to pay Mr. Morley a visit in his House that evening.

The Fates assuage their grim vocation with playthings,
little symbols, the flotsam and jetsam of chance and
coincidence, but sometimes they weight them with
mysterious or ironic values. The Fates had played with
Soeston's School Shield, snatching it from his watch-chain,
hooking it to a bracelet, snatching it off again and whisking
it back to Eton, where it now reposed on the Head
Master's table. The Head had himself once won the
School Pulling and he looked at it sadly.

Another little object seemed to be causing amusement
to the Fates, the broken charm which had come out of
the grave of a long-dead Egyptian, who had taken pains,
as was common in those days, with his grave, and gone

the length of cursing any interfering body by water and by fire. The Fates had once allowed an exploring British officer to interfere with it and to find a nameless grave for himself while on a shooting expedition. The curse had promised that many waters should come about the disturber of the sepulchre and when his friends went to recover his body from the spot where they had hidden it, a flood had already swept away all traces. The Fates had let his widow break the charm, rather than present it to the Museum which clamoured for it, and leave a half to each of her children as a memento of their father's last journey. When she died, the boy was sent home to England to an uncle who declared he had no use for a girl, and she was left to drift, was adopted by officers, and when her father's regiment left Egypt she had been last heard of drifting on the floating wave of white people who drift between East and West. She had drifted to London, but she always kept the broken charm on her wrist until the Fates snatched it off in a moment of sentiment never felt by her before, and sent it whirling to Eton in Socston's evening trousers. For some days it had been secreted in his bureau, touched and contemplated at appropriate moments. When curiosity conquered sentiment, he wondered what it could be and, as it had an oriental look, he took it to Ormton for expert opinion.

'What's this, Ormton?' Socston inquired. 'Oh, where did you find that? It must be part of the Egyptian truck that Darley fetched from home for me to sort. By the way, I have fixed his mummy heads. They had decayed a little owing to exposure in a damp conservatory. Gill will jump with delight when we take them to the Museum. As good as Great Auk's eggs to him,' and Ormton took the curious thing out of his hand. 'I will tell you what it means in a minute. But it's Darley's, isn't it?' 'It's not Darley's, it's mine,' said Socston, 'so don't mix it up with the rest of the loot.' 'I am exhibiting the mummy heads in the Library before supper,' went on Ormton with a specialist's fervour; 'Camdown's sending a couple of fags to fetch them on tea-trays. I am giving a little talk. I hope you will come. The British Museum would give anything for these. Darley's *pater* must have been a real explorer and dug them up before they had begun faking mummies in Paris.' Two grinning fags appeared at this moment, and Ormton slipped the charm into his pocket. 'Take these carefully down to the Library,' he said, placing a head on each of four trays. As the fags turned the corner of the landing, there was the sound of a scuffle. Some idiot had run into them and the horrified Ormton leaped to his feet as an audible and sacrilegious bump! bump! bump! was heard going down the stairs. 'Damn him!' muttered Ormton, who was too philosophical as a rule to be profane, 'I spent all night touching up those heads.' 'I bet the Dame will be at the bottom and will think we have really murdered Willum,' was Socston's happy thought. As they rose to investigate, a piercing scream shot through the landings. Philips was under the banisters and looked up, 'Oh, it's all right. It's only Cheener. The Mummy hit him in the eye and he is throwing a fit in Mrs. Sowerby's room.' Cheener's surprise could be pardoned. Many different objects had at different times rolled down Mr. Morley's stairs—footballs, lexicons, cans, Willum, hip-baths, but the head of a deceased Egyptian was a novelty. While Ormton delivered his lecture that evening to Mr. Morley's Debating Society, Cheener was put to bed feeling very queer indeed. It wasn't the fault of the mummy, but constant bullying had made him nervous. In default of good captaincy an undercurrent of oppression embittered the life of Mr. Morley's Lower Boys.

Ormton returned to his room feeling thoroughly satisfied. He decided to shirk Prayers, and having replaced the precious heads in the old hamper, began to turn over some of the miscellaneous stuff Darley had sent with them. He emptied and opened a boxful of coins, beads,

little gods and goddesses. As his finger passed through
them he suddenly stopped short. Ormton was a very
accurate and precise person. He could have sworn that
Socston had handed him a broken green-coloured charm,
and that for safety he had placed it in his pocket. Socston
had particularly asked him not to mix it up with the rest
of the loot, and he had particularly not done so. Yet
. . . there it was in the box, which he could have sworn
he had not touched for two days. He had been working
at the heads all the time. He sat and toyed with the
charm. It was not only similar, but it was actually
broken, identically the same, and yet . . . he felt in
his pocket and slowly drew out the other half, which
Socston had just given him. He put them together,
moved them with the end of a brush, and they became
one ! It was obvious that Socston had lied slightly when
he said his piece was not Darley's. He must have picked
it up on the stairs and pretended to believe it was his own,
for the two pieces made one very nice specimen together.
He felt sure it was genuine, and he recognised the symbol.
It was the god of the nether world. It was Death, and
smilingly he dropped a little refined glue between the
crack. He was very skilful, and behold ! it was neatly
and perfectly joined ! . . . His door burst open, and a
Lower Boy came in to say that Prayers were over, but
that the Man wished the whole House to assemble as the
Head wished to speak to them. Recalled from thinking
of Egypt to the terror of a big row that always haunts
Eton life, Ormton stood up with a shock. In school
history the Head never visited a boarding-house, and at
night, except for one thing, to perform an expulsion.
His blood ran cold, but with rather pleasant anticipations
at the same time, for he felt certain he was on the right
side of the law. He could, however, think of a number
of his friends who lived in considerable jeopardy. He
heard the Lower Boy leave Peter's room, and looked
in himself. ' Come along, Darley, the Devil's own rag.
The Head is waiting for you downstairs.' It was a

Friday night, and on Friday night Peter's head always blazed with Iambics. Though he had won his History Exhibition, he never relaxed his Classical efforts, and worked away as hard as though he were going to take Trials. As a leaving boy he was excused Trials, so that this supererogatory zeal was set down as utter lunacy. He had just finished his last set of Iambics at Eton. To him they were always a mixture of impossible signs to be jumbled and sorted into place. There were the aspirates, the accents, and the long and short quantities to work over and over until his page looked more like algebra than poetry. He had wrestled for two hours with a piece of Swinburne, and now it was done. It lay beautifully written in Greek on a clean sheet, and then a Lower Boy had burst in, asking why he wasn't at Prayers. Well, he felt no conscientious duty to be present at Prayers. He religiously hated Prayers, garbled by the Man, and punctuated by a few drawling Amens. ' Oh no, tell the Man I 've got a headache,' he told Ormton. ' I believe you are shamming to get off Trials. O Darley, what would your kind Tutor say ? ' laughed Ormton. ' I hear you haven't been seen for two days running in the School Library, and the Librarian is thinking of sending out a search party for you.' ' *Sap* yourself,' laughed Peter, as they both went downstairs. ' They will make you Museum charwoman in the holidays.' He had always liked Ormton. He, too, loved knowledge for the sake of knowledge.

The scene was to prove memorable. The House was standing uncomfortably to attention, waiting for the row. The Man was leaning over one end of the table, with his moustaches bristling against his pale face. He looked acidly at Ormton and Peter, and asked why they weren't at Prayers. ' Because I am a member of the University of Cambridge,' replied Peter, astonished at his coolness. The Man was better at Euclid than repartee, and let the matter pass. ' And you, Ormton ? ' ' Well, sir, I am thinking of turning Mohammedan.' ' Very bad reason, very bad reason,' said the Man. 'You will both do me a hundred lines.' Both laughed. 'Two hundred!' snapped the Man, like an angry auctioneer bidding against himself. The atmosphere was a fighting one. The Man then stated his case.

'I have called the House together, because the Head Master informs me that a great injustice has been done to a young boy at this House. A case of arrant bullying to Cheener, of which you bigger boys must have known.' Camdown, Peter, and Socston looked blank. They had never cared whether Cheener existed. 'Come, come, come,' chattered the Man, 'the Head wishes to have the names of the boys responsible.' The House was puzzled. Cheener had been kicked about by the Lower Boys a good deal, but he had never been smacked. He looked too puny and insignificant. What had he wanted to sneak about? Cheener was not present, and the House felt that his ills were imaginary. 'Come, come,' said the Man, feeling desperate, 'if it is a case of Cheener having to leave or the rest of the House, the Head has told me it will be the rest of the House.' A defiant hiss shot down the ranks of the House. The Man began to splutter and talk very rapidly and unintelligibly. There was another hiss, and the Man rather ludicrously withdrew. A minute later he reappeared, with moisture on his glasses. But the House no longer hissed. Behind him stood the majestic figure of Edmond Warre. '*Deus ex machina!*' whispered Peter to Ormton.

The House quailed under his eagle glance, and his booming voice struck their souls as a clapper strikes wet laundry. Their courage oozed out of their heels. The sweat rolled from the brows of the less athletic. For a moment the absurd idea returned to Peter's mind that he was to be publicly congratulated at last on his Exhibition. 'Boys!' the Head began, 'a grave injury has been done to a boy in this House which requires the severest punishment, if the guilty can be detected. I refer to

z

the treatment which has befallen a young boy, an innocent and tender young boy, Cheener. I say that it were
better that a millstone should be hung round their necks,
and they be cast into the sea than that Cheener should
be treated as he has been treated. He is not present, is
he ? ' and he turned to the Man. ' No, sir, the Dame
has kept him in bed.'

' Has anybody here anything upon his conscience in
this most grave matter ? ' A Lower Boy, pallid with
fear, held up a hand that might have been pallid, but for
the inkstains. ' Well ? ' ' Please, sir, I accidentally
hit him this evening.' ' What did you hit this young
boy with ? ' ' I hit him with the head of a mummy
which I let drop. . . . ' ' Nonsense, you are leaving
your senses,' said the astounded Head. A long silence
followed. Then the Head said simply, ' Then I do not
think I can allow this House to continue as a part of
Eton.' It was the major excommunication. Good God,
was he going to *sack* them all ?

He continued without a tremor in the voice, which
became like the roll of a drum. ' I am also receiving
complaints that boys from this House are throwing
stones at house-boats and frequenting dance halls at
night as far away as London. May I ask any boy who
was foolish enough to attend a subscription dance last
week in Clarence's Hotel to come forward ? ' Not a boy
moved. Half the House could guess or knew to whom
he was referring, but loyalty would not allow them even
to glance at Socston or the Baboo. Socston often
wondered afterwards whether, if he had given himself
up at that moment, he would have been *sacked*. But he
never dreamed that the Head carried weighted dice in
his hand against him. ' Whose is the inscription on this
Shield ? ' asked the Head, as he laid Socston's rowing
trophy on the table. In an agony of fury and fright,
Socston said, ' Mine, sir.' ' Mr. Morley,' said the Head,
' will you inform this unhappy boy's parents that I wish
him to leave the School to-morrow ? Eton is a boys'

school, and when boys seek for women it is time they left
and went their way as men.'

Mr. Morley bowed, feebly associating himself with the
penalty, as though he had incurred none himself. ' Who
was the other boy or boys on this foolish escapade ? '
asked the Head, and Morley darted furious and futile
eyes up and down his wretched House, who returned fire
with a stony stare. The Baboo's dusky features alone
concealed any change of colour. His oriental eyes and
half-sensual lips were tightly closed. He had reflected
in a flash that as he had left nothing behind, there was no
proof. The House knew, but he knew that no Englishman
sneaked without becoming lower than a Hindu pariah.
He was not wrong in his calculations. No voice spoke,
either then or ever afterwards. The law which bound
them was a law stronger than colour, stronger than Christianity, stronger perhaps (though who would dare put it
to the test ?) than death. No Etonian will denounce a
fellow to a master, even though he has injured him or
left him in the lurch. Even the weakling Cheener, it
appeared, had refused, after his parents had discovered
his body was covered with bruises when he came home
for Leave, to blab a name to the Dame's queries and the
Man's threatenings. The Baboo placed his Eton life in
the hands of his fellow Etonians, and it was secure.

Without a word the Head turned and beckoned Mr.
Morley to follow him,' ' Mr. Morley,' he said gravely,
' I had intended writing to you, but this opportunity
makes it, I will not say easier, but less troublesome. The
School is grateful for your excellent teaching in school.
It has always been excellent, but I do not wish you to
continue your Boarding House after this half. Good-
night.' And the Head strode into the dark green twilight
of summer. Of the two men he was at heart the most
deeply grieved. He passed slowly through the School
Yard like a stricken stag. When he came back to his
rooms in the Cloisters, he knelt and prayed as he had
never prayed in Chapel under the gaze of the boys.

Simply and genuinely he prayed with all an Old Etonian's love for the School committed to his charge. By the time the Head rose from his knees, Mr. Morley had quite recovered himself, and was carefully correcting mathematical extra-works for Army Class IV. Only the good God, who created the universe on sound lines of geometry knows how bad extra-works can be, and Mr. Morley soon forgot the troubles of his House as conscientiously he traced and retraced the erring calculations of Army Class IV. The great Clock boomed midnight, and Mr. Morley slept the sleep of the happily insensitive. But the Head slept not, and the Clock boomed to him all night.

The next day was a grim day for Morley's. Mr. Socston arrived by the first train, summoned by telegram. Socston's anger and shame were only relieved by a humorous wonder how his father would take it. After all, his father had always been urging him to get *swished*, and implying the family disgrace if he failed to pay his kneeling respects to the Block before he left Eton. Well, all he could say was that he had a little overdone it, and gone one better than a *swishing*. Besides, it was rather a fine thing to be *sacked* for so daring a feat. It wasn't for immorality, and here poor Socston's heart felt a qualm. An innocent fellow as he was, undone by athletic pride and the oriental flattery of the Baboo, he began to wonder whether he had done wrong in making love to that girl. She looked so young and pretty, he felt she could not be bad. And they had done nothing but exchange souvenirs, that unlucky School Shield. He could not imagine how the Head could have obtained it, unless Mouler, yes, the jealous Mouler, must have sneaked. And his blood boiled. For the first time in his life he desired to kill a human being with a healthy and almost Christian desire. The best in him craved Mouler's blood. He immediately spread his suspicion through the House, which showed him the greatest sympathy. Only the Baboo lay low, lower than the serpent that draggeth his belly in the dust. Nobody would have known that the Baboo

ever left his room that night or was a member of the House
at all, so noiseless he became, so meek, so ingenuous, so
guileless.

Socston finally decided that his father would rather
enjoy the situation. He realised that in the School he
was the hero of the hour, and sat languidly swinging his
legs on the letter table receiving the sympathy of his
rowing friends. Two *Pops* called, and reiterated that
it was a damned shame, and hoped he would continue
his rowing career at the University. Between schools,
which he did not attend, his father arrived, and announced
that he was cut off with a penny, and could choose
between a ticket to Canada, third class, or becoming a
night porter at Clarence's. The Eton patriot took the
line of the Bishop whose son reaches the Divorce Court,
and he took the line very vigorously. ' Well, you always
wanted me *swished*, and I hoped I would be this time,'
said Socston humbly. ' I didn't send you to Eton to be
expelled,' howled the indignant father. ' To think that
I, who was in the Field, in *Pop*, won the Racquets——'
' And the Newcastle,' interjected his son sarcastically.
Mr. Socston raised his hand to strike, and catching the
eye of his handsome boy, who, after all, was putting a
very plucky face on it, relented. His hand fell, and he
burst into tears. ' Cheer up, Dad, I don't mind you
cutting me off with a penny. I will make good somewhere. They shall be proud of me yet. *Floreat Etona,*
I say, and damn the sneaks ! ' ' Well, come and see
your Tutor, Lamb, not Morley, and see if we can get
him to go to the Head.' They passed through the deserted
Eton street in the hush of Mid-day School. Only the
Sixth Form Praepostor passed like a brilliantly attired
diplomatist from room to room. Nobody but the School
Clerk noticed the tears bedewing father and son.

They found Mr. Lamb not unexpectant. He had
already been an hour with the Head, doing his utmost
to save his pupil, but he had found the Head immovable.
Mr. Lamb was gentle, courteous, unchiding, but pessi-

mistic. 'The Head places the honour of the School above any single House, much above any individual boy. But the disgrace will be shared. I may tell you privately that this morning the Head decided on the removal of eight boys from Mr. Morley's in connection with some bullying.' Socston gasped. 'Why, there won't be anybody left to play for the House in the Football Ties!' 'Even that serious possibility has been considered,' said Mr. Lamb, with a sad smile. 'Are they going to get Leaving Books?' asked Socston. 'That has not been settled by the Head yet.' 'Surely he will not refuse my poor boy a Leaving Book after winning the School Pulling?' pleaded the father. Mr. Lamb must have raised the point already, for he looked dubious. 'Perhaps if you went to see him, but he will be busy this afternoon, as the parents of eight boys are expected at any moment. I am afraid we shall have a very sad afternoon.'

Socston and his father went towards the School Yard. With lowered voice Mr. Socston asked the School Clerk if he could procure an interview with the Head immediately. 'You know who I am. I am Socston, who was in the Field.' The Clerk pitying entered the presence. There was nothing happening at Chambers, and the Clerk came out. 'You may come in for a moment.' It was irregular, but the Head was not afraid of parents. There was no need to explain the situation. 'May I ask that my boy should carry away a Leaving Book?' The Head replied 'No.' 'May his name be cut on the panelling?' This was an unofficial matter, and the Head referred him to the Clerk, who stood in the doorway. 'Let this be a very terrible lesson to you, my boy,' boomed the Head, not unkindly. Father and son withdrew. 'Give me a half-sovereign to pay for my name to be cut,' begged Socston, and his father, forgetting his financial threats, silently shed a gold obol into his hand. It was like the fee which the classical dead gave to Charon. 'Don't forget my name,' said Socston a little huskily.

The School Clerk shook him by the hand. 'Don't worry, sir, you're not the first to go sudden, and we know there were others, but we can say nothing. It's all known on the railway. All you've got to do is to go out to India or South Africa and win a D.S.O. Then they'll forgive you, and I'll find a place for your name where your friends will be proud to look for it.'

'Thanks awfully,' and Socston turned aside and wept bitterly. His father sent him to finish his packing and went to sleep the bitter night himself at the White Hart. Bitter were the thoughts of the father, thrice bitter the reflexions of the son. He had to brace himself while he watched Mrs. Sowerby stripping his room of trophy and print. The rowing photographs, the boating caps, and Fourth of June straw hats, with the artificial wreaths and the silver emblems of the boats in which he had rowed—*Alexandra*, black ribbon and silver escutcheon; *Britannia*, bright blue with the lady off the penny for emblem; and finally the glorious *Victory* and her anchor. His rowing sequence was broken. He knew well what might have followed, the peerless light blue blazer and white cap, and Henley oar, and perhaps the cap of the Captain of the Boats. He was so young, and so near the Eight. But it was never to be, and after sending all his books to the School Pound, he distributed his pictures, some personally, and some with a note. The photograph of himself and Crake as winners of the Pulling he left in the Baboo's room with a word of farewell. He bore no malice, save to Mouler, and he forgave all who had injured him. He left nothing in Peter's room, not that he disliked him, but that he felt ashamed. He could not bear to face his pitying and virtuous look. He refrained from saying good-bye to the Dame, though he understood the Dame had selected a Prayer Book as a form of leaving present. He remembered Willum, though he could, in view of his father's threat, hardly have afforded the ten shillings he gave him. He fell into reverie, broken by the sound of the cab rolling out of Wise's Yard. Slowly he rose and passed down the old lead-carpeted stairs, down the familiar landings, glanced up the well-known passages. The Man's green baize door was shut. He stood for a second, and turned on his heel. He received his valedictory from Willum, whose throat was scarlet with suppressed emotion. 'Hope you will meet Mr. Mouler in the Army, sir,' he said. 'I always thought he was no gentleman.' He had apparently overheard the story. Indeed the House had buzzed with gossip, and Mouler, had he returned, would have found himself lynched in Barnes Pool. Not a murmur was raised against the Head. He could not have done otherwise. But Socston had been the victim of treachery, and his friends had decided to make his departure memorable. As the old fly, driven by the old leering flyman, drove out of Wise's Yard, a subdued cheer arose from the street. Socston found his leaving much delayed by the number of friends who wished to shake his hand. There must have been fifty boys round the cab, and one held the horse's head until from a top window of Morley's a magnificent bouquet tied up in the House-colours could be dangled, and then solemnly lowered into the cab. Willing hands untied it, and it became part of Socston's luggage. Socston rose and made a low bow, which was received with tremendous cheering. The road was now becoming blocked as for a *hoisting*, and boys on their way to the River, or to bathe, remained to join in the cheers, though most of them could not have explained the cause. Rice appeared in surreptitious bags, and clouds of confetti began to descend from the windows as the common cab drove away like a vehicle of eternity. Peter had not returned to the House, for a sufficient reason perhaps. He had been 'sent up for good' a second time, and during 'after twelve' he sat in Mr. Lamb's deserted pupil-room transcribing the verses letter by letter upon the College vellum. It was a simple subject. A Psalm had been set for Latin Lyrics, and Mr. Lamb had so steeped him in the daintier metres that the verses almost ran off his pen.

It was an infinite pleasure to write the crisp, neatly-scanning lines, and to exercise a certain sweet pride of authorship. Peter felt it would be amusing to confront the Head with a second set of verses during the same half. He might say something at last. Mr. Lamb was charming. ' A very unusual honour. A real distinction. I believe Ullathorne, K.S., is the only other boy to share the distinction this half.' And he signed the azure-stamped card. ' Good boy, very good boy. Your Tutor likes good boys.' As a matter of fact they were both thinking of the same thing. From one mind to the other flitted the same thought . . . Socston ! Both felt a clutch at the heart, and then Peter burst into tears. ' It 's a shame, a horrible shame. We all know he didn't want to go to London, but he was persuaded. They dared him. Nobody is *sacked* who deserves it, and the fellows who don't deserve it are *sacked*.' Mr. Lamb looked troubled. ' I am afraid it is too late now to do anything. The Head Master is very just, very just when he is roused. I spent two hours with him, and we went over all Socston's career. It was unlucky the Head remembered that he had been out on the Fourth of June, his first year as a Lower Boy.' ' I wonder if we couldn't get him his Leaving Book after all,' said Peter. ' I thought with your permission that I would ask the Head to send it to him instead of the book which he will owe me for my third send-up.' Mr. Lamb put his hand on Peter's shoulder. ' I like you for that, but the Head couldn't possibly understand that way of reasoning.' ' Perhaps it isn't reasoning,' said Peter. ' It 's too mediaeval for modern Eton anyhow. I am afraid you must take your prize. *Palmam qui meruit ferat !* '

Peter sat astonied. ' I have got a prize for you, Darley,' said Mr. Lamb, ' which I was going to give you at the end of the half, but I should like to give it to you now.' Peter followed him to the familiar old room in Saville House where he and Socston had stumbled together through their first lesson in Greek Testament. The old parrot eyed him very wisely as he came in. He had been ruffled by too many pens thrust through the bars of his cage to take kindly to any boy. 'Have you been reading *Poetae Graeci* this half?' Peter nodded. 'What did you like best?' 'The Dirge for Heraclitus, sir.' 'Well, you will like this book, *Ionica*. Do you know William Johnson's translation of the Greek? I will read it to you:—

> "They told me, Heraclitus, they told me you were dead,
> They brought me bitter news to hear and bitter tears to shed.
> I wept as I remembered how often you and I
> Had tired the sun with talking and sent him down the sky.
> And now that thou art lying, my dear old Carian guest,
> A handful of grey ashes, long long ago at rest,
> Still are thy pleasant voices, thy nightingales, awake;
> For Death, he taketh all away, but them he cannot take."'

Peter recalled the Greek, and said simply, 'Yes, it makes me think of my friendship for Socston.' The pathos of Friendship and the beauty of letters dawned upon him in the one moment. 'You were very attached to him, I feel,' said Mr. Lamb sympathetically. 'Yes, we were close friends at the beginning, and when he had no use for my friendship, I must have come to love him.' 'Never mind,' said Mr. Lamb cheerfully. 'But I do mind, and I always will mind,' said Peter.

After his Tutor had looked through the fair copy of his 'sent-up' verses, Peter walked round to the Cloisters, where he felt anxious to acquaint his understanding friends with his further success. He was received with both gusto and refinement. Mr. Thackeray was pleased to read and comment on his verses, also to talk mildly of the translator of Heraclitus. 'He wrote many wonderful things, such as an epigrammatic guide to English History and the gem called *Lucretilis*, which I think, if found at Herculaneum, would be classified as Horatian.'

'How parabolic,' suggested Mrs. Thackeray. 'And now, Mr. Darley, how surprised the Head Master will be by your second appearance this half. He is bound to regard it as symbolic of the inverse square operating in Mr. Morley's.' Peter nodded, for he knew that she meant that the work of the *saps* in a House like Morley's was in inverse ratio to the idleness of the idle. ' Mr. Darley, can you not read your verses aloud, or are they reserved for the ears of the Head Master before they are made meat for moths ? ' Peter did not wait for Mr. Thackeray's gentle assent to begin declaiming his verses. ' How beautiful ! They appeal even to the illatinate. We are most touched that you should have thought us worthy to hear them.' And then closing her eyes, as though uttering a dark saying, she continued, ' If I may speak reverently, you seem to me to have brought us an unguent before burial. We are both old, very old.' Peter rose to say good-bye to his dear friends, and strolled back to Morley's. He could not help thinking that Charleston's epigram was right when he said, ' There are two great women in Eton. Miss Evans is a great Dame, but in the Cloisters you will find a *grande dame.*'

That evening he took tea with Charleston at Miss Evans's. He could not help comparing the two great old ladies, so remotely different but so strangely part of the Eton world. He noticed Miss Evans's head trembled a little from old age, as she performed her soundless laugh. The old gaiety was there, but as she mentioned the great row she became formidably grave. Charleston was cynical, but she tolerated his casual manners because they were graceful. Peter only wished to God he had been at her House. He returned to Morley's, wondering what humorist could have sprinkled his unlovely portals with confetti.

CHAPTER XXVI

FIRE !

THE School was little affected by the clearances from Mr. Morley's. As pheasants streaming over a rise of trees have no time to notice those that fall to the guns, and as forest trees grow into the gaps of a storm, so are the expelled forgotten at Eton. Houses in their fierce rivalry at games keep their eyes too closely pressed to the goal to notice the collapse of the insignificant or the departure of the uncrowned, and Morley's was remarkably a House *sans* caps and *sans* cups.

Morley's was so much out of the main current of the School that nobody cared whether the House lived or died. The deeds of Morleyites did not call for Eton's admiration. Socston's escapade made a ripple, and his dramatic departure was interpreted by nervous authorities as a riot in favour of immorality. *Pop* were asked to inquire into the matter, which they did by performing a few summary executions with the cane on the ground that the crowd had incommoded the entrance to their rooms. The wholesale expulsions interested the School considerably. The procession of weeping parents in cabs was diverting even on an Eton half-holiday, and the expelled, once the uncertainty of their fate was settled, created a sensation by rushing round the Playing Fields to inform their friends of their fate and enjoy the chivalrous humour such a communication naturally afforded.

But for the unhappy parents it was a very much sadder affair. They had arrived in different stages of anger and despair. Several brought letters from their solicitors,

At least one family lawyer was brought as far as the waiting-room at Slough. One anxious mother had calculated on the effect of a sympathetic telegram from her rural Dean, and another had telegraphed for action to be deferred in deference to her friendship with several Duchesses. But passionate entreaties and humble threats were of no avail. The manner of the Head was aloof and almighty, and he conscientiously abashed fathers who were already bashful and quelled mothers whose hearts were already breaking. And so the blackest day in the history of Morley's House came and passed.

The most absorbing event at Eton is the quickest absorbed, and the tail of one vanishes down the throat of the next. Like a thousand rivulets the lives of a thousand boys mingled in the one steady stream. Rivulets withdrawn or diverted could not be missed in the flow. The least and the greatest passed without leaving a trace on the Eton sand. Captains could go away and be forgotten by the very ones who leaped into their place. God only knew what became of the temporary gods of the Eton world. The rank and file of the School left little except the carved letters of their names in symbolic return for the mighty impress Eton had made on them. The entire human contents of Morley's House might have been transferred by Sinbad's rocs to the Arabian desert without altering the stride of the School, or postponing an hour in the time-table, or a cricket match, or a heat in the rowing of the House Fours, of which the Final was to be contested between Munfort's and Jenkinson's on the very Saturday following the Black Friday, which had wrought such havoc to Morley's.

On Saturday morning Mr. Socston, after spending the night at the White Hart, removed his son, in spite of all entreaty to be allowed to see the Final of the House Fours. The bitterness of the situation did not touch Socston until the train rolled over the Railway Bridge, and his last look had been cast to Rafts. There were the

roofs of the boat-houses. There was housed the beautiful
shell of the *Victory*. There, no doubt, was 'Brocas
Bill' polishing his oar for another to drive through the
water. He felt like an Admiral pulling down his flag
in the prime of life. As the train ran along the Arches,
he could see Brocas Clump hanging like a bright green
thunder-burst over the dried fields, and Eton Parish
spire hid in the green gossamer of a giant aspen-tree.
And beyond Athens he caught a last glimpse of the
deserted River, running without fleck or foam, poising
its everlasting strength against the generations of boys
who grow up like the grass that perishes beside its banks.
Cloud shadows were passing as quickly across the fields
as his own days at Eton, and for the first time the torrent
of boyish impressions was checked in his mind at Memory's
weir. He remembered coming as a new boy, full of vain
expectations and pessimistic dread, the Entrance Examination in Upper School, meeting Mr. Lamb with Peter for
the first time, the first construe, the School Yard, the
wine-tinted battlements, the whirling pigeons, and the
boys massing for Chapel or Absence under the great
Towers. Then he recalled with a fervour he had never
felt before the wheezy little rooms and smoky passages
of Morley's House, Charley Wise's Yard outside, the
occasional rumble of cabs and horses, and the leering old
flyman, who had just driven him and his father back to
the Station. He remembered past triumphs, the Steeplechase he had run as a Lower Boy, and the School Pulling
he had won only a few weeks ago. He pictured himself
carried once more on the necks of *Pop* and, as it all faded
from his grasp, his desire for athletic glory and popularity
became passionate. He realised that only what is lost
can be loved perfectly. At Slough Station he knew that
he had crossed the bounds, and was an Eton boy no
more.

As the train rushed on to the main line, he thought of
the coming night on the River when Crake would be rowing
for the House Fours, the greatest of trophies that a House

could snatch from the face of the waters. How he envied
Peter who, though colourless, was still an Eton boy. As
he thought of him sitting and stewing in his little room,
foggy in winter and fuggy in summer, he could have cursed
him. He felt he hated the boy whose friendship might
have saved him, whereas the girl he had loved at sight
had brought about his ruin. Even if he never saw them
again, he could not help connecting both curiously in his
mind. He looked out upon the unlovely parts which
surround the prison of Wormwood Scrubbs, and surmised
he would probably end there. He felt like a pilgrim
thrown from Paradise and left to shift for himself under
infernal conditions. He found himself thrust into the
sudden shadow of Paddington Station. He drew an Old
Etonian tie out of his pocket, and with no other cuirass
stepped out to face the world.

That night an enormous crowd came to watch the Final
of the House Fours on the River. *Dry-bobs* put aside
their eternal practice at nets, and the River was cleared
of all other craft. Masters abandoned the correcting
of Trials papers, which were recurring with the baleful
precision of decimals. Jenkinson had not been well,
but he came down to the River in a cab, with his faithful
butler and Peter, whose last desire at Eton was to see
Jenkinson's victory. The cab stopped at Cuckoo Weir,
and Jenkinson was lifted out like the Celtic chief, who,
in spite of wounds or lumbago, was carried into battle
on a shield. It was a tense moment for his House, and
the butler's shakiness transferred itself to Jenkinson,
who was not the steadier for Peter's quaking support.
They began to suffer from those qualms which visit
rowers and the friends of rowers before the starting of a
race. The seething crowd moved up and down the trodden
tow-path for vantage to view the start, and yet obtain a
start of the runners, who cover the whole distance, shouting to their friends from the bank.

'There they are ! coming round Upper Hope to the

start,' cried Peter. Jenkinson's House accompanied them, and merged in the crowd which was watching the three Fours moving upstream into position. Jenkinson, Peter, and butler moved down the bank, throwing a nervous look behind from time to time. 'I heard the boys' maid say they had a very good tea, sir,' said the butler, to ease the awful moment. Jenkinson showed relief. 'A good tea, how jolly! I never thought of ordering it. How wrong of me!' He was now suffering from excitement more than lumbago. 'I hope they had something with their tea,' he added. 'Yes,' said Peter, 'I am sure they did. There can be more in a cup of tea than is dreamt of in your filters.' It was only better than saying nothing, and Jenkinson smiled feebly. 'If you mean brandy, say so.' His pale face became lit with an amused tolerance, which disappeared as quickly as a zephyr dipping on and off water, as a shrill discordant howl signalled that the race had started upstream. A keenness as of the east wind caught his nobly drawn features into immovability.

Three rowing Fours had begun to move rapidly abreast. Abreast they shot past Athens, and lengthened into over-lapping procession while a frenzied crowd ran, gasped, shouted, barged, and dodged for room on the towing-path. The perfect dignity and time of the well-trained rowers might have induced a stranger from Mars to believe that the contest was really being fought on the bank, while the referees and limited spectators were swinging comfortably alongside in their boats. The strife was so evidently fiercest on the land. Then was fulfilled the Greek epigram, which expressed wonder at the groans of the spectators compared to the silence of the agonists. The different supporters screamed, entreated, and threatened, uttering whatever syllables might possibly encourage their own Boat and dismay the others. Lower Boys were jostled into the reeds. Runners were tripped flat. Mr. Flinders drove his wheel into the water, and followed on foot shouting cast-iron instructions to Jenkinson's

terrified cox. *Pops* and Upper Boats, speaking through
megaphones, kept pace with the boats without over-
distress to their wind or toilet. Far behind the ruck
of runners a lonely figure hobbled through the dust,
supported by Peter and his butler. ' They are holding
their own,' he gasped. ' I can see no more. Oh, what
a *scug* I am ! ' ' They are leading ! shooting ahead ! '
lied Peter, who saw nothing. All three Fours had disappeared round Sandbanks, hugging the inside station,
disputing every corner, and spurting downstream. Only
a low distant murmur moving across the fields indicated
where they were. Jenkinson, Peter, and the butler
waited agonising minutes till they should swim into sight
again. The result would be judgeable by then, for the
winner would probably be well ahead. But if the Fours
were still close together, oh, the physical agony in thwart
and the mental pain on tow-path before the decision was
made. Jenkinson's emotions were more than those of
critic or spectator. The life which he had lived for
others was approaching its climax. The great rowing
trophy for his boys meant more to him than his Newcastle
in the past. For ten years he had built his House, mould-
ing, polishing, placing every brick. Ten years ago he
had sat in his study at ' Drury's,' with his butler watching
the first boarder arrive. He had always apologised to
his boys for being a duffer at games, so it seemed strange
how quickly his House had swept into the front rank.
Fast-hand bowlers and graceful oars seemed to grow under
his care. Yet all he had been able to do had been to
encourage and feed their minds, which he had done in
scores of ways outside the dull routine of work. In
many instances he found the strong body had grown to
accompany the bright mind. Some of his boys would
pass for Greek gentlemen, fair and good. Smoking and
drinking he had eliminated by the force of his contempt.
By furious toil and training his boys had begun to wrest
trophies from the School. There arose Crake, a delicate-
looking American, who arrived talking French, but under

AA

Jenkinson's sanctioning enthusiasm had taken to rowing. In three years he had won the School Pulling, and marked Jenkinson's as a great *wet-bob* House, and now, with a burst of rowing talent, Crake and three others were challenging the crown and headship of the River. A Pindaric Olympian Ode was stirring through Jenkinson's old Classical cranium. With Peter dragging him, he managed to cut along Cumberland Creek and reach the Railway Bridge.

'There they come!' shouted Peter, who was watching the distant turn like a Greek watchman in Aeschylus, 'two lengths ahead! I am sure they must be yours, sir, because they are rowing so well.' Jenkinson smiled a little grimly. 'I hope that is the real reason, Peter.' The leading Four drew closer down the river three lengths from the frenzied pursuit of second. 'I do believe those are our colours on their blades,' mentioned the butler quietly in the tenseness. Jenkinson waited till he was sure. Yes, they were his own beloved boys rowing for dear life the race of their lives. A perspiring remnant of his House ran like demoniacs on the tow-path. As they passed Jenkinson they shrieked his name. 'Well rowed, Jenkinson's!' The glint of victory shone in the old scholar's eyes, and he murmured the Greek chant for victory once or twice, '*Nikomen, nikomen.*' Happiness and the soft radiance of love cast all trace of illness from those features. The youthful beauty of his own school days returned, and he became transfigured in Peter's sight. Peter thought to himself that if the face of the headless Victory of Samothrace were ever found, it would be like Jenkinson's at that moment. He looked at him, little thinking that he saw him for the last time. Then he ran off, shouting, 'Well rowed, Jenkinson's!'

The race flashed past in no time, though for five minutes *Pops*, umpires, stragglers, and partisans continued to flow along the path. Jenkinson kept his eyes fixed on his crew, as they passed under the Railway Bridge, and on the cloud of dust, which marked his supporters cheer-

ing and shouting as one man from the bank.   He watched
them all with true admiration, little dreaming that he,
the lumbago-stricken, was the inspiring energy in the
boat, the protathlete among the runners, and the chore-
gist of the shouters, who shouted, ' Jenkinson's !   Good
old Juggins ! ! Well rowed Jenkinson's ! ! ! '   No House
can achieve without a leader, and Jenkinson was the
inspired leader of his House, though he hardly knew it
himself.   His crew kept up their lead until they were out
of sight.   Five minutes later he reached Rafts, and
victory was confirmed to him by delirious Lower Boys.
' How jolly, how jolly ! '   And without wishing to share
in the pæan of jubilee, Jenkinson hobbled home, and
waited in his study to overhear the street thunder of the
School engaged in *hoisting* his House Four.   That evening
he was careful not to overhear too much of the sound of
revelry that went up in his House, and he read Pindar
till midnight.

Mr. Morley's House must have presented a striking
contrast that night.   Decimated and disheartened, it
preserved a silence, almost as of the grave, while from
Jenkinson's went up, not fifty yards away,

> ' the shout of them that triumph,
> the song of them that feast ! '

Sleep came to both Houses, but not to all their inhabitants.   Cheener had not been well since the shock
which his nervous system had received some days past.
His Dame had insisted on his ' staying out ' of school,
and even on his being excused Trials.   The expulsion
of so many for an attempt to bully him had had rather
worse results on him than on those dismissed from the
School.   He had remained terrified and brooding in the
sick-room that day and that evening until the agonising
fears of the unknown had invaded his brain and self-
control had slipped from his puny grasp.   He heard the
Clock strike midnight, but he could not sleep.   Influences
unknown and unconscious moved in his mind, and he

became aware of an encircling horror, against which it was necessary to struggle. He rose in his sleep and felt toward his fireplace. He was seized with a craving for light. There were no embers on the fireplace, only the paper screen which covered the space during summer. He began tearing it up. He struggled into the passage with the crumpled paper. Somewhere at the end of the passage he knew he would find a low-burning gas-jet. With a sigh of relief he caught sight of the pimple of blue flame. He lifted the paper to it and watched it burst into blaze. The paper reddened and blackened before his fascinated eyes. He dropped the lighted ash into a dust-bin. Other papers, old exercises, and book-covers caught alight. The fire relieved his nightmare, and he sighed in his sleep. He struggled back to bed. . . . The Clock struck two. Eton slept as heavily in the summer dawn as in the wintriest and darkest night. Boys and masters slept, and the rosy-fingered dawn dropped a silvery muslin between the dark and the day. A first faint red-tipped far-off sleepy little cloud peeped through the sepia. The sun rose like Humpty Dumpty on the wall of the world. Nothing in Eton stirred except a wisp of smoke which rose unnoticed over Morley's. For a while it hung like a string dangling in the air before dissolving in the first flush of the sun. Then a puff of smoke followed, and then another. Without a sound or a splutter, the fumes escaped into the clear ether, and shot brownly against the light of morning. Within the battered and burrowed old House, the rose of smouldering fire threw its red foliage from panel to panel, and from banister to banister. Running sparks crept into the crannies of the bricks, and revelled in the dry woodwork. The glow grew white under the old leaden carpets, and melted them in dripping bubbles down the stairs. Nowhere did it burst into open flame; but the red fringe ran like a silent cancer revealed under the myriad-powered microscope. Within the showy stucco exterior the red growth glowed and increased until the timbers were crumbling to ash, and a great volume of smoke, not finding ready egress through the roof, poured down the landings and penetrated under doors and through keyholes. Boys began to cough in their sleep, but habit did not permit Mrs. Sowerby to rise a second before half-past five, and the morning was still young. The smoke clustered thickly, and the minutes passed solemnly on the face of the old School Clock, who alone saw and uttered his quarterly warning in vain. Boom . . . boom . . . boom . . . boom . . . It was four o'clock, and a fine morning.

Philips had left his door open that night, with the result that his room became quickly filled with smoke. He was the first to wake, and naturally guessed a practical joke. If they were trying to smoke him out he felt he had better get up. He rolled out of bed into consciousness and sniffed soot. It was a very unpleasant form of joke. He opened the window and looked between the bars. Brown, billowy smoke and a dead silence ! He hurried into the passage and caught sight of fire. ' Fire ! ' he shouted, and banged at every door on the landing. Sleepers rose as for Early School. ' What the hell is up ? ' asked a few dazed Uppers, coming into the passage. ' Hell chiefly, I should think,' answered Philips. ' Hadn't we better get the Lower Boys out of the House ? ' Camdown strolled on the scene in pyjamas and a House Blazer, and asserted his Captaincy. ' Rout out everybody,' he said. Lower Boys were collected, half-dressed, with streaming eyes, and ordered to bolt. The front door was smashed open with the metal bell and pokers. And in this darkest moment of Morley's House none showed eagerness to save himself before others. The fag masters picked up and carried out into the street the fags they had unmercifully fagged and beaten the day before. The Captain of the House stood on the bridge of smouldering wood, till the House was emptied. There was no alarm, only a cynical amusement expressed in the phrase, ' Well, the rotten old House is on fire at last ' Others

asked, ' Where is the Man ? ' and Willum, with his gills,
it was remarked, for the first time white, reported that Mr.
Morley was saying *Absence* in the next House entrance.
Mrs. Sowerby passed out, correctly dressed, amid a cheer.
She had already made up her mind that the presence of
the Dame would act as an instant extinguisher, but the
Dame was below distributing sweaters on the theory that
if the Fire Brigade arrived the boys would get wet. The
House was abandoned in good order and with good spirits
by her crew. Where youth is, there is no fear.

The Man went on counting and recounting the Lower
Boys in the street amid the sympathetic interest of the
School, who had been roused out of bed in great numbers,
and were gathering in their overcoats and slippers to
watch the vain efforts of three Fire Brigades, one
engine in time being always more effective than three
coming late. Ladders and escapes were hoisted. Hoses,
however, were laid, and a good deal of water distributed
on the burning or burnt embers. Mr. Morley had counted
the Lower Boys three times to his satisfaction, and, with
the help of the School Clerk, was calling the roll of Fifth
Form. Camdown did not answer to his name. A cry was
raised, but the Captain was seen standing on some out-
houses, tragically surveying the scene with crossed arms.
As the roof showed signs of collapse, he turned slowly on
his heel, dropped into the yard, and emerged in the
street. There was a faint cheer, which was lost in the
Man's sudden inquiry for Darley. Nobody remembered
having seen him that morning. Then somebody thought
he was on Leave, but the Dame, having been disinterred
from a neighbouring house, could not swear that he was
on Leave. Camdown and Philips ran round to the yard
amid a hail of sparks. Firemen followed them with a
ladder, which was raised out of the yard to Peter's window.
It was easy to scramble over the low stable roof and haul
the short ladder after them. Philips wildly remembered
the last time he had climbed that roof. It was on the
Fourth of June, when they had broken out three years

before. They had used Peter's room then, and he knew there should be no difficulty in entering by the window. Camdown was already smashing the panes with his bare hands, and tearing at the bars, but his efforts to enter were unsuccessful. He turned round on the ladder and shouted 'Bars! iron bars! I can't get in. We must try the stairs.' It was only too true. Since the famous expedition bars had been carefully fitted to the window sashes, and the smallest Lower Boy could neither enter nor get out. The flames had died down under the tardy water supply, for the River, loved of the boys, had come to the rescue, and Thames waters were being pumped in liquid, hissing torrents in every direction. Several boys were then able to enter the House, headed by Camdown and the anxious House master. Though the landing was blackened, Peter's room had not been touched by fire. Eager hands burst into the stifling little den. The weakened door was torn off its hinges. From the crumpled bed a white arm was stretched in the air. Peter lay there as though asleep. Camdown cried to him to wake up, and lifted the blanket from his face. 'Time for Early School!' cried Philips desperately, but for the first time in his Eton career Peter Darley did not rise.

The Doctor had arrived at the window with a ladder, and the whole window sash was removed. Examining the still body, he realised that he was dead, and throwing a blanket over Peter, slowly carried him down and laid him in the pupil-room, which had survived. There was no mark of fire on the body, only a slight smell of smoke. They left him on the inkstained desks. The School Clerk had already marked him as absent, and when the worst was confirmed, it was felt that he alone could inform the Head Master. He alone possessed a key to the Head's rooms, and in the grey light of morning he penetrated to the bedside, and told him that Morley's House was burning. The old man leaped out of bed, and roused the household, ordering fires to be lit and hot coffee to be prepared. In a moment he was all energy and strength. Then the School

Clerk braced himself to strike. ' I am afraid there is a boy missing.' The Head stood still. The Clerk went on, ' I have seen his body.' The Head strode forth as the shepherd who goes out desirous to die that he may save his sheep. A silence of death fell upon the Cloisters.

The survivors were collected and brought to the Head Master's house, while the news of death spread rapidly through the School. And the summer day grew exquisite with flower and leaf. Insects and scents filled the air. A breeze filtered through the shaggy green branches of the elm-trees, and the River, running with crystal speed through shallow and over depths, embraced the whole Eton peninsula with a quivering arm of love.

With unusual quiet and thoughtfulness, the School continued their work. Fortunately Darley was an orphan, and no parent had to be summoned. All suffered, but the full crushing weight of the tragedy fell upon one, and upon the broadest shoulders in the School. Edmond Warre was a stricken man from that day. He never was the same again. It was not that he knew the boy personally, but that he felt he was a member of the flock entrusted to him, and Eton had suffered loss. Blame was accruing from every side. Newspapers were blazing the news across the world. Photographers were on the spot, and reporters were already at their ghoul-like task of gathering details of the disaster. The survivors of the House remained under the Head's roof until provision could be made to distribute them among other Houses. Silently and sadly the boys trooped into the gloomy Cloisters, and sat in the Head's rooms, looking out on the beautiful garden, otherwise walled from passing eyes. An ancient mulberry-tree drooped over the turf, rich with the promise of foliaged fruit. A cedar-tree rose against the distant background, with smooth green branches stretching like the mighty stairs of Jacob's dream, up and down which passed the unnumbered musical hosts of summer insects. Within the building there was no sound

heard save of the Head's voice murmuring in hushed
conversation from time to time with the Clerk or the
masters, who came in to discuss vital matters. Dread
questions of responsibilities and coroners and inquest
had arisen. The outside world inconsiderately demanded
to know the origin of fire in summer time. Was it due
to gas or electricity ? Where was the Fire Brigade, and
why were the windows barred ? Hundreds of parents
were stirred on these points. Schools all over England
had begun to remove bars, and to erect fire escapes.
Eton had paid the sacrifice to secure safety for others.
Within the hive of life stood the one blackened shell.
To the fretting of the outer world the Head turned his
back, immuring himself in the Cloisters, and by Doctor's
advice declining all discussion or interview. In conscience he felt free, for he had recently circularised the
Houses on fire drill and fire escape. The eagle was
mewed indeed, and a great wave of sympathy went to
him out of the present and the past. The awed boys
beheld the bowed figure that no opposition could quell,
and no enmity lower. The triumph of his great career
seemed blurred. Their captain was stricken as he
entered port. ' O be favourable and gracious unto Sion :
build thou the walls of Jerusalem,' had been his text, and
with his own eyes he had seen the walls of Eton stand
broken and blackened under the sight of Heaven. Could
it be true ? There had been a fire in a House in 1900,
and the great fire in the Buttery in 1865, but no life lost.
The third fire had visited his Eton, and death had come
sooner than the firemen.

Ullathorne and Charleston met after twelve, and
obtained leave to visit their friend's room and look at his
face once more in Mr. Morley's pupil-room. The old staircase was burnt, and the sunlight was pouring through the
broken windows on every floor. One side of the House
had collapsed internally, and the smoke of the embers
rose into the unpollutable. Cautiously the two boys
climbed on a ladder to Peter's empty room. It was so

like hundreds of other Eton rooms, undistinguished save by the 'sent-up' cards, proudly glazed and framed on the wall. The last set of verses was still on his desk, ready to be shown up at the meeting which Peter had hoped would lead to a real acquaintance with the Head Master. Ullathorne glanced at them, and gravely read out the Psalm verses and the Latin version, one by one. The motto chosen for the exercise was taken from a hymn :—

> 'He plants his footsteps in the sea
> And rides upon the storm.'

The version was of Psalm Seventy-Seven :—

'The waters saw thee, O God, the waters saw thee and were afraid : the depths also were troubled.

'The clouds poured out water, the air thundered : and thine arrows went abroad.

'The voice of thy thunder was heard round about : the lightnings shone upon the ground ; the earth was moved and shook withal.

'Thy way is in the sea, and thy paths in the great waters : and thy footsteps are not known.

'Thou leddest thy people like sheep : by the hand of Moses and Aaron.'

The Latin ran :—

DARLEY.   LATIN VERSES.

> *Vidit, o Metuende, te*
> *Regium pelagus : statim*
> *Percutit metus aequor et*
> *Subter alta moventur.*
>
> *Ille fundit aquas graves,*
> *Ille dat tonitrus ; simul*
> *Dira fulmina per polum*
> *Dissipantur hiantem.*
>
> *Nubibus tua vox tonat,*
> *Qua tremens resonat polus,*
> *Nimbus igne micat tuo,*
> *Terra contremit omnis*

Tendis in pelago viam,
Trames est tuus in mari:
Quis potest tacitos gradus
Nosse praetereuntis?

Ducis ut timidos greges
Moysis et famuli manu
Trans aquas populum tuum
Barbarosque per hostes.

'I think they are wonderfully symbolic,' said Ulla-thorne. 'Fire and water have accompanied his passing to another land. Thank God, he cannot have heard the streaming water or felt the burning fire. May he rest in peace!' Both boys were on the verge of breaking into tears, so lonely and yet so familiar the room appeared. It was exactly as it had ever been, whenever they paid him a visit—a *sap's* den. Charleston opened the bureau and began placing the well-used books in order. The touch of the dread visitant had shed a pathos on its humdrum contents, the inky grammars and classical texts, the box of coloured inks, the time-table fastened by drawing pins to the flap, the last piece of Broad rule torn off for use and left folded in the blotting book. In one of the pigeon holes lay the curious green charm which Ormton had mended with such care, and brought back, as he thought, to its rightful owner. Ullathorne picked it up and examined it. Without a word he crossed himself as they both descended to the pupil-room, outside which the policeman on duty in the College was standing. The Man, pitifully distressed, and unequal to the new sling which fortune had dealt him, was trying to collect fresh information from Willum, who had not sufficiently recovered from the shock of the fire to be intelligible.

Peter lay shrouded by a blanket across the pupil-room table, from which the last extra-work and the last *poena* had not been cleared. His unclosed eyes sought the ceiling, from which so many hard-pressed mathe-maticians had sought inspiration in other days. The stained, deserted desks were tragic as no church benches could be, and the blackboard from which somebody had half rubbed away some chalked figures was more solemn than draperies of crape. Both boys knelt for a moment and prayed where prayer had never been offered before. ' I found this scribbled in his *burry*,' murmured Charleston. ' It 's only a scrap he must have written when he was reading the Epitaphs in the Greek Anthology the other day.' Ullathorne took the Broad rule and read the scrap of doggerel, faintly parodying the most exquisite short poems known to the world. It read simply :—

> ' Stranger to Eton, a *sap* and misanthrope lies here,
> Shunned of all, yet only to the Muses dear.'

Neither of the friends could bear to speak to the other. The mask fell from one as quickly as the pose left the other. Ullathorne's ecclesiasticism became fused with poignant grief. Charleston's scorn for one world and professed disbelief in the next were melted in that moment. Both went their way with their hearts made like the hearts of new boys again. They were back at the beginning, back to their first day when the same cab had driven them all full of innocent wonder into the world of Eton, and dropped one of the three at the door of Mr. Morley's. And now one would never walk with the twain. They were divided for ever.

The whole School assembled in Chapel to pay Peter Darley the passing honour of funeral rites. The bell, which day by day gathered the School together like the ringing tocsin of Life out of the Houses and passages, out of the lanes and corners of Eton, began to toll the note of Death. And while afternoon was at its brightest, the work and the play of the School stood still. Sadly and solemnly the lines of boys took rank, and stood rigidly in that gigantic sarcophagus of Upper Chapel, that bright-glazed sepulchre into which the strife and hum and noise of Eton never penetrates, leaving it to the memory-stricken visits of Old Etonians, and the haunting of the older

dead. Dr. Lloyd was playing the slow Funeral March
as the Sixth entered with downcast eyes. Like dread
visitants rising from the darkness of Hades, the Head,
Provost, and Vice-Provost followed in their funereal
robes. Organ and choir broke into the piercing solemnity
of the Burial Service. How different the great East
Window seemed when it hung as the jewelled setting to
Death. The pain of God symbolised in the centre light
drew the grief of the School to itself like a magnet of woe.
As Ullathorne glanced at the majestic, stark-white Cruci-
fixion, he seemed to see in John and Mary no longer the
hieratic figures of Holy History but some young mourning
Tutor, some weeping Dame glazed from their midst. And
the very Apostles and Evangelists in the surrounding
lights of glass seemed suddenly transfigured into celestial
Provosts and unearthly Head Masters, while the scene
of the Ascension became the sign and symbol of the
passing of a boy from among the company of his kneeling
Eton friends. Between the leaded embroideries of
coloured glass the sheafs of stonework pillars echoed the
sad chant of the choir. The Psalm was ending on their
lips :—

'For a thousand years in thy sight are but as yesterday :
seeing that is past as a watch in the night.
'As soon as Thou scatterest them, they are even as a
sleep : and fade away suddenly like the grass.
'In the morning it is green, and groweth up : but in the
evening it is cut down, dried up, and withered.'

The music notes melted away as transient as the
generations of boys themselves, but the stone and
coloured glass seemed to linger with the strength and
hue of something eternal underlying their substance.

With ruffled hair and unruffled dignity, the Provost
read the time-honoured challenge to Death out of the
First Epistle to Corinthians, and Death, who is no more
mindful of Provosts than of small boys, accepted the

challenge, and breathed his chill breath about the old men in the canopied stalls of position and honour, while the choir sang, ' On the Resurrection morning, soul and body meet again.'

The School were deeply stricken, but knew how to present a gentlemanly appearance in face of Death. Neither the maudlin nor the cowardly showed in the faces of the boys. Their Etonian fathers and forefathers had all had to meet the invincible one. Happy would they be in their turn if the duel was sharp and short, if they met him splendidly in the open or diced him for their lives at some of Life's Damnation Corners instead of hugging him through slow years of sickness and decay. That he could throw a cast of the javelin in their midst had taken them horribly by surprise. For the first time many realised that they had other enemies than the traditional foes on the River and the cricket field. As they entered the Chapel, they had seen the lilies sent by Harrow School. The old bitter rivalry could never be the same again. It faded away with those fading flowers as the mortal enemies became immortal friends. They realised that there was no gulf between the two Schools, when Death was in the field, and that even among themselves the carefully guarded partitions could be shattered at a blow. One of the least and most unnoticed of their number had only to be lost to become precious to all. . . . It was time to leave. The great Chapel, which had entered often with stronger ties than home buildings into their lives, was revealed for the moment as the solemn ante-chamber of Death, out of which they were proceeding into the waiting world outside. As they left their seats the Dead March in Saul died down, and with the last rush of sound the careering pigeons returned to settle on ledge and pinnacles. The whole School was in motion. They seemed to have heard the last Requiem for all Eton's dead, for the slain in the Crimea, commemorated in the Antechapel, and for those being slain from week to week in the African veldt. Slowly the School poured into the familiar Yard and into the long Walk as though their generation had been consecrated by the Service they had attended, and as though they also were doomed to pass through some far-off and fiery harvest, of which the first fruits had been mysteriously reaped before their eyes.

Jan. 1920—*Sept,* 1921,